LORD QUILLIFER

QUILLIFER

BOOK THREE

WALTER JON WILLIAMS

LORD QUILLIFER

SAGA PRESS

LONDON SYDNEY **NEW YORK** TORONTO NEW DELHI

SAGA PRESS
AN IMPRINT OF SIMON & SCHUSTER, INC.

1230 AVENUE OF THE AMERICAS, NEW YORK, NEW YORK 10020

For Kathy Hedges

COLDWATER

GLENFIRTH

WEST MOSS

STEDLAW

MINNITH PEAKS

BLACKSYKES

HYTHE ORDIC

R. SAELLE

KINGSMERE

ABERUVON

ALLINGHAM

MOSSTHORPE

INNISMORE

FORNLAND

SELFORD

THE TOPPINGS

Sea of Duisland
(Mare Postremum)

INCHMADEN

WHELARGID

WEST RANGE

NEWTON LINN

R. OSTRA

USKMORE

ETHLEBIGHT

AMBERSTONE

PENARTHAR

MUTTON ISLAND

GANNET COVE

REALM OF DUISLAND

AVEVIC

FERRICK

STANPORT

BONILLE

LORETTO

EXTON SCALES

HOWELL

MANKIN CLOUGH

PECKSIDE

KINGS MAGNA

LONGFIRTH

R. BROOD

DUN FOSS

PONTKYLES

AKEVAST

CORDILLERIE

WINECOURT

L. GURLIDAN

LIPPHOLME

DEUBEC

HAVRE-LE-CREAG

BRETLYNTON HEAD

MELCASTER

CASTRAS

COSTANTON

DUNNOCK

THE RACES

N

W   E

S

CHAPTER ONE

You rested your cheek upon your palm as you sat at the table, your expression a mixture of disdain and weariness. "I have been traveling this world of yours, Quillifer," you said, "and I find it a dreary place, where the debased inhabitants employ themselves only in making it drearier." Contempt laced your words. "What have your cannons and galleons, your astrolabes and hairsprings brought you but fruitless and thoughtless activity? And your printing presses serve only to better distribute to the world your own sad ignorance."

"Our ignorance is hardly our fault," I pointed out. "And you could lessen that ignorance, were you so inclined. For you were created with the world and know many of its secrets. How much could you contribute to our metaphysics, our history, our natural philosophy?"

You waved a scornful hand. "You think me as old as the world? Nay—my kind grew up alongside yours, and in the early days we dreamed together, and we built together. But my people learned wisdom, and yours never did." You laughed. "Over many centuries I tried to improve you," you said, "but you remain obstinate in your foolishness, and now I find your whole race irredeemable.

Why should I take up that useless task again, when I find you all unchanged, and as witless and savage as the first human to come blinking from the shadows of the forest into the dazzling light of the sun?"

I reached for my crystal goblet and held it glittering in the light of the candle, bubbles rising like worlds in the golden wine. "I think you need an occupation," said I.

Mischief glittered in your green eyes. "Besides tormenting *you*, Quillifer?"

"Surely that grows as tedious as the rest of your dealings with humanity," I said.

"You have not yet ceased to amuse," you said. "Your wrigglings, your plottings, your absurd ambitions." I sensed a shift in your mood, as if a tide had changed behind those sea-green eyes. "Yet perhaps I will cease my plots for a time. They are hardly necessary now."

"I would be very pleased should you no longer seek my downfall," said I, "but how is your intervention no longer necessary?"

Your forest-green satins rustled as you took the wine-cup from my hand and drained it. "A second-rate vintage at best," you said.

"I think you are evading my question."

You lifted your cheek from your hand in order to better regard me. You tossed your head, and your red hair blossomed briefly beneath its circlet of gold, then fell back into place. Your mossy scent wafted through the night. "Consider your position now, Quillifer," you said. "You live at court, where every jest is malicious, scandal lurks behind every tapestry, the very air breathes conspiracy, and a dagger is concealed behind every smile."

"Indeed," said I, "the court at times resembles a congress of fishwives, only less well-mannered."

"Fishwives are less inclined to poison and murder." A corner of your mouth turned up in a smile. "Whereas you, Quillifer, are at your zenith. You are the favorite of the Queen as well as her secret lover. You are a Knight of the Red Horse and the new-made Count of Selford, which is a title formerly employed only by members of the royal family. You sit on the Privy Council, and even the hoariest statesman or the most regal duke is obliged to reckon with you. Do you think they love you for it?" Again you laugh. "Every courtier hates you and wants to be your friend, and those to whom you offer favors grudge the thanks they offer you."

I contemplate my empty goblet. "You think I don't know it?"

"I think you believe that none of that matters, so long as you have the love of the Queen."

"And does it?" I decanted more wine into the cup.

"I think you may not live in a world of whispers and enmity without suffering some loss," you said. "And in your position, to suffer any loss is to lose all, for once you are shown to be vulnerable, your very friends will become wolves and tear out your throat. You have risen as far as you can, and from this point you may only fall." You held up a hand. "The matter is inevitable, and I need not intervene."

"Oh," said I, offhand, "your premise may be somewhat in error. I may rise farther still."

Your barking laugh was incredulous. "What—you think you can marry the Queen?"

"It matters not what I think," said I, "it matters what the *Queen* thinks."

I sipped the wine. It *was* a second-rate vintage, but then, I had got it from the palace butler, who was probably trying to put me in my place.

"If the Queen marries a butcher's son," you said, "she would lose her authority faster than if she had run naked after hares armed with a pruning-hook."

"You offer a striking image," I said. "Have you met many monarchs who pursued game in such a manner?"

"One," you said, "and she was not a monarch for long."

Again I sipped the wine. "There remains the question," I said, "as to whether I am a butcher's son or the Count of Selford."

"The nobility think they know the answer to that question," you said. "And it is not an answer that would please you."

"I care not if they please me," said I, "so long as they hold by the Queen."

"The Queen has a government," you said, "and those not in power will form an opposition. But do they oppose the Queen's government, or the Queen herself? At some point these boundaries become indistinct."

"There is no alternative to Her Majesty," said I, "but submission to a foreign power. Even those opposed to her choices will hold by her."

"And they *will* hold by her," you said, "so long as she doesn't do something as mad as to marry you."

"I'm sure the Queen knows best." Though I admit that your certainty made me uneasy.

I had sent Master Redbine, a retired member of the College of Heralds, to my home city of Ethlebight to pursue inquiries about my ancestors, in hopes of finding a vine of nobility, however slender, wrapped about my family tree. If I could convincingly offer a noble ancestor—preferably from an otherwise extinct house—then I might ease the resentment of my supposed peers.

I was not entirely proud of this stratagem, for I had no wish to debase myself by making some false claim of nobility in order to gratify the prejudices of some well-bred, fleering coxcomb; but insofar as it might keep the peace in Her Majesty's council, I would make the attempt.

And of course half the nobility based their pretensions on invented genealogies, so I would find myself in the very best company.

You looked at me with your emerald eyes. "Your lover comes," you said. "And though I despise all your women, I think I despise Floria the least." Your lips turn up in a self-satisfied smile. "Perhaps," you add, "because you will not keep her long."

And then you were gone, and I turned to the secret, silent door through which Her Majesty soon emerged.

Floria wore a dressing gown of royal red satin and matching high-heeled sandals with bows. Her ladies had bound her ill-tempered dark hair with a ribbon, but it was already escaping its bonds. She carried a candle in her hand, with which she had lighted her way down the secret passage to my room. The great white castle overlooking Selford has its share of such passages, through which Floria's father used to visit his many mistresses.

Floria lifted her chin, and her nostrils flared as she tested the air. "What is that scent?" she asked.

"Labdanum, I think," I said. "I had an otherworldly visitor."

Her brows lifted in amusement. "Your fairy?"

"She isn't a fairy, as I understand fairies," said I. "A goddess, perhaps, and certainly a nymph, a nereid as proudly inconstant as her watery element."

Floria walked across the room and drew the bar across the door. "This won't keep out a goddess, I suppose," she said, laughing, "but it will do well enough against sublunary invaders."

I took the candle from her fingers and placed it on the fireplace mantel, pink marble carved with gloxinia and camellia, ornament suited to a monarch's mistress. Floria's bright galbanum scent flooded my senses, overwhelming your own earthy fragrance. Floria's face was turned up to me, an opalescent shimmer in the dim light, and I kissed her lips. I lost count of time for a moment, and then Floria sighed and rested her head against my chest.

"I don't know if I fully believe in this Orlanda of yours," she said, "but I suspect any woman who visits you at this hour."

"It is you I adore," said I, "and it was the nymph I rejected, which accounts for her malignancy."

Floria frowned. "Malignancy?"

"It's a new word. I made it up."

"Do we not already have good words for such a sentiment? 'Mallecho,' for example?"

"Would that make Orlanda a mallechist, then?"

As I attempt honesty whenever I think anyone might actually wish to hear the truth, I have told Floria about you, including the fact that you served her in the guise of the Aekoi Countess Marcella, who vanished when I unmasked you at the beginning of the rebellion against Viceroy Fosco. It seemed only just, that she should know she was the lover of a man cursed by a being extramundane, and that she should not be surprised by any extraordinary hostility directed against me.

She does not entirely believe me, I think, but is at least convinced that I believe in your existence.

"You need not fear her," I told Floria, "for she has promised not to injure anyone I love, and I love you utterly."

She looked up at me. "Yet you say she is inconstant. May she not retract that promise?"

"If she does, that will end her torment of me, her chief amusement in this world. For rather than risk one I love, I would make an end of myself immediately." I smiled. "You begin to sound as if you believe in Orlanda."

"Perhaps I do. Though I do not care to think that my safety is bought with such danger to you."

I laughed. "Kiss me, love! For all her mischief has done is bring me to your arms."

We kissed, and embraced, and went from there to other things, as you surely know if you were watching from some invisible perch. For I have noticed that, though you say that you hate and despise my lovers, you nevertheless maintain a great interest in them, and in our doings together.

It is almost as if you are jealous.

CHAPTER TWO

In the council room there was no throne or canopy of state, but the Queen's high-backed chair was placed on a platform that allowed her to overlook her councillors, an arrangement which gave her an extra degree of majesty and proved useful in wrangling a score of quarrelsome lords. She was the smallest person in the room, and the only woman, and thus made the utmost out of every advantage she could find, which included swaddling herself in clothing suitable for a goddess. She dressed in royal scarlet and gold, the heavy silk studded with gems and woven with gold wire. A carcanet of rubies circled her throat. Jewels glittered on her fingers and shone on the small crown she wore atop her head. Her face and hands had been blanched with egg white and talcum mixed with ground pearls, the latter of which gave her complexion an unearthly opalescence, as if she were a celestial being that had just taken a dainty step off a passing cloud. Her councillors wore their own silks, chains, jewels, and finery, but she glowed at their head, a being half-divine—majestic, awesome, and apart.

I, who knew the private Floria, was awed daily at her transformation. In you, nymph, I know an actual divinity; but beside Floria sitting in state, you seem whimsical and capricious and not entirely convincing.

The council room was above the Inner Ward of Selford Castle, and light entered through a clerestory and illuminated the carved royal arms above Floria's head, the tritons of Fornland quartered with the hippogriffs of Bonille, with an inescutcheon of the red horse of the Emelins. Light blazed along silk tapestries depicting the martial deeds of Floria's ancestors. Richness and magnificence surrounded us, and Floria, her pearlescent face glowing above us all, was the figure from which all this abundance flowed.

The lords assembled rivaled the tapestries in brilliance. They wore satins and silks and velvets. Sleeves were slashed to reveal bright satin shirts in contrasting colors. Gems winked from fingers and were sewn onto doublets in glittering patterns. Purfled velvets, gold and silver thread, and gold chains of office shone bright.

By comparison to the others, I preferred to dress modestly, in colors bright or somber according to the season. To welcome the onset of spring, my doublet and trunks were green silk moiré, worn over immaculate linen. As I didn't want simplicity to be mistaken for poverty, on my fingers I wore the best of the emeralds I imported from Tabarzam, and above my golden chain of office I pinned a diamond at my throat. On my cap I fastened an aigrette with a star sapphire surrounded by sprays of brilliants.

I shone less than the others, but paradoxically I was the most noticeable. I own that this distinction somewhat flattered my self-regard.

The Privy Council had about twenty members, of which half held high office under Floria, while the rest were present because Floria valued their advice, or because they headed some important faction in the Peers. Not all members attended, for some were elsewhere on matters of state, and the Knight Marshal and Constable were in Bonille, readying their armies for war. There were no less than four dukes in the room, all kinsmen of the Queen, all placed somewhere in the line of succession. The royal line itself had grown confused over the generations, with so many cousins marrying one another . . . and thus each one of the dukes, and a good many other nobles besides, could offer a claim to the throne that went back centuries. If Floria should die without an heir, there could be a blood-soaked scramble for the throne as bad as the Cousins' Strife of two centuries ago.

The Philosopher Transterrene, an abbot named Fulvius, opened the meeting with blessings and chants. I had not been raised in the sect of the Compassionate Pilgrim, but insofar as the Pilgrim's philosophy was nearly universal among the nobility, I had acquired a primer a year or so ago, and memorized some of the most common chants so that I could mumble convincingly along with the rest.

"Long live the Queen!" Fulvius concluded. "Peace unto her ancestors!"

We repeated the formula, and I opened my folder and readied my pen to take notes. At each place at the table was a bottle of Q Sable Ink, made by my own company, and I opened my own bottle and took out some sheets of foolscap.

"Gentlemen, I wish you good morning," said Floria. "Most of you know that I have made an offer of peace to Loretto. I proposed to make Aguila my heir on the condition that he be raised here in Duisland, fostered to a member of the high nobility. Our emissary, my lord Lestrange, has returned with a message from Longres Regius, and I'm sorry to report that they have rejected my overture."

Floria had told me of this the previous morning, and while she spoke I kept a good watch on the members of the council to gauge their reaction. Most of the company were grim, but two of the dukes, Waitstill and Pontkyles, tried and failed to conceal their satisfaction. Both had unmarried sons who they hoped to match with the Queen and thus make themselves the grandsires of a monarch.

Chancellor Thistlegorm raised a hand. The white satin that marked him as a member of the Retriever sect matched well with his white hair and beard. Yet he was also a lord, and a proud one, so his satin was sewn with white gems, pearls, and diamonds.

"Your Majesty," he said. "Was the message rejected on all points, or only on certain grounds?"

"On all points," said Floria. "And with insult—for the message implied that once I had Aguila under my power, I would make away with him."

Outrage sparked among the lords. "The brazen-faced dogs!" said Lord Coneygrave, the High Admiral. He was a tall, burly man with an iron-gray beard and an underbite so pronounced that his lower teeth rested on his upper lip, which lent his countenance an unexpectedly feral air. He clenched a fist and snarled with those undershot teeth. "Ay, Your Majesty, we will return that insult with buffets and knocks, mistake me not."

Prince Aguila, Floria's nephew, was the son of Floria's elder half-sister, Queen Berlauda, and her foreign husband, Priscus of Loretto. When Priscus had gone to war in Thurnmark, he had left a kinsman as his viceroy, and this arrogant stranger had been so tyrannical that he soon had the nation torn between outrage and fear. So bloody was he that it was all I could do to manage the escape of Princess Floria to Selford, where she was crowned on Coronation Hill, then raised the entire nation against the viceroy and swept him from the country.

Berlauda and Priscus, in the meantime, had themselves been swept away by a sickness, and left behind an infant heir, Aguila, who in his cradle had been crowned King of Loretto and Duisland. Floria had made her proposal of peace to spare the nation a war, but now her hopes for a tranquil reign were over.

I knew she was not surprised by Loretto's refusal of her offer, and that her indignation was largely feigned, but I relished her performance, and thought that—if her sex did not forbid it—she could have made her fortune as an actor.

"These fine gentlemen of Loretto contemn the arts of peace," she said, her voice sharp, "and they despise us as swinish, foot-licking cravens." She thumped a fist on the arm of her chair. "Let us meet them in the field, then, and there give them such an abundance of war, such a storm of Fornland iron, Bonille steel, and Duisland courage, that they will turn in horror from the fray and beg us for the peace they so despise!"

I watched as the councillors' necks stiffened, as their eyes blazed, as their nostrils opened like those of a warhorse scenting battle. These lords were not peaceful men, and even their games—in the hunt, in the races over fields, in the tiltyard, and in the constant battle for precedence—they practiced for war.

"Well spoken, my Queen!" cried Chancellor Thistlegorm.

"Give me but the ships," said Coneygrave, "and I will burn and harry the enemy's land until there is naught left but ashes!"

Other councillors expressed a similar belligerence. Floria smiled her triumph from her seat beneath the arms of her ancestors.

"We may hope for victory in battle," she said, "but we must have that iron and steel, and the men to use them." She turned to me. "My lord Selford, kindly give us a report on the numbers of our forces, and as well our intelligence for the enemy."

I looked in my file and found the figures where I had left them. "Prince Tiburcio," I said, "has left Longres Regius to command the enemy's forces in the east, in Thurnmark and Sélange. Against us in the west, eighteen thousand enemy gather at Avevic, on the north coast, and at least fifteen thousand at Perpizon in the south, under Marshal Rutilan. A commander at Avevic is not yet appointed, unless it is intended that Admiral Mola command there, for he is present with his ships."

It had taken over a year for Loretto to raise these forces on their western border, for they were already fighting a bitter war with Thurnmark and its allies in the east. But now more nations had entered the fray, for each of those allies of Thurnmark had a list of its own enemies, Loretto diplomacy had persuaded them to join the conflict, and the opening of these new wars had caused Loretto's enemies to look to their own defense, and lessened their contribution to the armies arrayed against Loretto.

Furthermore it seemed that Loretto's invasion of its neighbor had somehow triggered a spirit of war throughout the continent of Alford, because wars had now begun that had nothing to do with Loretto. The Triple Kingdom had split, the two smallest elements of the commonwealth now in revolt against the largest and wealthiest, with the royal family itself divided. In the far east, Radvila had invaded Littov, and Durba was fighting a mostly naval war against Turo.

"The Knight Marshal musters eleven and a half thousand in Ferrick against Mola's eighteen thousand," said I. "The Constable has nine thousand to hold Castras against Marshal Rutilan."

"These forces seem insufficient," said Baron Scarnside, who spoke as if this was a novel idea of such striking originality that it could not possibly have occurred to anyone else in all history. Scarnside held the oldest barony in Bonille, and was unparalleled in point of pride. He held no office, but sat on the Council because his conceited opposition to Viceroy Fosco had got him thrown in the Murkdale Hags prison, which made him popular; and also because he represented those of the nobility with no deeds to boast of save those of their distant ancestors.

He despised me as a tradesman, but I did not feel singled out, because Scarnside despised practically everyone.

I donned my learnèd advocate face. "Your lordship makes a good point," said I, out of pure politeness. "But both the Constable and the Knight Marshal can be reinforced once the direction of the enemy's attack is made clear, and in any case we have of necessity adopted Duisland's traditional policy of forcing the enemy into sieges that will eat their strength and vigor while we raise forces elsewhere in the country to relieve our towns, and then to harry the enemy home."

"You say 'once the enemy's direction of attack is made clear,'" said Duke Chelmy. "But will they not come over the mountain passes, as they always have?"

This was a pragmatic question. In ancient times, when Bonille had belonged to the Empire of the Aekoi, the conquerors had built two military roads along the north and south coast, piercing the mountains that separated Bonille from Loretto, our enemy. Traditionally Loretto attacked along these roads, first clearing the forts we had built in the mountains, and then descending to lay siege to the cities of Ferrick and Castras.

That is why the armies of Duisland were commanded by two great officers, the Count of the Stable, familiarly the Constable, and the Knight Marshal. The Constable was traditionally of the highest nobility, and while the Knight Marshal was an office that could be held by someone of lesser rank, at the moment it was possessed by the Count of Emerick.

"We may hope the enemy comes over the passes," said I to Chelmy. "But the enemy have more ships than we, and they may sail clean around our mountain forts and land their armies on our coasts."

"Why can they not sail all the way to Fornland, land troops at the mouth of the Saelle, and march them right to the capital?"

"Your Grace," I said, "they can."

Chelmy blinked at me. A man in his thirties with black hair, a long jaw, and calculating blue eyes, Chelmy was another royal cousin, as well as a representative of a certain class among the nobility, for he had supported the rebellion of Clayborne the Bastard against Queen Berlauda seven years before. Chelmy's elder brother had fought and died in the sunken road at Exton Scales, passing the title on to him—though Berlauda had seen that title attainted and the family's possessions confiscated.

Chelmy had fled along with such of Clayborne's supporters as could get away, for any caught were executed or branded and sentenced to ten years at hard labor. Floria, acting very much against her instinctive loathing of traitors, had made the hard decision to use Chelmy and his fellow rebels, and had invited them to return, provided they took the oath of submission. Their property—if it hadn't already been sold—was returned to them, and those who had survived the years of hard labor would be forgiven the rest of their sentences if they joined the army. The result was a few thousand soldiers with the T for Treason branded on their faces, which must have made an uncommon sight when they passed in review.

Chelmy turned to Coneygrave. "Lord Admiral, can you not prevent these landings?"

"With enough ships, ay," he said. "But Priscus halved our navy, and cut off the head of Admiral Mardall when he objected. Yet I would engage the enemy if I could."

The Queen did not desire the others to accuse Coneygrave of any want of courage, and so she spoke. "I have ordered the Lord Admiral to preserve such ships as he has," Floria said, "until we can make up our numbers. There are many ships a-building now, great galleons of war, and the enemy's advantage in numbers will not last another year. Nor do my instructions encompass the navy only—I have also ordered the Knight Marshal and the Constable not to engage the invaders in battle unless they possess absolute superiority over the enemy."

"The navy is fully occupied convoying troops from Fornland to Bonille," the admiral added. "We do not want our soldiers to go without protection."

Indeed, I thought, if Admiral Mola were more aggressive, he could have blockaded us in Selford, and that would have left our armies in Bonille entirely on their own. That the enemy fleets had made no move suggested to me that they were being kept in reserve for an enterprise of some consequence, most likely an invasion by sea.

We discussed the war another hour, with many of the Council making suggestions and improvements that had to be declined for lack of means. In truth, we were recruiting soldiers and building ships as fast as we could. Normally we could buttress our forces by hiring mercenaries abroad, but the war between Loretto and Thurnmark had been over a year old before our rebellion in Duisland was ignited, and most available mercenaries had already found employment. It was fortunate that it was beyond Loretto's means to attack us in that first year.

But now forces were building on either side of our border, and soon that Fornland steel, Bonille iron, and Duisland courage would meet the massed pikes, fire-spitting guns, and high-vaunting chivalry of Loretto.

I thought we would hold our own so long as Floria remained safe on the throne and retained the allegiance of our commanders. And, as Personal Private Secretary, it was my task to ensure both the safety of the Queen and the loyalty of the officers and nobility.

And so I privately watched the members of the Council as they spoke, and privately judged their words and intentions, and privately compared them with the words and intentions reported by spies I employed in their households. For my task was to know their minds and their hearts, and all the little schemes and treacheries they employed against one another, all to anticipate the day when their treacheries would be enlarged enough to threaten the crown.

After which I, of necessity, would act.

Following the discussion of the war, the Chancellor of the Exchequer would offer a report on the kingdom's financial reserves. But before it could begin, the privy seal, Lord Waitstill, asked permission to speak.

Waitstill was a duke and a royal cousin, which accounted for his resemblance to Floria's father, at least as His late Majesty was depicted in his portraits. Waitstill was large and handsome, with a clipped yellow beard and blond hair rolling back off his forehead in waves. I felt a degree of tension between us, as I had killed his third son in a duel. Sir Brynley had challenged me after having been driven mad, part of a callous plot aimed at me by a fiery-haired goddess whose name, I think, would be superfluous to mention. I hadn't meant to kill him, and an investigation had cleared me of any fault, but Waitstill had less reason to love me than anyone at the table.

Nevertheless he was civil, and allowed his handsome face to show no enmity. I could not tell whether he believed that I was truly not at fault in his mad son's death, or whether he intended to take a more subtle course to revenge. My spies in his household reported no conspiracies beyond those the nobility were wont to employ against one another, for prestige, pride, or spite. Apparently my name never came up, which rather injured my self-regard.

"Your Majesty," he said, "in view of the contemptible answer your peaceful overtures received from the court at Longres Regius, I beg that you marry as soon as might be, with a view to securing the succession."

"Ay," said Lord Pontkyles, the Minister of State for Bonille. He was another demi-regal duke, and like Waitstill had an unmarried son whose appearance, he thought, would be greatly improved by the addition of a crown on his brow. "I beg Your Majesty to choose a husband, and quickly."

Floria regarded them levelly. "It seems to me," she said, "that my sister's most unwise decision was to marry."

"To marry a *foreign prince*, Majesty," Pontkyles said. "I confide that Your Majesty would be more sagacious."

"Yet a foreign prince brings alliance in his train," said Floria, "and a country at war needs allies. Perhaps I should travel to Thurnmark and marry the Hogen-Mogen."

Pontkyles blinked his small, greedy eyes, eyes that belonged more properly on a famished hog. This conversation had taken a turn he did not like, and he knew not how to steer it back on course. He was a large man, taller even than I, with a vast barrel-shaped body and a gray carpet of beard that spread over his collar-bones. He had been a great jouster in his youth, and had fought in King Emelin's wars; but I could hardly imagine him now at the head of a corps of soldiers, but only as captain of a company of tipplers and gluttons.

Waitstill stepped smoothly into the silence. "Your Majesty's jest is apt," he said. "For a Queen of Duisland to marry a mere Hogen-Mogen of Thurnmark is risible, not when there are so many more suitable candidates. Yet out of love for Your Majesty I urge you to choose from among them." He raised a gloved finger as he made his point. "A woman alone on the throne is vulnerable, no less in the matter of reputation. The enemy already makes the false claim that you have a lover, in hopes this will injure your standing with the people. Marriage would end these rumors once and for all."

I wondered at the strength of will required for Waitstill not to glance in my direction, for indeed I had been named by the enemy as the Queen's lover. Perhaps a few simple people even believed it.

"I know that my people of Duisland will not allow such poison to sully their ears," said Floria. "And the getting of an heir, I remind, is not without hazard. For was my sister not weakened by miscarriages and the birth of her Aguila, such that a fever carried her off?"

"Yet the heir lived!" blurted Pontkyles, no doubt dazzled beyond all prudence by the thought of a grandson with a crown impaled on his infant brow.

The other councillors regarded at him with distaste. Floria raised an eyebrow.

"I am pleased to discover how well my life is regarded by His Grace of Pontkyles," she said, and then her hazel eyes hardened as she glanced over the company. "Yet despite his tender care for my person, I am not now inclined to marry, and I beg your lordships not to raise the subject again."

Pontkyles flushed a furious red. Waitstill looked as if he'd bitten into something sour. Lord Thistlegorm, the Chancellor, spoke in a measured voice.

"Is it possible that Your Majesty will name a successor, so that the realm will not fall into disorder should an accident befall you?"

"I will not." Floria's voice was firm. "For if I did, the rest of you gentlemen would tear him to pieces."

Which was so true that no one dared to contradict her. Floria turned to the Chancellor of the Exchequer and spoke. "Sir, will you not enlighten us as to the current state of the finances?"

Which Sir Merriman Sandicup began to do, speaking in the languid, superior tones that so irked my ears but that had served him well arguing for new taxes in the House of Burgesses. I paid little attention, for I already knew the state of the nation's debt. The previous two winters I had been involved with Floria in the matter of taxes to support our war, and the borrowing that took place to shore up the kingdom until the new taxes could be collected.

The doors opened, and we all looked up from the drawling recitation of figures to see a cornet of the Yeoman Archers in his black leather jerkin and scarlet bonnet, which he promptly doffed in the royal presence. He paused a moment to allow his eyes to adjust to the light, and then he advanced along the table and paused by my chair. He leaned over me—his breath smelled of barley wine—and whispered into my ear.

"I have been told to fetch you, my lord," he said. "A dead man has been found outside the castle walls."

I turned and answered his whisper with one of my own. "Do we know who it is?"

"Not yet, my lord. But either he threw himself from the walls or someone threw him."

There was silence in the room as everyone strained to hear our whispers. Sandicup had his pen to his pursed lips in an expression of petulance. I put down my own pen and gathered my papers. "I beg pardon, Your Majesty," I said. "I am called away, I trust not for long."

"My lord of Selford has leave to depart," Floria said. "I will secure him a place by me at dinner, and trust he attends." In her eyes there were both curiosity and calculation, for she knew there were few errands that would call me away, and that all of them had to do with the safety of the realm.

I rose, bowed, and gathered my folder.

"Now," Sandicup drawled, "if Selford is quite done, I hope I may proceed."

I paused and put on my dutiful-apprentice face. "I am, and you may," said I, "though I believe you misstated last year's income from escheats. Remember that the Marquisate of Eldyn fell to the crown only after the New Year, after the court dismissed the precontract which would have legitimized the bastard son."

Sandicup smiled with white, even teeth. "True," he said, "though it makes little difference. For last year's funds from the estate were held in escrow by Eldyn's justice of the peace, and have already been rendered up to the Treasury. Yet I thank your lordship for this facticle and will amend my figures."

I bowed. "Your servant," I said.

His smile thinned. "And yours, I'm sure."

Facticle, I thought. That was rather good.

I bowed to the Queen and followed the guardsman out of the room and into the white glories of the Inner Ward. Over the centuries every sandstone surface had been ornamented and carved: There were leaves and vines, gods and fantastic monsters, the fierce bearded faces of wood-woses, and the gracious smiles of oreads. Shields were blazoned with the triton of Fornland, the hippogriff of Bonille, and the prancing horse of the Emelins. The upper reaches of the castle looked as if it were made of lace, or perhaps carved of ice.

The officer led me down a stair carven with a thicket of eglantine, then through a gatehouse into the Middle Ward. There he took me through a postern, and below me I saw Selford, rank after rank of rooftops stepping down the bluff to the River Saelle and the great bridge to Mossthorpe on the left bank. Wisps of smoke rose from the chimneys, and charcoal faintly scented the air. Farther downstream I could see a forest of masts surrounding Innismore, the city's principal port.

"This way, my lord."

We worked our way along the footpath beneath the castle's brilliant white curtain wall. There had been rain overnight, and my crooked little finger ached while clay gummed my shoes. Beneath the great lacy ramparts of the Inner Ward, a group of Yeoman Archers huddled around a man lying amid brambles newly green with spring. The soldiers parted as I arrived, and I looked down at the face of a stranger.

Strangers were not supposed to go pitching off the fifteen-yard-high battlements of the royal residence. Nor were strangers supposed to be in the Inner Ward at all.

"Does anyone know this man?" I asked.

The captain saluted. "No, my lord," he said. "None of us recognize him."

I suppressed a shiver as I stood over the corpse. He had died by violence, and he brought back a chill memory of battle, a cold, sere field with the red-streaked dead lying in heaps.

He had landed on his feet, I thought, but was then thrown over backward by the impact, so that his face remained intact even as the back of his head was crushed. Blood had pooled beneath his head, and his arms were thrown out wide. His pale palms gazed upward from the greening brambles. I thought the man was about thirty, with black hair and beard. Though death had turned him pale, still it seemed his natural complexion was dark. He had a straight nose with a hump in it, and there were silver rings on his fingers.

"Does he seem foreign to you?" I asked. Something about his

aspect, perhaps the dark complexion and the aquiline nose, suggested an origin abroad. He was well dressed, in a wool gown of deep blue ornamented with golden lace, a blue velvet cap that covered his hair, and shoes of brown suede. He had dressed well for creeping about the battlements at night.

I looked at the rings on his fingers. "Does he wear a signet?"

The captain bent to examine the man's hands. "Nay, my lord. But judging by these gems, he was not poor."

My skin crawled at the thought of touching the dead man, but I knelt and managed to examine the corpse's cold hands, which were soft and lacked the calluses of a working man. The body was stiff and I couldn't get a good view of the rings, so I turned the rings around so the stones lay beside the colorless palms. The stones on his rings were opals, garnets, a large baroque pearl, and a sizable table-cut ruby. I peered for a moment at a thumb-ring with a black onyx cameo of an eagle battling a serpent, the serpent's head buried in the eagle's breast, and then my eye was drawn back to the baroque pearl, which seemed set into the ring at an unusual angle. I touched it and felt the pearl shiver beneath my finger, then looked for a mechanism and found it. The bezel fell open in a hidden hinge, and I looked into the revealed compartment, and but was disappointed to find it was empty.

"A poison ring," breathed the captain.

I closed the ring and tried to pull it off the man's finger, but the body was too stiff and the ring would not slide off.

The captain and I then searched the corpse and produced a table knife and a purse with a modest amount of silver money, all minted in Duisland. I looked at the suede boots, which had thick soles, tall heels, and the toe and sole square in front. I thought they might be good for climbing—climbing walls, in fact, with the square-cut sole jammed between stones or bricks. I wondered if the man had been trying to climb the curtain wall when he fell.

I had once climbed a curtain wall myself. It was not a happy memory.

I examined the boots carefully to see if there was anything hidden in a hollow heel, but the heels were not hollow. "Does anyone know where they make boots like these?" I asked. "I don't think I've seen them in this country."

No one had an answer to my question. I rose from my crouch and turned to the captain. "Bear the body to the guardhouse," I said. "Parade your men past him, and see if anyone can recognize the fellow. He is like to have entered the castle with one of the musicians who entertained last night, or in the following of a noble or a minister."

"Yes, my lord."

"I'll want to examine those rings once they can be got off his fingers," I said.

He gave me a confiding look. "I'll see they don't disappear, my lord."

I looked at the white wall that loomed above us. While the Yeoman Archers lifted the body and carried it toward the postern, I examined the stone for any marks that might have been made by those squaretoed boots, and satisfied myself that the stranger had not tried to scale the wall. I suppose he might have fallen when trying to lower himself to the ground from the battlements, but I was inclined to think that someone had aided the man in his plummet to earth. If he were going to commit suicide, he didn't have to come to the palace to do it. He had come to meet someone, and that someone had made sure he fell.

I imagined that meant the stranger had known something that his killer wished to remain hidden. Very possibly the killing was a private matter and had nothing to do with the war or the crown; but I was sworn to defend the Queen, and I could take no chances that this was not part of some plot against her. Therefore I would discover whatever secrets were hidden here, and even if there were no treason, there would be law, and possibly even justice.

Kicking clay from my shoes, I went to find the Steward of the Castle, and told him to make it known that the castle servants should view the body in the guardhouse, in hopes they might recognize him. The steward said he would do this, though in a tone that suggested this would happen at his convenience and not mine. I went to my room and found there my varlet, Rufino Knott. A sometime minstrel, he was a young man with a sparse beard and turned-up nose, and he also served as my guitar master on those days when I had time for lessons.

He was folding clean shirts and linen, and putting them up in my trunk. He looked at me in surprise.

"My lord?" said he. "I wasn't expecting you. Has the meeting adjourned?"

"I was called away," I said. "And now I need new shoes."

Knott went to the wardrobe for another pair of shoes, then helped me change. I told him about the dead man found beneath the battlements.

"I need you to go to the guardhouse and give the man a thorough viewing," I said. "Then take a boat to Innismore and find out what ships have come into port in the last few days. Speak to the officers and ask if they've discharged a passenger, and if that passenger traveled alone."

"Yes, my lord."

I reached into my purse and gave Knott some crowns so that he could pay for his dinner and a glass of ale, and if necessary bribe a ship's officer. I emptied my bladder in the close-stool, then made my way back to the council room, which I found empty. I assumed that Floria and her council had gone to dinner, and so I walked to the banqueting hall, where the company were just finishing their meal. Floria had been joined by several of her ladies of honor—a Queen required a dozen at least—all wearing her badge of the double white impatiens. The other council members were accompanied by members of their families or their retinue. They had all been pledging the

Queen and each other with cups of wine, and the conversation was loud and buoyant.

Across the room from the royal seat was a gallery set just below the rafters, where ordinary people—underemployed laborers, well-to-do wives with a free afternoon, sailors from the port, visitors from the country—watched the monarch eat her dinner. It was a long-established custom that any person could watch the Queen at her meat.

I hastened to my own seat, on Floria's left, and bowed to her before taking my place and unfolding my napkin.

Questions glittered in Floria's hazel eyes. I leaned close.

"A stranger was found below the wall on the north side of the Inner Ward," I said. "He had been thrown from the battlements. You may hear a tale of a poison ring, but the ring was most likely used to carry a message."

"Yet poison cannot be ruled out."

"It cannot."

I realized that the room had fallen nearly silent, as all hoped to overhear my conversation with Floria. Floria waved a dismissal. "We will speak of this later," said she, "and in the meantime, I will make good use of the Yeoman Pregustator." Who was the Queen's food-taster, a small, melancholy gentleman who spent his working life waiting to die in some horrible, agonizing way.

A footman poured sauternes into my wine-cup, and I waved another footman over and asked if there were some portable item on the bill of fare. "Eel pie, my lord." Surprised that the royal kitchens would serve something so simple, I told him to bring me one.

The contents of the pie might have been simple, but the crust was not, for it featured a pastry sculpture of a trooper on horseback, with an embroidered ensign on the end of his wooden lance, the quartered tritons and hippogriffs of Duisland. I wondered how many seamstresses had been employed in stitching those little flags, to provide one small, colorful item of a meal soon to be forgotten.

The pie had no sooner been delivered than Floria rose from her seat, and we all rose with her. "Gentlemen, we will meet again at one o'clock."

We all bowed as Floria swept out, followed by her ladies. I plucked the flag and its staff from the pastry, put it in my cap, then gulped down the sauternes and carried the pie away in a napkin. I bit into the pie as the councillors and their retinue made their way to the lobby of the council room, often by way of the nearest close-stool. Two of the Yeoman Archers, in their black leather jerkins and red caps, stood guard by the council room doors.

His Grace of Roundsilver, the Lord Chamberlain, entered carrying his white staff of office. He was a small, delicate man with dark eyes, elegant features, and fair hair and beard turning gray; he wore a silk tunic that had been painted with a picture of elaborately posed humans who shared an intricate landscape with fabulous animals, a garment that made him look as fantastic as anything in the painting. He was a man of refined and exquisite tastes, with palaces full of beautiful objects: statues, paintings, cameos, gems, carved ivory, and jade. He worshiped Beauty in all its forms, and had purposefully avoided any responsibility or office until fifteen months ago, when he had opened his treasury to assure that Floria would be proclaimed Queen, and had then been rewarded with the Exchequer, an office he did not desire. Though he understood money and made successful investments that assured a manner of life as regal as that of the monarch, the province of finance was traditionally left to the House of Burgesses, and that required a commoner to manage it, so Roundsilver had shifted to the office of Chamberlain just before the Estates met the previous autumn. It was an office that suited him better, for he was now in charge of the royal household and its finances, and his experience in managing his own fortune and pos-sessions served him well.

Strange to relate, this elegant, refined gentleman of impeccable lineage was one of my few friends among the nobility. He and his young wife had received me graciously when I first came to Selford, a refugee from plundered Ethlebight, and he had been a faithful ally ever since, even when I was a scapegrace scarcely worth the alliance.

"Good afternoon, Your Grace," I said.

He nodded. "Good afternoon, my lord." He observed me closely. "You seem refreshed. Did you sleep well last night?"

"For some reason," said I, "I have the best sleep here in the castle."

"And you eat a hearty dinner, I see. For much of it resides on your doublet."

I brushed crumbs from my clothing. "How is Her Grace?" I asked. "I trust she is well."

"My lady wife will ride in the park this afternoon." He sighed. "I wish we were *all* riding in the park."

He disdained the letter *r* as plebeian, and so he spoke of "widing in the pawk." I was accustomed to this affectation and could deci-pher even his most recondite speeches, as when he might denounce "twoublesome twaitors shawking up webellion."

"And young Ethlebight?"

"Thriving." He tilted his head. "Do you know, Selford, I had no notion that having a child in the house would prove so diverting, even when he smashes my porcelain and knocks my treasures off shelves."

"I hope you will secure your valuables, Your Grace, or at least put them out of his reach."

"I would, but he has grown surprisingly adept at climbing."

I considered this. "I venture to suggest that if Ethlebight's nurse permits him to climb shelves, he should have a new nurse."

Roundsilver had his seat in the southwest, near my home city, and his young heir—not quite three years old—was known by courtesy as the Marquess of Ethlebight. I thought it absurd to shackle an infant with such a grand mouthful of a title, but such was the custom—just as if ever I had a son, he would be Viscount Someplace-or-Other. Dunnock, perhaps, after my manor in Hurst Downs.

The Duke of Pontkyles entered, and he brought his heir with him, the Marquess of Morestanton. Young Morestanton had inherited his father's height but not his gross, powerful body, and he posed gracefully in peach-colored velvet, a silver pomander in his hand. A dark beard, composing at most of a hundred hairs, drifted downward from his chin, and a wisp of a mustache floated featherlike above his upper lip.

"Roundsilver," said Pontkyles, looming over my friend. His small, swinish eyes turned to me. "Quillifer."

He should have addressed me by my title, as we were hardly on a first-name basis, and no doubt he thought he had scored a decisive strike on my dignity. But my dignity was more resilient than he expected, as was my invention.

"Pontkyles," I greeted. I turned to the son. "You know, Morestanton, my mother had a balm that would have been a sovereign remedy for those spots of yours. I can make inquiries of apothecaries in Ethlebight if you wish; they may have preserved her recipe."

Son and father both flushed scarlet, one from embarrassment and the other from anger, and before either could reply, Roundsilver gripped me firmly by the arm and pulled me away. "You know, Selford," he said, "we *must* discuss those leases."

While Roundsilver and I feigned interest in his invented leases, the other members of the Council entered. The hum of conversation rose in the room, and then the great bronze doors at the far end of the room swept open, and Floria entered, along with a half-dozen or so of her ladies, all wearing her white badge. Conversation ceased. We bowed and doffed our caps.

Floria and her procession passed partly into the room, then paused as her hazel eyes darted from one member of the Council to the next. We straightened and put on our caps. Pontkyles approached the Queen, his son in tow.

"Your Majesty," he said, "I hope you remember my son Morestanton."

For half a second Floria's eyes darted to me, and I read her thoughts, and did my best to suppress my laughter. For the last months, it seemed all the great lords of the land were hurling their sons at Floria's feet—or if not their sons, then brothers, grandsons, nephews, or their most distinguished selves. Some were schoolboys, some doddering graybeards, some drunken rakes, some witless fools lacking only a cap and bells. Now Pontkyles had thrust his son Morestanton into the ring, to be poked and prodded like a young calf at auction.

"Of course we remember Morestanton," Floria said. She had reverted to the royal *we*. She turned to the son and looked up at him. "Since we last met, you have grown to an inconvenient height. Our neck aches at the sight of you."

"I have nothing but compassion for your neck," Morestanton said, "which must alone support the weight of Your Majesty's vast responsibilities. But in any case, I have a duty to majesty"—and here he knelt—"and so I hope, as a proper subject, to gaze up in reverence at Your Majesty's countenance and relieve Your Majesty's neck at the same time."

Indeed, he managed to seem reverent as he knelt in his peach-colored satin. Floria looked down at him with an inward smile. "If only more of my subjects sought to save my neck," she said.

"You may count on your subjects," Morestanton said. "It is the foreign enemy from which we must shield you."

"I don't believe," said Floria, forgetting for a moment her *we*, "I have ever seen a shield so tall."

"The taller the shield, the better it will protect you, Majesty," said Morestanton.

"My subjects," said Floria, "will soon be in the field against Loretto. Will you join them?"

I suppressed a grin. Sooner or later, Floria would always ask whether her would-be suitors would join her army.

"I command a troop of demilances, Majesty," Morestanton said. "As soon as we can make up our numbers, we will take ship to join the Knight Marshal."

"We commend your resolution," said Floria.

"But until that time, I stay with my father here in Selford," said Morestanton. "I and my horses are at your service."

"We are obliged," said Floria. "But why would we need your horses?"

"I hope to show you, Majesty. I know that you enjoy the pleasures of the chase and favor horses both swift and audacious. Yet I fancy that I on my charger Dickon can keep your pace and maybe even beat Your Majesty across the line."

"Oh, a challenge." Her face took on an appraising cast. "Well, we shall see."

"Would Your Majesty care for a wager?"

"We will make no wagers until the war is over," Floria said, "for if we lose, the treasury could be deprived of the means to support our soldiers."

Her half-sister, Queen Berlauda, had been a gamester, had cost the treasury dear and become unpopular. Floria would not so court the people's displeasure.

Morestanton reached up to his peach-colored bonnet and withdrew a feather from his cap-badge. "Will you wager against this partridge feather?" he said.

Floria examined the offering. "The treasury can spare a feather," she decided.

"Were I so lucky as to win Your Majesty's feather," said Morestanton, "I would treasure it, and wear it next to my heart."

"It would grow frayed that way," Floria said. "Either the feather—or your heart."

She swept on into the lobby, leaving Morestanton blinking on one knee. I turned to Roundsilver. "A well-schooled young gentleman, don't you think?" I said.

"He held out longer than most," Roundsilver said. "He kept up with Her Majesty, till the very last."

"As will his horse, I suppose," I said. I looked at him. "Where *is* Morestanton, anyway?"

"Southwest Bonille."

"And why is there more Stanton in Morestanton than anywhere else?"

"There is also a Little Stanton in the vicinity, and an Upper Stanton—and, I believe, a Stanton-on-the-Lea. Plus of course the port city of Costanton."

"I see. Morestanton must have More. I will consider it a clue to his character."

More members of the council arrived, some with attendants, and Floria vanished into a circle of tall men. Lord Thistlegorm, splendid in his diamond-decked white suit, approached me and took me aside.

"Lord Selford," said he, "my daughters have come to town."

"I trust they will bring you joy," I said.

"They will. I rejoice in them." The Chancellor pursed his lips for a moment, as if he were arguing a difficult case before a judge. "My daughter Candice is seventeen," he said. "Perhaps it is only the fond eye of a father, but I believe her comely."

"I cannot believe your eye would deceive you in this," said I.

He looked up at me with that selfsame eye, no longer fond but ice-blue and calculating. "I should be delighted if you were to meet her," he said.

"Nothing would please me more."

"If Candice does not suit," he said, "I have another daughter, Emily. She is twelve. Should you prefer her, I hope—" He stroked his beard. "Well, I hope you might practice a degree of restraint, for a year or two at least, in the business of the marriage bed."

"I would do my best to oblige you," I said. "And the young lady, of course."

Since I had reached my present estate, any number of fathers had proposed their daughters to me, though so far, the offers had come from the knightly classes or the burgesses. Thistlegorm was the first of the nobility to propose a marriage alliance, and I knew his offer was not based on any measure of love for me.

Thistlegorm had been Attorney General under Berlauda, but Priscus and Viceroy Fosco had opposed the white-clad sect of the Retrievers, of which Thistlegorm was a prominent member. Fosco executed several of the Retrievers as an example to the others, but he allowed Thistlegorm to purchase his life for thirty thousand royals, most of which, I imagine, went into Fosco's private purse.

In order to pay the fine, Thistlegorm had borrowed, and had mortgaged much of his land. Floria had promised to repay the money but did so with a bill on the Treasury, which would only be honored when the Treasury pleased, and the Treasury would be pleased only when the war was over and the nation's finances restored. Floria had also appointed Thistlegorm Lord Chancellor, which was an office that came with certain traditional sweeteners and privileges that would help him recover at least a part of his fortune.

The Lord Chancellor was in charge of justice throughout the realm, and in Duisland, as elsewhere, justice cost money—some of which, as if by some subtle law of the universe, adhered to the Chancellor himself.

Apparently the money was not adhering as quickly as Thistlegorm wished, and he had decided to acquire the support of a wealthy son-in-law who might be expected to offer him loans free of interest. While

I sympathized with his plight, I had no intention of marrying either of his daughters, and I would have to give some thought concerning how to evade the delightful Candice without making the Chancellor an enemy.

As I smiled at Thistlegorm and inwardly calculated how I might escape his marriage schemes, I saw out of the slant of my eye a black-haired man enter the chamber, somber and scowling in the unbleached woolen robes of a monk.

I know not what attracted my eye to him, unless it was his air of decision, of a mind that had determined on an action and would not be swayed from it. His tonsure, which shaved all hair forward of his ears, had grown out a little, and his forehead and jowls were blue with bristle. Both his hands were hidden in his robes of unbleached wool. With resolute tread he walked toward the cluster of men about the Queen.

"Beg pardon," I murmured, and stepped past Thistlegorm. My nerves were taut as lute-strings, and the small hairs on the back of my neck prickled erect. I moved to intercept the newcomer, and wondered if I would arrive in time. I thought I would need a weapon, but I had none beyond the small knife I carried for eating. One did not go armed into the Queen's Presence.

When the monk's hand rose from his robes carrying a pocket-pistol, I cocked my hand over my right shoulder and hurled the remains of my eel pie directly into his face.

Eel and stewed vegetables exploded across the monk's face and the pistol instantly discharged. The bonnet of an elderly baronet flew into the air. I knew not whether the monk had a second pistol, so I had launched myself for the monk as soon as the eel pie left my hand.

I am a tall, strapping fellow, and as I ran to the monk, I held out my arm to the side and caught him under his chin with my forearm, which served to toss him backward onto the marble floor. Eel, stewed vegetables, and flakes of crust spattered the air. Choking, the monk landed on the back of his head and was promptly buried under several peers and a pair of the Yeoman Archers. The Queen was surrounded by burly noblemen and carried into the council chamber.

"Hold him," said I, perhaps unnecessarily. "Search him."

At that moment I looked no longer at the monk but instead surveyed the room to see if the man had an accomplice. Everyone stared back at me, stunned. I saw none who aroused suspicion.

"Take him to the guardroom," I said to an officer of the Archers. "Hold him there until he can be taken to the Hall of Justice." Four of the Archers picked the monk up from the floor and held him. He was blue and gasping from my forearm across his throat, and bits of my dinner trailed down his face. I looked at the officer. "See he comes to no harm," said I. "If someone is behind this, he may wish to silence his minion."

I confiscated the pistol from the floor and put it in my pocket.

"I will report to Her Majesty." I spoke to the room in general, then entered the council chamber, where Floria was being assisted into her chair by two of her ladies, who arranged her skirts and withdrew. She seemed composed, and as I made my bow, and her eyes lifted to mine, I saw the questions there.

A death, a shot, and possible poison. Were these a coincidence, or something else?

I would do my best to find out.

CHAPTER THREE

「T」he monk has confessed," said I. "The confession was voluntary—boastful, almost. His holy name is Aemilius, but he was born Jack Chess in Newton Linn, and was a monk in the Shining Refuge Monastery there till last month, when he left to walk to Selford and kill you."

Floria absorbed this, then nodded to herself. "Did he say why?"

"He is a supporter of Viceroy Fosco's religious policy and hates you for not cutting off the heads of Retrievers and other such recusants."

Her hazel eyes rose to mine. "He was not connected with the man fallen from the battlements?"

"I do not think so."

She sighed. "So that mystery remains."

Until Viceroy Fosco came on the scene, debates among the followers of the Compassionate Pilgrim had been polite and full of erudition. In his lifetime, Eidrich the Pilgrim had denounced the gods, denied that his philosophy was the result of any divine inspiration, and insisted throughout that he was naught but a man and his thought a product of observation and reason. But in the years since his death, many of his followers had proclaimed him divine, an emanation of the Creative

Force, and had invented a mythscape of demons, demigods, a celestial paradise, and a great many ingenious hells. White-clad Retrievers like Thistlegorm attempted to scrape the Pilgrim's thought of all these accretions and return to the philosophy of the man himself.

But in Loretto the King had proclaimed the Pilgrim divine, and persecuted those of contrary opinions, and Viceroy Fosco—himself a monk—had brought this persecution to Duisland until Floria's revolt had ended it.

"I will send men to the Shining Refuge," said I, "and see if anyone there gave Jack Chess the idea of using violence against the Queen. If the monastery is a shining refuge for Fosco's thought, we may have to sweep it clean."

Floria sighed. "And while you were listening to the confessions of this Jack Chess, I had to herd the council all the afternoon and keep them somewhat on topic despite the distractions of pistol fire in the lobby." She looked at me and laughed. "I wonder which of us found our duty more tedious."

We were in my room in the palace, lying at ease on the settee, I in my shirt, Floria in a silver satin dressing gown. The room was lit by candles and by a fire in the hearth, so flame lit our faces and danced in Floria's eyes. I sipped at a glass of apple brandy, and Floria a sloe-flavored cordial produced by our enemies in Loretto and smuggled over the border.

It is a foolish delusion to think that war inhibits commerce between the principals, for commerce continues but merely changes its character.

"Each of the peers," Floria said, "insisted on their right to make speeches at least as long as those of any other peer, even if they had nothing to say. At least Abbot Fulvius was silent, after his chant was over." Again she sighed. "I wanted to knock them on the head if they kept repeating themselves and get to the point, but they could not find a point with both hands. I was completely disgratified."

I was intrigued. "Disgratified? Did you just invent that word?"

"I did. I also liked Sandicup's *facticle*."

I shrugged. "That wasn't bad, for a beginner."

"I shall tell him you said so."

"I have a name for the man found dead this morning," said I. "I sent Master Knott to Innismore to see if any ship had carried him here, and he found the ship easily. The man gave his name as Antonio Luzi, and said he was from Pisciotta. He disembarked two days ago on a ship from that city."

"Gave he a reason for his journey to Duisland?"

"To visit a cousin in Mossthorpe. A wine merchant." I sipped my apple brandy, and spiced fire ran along my tongue.

"Will you inquire among the wine merchants?" Floria asked.

I sighed. "I suppose I must, though I doubt this merchant exists."

Floria looked into the fire, her face pensive, the rim of her glass of crystal lightly touching her lower lip. "I wonder if the *poison* exists."

"If so, I will discover it."

Reflected flames flowed across her face. "Someone has gone to great trouble to import this Antonio, and whatever he carried, from so far away."

"The court is a humming hive of rivalry and conspiracy," I said. "If there is deadly intent behind this matter, it is likely to be aimed at someone else, not at you."

"Yet it was my wall from which this man fell. He was in *my house*." Floria frowned down at her glass for a moment, then tilted back her head and drank off the cordial. She placed the glass on a cherry-wood table, then turned to me and draped herself across my chest. Her lips tasted of sloes.

"Perhaps I will don my quandias ring," she said, "though it is unhandsome."

"What is a quandias?" asked I.

"A stone found in the head of a vulture, said by the ancients to be of such great virtue that it guards the wearer against evil, most especially poison. My father gave it to me as protection. He wore one himself."

"It did not save him from the onset of the illness that killed him," I said.

"But neither was he poisoned." She tossed her head. "It may be nonsense, but people are known to believe nonsense. The belief may deter anyone wishing me harm."

"The Pilgrim make it so."

She drew back and regarded me. "A name crossed my desk yesterday, a name known to you."

"Yes?"

"Sir Edelmir Westley." She waited for me to react in some way, but I showed neither surprise nor anger, and she continued. "He has returned to Duisland from his wars abroad, and has written to me asking for employment. I am minded to give it, perhaps the wardenship of Dun Foss, if you have no objection."

"None in the world."

"I know he challenged you. It was said you slept with his wife."

"Sir Edelmir and I were friends, I think, or at any rate friendly," said I. "Westley had gambling debts, and the Count of Wenlock bought his notes-of-hand and forced Westley to chose between bankruptcy and challenging me. I now have proof of this, found in Edevane's files when I took his job. It will do no harm to tell Westley the notes will be burned if he does his duty, and Dun Foss is a remote enough post that he will have trouble losing a second fortune there."

Floria frowned. "I hadn't realized Wenlock's hatred of you burned so strong as to connive at murder."

"Wenlock's hatred is real enough," I said, "but it was stoked, I think, by supernatural means."

"Your fairy."

"She boasted of it."

Floria drew away from me a little. "Yet this tells me that Westley is willing to betray his honor for money. I think I will not give him a fort that controls a pass into Loretto. He may be Lord Warden of Uskmore Castle, or some other place the enemy will not invade."

I nodded. "Your Majesty is wise," I said. "Yet I feel sorry for his poor wife, cast away on that bleak coast."

Floria's answer was tart. "There is such a thing as divorce."

"Indeed." I had urged it on her when the extent of her husband's debts was revealed, but she feared scandal.

Floria again reclined against my chest. I kissed her forehead. Her galbanum scent drifted through my senses.

"Oh, I am too tired for pleasure tonight," she said. "But I would like to spend the night in your arms."

My arms encompassed her. "I will keep you safe," I said.

"I know you will."

"Yet I wish I could be as confident for our armies," said I.

"The warriors of Duisland are ever doughty," Floria said. "And we have many allies against Loretto."

"I doubt not our soldiers' courage," I said. "But I fear our commanders may not be our best choices. Neither the Knight Marshal nor the Constable has ever commanded an army, and Coneygrave has never commanded at sea, and has never even voyaged abroad."

I felt her irritation. "I thought we had already talked this subject unto death! There was good reason for every choice."

"I know the nobles must be appeased, but—"

She sat up, fire blazing in her eyes. "Drumforce hates the enemy with every atom of his body!"

Drumforce was no longer the Constable's name, but his name had changed so many times that people found it difficult to keep track. He had been Viscount Drumforce when his father, Lord Scutterfield, had been the Lord Great Chamberlain. But Scutterfield had been executed and attainted by Priscus and Berlauda, and the attainder meant that Drumforce became merely Amador Wending, a lone, furious commoner stalking through the drawing rooms of the capital. Floria had reversed the attainder, and now Amador Wending had his father's title of Scutterfield, though many people throughout had continued to call him Drumforce out of habit. There was no doubt that Drumforce, or Scutterfield, would do his utmost to destroy the forces that had killed his father, but he was barely thirty, and had never even fought in a battle.

"He will have experienced advisors," Floria said. "And his presence is a reminder to the soldiers of the evils we fight against. Arbitrary government, judicial murder, all of it."

"He could be a symbol without being in command," said I. "At least your Knight Marshal, Lord Emerick, has served in the campaign against Clayborne." Though he had not, apparently, ever crossed swords with the enemy, but remained in the reserve with his troop of dragoons. "If a noble must command," said I, "let it be Lord Barkin, who commands your Queen's Own Horse. He is a proved commander with experience fighting abroad, and he played an important role against Clayborne at Exton Scales."

"Barkin commands the horse, but he commands no votes in the Estates," Floria said. "And we must have those votes if we are to pay for this war."

"Victory will encourage cheerful payment more than will coronets on a battlefield."

"I have never seen a cheerful taxpayer, and neither have you." Floria gave me a baleful look. "You seem to think you would do better than my generals."

"I think I would do well—particularly at sea—but I would hate it. Exton Scales was the last battlefield I hope ever to see." Reflected fire glowed in her eyes as I looked at her. "And I would be desolate without you," I said. "Your presence on the campaign would make it bearable, but we cannot risk the life of the monarch. And so I will serve you as best as I can here in the capital, and keep you safe, even though I am so ill-suited to some of this work that I must clench my teeth and force myself to it."

"Do you know who was best suited to the work?" Floria asked. "Edevane."

Edevane had been Fosco's judicial assassin, a soft-spoken master of spies and informers who had sharked up false charges of treason against Scutterfield, Admiral Mardall, Sir Cecil Greene, and a score of others, and set their severed heads on pikes. He had also extorted those thirty thousand royals from Thistlegorm, his own attorney general, and more contributions from a dozen others.

"I would not have an Edevane in your office," said Floria. "I would have someone who hates these hateful things. I would have *you*, my lord of Selford."

I felt my heart dissolve into a black sea. "You may have me then," said I, "and have me forever, an you want me."

The next morning we rode to hounds. It was too early in the year for most four-footed game: The season for stag would not begin until midsummer. Does as well as stags would be hunted in autumn, as would boars. Rabbits were prey all year long, but shooting rabbits lacked the excitement of the gallop that Floria so loved and that I did not.

Rabbits are considered vermin, and that category included also wolves and foxes. It had been centuries since wolves had been seen in the civilized parts of Fornland, but that absence had left the foxen free to breed unchecked, and now they appeared in such numbers, they were hunted year-round.

Vapor streamed from the nostrils of the horses as we gathered beneath the white oaks of the royal park south of the city. The hounds, barking, tangled their leads in excitement. The Master of the Hunt, a baronet named Jackman, practiced a few calls on the brass horn that coiled around his shoulder.

The air was filled with the bouquet of the turf, the scent of the newborn leaves, the odor of leather and horseflesh. I stood beneath the trees holding my own horn, a horn that had once belonged to a cow and was filled with the hot whisky punch with which I hoped both to counter the cold and to fortify my own courage. I did not like the chase, for horses and I were perpetually out of sympathy with one another. When I was astride a horse, it was the horse that often mastered me, and not the other way around. So at present, I kept my feet on the ground and postponed the moment when I mounted and surrendered the sovereignty of myself to the vicious whim of a dumb brute.

Floria on her dapple gray waited amid her ladies, her doublet of scarlet leather buttoned up to her throat, gold-tipped points hanging like fringes from her shoulders, and her skirt all trigged out in a great sweep, as if it were already blown back by the passing wind. I noted she wore a partridge feather in her cap, in token of her wager with Morestanton. Morestanton himself rode a great black monster of a horse, high-stepping and proud, with a silver star on his forehead and a silver forefoot. His father ignored me, but Morestanton saluted me with his silver-handled whip like a well-schooled young gentleman, and I raised my horn in reply. The two made their way to the Queen, and doffed their caps when she glanced their way.

Following them came the Wilmots, two sons and a daughter led by their father, the Duke of Waitstill and privy seal. The duke nodded gravely to me in passing, as did the younger of his boys. The daughter and the eldest son were conversing and did not notice me.

All those who had been in the council room the day before were here, and many more besides. I looked from one to the other and wondered if any of them had brought Antonio Luzi from over the ocean, and for what purpose.

"Ho, Quillifer!" The Duke and Duchess of Roundsilver rode up abreast on matching chestnuts, manes and tails catching red fire in the rays of the rising sun. The duchess was a small woman my own age, with bright blond hair braided and coiled beneath a smart little cap tilted over one eye. She and her husband were dressed alike in scarlet leather doublets with a double row of gilt buttons—Roundsilver being the Queen's cousin, he was permitted the royal colors of scarlet and gold. Their saddles and tack glittered with gilding, and gems shone on their fingers and their caps. Roundsilver looked, as he always did, like an exotic bird imported from southern climes; but his lady looked, as she always did, nothing short of brilliant.

The duchess reined to a halt near me. Her cheeks were flushed, and her blue eyes sparkled.

"The first chase of the year!" she said. "How I've longed for it!"

"I hope it is everything Your Grace may wish," said I. "As for myself, I shall do my best not to fall off my horse."

"I hope you will attend Blackwell's play tonight," she said.

"Oh, I shall be there," said I. "For I understand I am to be a character in the drama, and I wish to see how well I am enacted."

"I think Wakelyn doesn't quite have your gift of facetious conversation," said the duke, "but then he plays the hero very well."

"I shall be pleased to see myself embodied as a hero," I said.

"Noble," said the duchess with a knowing smile, "and chaste."

"Chaste?" said I. "Well, I understand there is a first time for everything."

Jackman, the Master of the Hunt, brayed out a horn call, and the duke and duchess straightened in the saddle and looked ahead. "It begins," said the duke. "Time to mount, Sir Quillifer."

I drained my whisky punch, and the fire burned my throat. "I suppose I can avoid it no longer."

My groom, Oscar, had been standing nearby with my bay charger, Phrenzy. Acorns crunched beneath my feet as I walked across the floor of the park. Oscar's bushy hair flopped in his face as he bent with cupped hands. I put my foot into his hands and let him boost me into the seat. Phrenzy looked over his shoulder at me and bared his teeth in a snarl.

Phrenzy was an ill-tempered animal with a fierce hatred of both man and beast, but he had borne me through battle at Exton Scales, a confrontation with a dragon, and other hunts such as this one, and so far I had emerged alive from every hazard. I disliked riding Phrenzy more than any other animal, but I had to admit that the brute was lucky for me.

Oscar mounted his own steed and followed as I urged Phrenzy to walk in the general direction of the other riders. I kept my distance, however, because Phrenzy hated other horses as much as he hated humans, and he had been known to kick other mounts, or sink his teeth in them if they came too close. So I stayed a little apart, and kept an eye on my fellow hunters, and wondered if one of them had hurled a man from the Castle wall two nights ago.

The hounds were let off their leads, and the whippers-in urged them in the direction of the nearest covert. Miraculously they flushed a fox immediately and bayed after it like a great tawny tide, and we were off.

Since we hunted in what was called a park, you might imagine we rode in a civilized place, grassy and level, with an admixture of well-groomed trees. But this park was closer to a forest in its natural state, cut by streams, earthen banks and ditches, and old half-tumbled, moss-covered stone fences. There were bogs, lakes, stiles, and narrow bridges over obstacles. Much of the undergrowth was cut back, but by no means all, and it was easy to be whipped in the face by a bush or shrub, or for a horse's foot to be tangled in brambles.

My ride was frantic and bruising, for the fox was cunning, and was always circling, doubling back, or cutting a zigzag path through brush, but I kept my head down and let Phrenzy drag me over fences, ditches, and other obstacles. A fierce pain settled into my thighs and belly at the strain of galloping. I would happily have hung back and had an easier ride, but Phrenzy was now in command, and he was in such a combative and zealous frame of mind that he kept always toward the front. It was all I could do to keep him from riding down the dogs. About me I caught glimpses of other riders: Floria tucked in atop her large-framed dapple gray, her hair flying out like dark smoke; Morestanton grinning atop his huge black; the Roundsilvers laughing on their matched chestnuts; Jackman, red-faced, bleating out his horn calls.

After a league or more, the fox went to ground in its den, and the den was surrounded at once by a mass of hounds, all frantic to get at their prey. The riders circled wide and gave the whippers-in a chance to manage the pack. I reined Phrenzy in and tried to catch my breath. The fox's den was a clump of bracken set in a clearing within a grove of ash-trees, and the ground was carpeted with previous year's helical seeds. Phrenzy grunted out his frustration—he would happily have dug the fox out of its den himself in order to bite its spine in half. I knew he was in a dangerous spirit and tried to keep him away from the other horses, but I failed to notice the youngest Wilmot as he trotted past me, and I cried out a warning too late as Phrenzy sank his teeth into Lord Hunstan Wilmot's thigh. I yanked Phrenzy's head away from his victim and—as I imagined my having given the Wilmots yet another reason to hate me—I babbled out a series of apologies.

Lord Hunstan had cantered a few strides away to examine his wound. He pressed his gloved hand to his thigh and frowned, then brought the glove away stained with blood.

"Don't trouble yourself, Lord Selford," he said. "My wound is not severe."

Like his late, mad brother, who I had knocked from the rigging of the *Kiminge* in a duel with top-mauls, Lord Hunstan was a pale blond. He rode a copper-colored sorrel, and wore riding leathers in the Waitstill colors of white and green. He was, I believed, still under twenty.

Phrenzy gave out a breathy roar, as if to pledge his willingness to bite again. Again I yanked on the reins, less to command the beast than to divert him, perhaps, from his victim.

"I would offer you a handkerchief," I said, "but I daren't come near you with my charger in this mood."

"The bleeding will stop ere long," said Lord Hunstan. "Though I fear I will be sadly bruised."

"You should have a surgeon look at the wound," said I. "It may need stitches."

Lord Hunstan was unconcerned. "A surgeon would say that bleeding is needed to prevent the blood from stagnating. Your steed, by bleeding me, has merely saved me the barber-surgeon's fee."

He lifted his gaze from his wound and looked at me for the first time. "I was partly at fault," said he. "I came near your charger, which after all has a reputation for ferocity that I see is well deserved."

"You are gracious, my lord."

His eyes dropped to the holsters at my saddle-bow, and a frown appeared between his brows. "You carry pistols," he said. "Did you expect to shoot the fox?"

"If a horse falls and breaks a leg," said I, "I would spare it suffering."

"Ay." He nodded thoughtfully, and then his gaze shifted to the Queen, who sat atop her dapple gray, chatting to Morestanton. "Or perhaps you plan to preserve the Queen's life in the event of some assault."

"I am not a pistoleer, my lord," said I. "I doubt I could hit an attacker from horseback unless the pistol were pressed to his neck."

I did not mention the gentleman officers of the Yeoman Archers who had ridden through the park at dawn, to scout for danger, and who now made up part of the hunting party. It was best not to let the greatest in the land know they were under observation by a crew of armed, sharp-eyed men.

Lord Hunstan smiled. "You would need only let your horse fly at any assassin, and he would soon be dead." His eyes turned from the pistols to me. "I heard a man was found dead outside the castle walls," he said. "A man with a poison ring."

"Your lordship is well informed."

Lord Hunstan shrugged. "It is the talk of the castle."

"The investigation continues," I said, "and we will run his killer, like this fox, to earth."

"The Pilgrim grant you all success."

Our conversation was interrupted as Jackman loudly blew a call on his horn. The call echoed off the tall ash-trees. Lord Hunstan cocked an ear at the sound. "He calls for the terrier-man," he said.

His older brother, the Marquess of Brighthelm—pronounced "Brightum"—came trotting up on his chestnut, and gestured with his silver-handled whip. "Hunstan," he said. "Come."

"What is it?"

"Just come." Brighthelm began to trot away.

Lord Hunstan gave me an apologetic look and followed. I gave him a half-wave and let Phrenzy walk over the carpet of samara toward Floria's party. The Queen, I saw, was almost eclipsed by Lord Morestanton on his great charger. I made a half-circle around them, careful not to let Phrenzy within biting range of Morestanton's black.

"Well, Sir Quillifer," Floria said. "That was a fine chase, was it not?"

"I am gratified Your Majesty enjoyed it."

"Did your charger give Lord Hunstan an injury?"

I was not surprised Floria had noticed, for she had the sharpest eyes, and the most cunning discernment, of anyone in the realm.

"Lord Hunstan says the bite is minor."

"No assault by your Phrenzy is minor," Floria said. "Sometimes I think your horse is a demon in a bay pelt."

"Sometimes I think Your Majesty is right," said I.

Morestanton eyed Phrenzy, then shifted his own horse somewhat away. He turned to Floria. "I think our coursers are equally matched," he said. "I hope you will consent to a race on our return, with the stakes as we yesterday discussed."

Floria looked at Morestanton's black. "I cannot but think your charger will flag on our return," she said, "having to carry its own great weight, and you as well."

"I am not so heavy as that." Morestanton grinned. "I will wager you a peacock feather that you are mistaken, Majesty."

Floria nodded. "I consent to the wager, then."

I looked at Pontkyles, who seemed well satisfied at his son's place by the Queen; and then at Waitstill, who was displeased for the same reason.

The whippers-in had driven the hounds off the fox's den, to make way for the terriers. The terrier-man, a short, stout fellow in a blue coat and a tall black hat, appeared driving his light two-wheel cart, very like a cocking cart, with his animals in a box behind. He drew his cart to a halt, released his dogs, and led them to the quarry's den. The bracken was well trampled by this point, so the dogs saw the den well before they arrived, and they barked and strained on their leads. The terrier-man pondered for a moment, then released but one of his animals, who dove into the den with an eager snarl.

The riders, and the hounds, remained alert in case the fox had a back door to his bolt-hole and made a final dash for its life. But this was not the case, for soon the terrier dragged the fox out of his den by a hind leg, and at once the other terriers were released to finish the beast off. The Master of the Hunt dismounted, drew a short, curved sword, and, once the terriers were called off, bent to hack the fox to pieces. Morsels were given to the terriers as a reward, and the rest thrown to the hounds. The head and the brush were kept as trophies, though I knew not what was done with them. I had never seen the heads of foxen displayed on pikes, like the traitors before the Hall of Justice in Howel.

"It is like drawing and quartering," said Morestanton. "At least we spare the animal a hanging."

"Indeed," said I. "We treat our fellow humans with more savagery than we treat the vermin of the fields."

Floria gave me a sharp look over one shoulder—she was wary of any suggestion that she ruled through tyranny or brutality, as had her sister—but my remark had been general, and she soon decided I had intended no criticism either of her reign or her fox hunt. She returned her attention to Morestanton.

"Let us find a starting-point," she said. "And when the Master is not otherwise occupied, he can signal the start with his horn."

"Shall we follow the course of the hunt?" Morestanton asked. "Or ride straight for the finish?"

Retracing the fox's serpentine course would make for a much longer ride, as well as a more challenging one for the riders. I thought that Morestanton's big horse would flag before the finish, and that in a straight gallop he would have a better chance of victory.

"There is no straight ride in this forest," Floria said, "but let us make as straight a path as we may."

The two trotted some distance from the party. I followed, but stayed a respectful and watchful distance behind. I was not a party to the race, but I wished to keep a protective eye on Her Majesty.

Jackman wiped the fox's blood from his gloves, then remounted and put his horn to his lips. He waited a suspenseful few seconds, puffing his cheeks, and then blew a rousing charge. Floria and Morestanton spurred their mounts and disappeared in clouds of samara kicked up by their horses' hooves.

Phrenzy needed no urging to pursue, and soon I was at the head of a party of riders who were more than happy for another chase. Floria was correct that her path would not be straight, for the park was wild enough that the riders had to swerve around obstacles, or jump them; and the precise direction of the finish was uncertain at the start. Phrenzy began at a bruising gallop—intent, I think, on sinking his teeth into the haunches of Morestanton's black—but Phrenzy was no longer as young as once he was, and flagged before Morestanton's mount, which lunged into the lead at about the halfway point. The two steadily drew ahead, and I saw them only now and again, as trees and other obstacles blocked my view.

I wondered if Morestanton would try to retain his lead. If he dashed to the oak grove first, he would have the prestige of winning, and a partridge feather to wear over his heart; but it might serve his suit better to allow the Queen to win. I wonder what instruction Pontkyles had given his son in the matter.

Floria's dapple gray began to overtake Morestanton as the heavier horse started to fade, and I ran into the clear to see the two were dashing up to a watercourse, riding side by side for a wooden bridge that was only a single horse wide. I saw Floria bent low over her horse's neck, her whip slashing down, as she pulled a little ahead, but not far enough—my heart leaped into my throat as I foresaw a collision, with Morestanton's giant steed knocking Floria's gray off the bridge, the Queen thrown into the water with her horse atop her; but then Morestanton pulled his horse wide at the very last second, and the gray's hooves clattered on the bridge as Morestanton tried to leap the brook. Due to the unexpected change in course, Morestanton's charger had not managed to set himself properly for the jump, and Morestanton was almost thrown as his mount staggered on the landing. He and the black managed to recover, but they had no chance of catching Floria, who rode on without looking back.

For myself, I was still at the head of the group that followed the two racers, and I steered Phrenzy for the bridge—until a charger came out of nowhere and shouldered Phrenzy out of its way. My teeth clacked at the force of the impact, I swayed in the saddle, and for an instant I felt for myself the terror that I had just felt for Floria in her dash for the bridge as I imagined Phrenzy falling with me under him—but then Phrenzy leaped into the air, his hooves doing a little caper like a ballet-dancer hovering above the stage, and then he somehow landed square. Phrenzy had managed something like this once before, at Exton Scales, when he made a strangely delicate leap over a fallen horse and rider; and I had thought it a miracle then just as it seemed a miracle now.

Phrenzy gave a bellow of rage and charged after our assailant, and for once I was inclined to give my charger his head. Before us was a blue dun fully as large as Morestanton's black—and it may have been the black's father or near relation, for astride the great beast was His Grace of Pontkyles, Morestanton's father, vast buttocks planted like a pair of fleshy turnips in a bucket-like saddle. I felt a suspicion that Pontkyles had just tried to see off his son's perceived rival for Floria's favor, and I was firm in the conviction that I should seek justice in the matter.

We clattered across the narrow bridge, and Phrenzy seemed a beast enchanted, for he had cast off all weariness and was determined to catch Pontkyles or burst his heart in the attempt. Within a hundred yards, Phrenzy had achieved his goal, and sank his teeth in the blue dun's nates. Pontkyles's hunter gave a shriek and missed stride, which was all the opportunity Phrenzy needed to drive his shoulder like a battering ram against his victim's hip. Even though I was braced for the impact, still I was nearly thrown.

Only the blue dun's size and weight saved it from crumpling like a piece of parchment. As it was, the beast staggered, and Pontkyles came free of his seat and was only saved by his tall, bucket-shaped saddle, which barely managed to restrain his broad hips from taking flight. As it was, Pontkyles must have been terribly wrenched, and his foot lost a stirrup.

I decided against allowing Phrenzy to persevere in his revenge, for I did not wish to have to explain the presence in the hunting party of a dead duke. So I wrenched Phrenzy's head aside and kicked his flanks, and he gave a bawl of frustrated anger but for once obeyed. Ahead, Morestanton and the Queen were vanishing into the distance.

I caught up with them in the oak grove where the hunt had begun, after they had reined up and were trotting their horses in a wide circle. Phrenzy was near staggering with weariness, and he seemed grateful to be brought to a walk as the others of the party spilled into the grove. Palace servants were present with food and drink laid out on tables.

Pontkyles came in last, on his limping blue dun, and when his glance settled on me, it looked like a dark storm advancing across the horizon. And then Sir Merriman Sandicup, who held the Exchequer, came trotting up by me.

"I saw what you did, Selford," he said. "That attack of yours was a foul piece of work."

"Ah," said I. "Did you not see what Pontkyles did to provoke it?"

"You should have got out of the way."

I felt myself snarl, for my blood was still up, but some small element of caution restrained me, so before I spoke, I took a few deliberate breaths of air scented with the rising spring. "If His Grace had asked me," said I, "or somehow made his presence known, I would have given way. But instead he ran into me like the most blundering rider in the world. Or perhaps—" And here I put an edge on my words. "Perhaps he was not blundering at all but wished to do me some injury. So which do you think—is he a wretched rider, or a paltry, incompetent ruffian?"

Sandicup flushed scarlet, which made him look like a blazing firework candle, for his hair and beard were red. He had been chosen for the Exchequer because his shrewd use of money had turned his small fortune into a very large one, and—as a mere baronet—he was not, strictly speaking, a member of the nobility, and could sit in the House of Burgesses and manage the realm's finances. I own he had done well with the budget, and brought in most of what Floria wanted; but somehow I did not like him, and he did not like me.

"You should have given way," he said, and trotted off.

I inclined Phrenzy toward Morestanton, who was offering his partridge feather to the Queen. Phrenzy seemed too exhausted to attack anyone, but still I kept a safe distance.

"That was a pretty piece of chivalry on the bridge, Lord Morestanton," I told him.

"Her Majesty reached the bridge first, and fairly," Morestanton said. "It was only right that I surrendered the right-of-way."

"There was less chivalry elsewhere in the park," I said, "but no doubt your father will tell you about it."

He and Floria each gave me a questioning look, but neither decided to inquire further. Floria took off her cap and pinned Morestanton's feather to it. Then she removed her own partridge feather and handed it to Morestanton.

"Chivalry should be rewarded, sir," said she. "Take this from me, and should you win glory in the war, I will redeem it with a kiss."

Morestanton took the feather and raised it to his lips, then stuffed it into his doublet, somewhere in the vicinity of his heart. "Ever shall I treasure this, Majesty," said he, "and ever shall I try to prove worthy of the gift."

I was struck with admiration for Floria's art, her skill at managing these powerful men who surrounded her, her suitors in particular. *Serve me and go to war*, she said, *and if you succeed, you will be rewarded*.

By a sisterly kiss, apparently, but her suitors were at liberty to imagine something greater.

My groom Oscar arrived, and I dismounted and handed Phrenzy's reins to him. I helped myself to a mince pie with the royal arms imprinted on the crust and a pot of ale made in the palace's brewhouse. The brewhouse was in constant use, for nearly six hundred people were employed by the royal household in the palace and other properties near Selford, and most of them were paid partly in ale, wine, or beer, depending on the season. The ale had been enhanced with bay berries and alecost, a flavor that foretold the coming of summer, and the pork mince had been sweetened with dried prunes and apricots, and enriched with suet harvested from the kidneys of lambs.

It was a fine mince pie, yet not as good as my mother's.

I looked up from my flagon to see Lord Catsgore approaching. He was a sturdy man of middle years who, like me, wore his dark hair long and his face clean-shaven, a style that in his case revealed bright, confiding blue eyes and a wide, lipless mouth. Catsgore was Minister of State for Fornland, with his family seat in the far west near Uskmore, where his clan had long spread their power over the dark viridian valleys and stark seaside cliffs, holding dominion from their gray flint castle reared up on a spur of the West Range. He seemed to be one of those great lords who did not despise me, and we sometimes supped together as we worked on projects to benefit the people and prosperity of the West and my native Ostra Valley.

"Lord Selford," he said, "I wished you to know that I saw Pontkyles try to knock you and your horse, and that if your repayment of the offense becomes the subject of one of his complaints, I will be happy to bear witness on your behalf."

"I thank your lordship," said I. "I hope your testimony will not be necessary, for the last the realm needs is for Her Majesty's councillors to mewl and grumble in open complaint 'gainst one another."

"They will hardly stop now." Catsgore smiled. "It is viewed as a right, and nearly a duty, for men of rank to secure their own place by debasing others." He continued. "But Selford, should you ever sell that bay of yours, I hope you will let me buy him. Your Phrenzy is fierce and passionate, but he preserves his rider."

"I only hope Phrenzy will not change his mind," I said.

He stepped closer and took my arm, lowering his voice in

confidence. "I also wanted to warn you," he said, "about this visitor, this Albiz prince, Amadeu."

"He has written to tell Her Majesty that he will come," I said, "but I know nothing else about him." Nor much about the Albiz in general, other than they were said to be dwarfish, brown-skinned, and live in great carven cities underground.

"Amadeu is one of their chieftains," Catsgore said, "and hardly rates the title of *prince*. I fear he comes to lay a complaint against me and my family."

"On what grounds?" I glanced over my shoulder. "Perhaps we should speak to the Chancellor."

"I doubt it will come under the Chancellor's jurisdiction," Catsgore said. "Amadeu's case is so weak that he hopes to evade the courts altogether, and intends that Her Majesty will make an arbitrary ruling in his favor."

"And the dispute?"

"Title to lands. Lands that have been in my family for four hundred years, and which Amadeu will insist have always belonged to his clan."

"Who possesses the land now?"

"All manner of people." Catsgore was offhand. "These mountain coombs are remote, and folk have lived there for generations without asking anyone's permission, or wander from hedge to ditch after their flocks of sheep. There has never been a census taken, nor a survey."

Nor rent paid, I thought, at least to Catsgore. Though to a degree, he had my sympathy.

Land disputes based on ancient deeds were always filled with dangerous complexity, not least because of the way boundaries were described. A deed might say that the boundary followed the river till it came to the old pine, and then went westward until it encountered a stone wall; but in the centuries since the deed had been granted, the river had changed its course, the pine had fallen, and the stones of the wall had been robbed out by a neighbor to build a new barn. Proving anything in these cases was absurdly difficult and often required collecting depositions from the oldest inhabitants of the district swearing that the boundaries had always been thus-and-so, a procedure that took ages.

"And the law," said I, "gives certain rights to those who have lived on the land for generations."

Catsgore spread his hands. "But have they? They will *say* they have always been in the country, but they *may* be wandering herders who have just occupied the land, or violent clansmen who have burned out their neighbors in order to seize the property."

"I imagine a judge will take much convincing before making a ruling," said I. "And as for Her Majesty, I can't see why the Queen would make it her business to interfere."

"I thank you for this reassurance, Selford," said Catsgore. "And be assured that I will stand by you if Pontkyles makes any accusation against you."

"I thank your lordship," said I.

So were bargains made at court, in which neither party truly committed himself, but both understood one another perfectly. I was the royal favorite, and people were always approaching me in the hopes that I would influence Floria on their behalf. Sometimes I was offered money, which I refused, though I was not immune to the gracious presentation of a modest and tasteful gift, or to a favor involving a friend.

Those who attempted to win my influence had not, I think, understood Floria, who knew those around her better than they knew themselves, and whose decisions were based on that knowledge. If knowledge proved lacking, it was my task to supply it; but unless I offered some particulars the Queen did not already know, her decision was made without reference to my views, as her choices for military command demonstrated.

Floria and Morestanton turned their horses over to their grooms and walked to the refreshment table. I watched carefully as Morestanton offered her a cup of ale—all ale was drawn from the same barrel, so if the Queen were poisoned, so were we all. He also offered her a pork pie, but she declined and pointed to another. "This other has kindled my affections," she said, "I know not why." Morestanton hastened to bring it to her.

Her years at court had taught that food chosen at random was the least likely to prove deadly.

After our rustic feast, we remounted our horses and returned to town, walking and trotting alongside the hounds. Phrenzy had recovered some of his vigor, but he seemed content with the vengeance he'd wreaked on the blue dun and made no more assaults on his rivals. Lord Hunstan Wilmot ambled near me on his steed but was careful to stay out of range of Phrenzy's teeth.

"I hope your leg isn't troubling you, my lord," said I.

He was blithe. "It will be sore tomorrow," he said. "Well, it is sore *now*, but tomorrow it will be worse. But at least it has stopped bleeding."

I glanced ahead in the column and saw his older brother Brighthelm in deep conversation with his father. "What did your brother want with you?" I asked.

"Oh." He seemed embarrassed. "He didn't want me speaking to you. He hates you for killing our brother Brynley."

"And you do not?"

Hunstan gave the matter a moment's consideration. "My father received the report from Lord Edevane, with the statements of the witnesses. All agreed that Brynley provoked the fight, and that— well—he was mad when he did it." He looked at me. "Edevane could easily have condemned you in order to put my father under an obligation, but he did not. My father mourns Brynley but accepted the report." He shrugged. "And I respect my father's judgment."

"And Brighthelm does not?"

"He thinks Edevane's report irrelevant and your fault lies in your failure of respect."

"My disrespect is that I did not consent to be killed by a madman?"

Hunstan's answer was diplomatic. "I do not believe he has expressed it thus."

I had just about had my fill of well-born gentlemen who felt I should be honored to be ridden down by any duke who felt like trampling me, or to imagine myself flattered when I allowed my head to be beaten in by some deranged cockalorum with a grant of arms. But I concealed my indignation behind my learnèd advocate face and merely nodded.

"No doubt his feelings on the matter are complicated," said I.

Hunstan looked at me with pale eyes. "There is a thing about your lordship that I have remarked," he said, "and which I do not understand."

"Ay?" I waved a hand. "I am transparent. Ask your question."

"It seems that you are not—how do I phrase it?" He hesitated. "You seem unimpressed by us."

"Us?"

He waved a hand at the line of hunters trotting toward the palace. "Us," he said. "The nobility. My brother Brighthelm views it as disrespect."

"I like to think I respect people as they deserve," said I. "Her Majesty, for example, has not only my respect but my worship."

"A worship shared by all of us," he said. His words were almost an unwitting reflex, the reflex flattery of a courtier to the monarch.

"Just so," said I.

"But," said he, "we have *ancestors*."

"So does everyone," I said. "Only the Ghouls, I'm told, are created spontaneously."

"I mean noble ancestors," he said. "The Waitstill family has been titled for over four hundred years."

I put on my superior prefect face. "You *have* ancestors," I said. "I *am* an ancestor."

He seemed puzzled. "I hadn't heard that you were a father," he said.

"That is not what I meant," said I. "I meant that I am like that first ancestor of yours to be raised to the nobility. He had as obscure an origin as I, and by dint of luck and a deal of mother-wit earned himself a letter patent and a seat in the House of Peers." Hunstan still seemed puzzled, and so I added, "What, did you think that first Waitstill was born with a coronet on his head?"

"I had not considered it."

"Well," said I, "if he was, then so was I."

The hunting party took separate paths once it entered the city gates, as some, like the Roundsilvers, rode for their own homes in the city, while I followed the royal party up Chancellery Road to the great white castle on its bluff. We entered the Outer Ward in a clatter of hoofs and a barking of dogs, and I again turned Phrenzy over to my groom Oscar, then tramped in my boots and spurs to the Inner Ward to change out of my riding clothes. As I walked I eyed the dozens of people moving in and out of the castle gates, and the Yeoman Archers standing guard with their halberds, and I wondered how and when Antonio Luzi had walked past the sentries into the most guarded part of the Castle.

In truth, it wouldn't have been difficult. Hundreds of people lived or worked in the Castle, and many others came on business, and the guards couldn't know them all. As long as someone looked as though he belonged, he would pass the gate even into the Inner Ward—I had done this myself, walking past the guards when an apprentice lawyer, with a gown and cap. I had seemed to be someone's secretary or scribe, and as long as I did not call attention to myself in some glaring way, I was allowed to haunt the palace as much as I cared to.

It was much more difficult to get into Floria's private quarters, for few were allowed there, and the guards knew them all. Yet it was not a person who had to get close to Floria but poison, and poison need not arrive in the form of a stranger but in a posset, a cake, a sweetmeat, a hairpin.

CHAPTER FOUR

That evening *Escape from Laelius* was to be enacted in the castle's Great Reception Room. Courtiers walked through the Inner Ward, glittering in the declining sun. Hawkers sold pies and gingerbread, and grilled sausages sent their aroma into the air. A water organ played unearthly music that reminded me of whales singing in the Tabarzam Strait.

I approached the engineer Alaron Mountmirail and his wife Edith, the sister of the Queen's Gunfounder, the alchemist Ransome. They were an unusual couple, Mountmirail moon-faced and lanky, looking no older than eighteen, and Edith fierce, gaunt, hatchet-faced, and at least fifteen years older than her husband. The two were deeply in love, and she walked with both arms enfolding one of his, her stark face bearing an unaccustomed look of contentment.

"Mistress Mountmirail." I doffed my cap. "I thank you for the gift of your book. Of course I bought copies for all my captains, and for the Lord Admiral, too."

"I hope they con them with care," said Edith. "For I boast but little in saying that they are the best in the world, yet in the end are only as good as the navigators who employ them."

Edith Mountmirail was one of Floria's ladies-in-waiting, but she was seen little at court and instead spent most of her time at an observatory and mural quadrant that the Queen had built for her at Floria's old home of Kellhurst, in Bonille. With the quadrant, aligned with the meridian and said to be the finest in all of Alford, Edith carefully measured the height of stars and turned the measurements into tables. The tables, which would be superior to the error-filled tables now in circulation, could in turn be used by navigators to determine their latitude at sea, and to find their way home in bad weather.

The first volume of tables had just been published, and Edith had trained a group of assistants—all young women—to work with her on the second volume. I supposed they would all be up late tonight, wrapped in shawls against the chill, gazing at the heavens and jotting down numbers in a book.

"I thank you for letting us shelter at your house," said Mountmirail. "It is all a-bustle with preparations for your great feast, but our room is in a quiet corner, and there we can both work."

"I'm pleased the house is of some use," said I. "I rarely see it myself."

The house, Haysfield Grange, was one of the properties that Floria had given me, and was intended to support my dignity as Count of Selford. It was an old castle that had been converted into a manor by an industrious baron about a hundred years ago, but his family had died out, and the property had reverted to the crown. For the previous thirty years it had been inhabited by a series of tenants who left it dilapidated. For over a year I'd had workers polishing the woodwork, laying new tile, planting gardens and orchards, constructing a bath-house and a brewhouse, enhancing the kitchens, hanging tapestries, building a minstrels' gallery in the great hall, bringing in new beds, mattresses, and linens, and laying wines and liquors in the buttery. In a few days I would play host to the court in a day of games and entertainments, along with a great feast prepared by my cook, Harry Noach.

To make Haysfield Grange suitable for the court seemed a great waste of labor, for ere long I would be expected to pull the place down and build a great prodigy house in its place, with a hundred rooms, a thousand windows, and a dozen carved chimneys twisting into the sky. It was what everyone did with their country homes if they could afford it, and I suppose the Count of Selford could do no less than his neighbors.

Though I would wait till after the war to put up a new house, for now my money had better uses than to build a monument to my vanity—though of course it must be admitted that my friends thought me vain enough already.

I turned to Mountmirail. "Have you seen Blackwell?" I asked.

"Ay." A grin split his moon face. "I was able to suggest a few improvements to aid in the shifting of his scenery."

"I am sure he is grateful."

He looked over my shoulder. "The bellows there," he said. "I have not seen their sort before."

He was referring to the bellows of the water organ, two mounted side by side and operated by an apprentice, who stood on them and shifted his weight left and right to drive air into the copper reservoir. We strolled to where the musician, sweat gleaming on his forehead, played at his double keyboard. The apprentice, who seemed to be exerting himself far less than his master, rocked back and forth from one bellows to the next. Chords wailed from the pipes and echoed off the castle's stone walls.

"Why is there water in the air reservoir?" I asked.

"Water may not be compressed," Mountmirail began.

"Indeed?" said I. "Of this I was ignorant. I shall try to compress some and see."

Mountmirail was unperturbed by my interruption. "So water, which may not be compressed, is put in the bottom of the air reservoir. Air, which *can* be compressed, is pumped in atop it, displacing the water to a separate reservoir at a higher level. The water strives to return against the pressure of the air, thus keeping pressure steady within the reservoir. The air maintains a high pressure and enables the organ—" The organ gave a particularly discordant shriek and for a moment we clapped our hands over our ears. Mountmirail grinned and walked away from the screeching pipes. Now at a safe distance, he waved a hand.

"Enables the organ," he laughed, "to bless us with such music."

I looked over my shoulder at the organ's operator. "He is a damned poor minstrel," I said.

"Say rather that he is a poor composer," said Mountmirail, "for I've heard him before, and he plays his own music only. He has a new theory of modes illustrated by his compositions."

"Well," said I, "there are other organ players."

Mountmirail tilted his head and looked at the organ through the tight curled locks of his red hair. "I admire the genius of the water-reservoir mechanism," he said, "and I wonder if there is some other use for it other than making music."

"Blast furnaces?" said I. "They use trompes to push the air in now, and the trompes are powered by water."

"Or perhaps air pressure could be used to work machinery?"

"Again, we have water to power machinery, from triphammers to flour mills," I said. "It would have to be a powerful force of air indeed to be stronger than water running downhill."

Mountmirail bobbed his head left and right, like the organ apprentice striding on his bellows. "Perhaps I'll build a bloomery," he said, "and then we'll see if I can make some good pig iron."

"Nay, you shall not," I said firmly. I took his arm and steered him away from the water organ. "Your task is to build the Queen's Canal, and nothing else."

"Ay," Mountmirail conceded. "Yet if my experiment succeeds, you would be the first to profit by it."

"Let us deal with one enterprise at a time, Master Mountmirail," said I. "And start with the canal. We already know how to make pig iron."

In the last meeting of the Estates, I had finally managed to get passed a bill that would allow my company to acquire the right-of-way and build a canal from the River Ostra above Ethlebight to Gannett Cove on the south coast. Even before its sack by Aekoi reivers, my home city had been in decline, for its harbor had been silting for a generation, and now only small vessels could attempt the passage. Once the canal was built, the wealth of the upper Ostra would once more have a free passage to the sea, and Ethlebight could be rebuilt on the cliffs above the finest harbor west of Amberstone.

Construction of the canal had now begun, advancing from either end toward a meeting in the center. The lords and merchants of Ethlebight and the Ostra were heavily invested in the project—including Ethlebight's famous brickmakers, who donated generously but would earn their money back by selling their bricks to line the bed of the canal. Mountmirail had been made chief engineer based on his invention of an antihydraulic mortar that would keep the canal's lining from washing away, and now that the project was well begun had come to Selford to report on his progress.

"Those cliffs behind Gannett Cove are mostly shale," he said. "And shale crumbles well, and is easy enough to blast and shift. The spoil can be turned into shingles, or mortared together to make quays or firm roads or towpaths. But the shale won't stop crumbling just because we've finished digging our canal. There are small landslides all the time. I think we shall have to build a roof over the locks, because otherwise, falling shale will over time fill the waterway."

"You could plank over the right-of-way with wooden beams," I suggested. "And make the structure more artful later."

"Ay," he said. "I will order the beams, then, from Amberstone."

"And your rate of progress?"

He gestured with his right hand. "Progress has been greater on the western end, for the land is flat, and we can bring supplies in by water. We have gone six leagues, and should be adding another league every two or three weeks until we run into the Eldir Valley, where we shall be obliged to build an aqueduct to carry the canal over the ravine."

He swept to the other end of the canal with a broad gesture with his left hand, and almost knocked off his wife's cap. "In the east, we have barely finished blasting our way up the cliff, and now we must construct the locks to take the barges up and down. Though once that is done, and I have diverted a stream or two into the channel, we may advance fairly quickly, and carry ourselves forward on barges, far better than carrying the bricks up the cliff on mules."

I thanked Mountmirail for his report, and then I turned as someone touched my arm with a fan. This proved to be Lady Mellender, one of Floria's ladies, who before her marriage I had known as Chenée Tavistock. She had an engaging air and a pleasing overbite, and delivered her message with a confidential air.

"Lord Selford," she said, "Her Majesty would like to speak with you."

"Of course," I said. I turned to the Mountmirails. "If you will excuse me."

I left Lady Mellender to renew her acquaintance with the Mountmirails and walked into the Great Reception Room, a vast tapestry-hung chamber, always chilly despite the logs burning in the great carven fireplace. Almost immediately I knew trouble was at hand, for at Floria's right hand I saw a distinguished stranger. He wore a sequin-covered black doublet slashed to reveal a white satin shirt, and on his distinguished face I saw an expression of perfect amiability. He had a long head topped with gray curls, a formidable blade of a nose, and a beard of mixed gray and iron.

I realized at once that this had to be Dom Erasmo Resendes

Armaval, *Duque* de Gandorim, the new ambassador of sun-kissed Varcellos, and leader of an extraordinarily large and magnificent embassy that had just arrived on a galleon blessed by King Anibal himself. His commission, I had no doubt, was to marry Floria to one of his country's great superfluity of bachelor princes, all of whom were perpetually on offer to the royalty of other countries.

As I knew the *duque* hadn't yet presented his credentials to the Queen, he was no doubt here informally, though even if he were here in the character of a private individual, I very much doubted he would have refrained from making the opening moves in his regal courtship dance.

I approached Floria, bowed, and doffed my cap. "Your Majesty sent for me?" I asked.

Floria was seated on a magnificent gilded chair that fell just short of being a throne, and which was set with a few other chairs on a carpeted platform that gave her a superior view of the stage and its actors. Gandorim sat on her right, his body inclined gracefully in her direction. The chair on her left was empty, and Floria pointed toward it with her fan.

"Please sit with us, Lord Selford," said she. "And allow us to introduce to you to His Grace of Gandorim, who surprises us with his appearance tonight."

"Your Grace," said I as I took my seat. "I received a report this afternoon that your ship had arrived in Innismore. I hope you had a pleasant journey."

Gandorim regarded me with mild brown eyes. His gaze was direct but almost caressing, and he missed nothing, not the moiré pattern of my silk doublet, the gemstones on my fingers, the badge on my cap, or the lively antagonism that lay behind my attentive courtier face.

"The crossing was uneventful," he said. "You will be gratified, I hope, to hear that we encountered your ship *Sea-Drake*, returned from a successful voyage to Tabarzam. Your Captain Oakeshott sends his greetings, and I'm sure will make port tomorrow."

"I thank Your Grace," I said. "With our enemies on the sea, I have been anxious for all our ships." *Sea-Drake* had always been a slow vessel, and though she was well armed, I'd feared the enemy would catch her. Now it seemed as if my largest ship would soon be discharging its cargo in Innismore.

Gandorim cast a lazy glance at the stage. "I understand that you are the hero of this play," he said.

"I'm certain that any heroism will be expanded by a deal of fiction," I said. "The play is not even set in our country but in ancient history."

"And yet you did in truth rescue Her Majesty from her enemies," said Gandorim. "No amount of fiction can disguise that."

A small orchestra began to play from its place in the gallery. Floria's ladies drifted toward us, and I rose to help them onto the platform and into the chairs behind us. The audience began to settle into their seats, and then the playwright Blackwell stepped out to proclaim an address to Her Majesty.

It was the usual flowery dedication, better than most of the laudations that were ever directed at the Queen, but much the same in content. I ceased to pay attention almost at once.

Blackwell was an actor and poet as well as a playwright, and his long poem *Court of Laelius*, which viewed the reign of one of the Aekoi Empire's more appalling rulers as a metaphor for the rule of Viceroy Fosco, had been a sensation a few years ago. It would never have passed the censor and had been published illegally, but that made it even more popular, and it became a great success, and helped to turn the country against Fosco and Loretto.

After Floria had been crowned and Fosco driven from the country, Blackwell followed with *The Fall of Laelius*, mixing a savage attack on Fosco with a panegyric in praise of Floria. It was less successful,

I thought, in the way that sequels are often but shadows of the work that inspired them, but it had sold well.

Now Blackwell had added *Escape from Laelius* to his scope, a drama masquerading as the story of Floria's escape from Fosco's deadly net. Fortunately it contained enough fiction to pass the censorship of the Master of the Revels.

It helped that Blackwell had already written half of it, a single-act farce called *The Doctor and the Fever-Struck Princess*, which showed how a member of his own company, a boy actor called Bonny Joe Webb, had impersonated the imperiled Floria in her own house while the authentic Floria and I were fleeing over the Cordillerie as fast as our horses could take us. Bonny Joe was by far the most popular member of Blackwell's company, a beautiful and enchanting juvenile who could play man or woman, comedy or tragedy—and now he had become one of a very few actors who played himself onstage. In this play Bonny Joe not only played himself disguised as the Queen, he played the Queen herself.

My character was played by the company's leading male ingenue, Wakelyn, a stern-jawed fellow who was very good in the role of a man of action, or of a lover. Naturally I could not be the lover of the Queen in this drama, and so Blackwell had invented a lady-in-waiting for me to be enamored of, and who—once I had rescued the Queen, and got her crowned—I could then save from Laelius's dungeon, after Laelius himself, defeated and at bay, had toppled to his death from a cliff.

I thought the play was clumsy and overstuffed with plot, but the sub-story with Bonny Joe impersonating the princess was proven comedy, and the company had only improved it in the year since it was first played. The audience either liked the play or felt it was their duty to like it, and so there were ovations at the end of every act and after every one of Wakelyn's partisan speeches.

Rufino Knott and a band of minstrels performed in the courtyard between acts, and some of his songs were about me, and my adventures in the royal regattas and in Floria's escape.

Edevane foiled, and the princess unsoiled

The escape would reshape our realm despoiled.

On the whole, the songs were more truthful than the play.

"Upon my word, Lord Selford," said Gandorim after the final act, "it seems that you are the cynosure of the realm."

"I am a dog's tail?" For I knew that word came from the Old Aekoi *kynósoura.*

"I mean the word in its present meaning," said Gandorim.

"That *cynosure* is *premature,* I do *assure,*" I said. "I am merely Her Majesty's faithful servant."

"Please, Quillifer." Floria winced. "Let Blackwell provide the rhymes."

"As you wish, Majesty."

She turned to the stage. "I suppose I must congratulate young Master Webb for his impersonation of me."

"'From the Queen of Duisland to the Queen of the Stage, greetings,'" said I. Floria regarded me with mild eyes.

"Not bad," she said.

Floria stood, which obliged everyone else to stand as well, and I offered her a hand in descending the platform to the floor of the vast room.

I turned into the room and found there Lord Thistlegorm, all smiles, along with his daughters.

As befit the daughter of the most prominent Retriever in the realm, the two girls were dressed in white samite, the elder in a gown sewn closely with white pearls and silver galloons, the younger in a gown more girlish, with flounces and purfles.

"I am pleased to make your acquaintance," said I, "and I hope the journey to Selford was not too fatiguing."

"Not at all," said Candice, the elder. Her hair was pale brown with an admixture of bronze, and her dark eyes were downcast. I couldn't tell if she were shy, or if this brand of modesty was recommended in a young lady from a house devoted to the teachings of the Compassionate Pilgrim.

Her sister Emily was less reticent. "Did you really kill those bailiffs on the stair," she asked, "and then run away with the sick princess in your arms?"

"I killed no one on that journey." The lie came easily to my lips. "But Her Highness Floria became very ill in the Cordillerie, of the same sickness that killed her sister, and while I played nurse I was afraid the whole time that pursuit would overtake us."

Emily seemed unwilling to entirely abandon the subject. "But if they'd caught you," she said, "you would have fought?"

I smiled down at her. "It would have been my duty," I said.

With this she seemed satisfied. I looked at the stage, where the players had come out to meet the audience, and then turned to Candice.

"Would it amuse you to meet the actors?" I said.

I was on the alert for a look of horror, for actors of course were far beneath her, dandiprats and cullions notorious for immorality, but her downcast expression changed hardly at all. Once again her sister was more candid.

"May I meet Bonny Joe?" she said. "He's my favorite."

"I will do my best to introduce you," I said, "with your father's permission."

That permission granted, I took the young ladies to the stage, where other young ladies, and some young gentlemen as well, were clustered about Bonny Joe. He was still in costume as the Queen, and still retained some of his regal mannerisms as he addressed his courtiers. I did not wish to shoulder my way through his pack of admirers, and I saw Blackwell at a corner of the stage, and waved him over.

"Master Blackwell," said I, "I would like to introduce you to the Honorable Candice Thistlegorm and the Honorable Emily Thistlegorm. Mistress Emily would like to meet Bonny Joe, but I don't want to have to wrestle half the youth of Selford for a chance to say hello."

"I'll send for him," Blackwell said. He signaled to one of his stage-hands.

Blackwell was a tall man, narrow as a lance, with remarkable indigo eyes. His blond hair was concealed by a black wig to enable him to impersonate a murderous Ackoi emperor, and his beard was dyed.

"It seems you must cope with yet another triumph," I told him. "And I thank you for featuring me so well on the stage."

"You may thank the censorship of the Master of Revels for making you such a paragon," Blackwell said. "He insisted the insolence be removed from your character."

"I'm not insolent," said I. "I but employ the art of ironic observation, and to my sorrow the difference escapes some of my interlocutors."

"Ah," said Blackwell. "That must be the problem, then."

"What play will you write next?"

"A comedy, *Two Gentlemen of the North.*"

I laughed. "You continue our long theatrical tradition of mocking our northern cousins?"

He made a movement of his hand. "We shall discover the hidden virtues of our young stalwarts. For Wakelyn will once again have the lead, and he never plays the fool, and besides he must marry a Selford girl at the end." He gave me a look. "If I may beg a favor, my lord, could you praise Wakelyn's performance tonight? I would be in your debt."

"Lacks he confidence? This was hardly obvious from his performance."

Blackwell gave me a confiding look. "Wakelyn looks to the future. Bonny Joe grows older by the day."

"Ah," said I. "I comprehend."

For a professional theater company has certain well-established roles. At the head of the actors is the Great Tragedian, in this troupe a Master Archer. But the most popular members of the company are the male ingenues, who play usually the Hero and the Hero's Best Friend. Wakelyn had been the lead ingenue for half a dozen years, and was supported by the second ingenue, an actor called Lexter.

In addition there were the clowns, also very popular, and a few miscellaneous actors who specialized in character parts. Blackwell himself was one of these, and he often wrote himself a small but distinguished part, often a king or duke or judge, who stepped onto the stage at the end to sort out the other characters' misperceptions—or to bury the bodies, depending on the nature of the play.

But there were also the female ingenues, played by boy actors. Bonny Joe Webb was wildly popular, with an actor's skill beyond his years, but he would not stay a boy for long. If it ever came to the point when he was no longer plausible as a woman, he would step into a male ingenue's role, and then Wakelyn's primacy would be in jeopardy.

"I will praise Wakelyn till the heavens ring," said I.

"Ah. And here is Bonny Joe."

I presented Candice and Emily to the actor, and for once the words stopped in Emily's throat as she was confronted with her idol. But Bonny Joe was experienced at putting his admirers at their ease, and soon he was chatting to both young ladies. I saw Wakelyn standing at a corner of the stage and approached him.

"I thank you for making me look so well," said I. "You were far more handsome and virile than ever I was, and your performance will improve my standing as well as your own."

This flattery did not seem to astonish him. "The censor cut most of my best lines," he said, "but then I'm used to that."

"Surely," said I, "losing your lines provides an opportunity to *act*, rather than merely *speak*, your character's inmost thoughts. Clearly you were up to that challenge tonight."

"Well, I thank you." He blinked at me in surmise. "You show a fine appreciation for the actor's craft, my lord," he said. "I wonder, have you ever considered becoming the patron of an acting company?"

I looked at him in some surprise as I realized that Wakelyn was not going to wait for Bonny Joe to supplant him, but intended to desert Blackwell and the Roundsilver Players as soon as he could find a suitable place, possibly as head of his own company.

"It is not something I had considered," said I. "It would be a formidable undertaking, would it not? To recruit a suitable troupe of actors would be difficult, and even then, who would write the plays?"

"Your lordship knows there are a great many young poets in the capital," Wakelyn said. "And I confide you know also that these poets earn very little by their pen and would be happy to share in the bounty that a successful play would bring."

"But do they know how to write plays?"

"Possibly some would not," said Wakelyn, "but an experienced manager can put a good play together out of mere scraps."

"You make the business seem very simple," I observed, "yet perhaps it is still too complex, at least for me. My duties to Her Majesty allow me little leisure for the managing of theater troupes, and so I must decline the role of patron until the war, at least, is over."

If Wakelyn was disappointed, he was actor enough not to show it. "I fully understand, my lord," said he. "Yet should you change your mind, I would be happy to advise you."

I rejoined Bonny Joe and the young ladies, who had been nearly submerged by the pack of Bonny Joe's other admirers. The actor spoke pleasantly to these enthusiasts for a few more moments, then bade us a good evening, after which he went to the tiring-house to take off his gown and corset. Emily was aflame with excitement at having met her icon, and even Candice seemed more animated than the shy girl I had met earlier in the evening.

"Master Webb invited us to a party!" Emily cried. "Held tonight at the Dead Vile! Do you think we might go?"

I smiled. "I hardly think your father would approve of my taking you to a revel with a pack of actors, let alone at a tavern called the Dead Vile."

Emily was indignant at my response. "Bonny Joe hardly drinks at all!" she proclaimed.

"How do you know that?" asked I.

"It's *known*," she insisted. "Everyone says he's *abstemious*."

"The Dead Vile, however, lives up to its name. And here is your father."

Of course Emily asked Lord Thistlegorm for permission to go to the Dead Vile with the Roundsilver Troupe, and received the answer I expected. Emily protested, and instantly a battle of wills commenced between the child and the Chancellor. Since I could predict the outcome, I turned to Candice.

"Are you fond of the theater?" I asked.

"I go when I have the opportunity," she said. "But I'm only rarely in the city, and my father is very careful about what I can see."

Her Retriever father, noted for his devotion to the Compassionate Pilgrim, did not want Candice to see immorality onstage, but was willing to sell her to a rich husband who could help him pay his debts. My sympathy went out to her, but not so far that I wished to fall in with Thistlegorm's plans.

"Do you play music?" I asked.

She considered her answer. "I play the virginals, but I have no talent for it. Emily is much better."

In truth, she was making herself seem as colorless as possible. It occurred to me that this might be deliberate, and that she might be as enthusiastic about her father's plans as was I.

"Has your mother joined you in Selford?" I asked.

"She suffered a riding accident two years ago, and can barely walk. She prefers to stay at home."

"I'm heartily sorry to hear her recovery went so ill. I'm sure you must be a great consolation to her."

As I spoke, I saw over Candice's shoulder the figure of Lord Catsgore, his face set in an expression of blazing fury, as he stormed out of an arch that led beneath the minstrels' gallery. I looked after him as he stalked toward a door leading into the courtyard. I knew that his enemy, the Albiz Prince Amadeu, would arrive within days; but unless Amadeu, like Gandorim, had come to the play incognito, something else had prompted his choler.

A few seconds later, I saw the Duke of Pontkyles fill the doorway with his great bulk, and look after Catsgore with a pensive expression, one hand twisting a strand of his beard. Then he, too, passed through the arch, but strolled farther into the room, not to the courtyard after Catsgore.

Pontkyles and Catsgore were not particular friends, but I knew no reason why they should be at odds. And when I saw Rufino Knott near the archway tuning his guitar, I thought I should return Candice to her father and find out what had gone on beneath the minstrels' gallery.

Emily had been prepared to argue till doomsday for her plan to visit the Dead Vile, and Thistlegorm had run out of patience, and was simply repeating, "Nay, never, no." I thought that perhaps he would welcome an interruption, and turned to him.

"I beg your pardon, my lord, but I see that I have a messenger. I will keep you informed if it involves the Chancellery."

"Thank you, Selford," he said shortly. His argument with Emily had not improved his temper.

I bowed to the ladies, then made my way to where Knott stood overshadowed by the gallery. Over our heads, the royal chorale sang a motet while the theorbo marched steadily through the bass accompaniment. I spoke under the sound of the music, so as not to be overheard. "Did you hear aught of what went on between Pontkyles and Catsgore?"

"Only a little, sir," said Knott, "but what I heard was loud enough. Lord Catsgore did the shouting, and Pontkyles but protested that he hadn't done whatever Catsgore claimed he had done."

"And what was that, goodman?"

"I couldn't tell. But Catsgore was saying that even though he won twenty royals, he heartily regretted that game of cards, because he was playing with a brazen-faced villain."

I considered this in surprise. "Catsgore regretted that he won? And he accused no one of cheating?"

"Not that I heard, my lord, but I didn't hear everything."

"And Pontkyles took no offense?"

"I think he was mightily offended, but he uttered no threats and did not offer a challenge."

I considered this in my mind, and wondered if the quarrel had any pertinence to the troubles afflicting the realm, or whether it was just another dispute between noblemen, which in truth were common enough and usually came to nothing.

"They didn't mention what night this card game took place?"

"Nay, my lord."

I decided that anyone so extraordinary as to regret winning twenty royals deserved further inspection, though that inspection would have to wait another day.

Unless of course I could speak with one of the principals. Catsgore was, I supposed, in the courtyard.

I thanked Knott for the information and walked out to the courtyard. The water organ player had emptied the water from his reservoir, then taken apart his instrument and was putting it in a small cart. The hawkers were trying to sell what remained of their pies and sausages. I saw Catsgore with one foot on the stair that led to the battlements above, while he scowled into the court and squeezed the gloves in his hand, squeezed hard enough to whiten the knuckles. I approached.

"May I be of any aid to thee, Lord Catsgore?" I asked. "You seem discomposed."

"Discomposed?" he said, and then shrugged. His lipless mouth hardened into a thin line, and then he shook his head. "This Prince Amadeu will come in days," he said, "and slander me before all the court."

"You may count upon your friends, I'm sure," said I.

"Thank you," he said, and touched my shoulder in gratitude. "Yet the slander will be hard to bear."

"We public men must endure these things," said I. "When I was a private man, I could issue a challenge and fight anyone who defamed me. But now I am a councillor, and must endure in silence even when the entire nation of Loretto blackens my name."

"Ay," said Catsgore. "But the thought of having to abide these lying cocklorels makes my blood to scald my veins."

"I would offer to restore amity between you and His Grace of Pontkyles," I said, "but I hardly think he would listen to me."

Catsgore's blue eyes snapped to mine at the sound of Pontkyles's title, and it was a few seconds before he managed a reply. "He fleered at me," he said. "He said I would be obliged to answer the jibes of a dwarf."

"That was ill-bred of him."

"He was born beneath a peevish sign," said Catsgore, "and his choler is always high. He seeketh always after quarrel."

"And always he finds it," said I. "Well, I am sorry."

I offered Catsgore further condolence, but behind my hearty-lad face my mind was spinning. Catsgore had lied to me, about Pontkyles at least, and now I was obliged to discover why.

I returned to the great hall and viewed the gathering for a moment. Blackwell's scenery had been broken down and was being carried out to the carts. A gang of castle footmen, under the guidance of the Master of the Revels, stood ready to take the stage apart and carry it to storage till the next performance. Her Majesty had already left, along with her regiment of ladies.

I saw Candice speaking to Lord Hunstan Wilmot in one of the arches beneath the gallery. She was smiling and seemed far more animated than when she had spoken to me. I observed them for a while, then approached.

"I hope your leg is better, Lord Hunstan," I said.

"Oh, I shall limp for a few days," said he, "but I shall heal by and by."

Candice's eyes widened. "You're injured?" she said.

This required a certain amount of explanation, during which Candice grew more and more alarmed. "You must see a doctor!" she said. "Or at least a barber-surgeon!"

Hunstan seemed a little uncomfortable at this attention. "It is nothing," he said. "And I am already bled."

"I'll have our man cast your horoscope," said Candice, "and we shall find the proper treatment."

"It's already getting better," said Hunstan. "Truly."

I saw his brother Brighthelm glancing in our direction from the midst of a group of his friends, and then his face hardened and he began a determined walk in our direction.

"Your brother comes to fetch you," I told Hunstan. "I will withdraw and spare you being dragged away."

I bowed to Hunstan and Candice, and stepped away while Brighthelm glared daggers into my back. I went back to the courtyard, purchased a pot of beer from a vendor, and reviewed the day's occurrences. It seemed to me that I was puzzled now by a different series of events than had puzzled me that morning, and I wondered if this was progress.

I saw the tall, lean frame of the poet Blackwell looming over the smaller figures of the Roundsilvers, and I approached. I bowed to the duke.

"My lord," I said, "I have received an offer to join Your Grace in the rewarding occupation of patron to the arts."

"In what field?" Roundsilver asked. "Are you engaging a portrait painter? A poet? An architect, to rebuild your Grange?"

"Nay," said I. "For Master Wakelyn suggested that I become patron to a troupe of players."

Blackwell's indigo eyes fastened upon me with a fervid intensity. "Indeed?" he said. "And what will Selford's Players do for plays?"

"Wakelyn seemed to think playwrights were to be found in every alehouse," I said, "to be hired for a few pennies to produce verse by the yard."

"He thinks plays are easily acquired," said Blackwell, "because he has never written a play."

"Just so," I said.

Blackwell frowned at me. "What answer did you give Wakelyn?"

"I said that my work as Her Majesty's servant did not allow me the leisure to deal with a group of players."

"I thank you for that," said Blackwell, "and for this intelligence. For myself, I think that actors are more easily replaced than poets."

"Perhaps we shall soon find out," said I.

CHAPTER FIVE

esterday I looked into the lodging-houses of Mossthorpe," said Knott, as he poured my shaving water into the basin. "I found no sign of this Antonio using that name or any other."

Steam rose from the basin. I reached for the soap.

"Go down the river to Innismore," I said. "He may have been lying about staying in Mossthorpe."

"Ay, sir. And oh—there was a message."

He plucked the message from his doublet and handed it to me. I marked the sea-horse on the seal and opened the letter. I read the few words, then put the paper and the seal into the fire.

"When you are out," I said, "tell Greenaway to have his haquenai by the gate at six tonight."

"I shall."

I would wear my good cheviot overcoat tonight, I thought. Though the sky was now blue, my crooked little finger ached, and I knew that meant we would see weather in a few hours.

After I shaved and dressed, I walked from my apartment to the Middle Ward, where the Yeoman Archers had their barracks, and collected Antonio Luzi's effects, his rings, knife, and belt. I then walked through the Outer Ward, where the fox- and deerhounds were crowding around their feeding troughs, then down Chancellery Road to the College of Arms, that square, pale building ornamented with the shields of the cities and corporations of Duisland. I asked the pursuivant for Sir Robert Hillier.

Hillier, the King of Arms, was a thin man in black velvet with a straggle of white hair around his bald pate, and a gold chain of office around his neck. Despite the white hair, his eyebrows and beard were copper-colored. It was Hillier who had aided me in augmenting my arms when I was made a count.

As a knight, I had borne a simple shield, described in the language of the heralds as *Azure, a galleon argent a chief fir twigged argent, in chief three pens bendwise sable*. Which is to say a blue field with a white galleon, and a wide white stripe at the top with three black quills. The border between the stripe and the blue field was jagged in a way meant to resemble fir twigs, which became a heraldic pun, *Quill-in-fir*.

But what suited a knight did not suit the Count of Selford. My escutcheon was now much grander, and the shield was supported by a dolphin and a grave, bearded triton with a trident and a swirling, feathery tail. Above the shield was a count's coronet with strawberry leaves and pearls, and above the coronet a peer's barred helmet surrounded by an elaborately displayed lambrequin of blue and white—"mantled azure, doubled argent" in the language of the herald. Atop the helmet was a twisting torse of blue and white on which sailed a galleon Proper—meaning a galleon painted in its natural colors, as opposed to the pure white galleon on the shield.

The entire shield and its supporters were wrapped in the red ribbon that proclaimed me one of the Knights of the Red Horse, the highest order of chivalry in Duisland.

Below in a scroll was my motto, *Ego Memet Finxi*, which in New

Aekoi states that "I, myself, have created my very self," or more concisely "I have myself created," proclaiming that I and my achievement were the results of my own efforts, and not those of some ancestor.

A scroll above the galleon offered my slogan or battle cry, which had been the subject of controversy between myself and Hillier. I had suggested that a battle cry best suited to my character would be *What? Not Again!*, but he ruled against it with some prejudice. In the end we settled for *Editio Princeps*, "First Edition," another reference to my self-created character.

All the elements of my heraldic "achievement," as it is called, had been proposed, argued, vetoed, designed anew, altered, re-altered, and finally accepted, though with every appearance of reluctance. The debates would have been maddening if they had been with anyone other than Hillier, whose wit had enlivened our combat, and whose knowledge of vexillology, ceremony, rank, languages, history, and pedigree was comprehensive. He knew the nobility too well to be awed by them, and knew me too well to let me browbeat him into accepting all my ideas. Many of his objections came from my notions being too near those of my predecessors—he wanted my arms to be clearly my own and not borrowed from some noble who might have cause to resent my appropriation.

In the end, I managed true originality. I was the first person in Duisland, and possibly the world, to seat a galleon, Proper or not, atop a helmet.

Hillier took me into his study, pleasantly scented by leather, book-paper, and paint. Beneath the window was a tall desk on which he could draw and color a heraldic achievement, there was a less imposing desk for other work, and many shelves holding books, scrolls, and carvings of objects frequently used in heraldry—lions, griffins, bulls—so that he could paint them. The large window with its many small panes was painted with Hillier's own arms, which were intended to be the most complicated in the world. He had designed them himself as an exercise in elaboration, and with the intention of describing it using as many arcane heraldic terms as he could. The shield was full of objects: seashells, bull's heads, griffins, wood-woses, sheaves of wheat, martlets, spears, boars' heads, human skulls, Aekoi warriors, stars, and a mystical arm appearing out of a cloud and brandishing a broom, each of which occupied a single glass pane of the window. The objects appeared on a riot of colors, metals, and furs. The shield was divided into a dizzying array of compartments that were made even more dizzying by the variety of partition lines: wavy, thorny, engrailed, bendy, twigged, potenty, nebuly, indented pometty, dancy floretty, and others perhaps of his own invention.

Supporters were an allocamelus, a theow, an emmet, and a turul. Five open knights' helms sat atop the shield, each with its own fantastic crest. The description in the College records ran for hundreds of words. The motto was the simplest element of all: "Make Of This What You Will."

Hillier would never have permitted anyone else to have such an achievement, but he was King of Arms, and accepted and recorded the blazon on his own behalf.

"Welcome, my lord," he said. "Make yourself comfortable. I hear nothing but evil of you."

"In the past I was dismissed," I said. "Now that I am no longer dismissible, I am hated."

"Hatred of you is a pleasure which the entire world may share," said Hillier. "It is said that you are behind any number of sinister plots, though no one seems to know exactly what they are."

"That makes them all the more sinister, I suppose," said I, and then a thought occurred to me. "Is there a heraldic device called a 'plot'? I could have a Plot Sinister placed on my escutcheon."

"Alas, I do not believe there is such a plot," said Hillier.

"You are the only man in the city who doesn't," said I. "Either I'm going to overthrow the monarchy and replace it with some kind of republic headed by myself, or I'm Her Majesty's lover and am leading her into disgrace and misadventure, or I'm a brutish warrior and duelist who's lowering the tone of the palace."

"Don't forget," said Hillier, "that you're also an enchanter who has cast a spell on the Queen so that she is bound to obey you in everything."

I shrugged. "Well, only one thing can be certain. Her Majesty's failures shall be blamed on me, and credit for her successes will be usurped by the nobility."

"Such is the way of the world," said the King of Arms. "By the way, may I offer your vicious, depraved, and conspiratorial lordship a glass of wine, or a tisane?"

"The tisane, please," said I. "I have a long day ahead of me."

He rang for two tisanes, and I opened the yellow suede bag holding Antonio Luzi's belongings. I handed Hillier the ring with the cameo of the eagle and serpent, and he looked at it with interest.

"Is that device on anyone's shield?" I asked.

He pursed his lips, scratched his copper-colored beard, and then reached to his tall desk and picked up a glass that was lying there. He peered at the cameo through the glass, and shook his head.

"The snake bites the eagle on the breast," he said. "That is an inversion of the usual symbolism, in which the eagle stands for justice and the snake for wickedness. It would seem that wickedness is triumphant in this instance."

"Have you seen this before?"

"I would have remembered if I had," he said. "There's nothing like it in Duisland. If it is a device at all, it is foreign."

I sighed. "I feared as much. Do you have any references for the heraldry of Pisciotta? Or Basilicotto, or any of the states in that part of the world?"

"I do."

"Please consult them and let me know if you find anything."

"Ay, of course." He frowned down at the ring and held it up to the particolored light that came through his vast, complicated arms on the window.

"This is a matter of state," and said, "and there is some urgency." He made as if to rise. "I'll do it at once."

I put a hand on his arm. "We can enjoy our tisanes first. And then you can to go your library and help me with my sinister plot."

He smiled, settled back in his chair, and returned the ring to me. A page entered, bearing a tray with our tisanes. Scents of cornflower and orange peel freshened the room.

"Ah, here we are," said Hillier. He cleared a space on his desk for the tray, and then instructed the page. "You may *engrail* the tisane," he said. "And be sure not to make it too *bendy* or *wavy*."

The page poured in silence. Perhaps he was used to being commanded in heraldic puns.

"I hope the beverage is *potenty*," I said. "Though I fear our conversation is growing too *enarched*."

"The matter is *thorny*, to be sure," he said, and smiled as he sipped.

From the College of Heralds I walked further down Chancellery Road past the Tiltyard Moot to the Hall of Justice, where I sauntered past the allegorical statue of *Dame Justice in Triumph Over the Wicked*. The bailiffs on guard recognized me, and I made my way to the office of the Siege Royal, where I procured a bailiff and a set of keys. I then went to the cells, where I opened a low door and stepped inside.

Lord Edevane reclined on a settee with a book open before him, and he looked up at me with a start. He stared at me for a few seconds, frozen in an attitude of complete consternation, and then the surprise vanished behind his glittering spectacles. "Lord Selford," he said. "I was expecting Travers today."

"He may still come," said I.

"It's Friday. He usually comes on Fridays."

Edevane was a delicate-seeming man, nearsighted, with a mild voice and the dead, clinical eyes of a predator fish. He had been my predecessor in office, having served Berlauda, Priscus, and Viceroy Fosco as private secretary. With soft-spoken efficiency he had sown a crop of spies and informers throughout the realm, connived at the judicial murder of Chamberlain Scutterfield, Admiral Mardall, and other victims; and along with Fosco he had extorted money from Lord Thistlegorm and others in exchange for not dragging them before the treason court. At the approach of Floria's army he had fled the capital along with Fosco and the rest of the Loretto faction, but once in Loretto he had lingered near the border, and offered to make his submission and return to Duisland. Floria and I had offered him a conditional pardon if he would agree to return and confess his crimes. No doubt he considered this a formality, but I had convened a special tribunal under Judge Travers, who I trusted because he had conducted the Ethlebight assizes fairly and well year after year. The tribunal were given access to most of the documents and empowered to ask Edevane questions. They did not use torture, as Edevane had, but they were allowed to point out that, if he were ever caught in a lie, his pardon would be voided and his execution carried out. After a year, Travers was still finding questions to ask.

Edevane languished in prison, though he was kept comfortably, with his own furniture, carpets, books, hangings, and visits from his wife. He had been encouraged to write his memoirs, but preferred instead to answer only those questions that were put to him. When Travers and his commission finished their inquiry, he would be executed if he were found to have violated the terms of his agreement, and if found truthful he would be formally pardoned and sent to his little barony in Bonille, where he could spend his days surrounded by my spies, and peacefully engage in the rural pursuits, the hunts and chases, for which his ectomorphic frame was ill suited. If, that is, he could afford these activities, for the crown had relieved him of the money he'd extorted, and taken any property he'd bought since he had left his home to seek his fortune in the capital.

When I stepped into Edevane's place, I retained most of his spies, for it was useful to discover what went on in the great houses of the wealthy and powerful. I dismissed the professional informers and perjurers who sharked up cases against Edevane's victims, and dismissed as well the spy that Edevane had planted in my own household. I recruited agents to voyage to Loretto and discover what our enemies had in mind for us, and had even employed a few Duislanders to travel to Longres, swear allegiance to the infant Aguila, and report on the court and what other exiles intended.

I opened the yellow suede bag. "I wonder, my lord, if you know the meaning of this cameo."

I handed him the ring, and he held it to the light falling through his little window. From a shifting in the muscles near his eyes I could tell he recognized it, and from the way his eyes blinked I knew he was debating with himself about what to tell me. He turned to me and held out the ring.

"Did you find it on a poisoner?" he asked.

My heart gave a thump so rib-shattering that I was surprised he didn't start at the sound of it.

"It was found on a corpse," I said.

"Did he die of poison?"

"He died of a fall."

"You have forgot the ring." He offered me the ring again, and I took it.

"The man belonged to a kind of guild of poisoners," Edevane said, "based in Basilicotto."

I looked for a chair, for my knees felt weak. I pulled a three-legged stool toward me with my foot, and sat in it. "With your permission," I said. He nodded graciously, as befit the sovereign of the cell.

"What do you know of this guild?" I asked.

Edevane's voice was so soft that I had to listen carefully in order to understand him. "They claim to have discovered a number of hell-brews which will assure death, either instant or over time, and against which no antidote will succeed." He gestured with a hand. "Though the residents of Basilicotto are famed for their boasting, and I'm certain the claims are exaggerated. Their motto is *Tutto del Aquilo Possono Cedere dal Cielo.*"

"'All eagles will fall from the sky,'" I ventured.

"*May* fall, I think."

I looked at him. "You seem to know a great deal about this guild."

"It was my duty to know what poisoners might prove a threat to the realm," he said. "Though of course I never employed them." He looked at me through his gold-rimmed spectacles and raised an eyebrow. "Why would I, when the state already employed such a fine hangman?"

Having had some experience at being insolent myself, I recognized the insolence of this reply, and took a moment before asking the next question. "How do you contact this guild?"

He made an equivocal gesture with a hand, then closed his eyes behind his spectacles. "The details have faded somewhat. Let me remember."

"Is the information in the archives?"

His eyes opened again and fixed me with a forbidding gaze. "It is not the sort of thing one writes down. Please allow me a few moments to interrogate the pneuma of my cerebral ventricles."

I had no choice but to wait while he closed his eyes again and rested his head on the cushions. His thin chest rose and fell with his slow breathing, and the only way I knew he hadn't fallen asleep was because of the rapid tapping of the pads of his right fingers against those of his left.

"Roundabout means," he began finally. His voice was softer than ever, and I had to lean very close. "I believe one goes to an inn—the

Belvedere, in Basilicotto—and asks for a plate of fricandoes. The landlord will say there is no veal available, but one should insist. The landlord will say there will be veal tomorrow. Then one orders something else—assuming one actually wants to eat a dish prepared by poisoners—and then goes to one's room. One will be approached, though it may be several days."

His eyes opened. "I hope you have committed that to memory."

I nodded. "Belvedere, fricandoes, veal. Though I thought fricandoes were a beef dish."

"Only in Loretto, I believe."

I pondered this information. "This guild functions openly in Basilicotto? The authorities permit it?"

"That part of the world is awash in banditry, secret societies, and poison. Their history is full of it. Have you read *The Romance of Dom Leonardo*? It's not all fiction." Again he raised an eyebrow. "The authorities permit all manner of crime, and not just in Basilicotto."

"Especially if the authorities are criminals themselves," said I.

He closed his eyes again, and his fingers tapped against one another. "A usurper perhaps," said he, "like our present queen."

I frowned at him. "You dance near the brink, Edevane."

"We all do," he said, "we who wield power and serve princes." His eyes opened again. "And Floria is a potent prince, having donned her power as easily as her hand slips into a glove. I was right to fear her."

"If you had not feared her," said I, "and conspired against her life, she would not have rebelled."

"She would have, sooner or later, once she found the right instruments." He waved a hand languidly. "Roundsilver, Drumforce . . ." His eyes turned again to me. "Yourself." He permitted himself a sphinxlike smile, and closed his eyes. "You should fear her, you know. For the present she is grateful, but monarchs do not like to be reminded of their debts, and reasons of state can weaken gratitude and every other virtue."

"I see no sign that Her Majesty's virtue is fading."

"Princes are less free than you imagine. Less free than butchers' sons." Again those dead eyes regarded me. "There is only one way to retain power, and that is to be ruthless in the use of that power. Is it better for a prince to have her seat planted safely on the throne, or to cultivate the virtues of gratitude?"

"It is possible to do both," said I.

"Well," said Edevane, and his eyes closed. "We shall see."

"I will leave you to your meditations, Lord Edevane," I said, rising. "Please give my regards to Judge Travers."

He didn't bother to open his eyes. "I wish you a pleasant afternoon, Selford."

I encountered Judge Travers and a secretary on my way out of the building. The dignity of Travers's office was enhanced by his white hair and searching blue eyes, and by the judge's robe of black watered silk trimmed with otter fur. I handed him the keys to Edevane's cell.

"His lordship is pleased with himself," I said, "as I needed to ask him for a favor."

"Was he obliging?"

"Seemingly. He also warned me against the Queen's treachery."

Travers's white eyebrows drew together. "He preaches always this perfidious doctrine of wily and inevitable betrayal, all justified by reasons of state." He shook his white head. "It is a tedious attempt to mitigate his own crimes, of course. If he would abandon the speeches, his interrogation would be mercifully shorter."

"I wish you patience."

"Thank you, my lord."

As I left the Hall of Justice, I looked up at the bronze statue of Dame Justice, and wondered who I would send to Basilicotto.

My crooked little finger ached. Dark clouds dimmed the sun. Soon there would be rain.

"A crumster has brought Oliver Birdseye twelve thousand royals from the enemy," I said. "A separate cruiser brought ten thousand pikes and four thousand hackbuts, plus powder and ammunition. Also some small cannon, though he does not say how many."

I reported to Floria in her cabinet, a small room crowded with books and papers. A gentle scent rose from the spiced wine held in a gold cloisonné pitcher atop an inlaid table. There were two windows, one looking out over the Inner Ward, and the other into the next room, where two of Floria's ladies watched us through what Floria called a squint, but which I thought was called more properly a hagioscope. Whatever the name, this permitted us to be observed without being overheard, and thus allowed me to report to Floria in private while the witnesses guaranteed Floria's chastity to the world.

Floria was careful never to be alone with a man, unless the man was myself and she had come down the secret passage from her room. We took precautions that we would not be observed, as we also took precautions that Floria would not conceive. The world had what to my mind was an indecent obsession with Floria's virginity, and I doubt that anyone could explain exactly why this purely notional maidenhead truly mattered. An unmarried Queen was a wonder, as if a unicorn had reared itself up on a throne; and though Floria's sister Berlauda was a precedent, Berlauda had been married off to a foreign prince as soon as propriety permitted. A king could take lovers, and was practically encouraged to do so; but a woman was expected to cleave, if not to a man, then to an impossible ideal.

If the world knew that I was entertaining Floria in my chambers almost nightly, there would have come such a roar of outrage and indignation that Floria might be swept from her throne, and I to the treason court. Yet in what way would Floria offend, save that she had fallen in love with a man who in his turn loved her?

To avoid this fury I had to spend a few hours every week reporting to Floria in her cabinet, observed by some of her ladies, when I could as easily have made my report in my own chamber, and in my own bed.

"I have suggested that Birdseye should write to Longres and ask that more arms be sent," I said. "And more money, of course."

"Take care he does not ask for too much," said Floria. "He may reveal the deception."

"The council in Longres is so credulous that it would be difficult *not* to deceive them," said I.

"*Mundus vult decipi*," said Floria. The indirect light of the window glowed on the reds of her gown, the gems on her fingers, the unearthly luster of her pearl-enhanced complexion. I rarely desired her so much as when we were together in this little room, her sweet breath flavoring the air, our knees nearly touching. Yet I had to be the civil and proper courtier, and not allow so much as an under-eyed, secret, confiding look to pass between us.

"Indeed, an exile is a coney ripe for catching," said I. "The Pilgrim prevent me from banishment, for these exiles so desire that the country want them back that they will believe any story that promises Aguila on your throne, and themselves in a circle about it."

Oliver Birdseye was a wealthy gentleman from southeast Fornland who had been elected to the Burgesses from his district. I had made his acquaintance during the last meeting of the Estates, and thought him ideal for an adventure I had imagined, in which he would claim to be a loyal member of the Loretto party. He wrote to Loretto claiming to be a supporter of Aguila, and claiming also that when Loretto invaded Duisland, he would raise a rebellion if he were only provided with the means. After the reception of his letter, Birdseye had been visited by a spy who delivered him a cipher and a method of sending messages, and Loretto had delivered thousands of weapons based only on Birdseye's promise to make use of them. My own agents had followed the spy from Loretto and made note of everyone he met before he got on a boat and returned to his home.

"Birdseye says that he hopes I can send him wagons soon," said I, "because he has run into difficulties finding places to store his arsenal."

"The lord lieutenant of the county should be of use."

"Moving so many weapons directly from Birdseye's arsenal to that of the lord lieutenant might be too obvious. It is a large shipment and could be noted."

"Yet these weapons do us no good so long as they are stored in barns in the country."

I conceded with a wave of my hand. "Majesty, I will do my best to see them distributed in ways that go unremarked."

Indeed, I was already thinking that Birdseye could write to Loretto, claiming that some of his arms had been found and confiscated, and that he would need them replaced before he could hazard a rising. In that way movement of the arms to loyal strongholds could be explained.

I glanced through the hagioscope at the two ladies who observed our meeting. Both wore Floria's badge of the double white impatiens. One of the ladies was Lady Mellender, who had once been Chenée Tavistock, a poor relation of Floria's who had married well as a result of her majesty's influence. The other was a lady I knew less well by the name of Holdsworth. The former had her embroidery in her lap, and the other was reading a book. I recognized the sky-blue leather binding as belonging to *The Divine Words of the Compassionate Pilgrim, annotated by Brother Fulvius, Abbot of the Perfect Soul Monastery and Philosopher Transterrene to Her Majesty*. I recognized the book because I had been presented a copy by the author, as had practically everyone else of note in the Castle.

I made a note never to mention Fulvius or the Pilgrim to Mistress Holdsworth, for fear that she would expound on his philosophy until my ears sagged from boredom.

"Sandicup suggested you tried to kill Pontkyles this morning," Floria said.

"I did not," said I. "Phrenzy might have."

Floria's lips twitched. "I think you cannot blame attempted homicide on a horse."

"I blame it on Pontkyles," said I. "He and his big dun tried to bowl my charger over as we were about to cross the bridge. If I am not injured, it is because Phrenzy knows how to keep his feet." I looked at her. "Pontkyles wishes to clear the way to the throne for Morestanton and his damned partridge feather."

Floria's lips thinned with vexation. "I cannot have my ministers engaged in these vicious games."

"Talk to Pontkyles."

"No," Floria said. "I will talk to Morestanton. I will tell him that his father's behavior is blighting his future." She looked up. "Did anyone see Pontkyles's attempt on you?"

"Catsgore did. And, I assume, others."

"I am sick unto death of Pontkyles," Floria said. "He is always dropping hints about you, saying that there are some at court unworthy of my trust, that I would be shocked if the private life of certain of my friends were revealed, et cetera. It is as dull-witted as it is heavy-handed."

"You could dismiss him," I pointed out.

"And lose the support of his mesnie? His faction controls votes in both the Peers and the Burgesses."

I made an insinuant motion of my hand. "Dismiss Pontkyles, but buy his friends. Do you think they will avoid lucrative office on account of his pique?"

She shook her head. "Pontkyles is necessary."

I kept what I hope was a firm hand on my impatience. "So the pleasant little game of kill-the-royal-favorite must continue?"

She gave me a regal stare. "I said I would speak to Morestanton. Morestanton will curb his father."

"Allow me to tell you of another game, less pleasant," said I. "I spoke to Edevane this afternoon, and he confirmed my most harrowing suspicions." I told her of the poisonous brotherhood of Basilicotto, and I watched as her back stiffened, her chin rose in defiance, and beneath her lunarian cosmetic the color drained away. Despite the pallor I saw nothing but courage in her, in the determination that burned in her hazel eyes, in the resolution implied by the furious set of her jaw. We both knew there was only one prey in the castle worth the expense of bringing a poisoner from over the sea, and her name was Majesty. In that moment I knew that Floria was equal to the contest, that she accepted the challenge of the unknown poisoner, and was ready to spit in the eye of fate.

"There will be a closer watch on the kitchens, and on the wines," said I. "You did well this morning, choosing a pie at random from the basket."

"It was the prettiest," she said.

"You must make use of the Yeoman Pregustator. And make your carver taste a few of those morsels he carves for you."

"It is fortunate my appetite is small," Floria said.

"Your courage is not in doubt," said I, "and courage will be necessary, but what is most necessary is sense. You must stand watch on your own food and drink, and make certain that you never dine alone, but always in company, and that the food is shared by all."

Wry humor touched her lips. "If some gangling half-lawyer offers me a frumenty, I will decline."

Frumenty was a private joke between us, from the days when I had been a gangling half-lawyer.

There was a crack of thunder outside the Castle, and the light from the window grew dark as rain came pelting down. Floria leaped in her chair, and throttled a shriek. I felt a fist close around my heart, and my crooked finger throbbed. Her nerves were strung more tautly than I'd believed.

"I would comfort you, Majesty," I said. "I would hold you in my arms. But your ladies stand guard."

"I hope you all stand guard," Floria said.

"I hope to guard you forever," I said. "And to that end, I may stock my apartment with viands and wines, to provide a safe pantry for you."

Thunder again rattled the windowpanes, and Floria shivered. "Yes," she said. "I would appreciate it."

"If you will forgive me, Majesty," I said. "I have a meeting in town."

Her eyes were sharp. "At that woman's house?"

"We agreed that such a woman was needful," I said.

"We agreed," Floria said, "but that doesn't mean I like it."

"Your Majesty has my utmost devotion," said I.

"I will search you tonight," she said, "and if I smell another woman on you, I'll bite your throat out."

If she were making jealous threats, I thought, she had overcome her shock at the news of the poisoner. "I will consent to the search willingly," said I. "But for now, I must visit my mistress."

CHAPTER SIX

I walked to my apartment, rang for Rufino Knott, and told him he would could consider himself free till the morning. Then I took my old cheviot overcoat from the wardrobe and went out into the rain.

The overcoat was loot from the sack of my home city of Ethlebight. I had lost all my belongings in the fire that had killed my family, and had found the overcoat a few days later in the wreckage of a stranger's home. I never knew to whom it had originally belonged, but it had been a loyal companion in all my travels since.

The overcoat had a short cape that I could draw over my head as a hood, and thus hooded I made my way through the castle to the main gate, where I found Harry Greenaway waiting with his light carriage and haquenai horse. Greenaway owned a stables across the bridge at Mossthorpe, and had shown himself willing to privately conduct me about the city on errands where my own carriage, with my arms on its doors, would be insufficiently discreet.

The light body of the carriage was made out of boiled leather, and it swayed as I stepped into it. "Philpott Square," I said. An oilskin drape sealed the window from the weather, and I opened it slightly to let in fresh air and to view the inundation outside.

"Very good, sir," Greenaway shouted over the sound of rain pelting on the roof. He turned the carriage about on the deserted street, and with water flying from the wheels we descended Chancellery Road into the city. The downpour was such that the lamps on the carriage were useless, and the darkness was nearly complete, broken only when lightning clawed at the clouds above and the streets blazed up with a shocking brilliance, every brick and cobble picked out with uncanny light. Glancing behind during the flashes, I could assure myself that I was not being followed.

Philpott Square was in the northwest district of the city, an area full of tall, narrow town homes, each with a covered lane that led to stables off a courtyard behind. The properties were made valuable by the assumption that the residents could afford to keep horses. Greenaway carefully steered his haquenai down one of these alleys, and for a moment the drumming of rain on the roof ceased. When the drumming began again, I alighted and entered the house through an unlocked rear door. I shook rain off my overcoat and scraped my boots on the horsehair mat. The air was scented with rose petals.

"Come, sir," said my mistress. "Let me help you with that coat."

Lottie Forde was an Aekoi, and had the golden skin and gracile form of that race, but she had been born in Duisland, and knew only a few words of the Aekoi tongue. She had been raised in that caste of Aekoi women who served as companions of wealthy human men. Because no children could result from any such union, the women found themselves in demand, just as human women (I suppose) were in demand in the old Empire.

We had met at one of the *Bailes de Diversions*, the Assemblies of Diversions, elaborate balls staged by courtesans—human and Aekoi both—in order to attract male admirers. The women dressed with a brilliance otherwise seen only at court, swags and purfles and pearls, and wore jewels suited to a countess. They danced with regal airs, and despised any man who thought they could be bought cheaply. They wished to be courted, preferably with many gifts.

And so I courted Lottie. I found her a clever, knowing woman, taller than the average Aekoi, with translucent golden skin, long dark eyes, and a lifetime of experience in practicing her profession. I guessed she was about ten years my senior, though I felt it impolite to inquire. When I made my offer, those long eyes widened.

"I thought I had heard everything!" she said.

"Surely such a pretense," I said, "will be easier than the stress of maintaining an artificial devotion."

She considered the matter, still bewildered by the unprecedented nature of my offer. "I will require maintenance," she said.

"Of course," I asked. "Do you have a carriage?"

She gave me a sharp look. "I need a new one."

I smiled. "Were you not given a carriage last year by your last admirer?" Which was to show her that I was not to be gulled easily.

Her reply was quick. "The style of that carriage, all the heavy wooden sculptures of gods and goddesses piled atop the box, is no longer in fashion. One would be mortified to be seen in it."

Indeed, I had thought the carriage a monstrosity when I had seen it the previous summer. Lottie was a woman of taste, and deserved better. "I will give you a carriage, then," I said, "with no ornament to detract from your beauty. There will be four matched horses, and postillions in livery. But there must be an open top, so we may be seen together."

"Well," she said. "Perhaps I will discover if I can be content in something like retirement."

Negotiations continued, and we settled on her monthly stipend. She would live in a house I provided, and we would be affectionate in public, be seen in the Assembly Rooms, and in private we would laugh at the credulity of the mesnie.

For I knew of the rumors that I had made Floria my lover, and I knew as well that the rumors were true, however proper we might appear in public. But if I were to deny the stories, I needed a plausible story of my own, and therefore I must have a mistress.

The need was in part my own fault, but for the most part the fault lay with the credulous. I had fought duels, and rumor said the fights were over women. They weren't, but the proximate causes of the fights were obscure, and the ultimate cause involved a goddess who ruined the lives of her instruments as a willful child might destroy her toys, and who could hardly be offered as an explanation.

The Quillifer known to the public would not be without a woman for long, and therefore I must have a companion, and to be seen with her. Therefore I paid Lottie to be in my company, and rode through the park in the open carriage, and went with her to the theater; and I visited her house from time to time, and allowed my carriage to be seen there—not Greenaway's little coach but the four-horse carriage with my arms on the doors, and the two postboys and the two armed footmen in my blue-and-white livery. As I seemed to be a subject of fascination to everyone in the capital, word that I had an Aekoi concubine spread with the speed of a tide roaring up the Saelle.

When I visited we played music, I on my guitar and she on her virginals. We also conversed, which was a pleasure, for she was poised, had seen much of the world, and had much practice in the art of conversation.

At times I asked her about former lovers, some of whom were powerful men with whom I would have to deal, but she was discreet.

"It is not for your ears," she said. "How would you trust me, if I spread these tales?"

But now that I had a story for the public, I needed another for Lottie, for she alone knew my first story was false. So to her I claimed that I loved the wife of a powerful, violent, and titled man, and that my meetings with Lottie were a public drama intended to better disguise my surreptitious meetings with my lover.

"Really, my dear," said she, "this is not sensible. It is too like the plot of a play. Far better to have a simple arrangement with a member of my sisterhood than to go through such extravagant contortions."

"I cannot resist the demands of my heart," I said, with perfect truth.

Of course I corrupted her staff, to make certain she was honest in her dealings with me, and not spreading slanders behind my back. But her servants reported that Lottie's visitors were for the most part women of her own class, and their gatherings an excuse for reminiscence. She spoke of my generosity but little else, and said only that I was "a young man who knows not what he wants."

Lottie kissed my cheek and hung my overcoat on a peg, and we walked through the kitchen into the dining room. The furniture and the hangings glowed softly in the light of the lamps.

"He awaits upstairs," Lottie said. "He was hungry, and I don't know if you've had supper, so I provided food and wine."

"Marry, but you are a darling!" said I. "I've had nothing since morning!"

I kissed her painted cheek and bounded toward the stair, then paused with one foot on the tread. "The servants?" I asked.

"Gone till morning."

"Very good." I raced up the stair to find Barbosa waiting in the parlor, a lean man who smelled of tar and the sea.

"You have news?" I asked.

His dark eyes were troubled. "I do indeed, my lord." He spoke with the accent of Varcellos. "Admiral Mola in Avevic issued orders for the soldiers to board the ships on the eighteenth. He closed the port to prevent the news from escaping, but I had my lugger waiting, and we slipped away over the shoals on a midnight tide."

Calculations spun in my head. "The eighteenth was six days ago. Do you know where Mola was bound?"

"Nay, my lord. That is in Mola's head alone."

"Were you able to warn Knight Marshal Emerick?"

Defiance shone in his eyes briefly before he quenched it. "My lord, it is my task to report directly to you."

"I do not say you were wrong to come straight here," said I. "I wish only to know."

Barbosa reached into his cracked leather doublet and produced papers. "These are lists of Mola's troops, his warships, and his ships of burden," he said.

"We had best get busy," I said. I went down the stair and asked Lottie for paper and a bottle of ink, and while she brought them, I applied myself to the supper she had provided: cheese, nuts, spiced wine, fine manchet loaves, and a cold chicken.

We worked long into the evening.

A little after nine o'clock I departed the home of my mistress, and Greenaway's haquenai trotted out into rain-blighted Philpott Square and its black, looming plane trees. Lightning had ceased to play overhead, and the darkness was nearly unbroken, only the porch lanterns putting out a wan and uncertain light. The coach crept along as Greenaway felt his way along the square. From the square we turned south and began to ascend the bluff of Selford in the general direction of Chancellery Road and the Castle. A swift-running stream poured down the street, and the haquenai's hooves splashed in the torrent, its shoes slipping on the slick cobbles. A heavy carriage stood motionless on the right of the lane, the coachman slumped in his cloak on the box. Greenaway checked the horse to a slow walk as he guided the haquenai past. I had the oilskin blinds slightly open to provide fresh air, and as we approached the other carriage I looked into its window and saw a bright gleam in the pitch-black interior, as if a red eye were staring unblinking into my face.

I threw myself to the floor of the carriage. There was an explosion and a flash of light, and whirring projectiles tore through the leather wall of the coach and blasted horsehair stuffing from the cushions on which I'd been resting. The scent of gunpowder filled the carriage. Ears ringing, I waited a moment to see if there would be another shot, but instead I heard only the other driver whipping up his horses, and then the strange carriage rumbled as it began to forge its way uphill.

Rain poured through the ragged, plate-sized hole that had been torn in the carriage by a double handful of lead shot. I sprang up and reached for one of the horse-pistols that Greenaway had readied in one of the scabbards by the window, and I tore the blind away and presented the gun at the broad stern of the carriage as it gained speed. The wheel-lock spun, the rain failed to smother all the sparks, and with a crack and a gush of flame I sent a pistol ball after my attacker. I heard the ball smack into the back of the carriage, and then I leaned out into the rain to cry to Greenaway.

"After! After! But not too close." For I did not wish to be too near that carriage when the assassin reloaded his blunderbuss.

Greenaway whipped up his haquenai, but his single horse could not match the power of the four steeds that pulled the heavier carriage. Nevertheless I knew what awaited in the next street, which was a public fountain planted in the center of a small square, with worn statues of three maidens carrying pitchers and jugs, whose very presence would force the other carriage to turn left or right.

Left would bring the carriage toward the center of town, where it might vanish into the darkness and the tangle of streets. Right would bring it into a small district up against the city wall, or to one of the city's gatehouses; but the gate would be closed at this hour, and the driver and his passenger would have to bribe their way through on a rainy night, which would take a long while and attract attention to them. So I thought the carriage would go left.

Greenaway had loaded the carriage with weapons—this was not uncommon, for robbers haunted Selford at night—and I made my choice of those available. I rejected a sword as being too awkward for what I intended, and the second pistol as having only a single shot, and took instead a long dagger, which I stuck in my belt. I opened the left door of the carriage and felt the wind tear the door from my hand. My face was pummeled by a blast of freezing air and a bucket of rainwater. I made my leap into the road and ran up to where Greenaway was hunched on his box.

"Wait for me in the square ahead!" I shouted, and then ran on.

I saw a likely building coming up on the left—a tall, narrow house with a shop on the ground floor—and with the use of a column, a capital, a bressummer, an oriel, a keystone, a corbel table, a cornice, and a double-ogee bracket, I was able to scramble up to the gable wall, haul myself over the pediment, and find myself—rain-battered, wind-scoured—on the roof. The roof was slate and steep, far more slippery than the front of the building, and I had to clutch at the pediment to keep from being blown off. While I had learned to climb in all weathers on a voyage to Tabarzam and back, they do not have slate roofs on ships; I had not yet learned to manage on such a rain-slicked roof without being pitched into the gulf below. And so I was forced to adopt a straddle-legged stance, with one foot on each side of the gable, and to lurch along the rooftop like some drunken half-ape, secure in the knowledge that in the event of an accident I would not plummet to my death but merely be split in half like a wishbone torn apart by a pair of greedy children.

I tottered along to the next house, where I hoisted myself over the gable wall and discovered that the roof was thatched and offered far more secure footing. I ran along the roof while trying to keep the heavy carriage in sight, and through the driving rain I was able to see the carriage slow in order to make a sweeping left turn just before the fountain. I had been hoping that the darkness and rain were so all-embracing that the driver wouldn't see the fountain until he'd driven his horses right into the statues' laps, but the left turn was satisfactory enough, and I hoped he would turn again.

For if he bore on straight he would find himself in a road that would wind below the rock of the castle, and though there were lanes and alleys that would take him from that road into the heart of town, they were narrow indeed for a large coach, and the vehicle might find itself in trouble if it needed to make another turn. It were far better for the driver to turn left again, into a street of hairdressers and wigmakers called Tiring Lane, and descend the bluff to the vicinity of Philpott Square, before making a right turn and bearing on into the tangled heart of the city. But if the driver made that second left turn, he would pass beneath me, and there I planned to enjoy a reckoning.

I made a leap to another building, this one facing Tiring Lane, and held out an arm to shield my eyes from the wind-scourged rain. Just visible at the top of the road was the heavy carriage as its four horses walked through another slow left turn. My blood turned to a fire in my veins, and I burned with the need for satisfaction. I walked to the edge of the building and looked down into the street in hopes of finding a way down, then discovered a path by way of the gable end, a soffit, a corbel, and a pilaster, which allowed me to drop onto a balcony overlooking the lane.

I drew back into the darkness as the carriage, moving faster now it rolled downhill, came clopping along the cobbles. The driver was a shadow atop a shadow. As he neared I drew my dagger, stepped forward to put a foot on the balcony's wooden rail, and waited. The driver's attention was fixed on his four horses and the dangerous road, and he failed to spy me. The horses passed beneath me—I could see their steaming breath and smell their rain-matted hair—and then I leaped out onto the roof of the carriage, my caped overcoat flying out behind me.

I was afraid of sliding on the wet surface and shooting off the far side of the carriage onto the cobbles, which would have provided fine comedy as well as making myself a perfect, sprawling target for the passenger's gun, so as soon as my feet contacted the surface of the carriage I dropped to both knees, and managed to slide to a halt. I came down with a crash, and the carriage swayed beneath my weight. The driver turned to see what had just landed on his vehicle, no doubt expecting roof-tiles or the limb of some tree, and that made him a perfect target for the pommel of my dagger, which I drove with my full strength into his skull behind his ear. He gave a huff of breath, dropped his whip, and slumped forward over the reins.

I intended next to get into the body of the carriage, swinging myself through a window if possible, or if necessary opening a door and leaping in boots-first. In either case my dagger would have an advantage over the assassin's firearm, which would be too long to use in the carriage—and I planned to be too quick to allow him to draw another weapon.

Homicide was not my intention—I intended at most to wound, so that I could capture both the driver and his passenger, and discover what plot was behind this attempt on my life.

In the end it mattered not what I had planned, for I had reckoned without the curse placed on me by the equine race. The driver's falling whip, I think, had got tangled with the legs of the near wheel horse, and the creature bucked and thrashed and succeeded in throwing the whole team into a panic. The steady, retarded pace of the horses was all that had kept the carriage from rolling free down the hill, then either ending up in the river or, most likely, breaking itself to pieces against some structure, but now the horses ran blindly down the slope. I was almost flung from the carriage as it lurched, and I managed to maintain my position only by hanging on to the pinecone-shaped ornamental bronze projections that decorated the carriage top and were intended to anchor the ropes that would secure any cargo. It wasn't long before I regretted this, and wished I had slid off the back while there was a chance to do so safely, for the carriage pitched and rolled, swayed and thundered, while sheets of rain pummeled me and left me half-blind. The passenger stuck his head out of the window and bellowed at the driver to slow the damned horses. He seemed unaware of me, and I caught a glimpse of a silhouette with a pointed beard and long hair, features shared by half the men in the kingdom; and then the coach lurched and he was hurled back into the interior. I considered crawling somehow onto the driver's box and taking the reins myself, but I had never tried to drive a four-horse rig, and I decided that even if I survived the climb onto the box, I could only make the situation worse.

We had been galloping less than half a minute when the front right wheel went up a curb, then scraped along the stony side of a wig-maker's shop. I flattened myself to avoid being scraped off the coach by the upper storey of the building, which was jettied out over the road, but a corbel caught the driver as he slumped over the reins, and threw him atop me. I heard his neck snap even over the sound of the clattering wheels.

Another lurch, and the right front wheel came free and bowled down the road ahead of us. The carriage dipped, the axle dug into the cobbles, and in a shattering of wood and glass the carriage went right over on its top. The two rearmost horses were hurled atop one another and screamed in terror. I found myself in the air, weightless as a shuttlecock, and tried to tuck myself into a ball. I landed on my back on something soft and warm, and there was a horrific shriek right next to my ear, and a hideous stench. Something squirmed beneath me and threw me into stinking muck, and I lay stunned as the wrack of the carriage was dragged on by the two horses still on their feet until it jammed on something, and then lead horses bawled and reared and tried to break free, but failed.

Rain beat down onto my face. Slowly my chastened thoughts crept back into my brain, and I raised my hands and felt myself to see if I could detect any injury. I found none, but my whole body was in pain.

I also began to recognize the stench that surrounded me, and I realized that I had landed in an alley, on top of one of the pigs that were allowed to wander the city and consume its waste. The terrified animal had fled and left me lying in its filthy bed.

That there might be humor in this episode escaped me at the time. I lay for a while, listening and wondering if the assassin had survived the wreck, and if I should make some attempt to capture him. But I'd lost my dagger, and I thought it best to remain hidden in the dark alley for a while and do my best not to attract the killer's attention, assuming of course that he hadn't been broken to pieces in the crash.

After a few moments I dragged myself to my feet, and pulled my coat's cape over my head to keep the rain from cudgeling my brains. I approached the carriage with care. It lay half-broken on its top, and I noted that the door on my side was lying open. The horses had ceased their panic by this point, but at my approach one gave a snort of alarm, and the team again tried to break free. Under cover of their noise I crept to the carriage, glass crunching under my boots, and then I bounded through the door and into the interior. Round lead bullets lay spilled under my feet, but I managed not to trip on them.

The assassin was gone, but I found his weapon, a long bell-mouthed blunderbuss. Its slow-match had been extinguished by the rain or by the tumbling of the coach.

When that blunderbuss had been fired at me, it had been loaded with so much ammunition that I imagined the discharge had knocked the assassin on his backside. In any case I hoped it had.

There was nothing left for me to do but drag my aching body through the pouring rain to Greenaway's carriage, then continue my journey to the castle. As I limped along, my boots splashing in the torrent running down the slope, I considered how well this attack had been planned.

All the world knew of my visits to Lottie Forde, and clearly someone had followed me there and back, well enough to learn the routes that my carriage would take. I had taken Greenaway's carriage and not my own, but the assassins knew about Greenaway or had someone watching Lottie's house. The ambuscade had been well planned, with the large carriage forcing Greenaway to slow and take a narrow route around.

They had not planned for the rainstorm which had darkened the night, which caused me to draw the oilskin window shade almost closed and made it impossible for the assassin to aim—though if I had been followed over a length of time, the killer would have known that I normally sat facing forward, and he packed his weapon with so much shot that I was bound to be hit, if not killed outright. Had I not seen the slow-match burning in the serpentine lock and thrown myself out of the way, I would have lost my head.

The plan argued that my attackers were experienced at conducting murder. It also argued that, while someone had paid a pair of murderers to send me to the next world, that same person hadn't at the same time gone to the trouble of hiring a foreign poisoner, which meant in turn that there were two plots, aimed separately at myself and at Floria.

The only consolation to my long walk in the rain was that most of the pig's filth was washed from my coat. I found Greenaway sunken on his box, half-convinced I was lying mortally wounded in some lane. I assured him that I remained among the living, and had him take me to the castle.

I returned to the palace as the clock above the gate struck eleven. The rain had turned bitter cold, and the guards were huddled around the fire in the gatehouse. I sent Greenaway into the courtyard to turn his carriage around, while I dismounted, went into the guardroom, and asked for their officer. A lieutenant of the Yeoman Archers was roused out of his cot in the next room, and I told him that he and one of his company needed to take Greenaway's carriage to Tiring Lane, where they were to guard an overturned carriage until they were relieved sometime after dawn.

Neither the lieutenant nor his men were pleased by the prospect of spending the rest of the night standing guard in the pouring rain, and he plainly considered declining the honor, then just as plainly reconsidered the matter of disobeying one of Her Majesty's ministers. He and one of his guards fetched oilskins and were soon bowling away in Greenaway's carriage.

I borrowed an office off the guardroom and wrote my dispatches, then gave them to messengers who soon carried them away into the rain. The officer then fetched a cadet with a lantern to light my way to the Inner Ward.

Water trailed from my cheviot overcoat as I entered my apartment and found Floria drowsing on the settee, lying beneath my warm woolen boat cloak. Her dainty slippers, with their dangling ribbons, were tucked beneath the couch. I locked the door, and as quietly as I could drew off my overcoat, hung it on its hook, and walked to my bed to pull off my boots. As I placed them as silently as possible on the carpet, I saw the lamplight glimmering in Floria's eyes as she observed me.

"I have been all night on Your Majesty's business," I said.

She threw off the boat cloak and sat up in a rustle of her gold satin dressing gown. "And I have been on yours," she said. "At dinner, I told Morestanton that his father's conduct at the hunt had brought him into disfavor, and I set him and his father low on the table while I sat next to poor limping Lord Hunstan and made much of him. Which I did again at supper, to make the point again."

"Waitstill must have been delirious with joy."

"If so, he concealed his delirium well—but I saw him smile, and that is rare enough." Floria shook her head. "The son was tedious, though. All he wanted to talk about was you."

I laughed. "He made a dull subject of me? How impudent of him."

"He wanted to talk about ancestors, and whether some fate had destined you for a coronet."

"You were the name of that fate," said I. "I did not ask for a peerage."

"I can take it back, an it offend you." Floria reached for a cup of wine that rested on a table, then wrinkled her nose. "What is that smell?"

"I slipped in the rain and landed in some muck." I rose and picked up my boots. "Allow me to remove the source of the offense."

I had decided not to tell Floria about the attempt on my life. She had received enough bad news in the course of the day, would receive more tonight, and my tale of two carriages and a blunderbuss could wait until the morrow.

I took the boots and my overcoat, opened the door to the secret passage, placed them in the hidden corridor, and closed the door. I turned to see Floria give me one of her darting glances from over her goblet's rim. I noticed a large silver ring on her thumb, with a muddy-looking stone upon it.

"Is that your quandias?" asked I.

She held out her hand to look at it. "Ay. It is not a pretty gem, is it?"

"So it guards you, it may be as ugly as leprosy."

She took another look at the stone, and then her glance darted to me. "And what business of mine have you been about?"

I returned to the bed and sat. "I met with one of my agents," I said, "who reported that Admiral Mola ordered the soldiers to board ship on the eighteenth."

She rose from the settee, a frown of calculation on her face. "So the northern fleet is at sea," she said.

"If weather permits, ay."

She sipped wine from her glass. "And I surmise the western fleet would have sailed about the same time. And the enemy will not fight their way through our border forts but instead land on the coast."

"That is how I would order it, were I the enemy. Though that stratagem carries with it many risks, for if the enemy army is defeated, it may be butchered before it can escape to the ships."

She paced back and forth, and I enjoyed the sight of her small feet, in their silk stockings clocked with white impatiens, pacing back and forth on my carpet.

"I have writ to the Lord Admiral," said I, "suggesting that he ready the fleet for sea. I wrote as well to the lord lieutenant of the county, and to the wardens of the forts on the lower Saelle, in case the enemy are so bold as to attempt the capital. I have sent to the Constable and the Knight Marshal, and the messengers will leave soon after sunrise, when the tide shifts."

Floria's glance was sharp. "Drumforce and Emerick have not this news?"

"Not unless they have their own intelligence. My messenger came this morning direct to me."

"And is lodging with your Aekoi woman?"

"I think she is very much her own Aekoi woman," said I. "But ay, he shelters there until I can best decide how to employ him. He's no longer needed in Avevic."

I realized that I should put a guard on Lottie. The assassin might break into her house in order to ambush me when I paid my next visit.

"Well, you know how best to use him." She stood over me, frowning. "It seems you have done all that can be done this night."

"I hope so, Majesty."

There was a moment's pause, and her frown relaxed. She reached out her hand, and caressed my neck beneath my long hair. "Have I not told you to leave off this 'Majesty' when we are together?" said she.

"I want not to make a mistake," I told her. "I would rather call you 'Majesty' here than 'dear heart' or 'lover' in the council chamber."

"I almost want you to do it," she said softly. The wine was sweet on her breath.

"I will," said I, "but when I do, I wish it not to be an accident."

She bent to kiss me, and then swirled her dressing gown about her and sat in my lap with a rustle of satin. I slid my hands beneath her gown and felt her body through her silken night dress, the warmth welcome after the chill night. We kissed for a long moment, and then she drew away and offered me a sip from her goblet. I drank, the sweet perfume of the wine rising in my senses, and then as Floria took her own sip I kissed her below the ear, and she shivered.

"Marry me," I said into her ear, "and we may stop all this concealment, and live in joy for all our lives."

She sighed, and looked down at the carpet. "Do you so wish a crown, Quillifer, that you would raise such a storm about us?"

"I do not wish a crown at all," I said. "I forbid you to repeat your sister's mistake. I wish you to be my sovereign all my days, and to be of some use to you withal. And as for the storm following our marriage, it would be over in weeks, because some new storm would break, and attract everyone's attention."

"And you and I would be blamed for that storm," Floria said, "and every storm that came after."

"We would ride each storm safely," said I. "For no one can defeat us once we are together."

Floria's hazel eyes gazed into mine. Reflected lantern-flames shimmered in her glance. "There must be victories first," she said. "The enemy must be driven out of our country, and then I will be firm enough on my throne to follow my heart."

"Then give me a commission," said I, "and I will sweep the enemy before me, for no one will have better reason than I to crown you with victory."

She put her arms around my neck. "Would you leave me, then, to risk your life in battle?"

"I would risk anything for you." I kissed her. "You know I have Robertson and his friends standing by in Innismore. A warrant from you, and I could bring you the first laurels of your reign."

"Much depends on the enemy's cooperation," Floria said. She looked down for a moment, then shook her head. "We must wait for the news, and then we will see what can be done."

"Ay, I will wait," said I. "But when the time comes, I will beg you for the commission."

"The enemy assault may be repelled," she said, "and then you need not risk yourself."

"That will be victory for you, if it happens," I said, "and nothing but more victories to come."

I kissed her, and she relaxed into my arms. She put a hand on my cheek. "Be at peace," she said, "for I know we will be happy together, no matter what fortune brings."

CHAPTER SEVEN

The next morning the sky was blue and cloudless, but ponds and lakes filled the squares and courtyards. A half hour past dawn I returned to Tiring Lane in my proper carriage, with my arms on the door and two armed, liveried footmen on the rumble. The horses' breath steamed in the wintry air. I brought the two shivering Yeoman Archers, officer and man, a large napkin from the castle kitchens filled with ox tongue pies and a wedge of Stedlaw cheese.

"Enjoy your breakfast," I told them. "You'll be relieved in a few minutes, and then you can get some ale and some sleep."

I had brought my varlet Rufino Knott and two fellows from my office. These were spies, one gray-haired and dogged, and the other young with a blithe, nimble mind.

I looked first at the horses. All four were bays. One was dead, and the Yeoman Archers had freed the others from the wreckage and tied them to a rail. They were sodden and miserable, and seemed thoroughly ashamed of their previous night's adventures.

I turned to the first of my spies. "Go to all the stables," I said, "and find out who's missing a team of four bays, and probably the carriage that goes with them."

"Yes, my lord." The gray-haired man looked resigned. That errand would keep him on his feet all day, trudging from one point to another, for while stables attached to private dwellings were allowed in Selford, none were permitted which rented horses and carriages. These were found across the great bridge in Mossthorpe, or outside one of the gates to the south, and these were on opposite sides of the city.

I examined the outside of the wrecked carriage and found the maker's mark stamped into one of the iron supports for the box. The mark consisted of two carriage wheels and a stylized lightning bolt. I pointed it out to the younger of my two spies. "Find out who uses this symbol," I said.

"Yes, Lord Selford," he said. "But where do I look?"

"Is there a carriage-makers' guild?" I asked. "I wouldn't be surprised if there were."

The man seemed baffled. "I don't know, my lord."

"There is a carriage builder on Ottwyn Street," said Rufino Knott. "You could inquire there."

"Be sure to give them the details of this carriage," said I. "Color, body style, those pinecone-shaped ornaments."

"Yes, my lord. But what is the body style?"

I peered at the splintered wreckage and tried to envision it whole and set on four wheels. "I'd call it an imperial," said I.

"An imperial. Thank you, my lord."

This was very likely a useless errand, for the carriage was not new and might have had half a dozen owners by now. Yet every approach to the problem must be examined, and I was thankful that someone else would have to do the examination.

The dead carriage driver was sprawled in the gutter, his head almost carried away from his body by his collision with the upper floor beam. I looked at the body—unshaven, straggling hair, a powerful torso combined with a superfluity of chins—and failed to recognize him. I searched the body and found a little money, a savage-looking knife sheathed beneath his left arm, and a pocket pistol. I stowed all these in my own pockets.

"Goodman Knott," I said. "I need you to discover this fellow's identity."

"I shall do my best."

"When the wagon turns up," I said, "you might take the body to the castle and ask if you can parade the Archers past him. If he's connected in any way with the palace, I need to know it."

Knott tilted his head and viewed the corpse critically. "Ay," he said, "though I don't see him in the castle, frankly."

"I agree. Yet still."

He sighed. "Oh, ay, it must be done. But where then? The morgue?"

"The Hall of Justice," I said. "He seems the sort to have spent time there, in one capacity or another. He was, after all, a murderer for hire."

Knott continued his examination of the driver. "He has not been branded, nor docked an ear or a finger. So either he served the law in some capacity, or he was a very successful murderer and left no witnesses alive."

"Perhaps he just drove a carriage for the real killer. In any case . . ."

"Ay," Knott said. "We must find out what we can."

Glass snapped beneath my boots as I walked to the upturned carriage, then crouched and crabbed inside through the open door, immediately stepping into a shallow puddle. The interior still reeked of discharged powder. I kicked lead shot out of my way, the splashes echoing in the small space while the water cast shimmering golden reflections across the sodden, wrecked interior.

In the coach the blunderbuss remained, and lay near a flask of gunpowder and a wide-brimmed hat, somewhat crushed. I took up the hat, drained the water from it, tried it on my own head, and found it far too small. The long hairs that I drew from it were brown.

So, the assassin had a small head, long brown hair, and the pointed beard I remembered from the previous night. All features he shared with at least two in every five men in Duisland.

I was narrowing my search.

I stuffed the hat beneath one arm, took the flask and the blunderbuss, and crouched to leave the coach, at which point I saw a smear of blood on the door frame. This I examined closely, and saw that the assassin had been cut by glass shards remaining in the window frame after the glass itself had shattered. I hoped he'd given himself a good slashing scar right across his face.

I placed the assassin's belongings in my own carriage. A glance up Tiring Lane showed a two-wheel cart carrying another pair of Yeoman Archers, which drove toward us and pulled up as close to the corpse as could be managed. Once the corpse had been exchanged for the soldiers, the driver would be carried up to the castle to be viewed by the guards and anyone else who cared to venture a glance.

I did not care to watch the embarkation of the body, and so I hoisted myself into my own carriage and asked the two shivering sentries if they would like a ride back to the castle. They were surprised to be invited, and greater was their surprise to be invited to share the interior with me, instead of being made to ride on the roof.

I had been made to ride on the roof of a carriage once, by a dithering apothecary who took too solemnly his own self-importance, and I had not cared for it.

So I made room for the two soldiers, and I asked them where in the realm they were from, whether they had families in the capital, and what they had heard about the man fallen from the battlements three nights before. They had heard a great deal about poison rings and conspiracies, and for the most part assumed the conspiracy was based in Loretto.

The private soldier offered a melancholy resignation. "Now, because of this, we must patrol the battlements at night, no matter the weather."

"Why were the battlements not patrolled before?" asked I.

The officer answered. "Because no one has ever tried to get in that way," he said. "How could you climb a fifty-foot curtain wall in the dark? Much easier to walk through the gate dressed as a lawyer or a musician, or come in with a delivery of flour or wine—and I am certain that is how our stranger entered. We guards can't know everyone."

Alas, that made far too much sense. I offered consolation on the extra duty, and reminded them that, while patrolling or at any other time, they should report anything suspicious to me. They both assured me that they would.

I alighted at my offices, which were not in the castle but across Chancellery Road, in the sprawling archive complex. The original archive building was of the same white sandstone as the castle, broad-shouldered and solid, three storeys tall with bronze statues of great thinkers frozen in the act of contemplating their niches; but as the archived documents expanded over time, more buildings were constructed to hold them. Fire was strictly controlled to prevent the documents going up in smoke, and there were heavy doors separating each room, to prevent flame from finding its way down corridors.

My offices were in the original archives building, which was the only one with fireplaces that might serve to warm the folk working there. I greeted the porter at the door, then went up a zigzag stair and past another porter into a room where the clerks and scriveners toiled with paper and quill. Few were present this early in the morning, and huddled in cloaks or cassocks they worked at their desks. Save to glance at me over their spectacles, they paid no attention as I walked through the long room.

Throughout the office were shelves with documents wrapped

either in red or blue ribbon—"Blue ribbon is used for matters that are still in progress," Edevane had once told me. "Red ribbon for those matters which have reached a happy resolution." A happy resolution, for Edevane, had often involved beheading or hanging, but during my tenure I believe I had somewhat improved the tone.

Sitting on a bench outside the door to my private office I saw my deputy, a client of Roundsilver's named Jeronimy Bledso. He was a former monk who had left the cloister for the world of the profane, and when Roundsilver had explained his situation, I had been happy to employ him. His balding head held a first-class set of brains, a cold appreciation of his fellow creatures, and a capacious memory that could hunt down any scrap of paper that had ever passed beneath his gaze.

Bledso carried a stack of bundled papers that would be my morning's business. All were bound in blue ribbon.

Waiting on the bench with him was my schoolfriend Theophrastus Hastings, who I had known practically all my life. He was one of a number of people from my home city of Ethlebight who had come to the capital in hopes I could advance them, and who I tried always to oblige. Hastings was a handsome youth, tall, with an easy grin and a tawny mane of hair—he had always been popular with the ladies, and now lived as the pampered guest of an attractive, well-to-do widow. Other than his knack with women, he had little to recommend him. He was neither a clerk nor a scrivener, and he was too open and amiable to make a spy—and besides, spies ought to be anonymous, and his good looks were too memorable for him to hide behind. So I used him to deliver messages, not the most exalted of tasks, and made less exalted by the fact that he did not yet know his way around the city, and had to be given careful directions.

"Master Bledso," I said, "I'm afraid I must see Goodman Hastings first, after which I will be at your service."

Bledso bowed. "My lord."

I unlocked my office and waved Hastings to a chair. "Well, Theo," I said, "I will be sending you to Basilicotto."

"Where's that?" he asked.

I told him. He seemed doubtful. "I don't speak the language," he said.

"You will have the whole of a voyage to study it. It's derived from Aekoi, and you studied Aekoi in school."

"Not very well," Hastings admitted. "You will remember I was often thrashed for my inability to construe, and I must confess that those floggings failed to beat any of the knowledge into me."

"It will come back to you," I said. "And in any case, all you have to do is travel to a certain place and deliver a document."

"Should I wait for a reply?"

"That should not be necessary. Now if you will allow me to write the letter, I will give you some money and send you on your way."

He cheered at the mention of money, and kept his fidgeting to a minimum as I took a pen and wrote.

> *To the Masters of the Falling Eagle, from Sir Quillifer, Lord Selford, Greetings:*
>
> *As secretary to Her Majesty, I regret to inform you of the violent death in Selford of the man who called himself Antonio Luzi, believed to be of your brotherhood. He was lured to a remote part of the Castle at night and thrown over the battlements to his death, after first being relieved of his possessions, including any messages or packages he hoped to deliver.*
>
> *It is likely that he was murdered by his employer, who killed him in order to take possession of whatever he had brought to Duisland.*

It is to be hoped that you will take suitable precautions should that gentleman attempt again to hire a member of your guild. Of course you might also wish justice for your lamented brother, in which case I wish you every success.

Yours fraternally,
Selford.

Of course my letter was written in the tongue of Duisland, which was unlikely to be understood by the directors of the poisoners' guild. I did not know their language, and could not have the letter translated because I couldn't trust any translator with the knowledge contained in the letter. All educated people could read New Aekoi, however, so I translated the letter into Aekoi with the help of a grammar, then made a fair copy in my best hand. I sanded and sealed it, then handed it to Hastings.

While I began a blaze in the fireplace with my two draft copies and some kindling, I told Hastings about the Belvedere Inn, the fricandoes, and the lack of veal. "When you are contacted," I concluded, "you should give them this letter."

"Of course," he said. "Now Quillifer, could you explain about the veal again?"

I threw a log onto the fire. "I shall write it down for you," I said. "Though you should memorize the instructions and destroy them before you arrive in Basilicotto."

"Of course," said he.

For a moment I reconsidered sending him, but then I thought it was probably a fool's errand in any case, and so I might as well send a fool on it.

I gave him a bill for seventy-five royals, which should easily buy him a trip to Basilicotto and back, with enough left over to buy a modest cottage once he got there. He accepted the bill with pleasure, then asked what ship he should look for in Innismore.

"You must go to the port and find your own ship, friend," said I. "Our navy is not so large that we can hand you a vessel all your own."

I embraced him, then told him to take the bill to our friend Kevin Spellman, who served as the Queen's cofferer. Unlike the banks and money-lenders in town, Kevin would give him full value for the bill.

After he left I wrote a note to Hillier at the College of Arms telling him that the eagle-and-snake emblem was the badge of a guild of poisoners from Basilicotto, and that his investigations should start there. I wrote another letter to Lottie Forde, warning her that I had been attacked after leaving her house the previous night, and telling her to beware until I sent her a pair of guards. I would have to find these bravos myself, as I could hardly charge the Exchequer for guarding my mistress. I then welcomed Master Bledso and his stack of papers, and gave the letters to him with instructions to have them delivered.

I began opening the files in blue ribbon. In the upper left corner of each I made one of the four marks that had been used in the archives for centuries. One, for use when the document had been strictly informational, meant simply that the document should be filed. The second, used when the contents of the document were of minor import, signified that a scrivener should draft a polite message acknowledging receipt. The third indicated that an acknowledgment should be sent, along with a request for further information, which request I penned in the margin for copying. These documents when drafted I would sign myself. The fourth meant that the documents would require a personal answer from me, which I would dictate or draft depending on circumstances.

Any documents that contained information too dangerous for the archives were fed to the flames.

These, I reflected, were now my days. Once, I had sailed the seas in my own ship, I had made a fortune, I had traded in gems on the Street of the Shining Stones in far Sarafsham. I had fought duels, and I had caressed beautiful women. Now I worked in an office, annotating stacks of paper and committing to memory an absurd number of facts, all in hopes of preserving the woman I loved. It seemed ages since I had paid attention to my own affairs, though it must be admitted that these affairs were managing perfectly well without me. I was the Count of Selford, and with the title came the deeds to many properties scattered through the kingdom. Floria had been generous, and I had personally visited only a fraction of my estates, but they sent me money whether I visited them or not.

I put much of the money into the canal I was building in Ethlebight, and much of the rest into building ships. Some were privateers to harry the enemy, some were large galleons for the trade to Tabarzam, some were intended as warships that I would loan to Floria's navy for the duration of the conflict.

For myself I spent little, at least in comparison to other great lords like Roundsilver or Waitstill.

When the war was won and Floria safe, I would become the most free-spending lord in the kingdom.

I had worked through a third of the pile before I had my first interruption, in the form of the younger of my two spies, who had been sent out on the trail of whoever had made the wrecked carriage.

"Bad luck, my lord," said he. "The carriage was made at the works of Sanders and Sons, which burned down eight or ten years ago. The family left the city to build carriages in some other town, but my informant knew not where."

That was unfortunate, but I knew the carriage was old and the trail unlikely to lead anyplace useful. I thanked my informant and gave him some silver to drink to the health of the Queen.

He had been gone scarce half an hour before my other spy arrived. "I was in luck, Lord Selford," said he. "The carriage was rented four days ago from Bertram's Livery in Mossthorpe, by someone who called himself Timothy Hewes. That's Hewes with a *W*."

"Did Hewes have a companion?"

"Nay—or if he did, Master Bertram did not wish to admit it. I thought Bertram was too circumspect in his answers, as if he might have something to hide."

"Thank you." I rang for Bledso, and when he came into the office, I asked him for any file on Timothy Hewes, and anything about a Bertram of Bertram's Livery in Mossthorpe. Then I turned again to my agent.

"Did Bertram regularly rent to Hewes? How did he know that Hewes could handle a four-horse team?"

"He said that Hewes once drove for a local gentleman who boarded his carriage and team with Bertram."

I sighed. "I don't suppose he remembers the name of the gentleman?"

"He did." My spy seemed surprised. "The gentleman was a Master Pennyroyal, who died six or eight years ago, of a griping of the guts."

I wanted to sigh again. "I suppose there were no heirs."

"There was a daughter, married to a wine merchant. Bertram didn't recall their names. They sold Pennyroyal's house and property and moved to Havre-le-Creag."

Which was in the heart of Bonille's wine country, so I imagined that part of the story was true. "Do we know where Hewes lived?"

"No, my lord. I'm afraid not."

There was a soft knock on the door, and Bledso entered. "I found the file on Hewes, sir."

"Was he a criminal?"

"No, my lord. A perjurer."

Which placed him in that elite corps of plausible fellows who loitered about the Hall of Justice in hopes of making themselves useful to litigants by swearing black was white and that the finest silk suit could be made from the cheapest pursers' slops. According to his file, Hewes had been employed by my predecessor Edevane in bringing people to the treason court of the Siege Royal, then swearing them over to the hangman.

I had dismissed the perjurers when I kissed hands and took my office, and for a moment I wondered if the attempt on my life had been personal, if Hewes hoped he might be employed again under a less-scrupulous chief.

"Let us look at the trials and see if Hewes worked with any other perjurers," said I. "The fellow who shot at me was someone Hewes knew and trusted, or so I imagine."

Bledso discovered the appropriate files, and we found the names of half a dozen of Hewes's colleagues who had been his partners in the business of ruining innocent men. I turned to my spy.

"Go fetch some thief-takers," said I. "Run these lying dogs to their dens, then drag them to the cells."

My agent smiled. "With pleasure, my lord."

"And if any of them have long brown hair, pointed beards, small heads, and a recent laceration, probably on the head or hands, then you must alert me instantly."

His eyes widened. "Small head? Very good, my lord."

"The Pilgrim speed you," I said.

Bledso and I returned to our labors. One of the documents on my desk was from the Steward of the Castle, reporting the names of those who lodged in the castle the night the assassin was thrown from the walls. I had asked for the list days ago, and was on the verge of asking His Grace of Roundsilver to spur his deputy's efforts, but here the list had finally come, and I saw why it had taken the steward so long to assemble it.

There were many names on the list, including my own. Any noble or senior officer of the crown was entitled to request lodging in the castle, and if a place was available, it would be provided. Most of these rooms were small, cramped quarters, barely large enough for a bed, a washstand, and a wardrobe, but some larger apartments, like mine, were available for those favored by the monarch. Those who took up lodging generally had servants, and these were accommodated in the dormers of one wing of the palace.

Living in the lower reaches of the castle were the Gentleman Pensioners, a band of gray-bearded men who had served the monarch for decades, in roles as varied as architects, butlers, or heralds. Loyal and honest service to the crown was usually rewarded by poverty, and so these were dependent on Her Majesty for their lodging, clothing allowance, and "bouge of court," a term that encompassed their fuel and food, the latter of which was often the broken remains of royal feasts. The Pensioners also formed a kind of militia to guard the Queen's person, but as very few of them had ever been soldiers, they were not to be counted on for much. Indeed, their fortnightly drill in the castle courtyard was the cause of much merriment to anyone who had the joy of observing them.

Important servants of the royal household, like Floria's gentle-women and grooms, also lodged in the Inner Ward, though most servants lived in their own quarters in the Middle Ward. Also in the Middle Ward were the Yeoman Archers and—when they were not at war—the Queen's Regiment of Horse and the Royal Regiment of Artillery.

Yet most of these mattered little, for few of them could afford to bring an assassin from across the sea. For that, I had to consider the most privileged residents of the castle.

On the night the assassin died, the Roundsilvers lodged in their palace in town. The other high nobility normally would have done the same, but there was a Privy Council meeting that next morning, and only Catsgore followed the duke's example and slept at his own lodgings. Lord Thistlegorm the Chancellor had lodged at the castle, as had Waitstill the Keeper of the Seal, along with his wife and his two sons Brighthelm and Hunstan. Pontkyles had slept at the Castle along with his son Morestanton, as had Sandicup, Lord Admiral Coneygrave, Duke Chelmy, and Abbot Fulvius the Philosopher Transterrene.

As I would not have cared to meet an assassin alone on a dark night, I looked also to see if any of Her Majesty's guests had been accompanied by some burly servants, perhaps to knock a stranger behind the ear and then pitch him through a crenellation. All the privy councillors had brought at least two men, though I couldn't tell from the lists how many of them were rudesbys suitable for grappling with a professional murderer. The file did not even include their names, reporting only something something in the style of "Adm. Coneygrave + 2 varlets." The varlets would have been in livery, of course, which would have identified them well enough as belonging to the Admiral and nullified any reason to know their names.

I called in Bledso and asked for the files on the households of the privy councillors. He bowed and withdrew. I returned to my correspondence and worked for half an hour until a page told me that Rufino Knott wished to see me. Knott bounded into the room, a pleased smile on his face.

"My lord, I have discovered much!"

I cocked an eye at him. "What can you tell me about Tim Hewes, then?"

Knott's smile faded. "Someone has already brought you that name."

"I know his name and his record," said I. "I know the names of some of his associates. I know not where he lived, nor the full range of his acquaintance."

Knott drew wax tablets from his jerkin. "The folk at the Hall of

Justice knew him well and spoke at length of his—of his virtues, as they might be called. They spoke in an admiring way of his invention and ingenuity, his skill at convicting others without implicating himself."

I considered this. "Did any of these—these admirers—have a recent wound?"

His eyes widened. "On the forehead? Crudely stitched?"

"The forehead or anywhere. Did he also have long brown hair, a beard, and a small head?"

"I did not judge the size of his head, but he had a beard, and hair past his shoulders. He also had some injury to his shoulder."

Possibly, I thought, because that shoulder had been kicked by an overloaded blunderbuss. I began a frantic search through my papers. "Did you get the man's name?"

"Freothulaf Post. A name so unusual I remembered it."

It was not a name mentioned in Hewes's files. I reached for my pen.

"Master," I said, "you must run to the Hall of Justice, find some thief-takers, and secure the person of this Post."

"Right away, my lord." He put his wax tablets on my desk. "But take these first—names of Hewes's associates."

"Thank you," I said. "And now, Knott, if you please—run!"

Run he did. I copied any new names onto a piece of paper, and sent out an order to have them all arrested. Bledso returned, with the files on the members of the Privy Council, replete with information provided by members of their households. But of course each of the great lords has hundreds of servants all told, not all of whom know each other, and no doubt some of these are fit young men well able to clout a foreigner with a club and hurl him from a wall. It is not unusual for nobles to keep men around for the purpose of intimidating their enemies, which was why so many footmen go armed, and why a tall, intimidating footman is paid more than a short one. All I could do was assure myself that none of the lords seemed to be employing convicted criminals, and though I could not prove this conclusively, at least I could find nothing in the record.

I heard the castle clock ring noon, and my stomach rumbled in response. It had been many hours since the morning's bacon pie, and I needed to report to Her Majesty in any case. With the solid, reassuring sound of six steel bolts shooting home, I locked the secret papers in a special cabinet, then locked my office on my way out.

The lobby outside the great hall was bright with lords and ladies, but it was Chancellor Thistlegorm in his white satin who approached me as I entered. I bowed.

"There is much activity at the Hall of Justice," he said. "Men taken and confined without proper warrants, I am told. Bound, I suppose, for the Siege Royal?"

"A plot against one of Her Majesty's ministers," said I. "You will have a report by the end of the day."

Disapproval creased the lines on either side of the Chancellor's nose. "I would prefer that the proper forms be observed, Selford."

"I quite agree with you," said I. "But the double handful of bullets fired into my coach last night has broken my patience."

He looked at me in surprise, and his blue eyes went wide. "Is this connected with . . . with that other matter?"

"I intend to find out, my lord. I know now the whoreson who shot at me, the thief-takers are out, and once we apprehend him, we shall wring him dry."

At that moment, the doors that led to Floria's apartments boomed open, and we all turned and bowed as the Queen entered, her ladies arrayed behind her in a V, like a formation of flying geese. The doors of the great hall were then opened to allow us to enter, but everything paused as Floria stopped her advance and walked to me.

"You will report to me later, Quillifer," said she. "Come to my cabinet after dinner."

I surmised she was not pleased with me. I hadn't told her about the attack the previous evening, and now I imagine someone else had, perhaps offering opinions unflattering to me.

"Your Majesty," I said, and bowed again. She took her place at the head of her ladies, and came into the hall as trumpets played a sennet.

The rest of us entered more slowly, as it had to be done in order of precedence, with the dukes first, followed by the lesser lords, the knights, and then the commoners. In general we sat in this order as well, though Floria sometimes chose a companion or two to sit by her, and it was permitted for a higher-ranking lord or lady to invite a lower-ranked guest to dine with them.

I was the most junior count in the kingdom, but that at least put me ahead of Baron Scarnside and his pretensions. It seemed that today I was fated to sit between Scarnside and the dowager Countess Scudmore, who was elderly and very deaf. Scarnside made a point of turning away from me and speaking to the person on the other side of him. The countess tried to make conversation with me, and I suppose it was her deafness that caused her to shout like a boatswain giving orders against the shriek of a three-reef gale. She asked me if I knew this marchioness or that baron, or some other person, I suppose, from her past. Not only had I not encountered any of them, I suspected most of them were long dead. Nor did she have anything interesting to say about any of these acquaintances, but on hearing I knew not the first, then progressed on to the next, and so on.

I was famished and applied myself to my dinner. First came a pottage of lamb accompanied by a posset of curdled cream, sack, and ale. Then came plates of oysters and offerings of gurnards stewed with white wine and spices. Next artichoke pies arrived, followed by a capon larded with lemons, and served in a sauce with dates, currants, almonds, sugar, and sweet butter. Then came a carbonado of mutton, pasties of marrow made to look like pease pods, a fricassee of rabbit, and a black pudding. Last were candied eryngo roots, a custard with almonds and artichokes, and an almond cream served in a bowl of sugar-paste. With each remove came its own wine, gold or ruby-red, most sweet to match the sugar, honey, and dried fruit in the dishes; and every dish was ornamented with pastry sculptures, the skins or heads of animals or birds, marchpane fantasies, or gold leaf.

Now that the days were growing longer, the cows were giving again, and it was a pleasure to have so much cream on the table.

I glanced up at the public gallery and the crowd of ordinary citizens who had each paid a penny to watch their Queen choose from the flotilla of platters that passed before her. The dinner was more than anyone could possibly eat, but the point of these feasts was not to fill bellies but to celebrate the Queen's generosity and magnificence before her subjects. For an ordinary weaver, saddler, or alewife, the parade below the gallery was like a glimpse into fairyland, and could only enrich the idea that the Queen and her companions were a species apart, placed above them by some heavenly dispensation to reign graciously and infallibly over them.

As one of these demi-divine companions, I found myself skeptical of this theory of government by cookery. I knew all too well the flawed instruments that were Floria's councillors, and I had never seen them alight into their places from a bridge of rainbows.

Yet Floria must be supported, and these were her supporters. If they failed, the kingdom was lost, Floria was lost, and my heart was lost with her. If lavish dinners would keep her on her throne, it seemed but a small price.

At least nothing was wasted. Anything not eaten ended on the table of the Gentlemen Pensioners, and the leavings of the Pensioners, if any, were distributed to the poor.

Though I listened as the dowager countess bellowed at me, and mused on what the people in the crowded gallery must be thinking, I kept also a watchful eye on the Queen, to make certain she was keeping a close watch on her food. She chose her morsels with care, watched as her carver sliced her meat, and offered these slices first to the carver and the Yeoman Pregustator. Her wine was poured from the same flagon as that of her guests. Furthermore she ate sparingly at these vast feasts, and took nothing from most of the platters, which made any poisoners' calculations that much more difficult.

She had learned the first duty of a monarch, which is to survive.

Scarnside turned to me and gave me a look of disdain. "For heaven's sake, Selford," he said, "you eat like a wolf. Save some for your neighbors."

"It is hungry work, doing the Queen's business," said I. "Why, in the last twelve or fourteen hours I have survived a murder attempt, climbed aboard the assassin's carriage as he fled, knocked the driver unconscious, was thrown from the carriage after it lost a wheel, began an investigation, discovered the identity of the driver, and then was led to the identity of the assassin, who I expect to arrest before the day is out. I think I have earned my black pudding." I raised an eyebrow. "What have you been doing in that time, my lord?"

He sneered. "Everyone knows you boast, Selford."

"Perhaps I do. But it seems to me that I have accomplishments worthy of the boasting." I shrugged. "Do you?"

"Anyone," said he, "absolutely anyone, could do what you have done."

I put on my respectful apprentice face. "If anyone could have, it is astounding that someone hasn't." I held up a bit of black pudding on my fork. "For instance, I rescued Her Majesty from Fosco and Edevane and carried her across Bonille and the sea so that she could be crowned here in Selford. If anyone could have done that, why didn't anyone?" I looked him in the face. "Why didn't *you*? You were in Howel at the time. You had far more resources than I. So—seeing an innocent member of the royal family about to be falsely accused and murdered—why didn't you act?" I forked the black pudding into my mouth. "Hm?"

"Because Fosco had me locked away in Murkdale Hags!" he snarled, and turned away from me. "*Insolence!*" he barked to his neighbor.

I swallowed my black pudding. "Well," I shrugged, "I suppose a time in prison is a better excuse than most." I returned to my dinner.

I had barely started my custard when Floria rose from the table, and we all had to rise with her. The doors swung open. The meal was over, and Floria and her ladies began her progress to the lobby. We had all to file out in the reverse order of our arrival, and so there was a certain amount of shifting about as we all tried to find our places. Thistlegorm, who ranked just above the dowager countess, saw me and gave a wave. "Selford!" he said. "I trust you will send me that report?"

"Of course," I said, "I—"

At this point, the dowager countess turned to me, her face in an attitude of astonishment. "Selford? *You* are Selford?" Her voice rose to a bray. "You're *Quillifer!* You're the Queen's *lover!*"

Unfortunately this came at a lull in the conversation, and her words rang from the great oaken beams of the ceiling. I looked up at the gallery and saw the observers staring down in shock and growing surmise.

I stepped closer to the countess and stared down at her.

"I hardly think Her Majesty would make such a poor choice as me," I said into the room's utter silence. "But if she did, the announcement would be made in a more fitting wise, and not by the demented howl of a drunken she-monkey!"

She gaped at me. Her daughter-in-law, the current countess, came rushing from where she had been talking to Catsgore, and took the dowager by the arm.

"I'm very sorry, my lord," said she in a breathless voice.

I glared at her. "Take her away," I said. "And don't bring her back until she's fit for the royal presence."

She bustled the dowager away, breaking the order of precedence by knocking a few dukes and a marchioness out of the way. I heard the old lady's complaint as she was pushed through the door.

"But everyone *knows!*" she boomed.

"Hush!" said the countess. "Don't you understand? He's the Queen's assassin!"

"Ah," said I, and looked into the inquiring faces of the crowd. "It seems I have a new title. Or perhaps two."

"'Drunken she-monkey' was good," Floria said.

"It was kinder than she deserved," said I.

The Queen's galbanum scent wafted in perpetuity through Floria's cabinet. Again a pair of her ladies observed us through the hagioscope. They were paying little attention, chatting merrily over their cards as they played a game of all fours.

"I hope the dowager's rantings did not distress you," I said.

Her lips thinned in vexation, then she shook her head. "It will be the sensation of a few days, no more," she said. "As the enemy are at sea, we will soon have news more urgent than the maunderings of some old fustilugs."

"I hope that is the case, Majesty." I put on my pious anchorite face. "'Everyone *knows*,' she said."

"Everyone *speculates*," Floria said. "That is a different matter."

"Yet if everyone thinks of us as lovers," said I, "it will be less of a shock when we marry."

There was a pause as Floria viewed me narrowly. "Someone tried to murder you last night," she said. "And yet you told me not, and you let me hear it from Sandicup this morning, complete with an insinuation that you were the target of a jealous husband."

"I brought news enough yestereve to trouble your sleep," said I. "I knew nothing about the attempt other than it had misfired, and all I could have told you was a number of questions without answers; but now I can tell you there have been arrests, that I know the name of the man who shot at me, and that he will soon be in custody and we shall discover the movers behind his action. I needed but a little time to bring the matter to a resolution."

Anger blazed in her hazel eyes. "That does not excuse you, Quillifer. Either we are united in our love or not. If someone is trying to murder you, I have every right to know it, and as my heart touches the matter, I have every right to be concerned—and if the knowledge keeps me from rest, then at least I will lose sleep in a good cause. For both as a queen and as a woman, I treasure you and find you indispensable."

I felt my blood surge, and for a moment my brain filled with writhing snakes, and I was unable to find words.

"You see me penitent," I said finally. "I wished to spare you distress, and instead I incurred your displeasure." I glanced through the hagioscope at those two ladies, who laughed as they finished their game and gathered the cards. "If we were not observed," I said, "I would throw myself at your feet and beg your forgiveness."

"I need not gestures, Quillifer, but plain truth. Think not to play your games with me. We may not have secrets from one another."

"I have always told you the truth, Majesty," I said. "Even when, as in the matter of the nymph Orlanda, it made me seem like a madman."

"Then let us hear the truth of this matter," she said.

I gave my report. She was perturbed by my pursuit of the assassin in his carriage, which I'm sure she viewed as reckless, and when I told her of the wreck and of being saved only by virtue of landing on a pig, I saw the set of her lips and knew that she did not find the story amusing. So I hastened on to the identification of the carriage driver, and then to the assassin himself.

"I hope by now Post is in a cell," I concluded. "If not, he soon will be. Then we will discover who hired him."

"Who wishes you dead?" Floria asked.

"Most of the Privy Council, I think," said I. "They would certainly applaud my quietus. But who would actually stoop to kill me is a separate matter."

"Is the man who hired Post the same man who paid for the poisoner?"

"I think not. The poisoner was brought into the country by a man of great means with connections abroad, while I imagine Post and Hewes were bought by a handful of silver, by someone familiar with the lesser denizens of the Hall of Justice."

"A lawyer?"

"A lawyer. A judge. Even a bailiff. But of course a lawyer acts for another, does he not?"

Floria shook her head. "There are too many possibilities, Quillifer."

"That is why I hope Post is now awaiting interrogation in the Hall of Justice. But it now occurs to me to ask your very own question: Who wishes *you* dead?"

She offered a thin-lipped smile. "The entire nation of Loretto, I suppose. And those of our own country who support Aguila."

"Ay." I nodded. "But for any Duislander to support Aguila would mean supporting our occupation by a foreign power. And therefore I wonder if there might not be some other cause to which a Duislander can attach himself."

Floria seemed intrigued. "Such that he would desire my death?"

"Ay. But I hesitate to offer this hypothesis, for it touches on secrets so closely locked away that you may never want them broken free, even in the security of this room."

Floria nodded slowly as amusement touched her lips. "And we have just sworn never to keep secrets, have we not?" She laughed. "You have won the game, Quillifer, and set and match as well." She raised her fan in a benevolent gesture. "You may offer your hypothesis."

I took a breath, and with it a grip on my courage, for I knew the likelihood of Floria's anger.

"Perhaps the poisoner was hired not by a partisan of Aguila the First," said I, "but of Emelin the Sixth."

She stared at me in shock, and then I saw swift calculation race behind her eyes. "Ah," she said. Then she, too, took a firmer grip on herself, and spoke. "Enlarge," she said, "if you will."

When Floria's half-brother Clayborne rose against Queen Berlauda, he did so not in his own name but in that of the infant he claimed was the son of the late King Stilwell and his fourth and last queen, Laurel. This supposed prince, as the only legitimate male heir, was claimed the rightful king of Duisland.

Since young Queen Laurel was never seen, and the babe, which *was* seen, could have been anybody, Berlauda had always denied the existence of a royal prince; and after Clayborne's defeat and the march of the Queen's Army into Clayborne's capital, nothing more was heard of the child or his mother, both of whom had vanished like a midsummer dew beneath the rays of the sun, and the whole matter was then wrapped in deep secrecy enforced by the full power of the state, so formidable that people only spoke of the matter in whispers.

"Suppose that the child exists," I said, "and that some lord knows it, and has access to the babe. Might he not think that if you were made away with, he could become the next Clayborne, and bring Emelin the Sixth forward to make himself the true power in the land?"

"It is not possible," Floria said.

"Because the child never existed?" I asked. "Or because the child is dead?"

"Quillifer." Floria's tone sang a warning. "You are meddling with a highly charged secret of state."

I glanced at Floria's two ladies, and saw they had begun another game of cards, and were not watching us. "I will withdraw the questions if that is what you desire," I said.

"I will answer them," she said, "if only to convince you that my sister may have been ill advised, but that she was not a monster." She raised an admonitory finger. "But your inquiries can go no farther than this. If you so much as ask the right question even to the wrong person, you will create chaos and uncertainty that we cannot afford, and a hundred would-be Claybornes will search the land to produce plausible-seeming contenders for the throne."

"I understand. I will not mention the child outside this room and out of your company."

Floria settled into her chair, sighed, and visibly composed herself. "The child was real," she said. "That foolish chit Laurel gave birth and died of childbed fever a week later."

"And the child was male," said I, "else we would not be having this conversation."

"It was Clayborne who had the boy crowned in his cradle," Floria said. "If Clayborne's rebellion had swept my sister aside, I don't imagine the child would have lived long—and after his death, Clayborne would have had the Estates declare him legitimate and made himself king sooner rather than later."

"What became of the boy?"

"He was in the palace, locked away and guarded, when the Knight Marshal captured it. Berlauda decided that it was too dangerous to acknowledge the child's existence, and so the boy was given to Chamberlain Scutterfield, who fostered him out to gentry in Bonille. Unless he's met with accident, the boy is still alive and knows nothing of his origins."

I considered this news. "Edevane and Fosco killed Scutterfield. Does anyone else know? Scutterfield's son Drumforce?"

"The secret died with Scutterfield. He did not tell his son."

"It disturbs me that we do not know where to find this child," I said. "Yet he must have had servants—a wet nurse, other nurses, a cofferer, an entire household."

"The boy was only months old, Clayborne was keeping him close, and his household very small. Scutterfield took the boy away from them, and both rewarded them with gifts of silver and terrified them with threats of imprisonment and murder that they have not testified from that day to this."

I contemplated this story. "How is it you know of this?"

Floria turned to glance out the window. "Berlauda and I were the most directly concerned. We two and Scutterfield dealt with the business ourselves. Berlauda insisted that the child not be harmed but instead sent to the country and forgotten."

"A lost prince, raised without knowledge of his heritage," I mused. "It is an element of a romance."

"Romances are less pleasant when they venture into the real world," Floria said. "For what are romances about but misunderstandings, battles, murders, conspiracy, and thwarted love?"

"Duke Chelmy was one of Clayborne's partisans," I said. "And now he is here under your amnesty."

Floria's glance darted to me. "You have spies in his household?"

"Of course."

"And there is no cause for suspicion?"

"Other than his old allegiance, no."

"Does he keep company with any other members of Clayborne's party?"

"None but the servants who shared his exile."

"Ah." A sudden gleam shone in Floria's eyes. "Where did he spend his exile? Was it by any chance Basilicotto?"

I laughed. "A damning surmise, madame, if true. But alas, he went in the other direction, to Radvila and the Three Kingdoms, in the company of the Countess of Tern."

"He was with Clayborne's mother?" Floria was amused. "No wonder he wanted to come home."

"I will increase my scrutiny of his household."

Again she pointed her fan like a weapon in my direction. "I charge you, Quillifer," said she, "to direct no questions to your spies about the boy or the rebellion itself. If information comes to you regardless, then we may decide how to act upon it."

"I shall ask no such questions, Majesty," said I.

Floria propped her fan on the edge of her chair as if it were a scepter. "Have you anything else to report?"

"Nay, Majesty."

"Then you had best go find this Freothulaf Post and find out who paid him to kill you."

"I will do so with pleasure, Majesty."

She rose, and I rose and bowed. I slid open the bolt on the door and opened it, and bowed again as Floria made her way out to the thump of the guards' boots as they straightened to attention. As she walked, Floria visibly donned her grandeur, no longer my intimate but a regal, commanding woman, dazzling in her jewels, glittering in her raiment, a formidable monarch who could send armies into the field, outface a room full of councillors, freeze courtiers with a glance.

I paused to admire her for a moment, then began my walk back to my office in the archives. I had just passed into the corridor when I encountered Her Grace the Duchess of Roundsilver. Because of her husband's nearness to the throne, she was allowed to wear the royal scarlet and gold, and over her bright hair she wore a scarlet velvet hat with a gold badge, and her gown was scarlet with gold thread shining in the ferny brocade like droplets of sunshine.

"Your Grace." I bowed.

"Quillifer," said she. She took my arm and walked with me. "I hope Her Majesty was not too upset by the event at dinner."

"I believe there was mention of 'the maunderings of some old fustilugs,'" said I. "In truth, I think Her Majesty has decided that there are other matters more worthy of her attention."

"The enemy now on the sea."

I looked at her. "You heard?"

"My Lord Admiral told us at breakfast this morning. Then he took his barge to his flagship."

"I suppose it was not a secret, though now that the news is out, there will be absurd rumors of night landings, skirmishings, and the smoke of burning towns visible on the horizon." I reflected on this, and shrugged. "Though it may divert attention from the nonsense spoken at dinner."

I felt her hand squeeze my arm. "I hope that business does not make it difficult for you, my friend."

"Prating cokes will talk," I said, "but then they always do."

"The Queen loves you, Quillifer," she said. "And you plainly love her." I stared in surprise as she spoke on. "It makes me happy for the two of you," she said, "but it makes me sad also, for a monarch must wed as benefits her nation and not her heart."

I considered this as we walked side by side. "Have you heard aught?"

"Ambassador Gandorim is here, is he not?"

"Ah. I understand."

Again she squeezed my arm. "Fight well, my friend," she said. "Never doubt Floria's love, or mine. I will help you any way that I can."

I bowed very low and raised her hand to my lips. "You are a constant friend," I said, "and a far greater champion than I have ever deserved."

She colored a little. "I remember the gangrel who turned up on our doorstep a few years ago, an exile from plundered Ethlebight with battered clothing and only a few possessions in a sack on his back."

Those few possessions on my back had included silver stolen from the bandit chief Sir Basil of the Heugh, but I did not feel that a regard for facts should stem the torrent of Her Grace's praise.

The duchess looked up at me in a kind of delighted wonder. "But to view you now! A great lord, owner of castles, ships, and gems! You have risen high."

"Ay," I conceded, "I am high. But I am supported by the most slender bough, and if it break and I fall, I may envy that tattered gangrel you so fondly remember."

"Slender bough?" She laughed. "You are supported by the strongest bough in the kingdom, the Queen's majesty herself!"

"Yet, as you just said, a monarch must act as benefits her nation. And if a nation demands my head?"

Disdain touched Her Grace's lips. "The *nation* demands not such a thing. A few jealous men, perhaps, and these are easily warded by a canny, sharp-witted likely young fellow, who I remind is not without allies."

I turned to her. "I apologize for this wayward humor of mine," said I. "I am grateful for every friend I have in this world."

"And someone has taken a shot at you, which just may have disturbed your composure."

"On the contrary. Unlike my life at court, that shot was an act which required but a simple response. It was a relief to go chasing that carriage through the rainstorm."

She looked up at me. "Did you really?"

"Of course."

"But you didn't catch him?"

"Caught one assassin," said I, "but not the other."

She gave me a wistful smile. "At least you can console yourself that somebody thinks you are worth murdering."

"That's not new," I admitted. "It seems to be a special quality of mine that people always wish to kill me."

"And your friends will try to preserve you," said she. "If you let them."

I laughed. "I will let you know, then, next time I need to chase a runaway carriage full of killers."

She gave a little bow. "I will be pleased to offer any assistance."

"You have my thanks in advance." I bowed again and again kissed her hand. "If you'll forgive me, I must go to the secretariat."

Her brows rose. "Secretariat?"

"It's a new word. I made it up."

She laughed. "Ah. From the Loretto *secrétariat*."

"Just so, but I was thinking more of the Aekoi *secretariatus*."

She tilted her head. "One derives from the other."

"Just so. Till tonight."

I returned to my office to find Rufino Knott waiting for me at the door. "I haven't been able to find Freothulaf Post, my lord," he said. "But I've alerted the guards at the gates and on the bridge, and I've sent to warn the watermen in case he tries to escape by the river."

"Let them know there is a reward of a hundred royals."

He laughed. "For that sum, half the men in this town will knock the other half on the head, drag them to the cells, and insist their victims are this Freothulaf."

"Yet one of these will truly be the rogue, if he has not already fled the city."

"Aye, my lord." Knott presented me with a folder. "I took the liberty of asking Master Bledso for Post's file."

I took it and found it light. "There is little here."

"Then there is more that is hidden." He began backing away. "I'll hasten to spread word of the reward, sir."

I waved the file at him as he left, then unlocked my office door. I took the other documents out of my strongbox, then sat down to examine what was known of the life of Freothulaf Post.

What was known was little indeed. Post was a native of Selford, and had first gained the attention of the catchpolls when he was a member of the Game Cockerels, a group of lawless renegadoes who engaged in pitched battles with another, more established group called the Ramscallion Roaring Boys. Early in Berlauda's reign, the leaders of these groups had been rounded up and hanged by Lord Thistlegorm, who was then Attorney General; and at this point Post's career began, in a strange way, to parallel my own. Facing perils to my life, I had decided the safest place for me would be in the midst of the Queen's Army; and Post too joined the army to preserve his neck. We had fought together at Exton Scales, though I had not known him, and afterward we made the most of looting the homes of rebels in Howel, for which offense he was arrested and flogged, and I was enriched.

Afterward Post seemed to have worked irregularly as a thief-taker, but otherwise he left little trace. He did not, like his friend Hewes, make a profession of perjury, and I thought it likely that he earned his living as a bully-boy for usurers or criminal gangs.

But there was little real information. It was not known where Post lived, or where he spent his time, or in what company, or who employed him.

The reward, I thought, would loosen tongues, and then much would be revealed.

That afternoon I received a message at the Secretariat that caused me to rush to Innismore. The privateer *Able*, which I owned together with Kevin Spellman and his family, had arrived in port with two prizes taken on its latest cruise, and I was required to sign some documents for the prize court.

I took my carriage across the bridge to the left bank, then rode to the Mercers Lodge. The Honourable Companie of Mercers occupied a splendid guild hall in Selford, with dignified servants in livery, meals served on silver plate, and polished wood panels hung with portraits of distinguished guild masters of the past. In contrast the lodge in Innismore was a place for business and bustle, and featured rooms for meetings with desks, paper, inkwells, and quills ready for use. A notary was on hand to give advice on legal matters, or to witness documents, and there was a wall whereon were listed the prices of commodities in all the ports of the world.

Kevin and I met with Captain Langsam in one of the smaller meeting rooms, and he brought the papers and bills of lading taken from his prizes, a pair of pinnaces laden with wine, brandy, silks, and rice. The prisoners had to be marched ashore into confinement— the officers would be held until exchanged, and the ordinary sailors would be offered a choice of imprisonment on one of the hulks or a term served in the Queen's Navy.

The business took only two hours, the notary was called in to witness the lists of sailors and lading, and then we adjourned to a nearby tavern for pots of ale. I offered Kevin a ride to Selford in my carriage, and he accepted. We said good-bye to Captain Langsam and embarked for the capital.

Kevin and I had been friends since our school days, and his family had been captured in the same Aekoi raid in which my own family died. I had managed to bring help to the city, help him ransom his family, and to invest somewhat in his family business, so that we now owned ships and cargoes together. His father was now a Member of the House of Burgesses, representing our home city of Ethlebight, and Kevin himself was the cofferer of the royal household, which meant he paid everyone in the palace who worked for the Queen. This put him in an ideal position to receive information, which he could pass to me, and also to make a small fortune for himself, by making loans to the palace workers and charging interest, which he could always deduct from their wages.

My friend dressed splendidly from his lace-topped boots to the nodding plumes on his hat, for his family imported silks and velvet, and his clothing was intended to drum up business. He was a sturdy man, fair-haired, and success was making him a little portly. We spoke a great deal of business on the return journey to the capital, but as we passed through Mossthorpe I saw a crew of grim-faced swashers marching down the road, armed with cudgels. I recognized at least half of them, for they were the Roundsilver Troupe with the lean form of the playwright Blackwell in the lead. I opened the door of the carriage, told the postillions to stop, then jumped out to join Blackwell on his march.

"What's toward?" I asked.

His indigo eyes were set in a fierce glare. His blond hair was tied back; his gloved hands gripped a cudgel.

"Wakelyn was dismissed from the company," he said. "But when he left, he stole my foul papers."

"Your what?"

He snarled. "The drafts of my next plays. These are the only copies in existence, for fair copies have not yet been made."

"You come to retrieve your papers?"

"We have just found where the glass-gazing rogue is hiding. I will beat my verses out of him."

We had come to Mossthorpe's fish market, and Blackwell turned and began to walk between the stalls. An inn, the Jolly Fisher, stood at the far end of the market, its gables capped with a fringe of thatch. The market, normally a bustling place, fell silent as it was invaded by a silent, grim army.

"Quilliter!" Kevin called out from behind me. I turned and waved him forward—and then, after I reckoned the consequences of a member of the Privy Council being caught up in a brawl, I slowed my own pace and let Blackwell's mob march ahead.

"What's happening?" Kevin said as he joined me.

"Master Blackwell is after some stolen property."

Kevin was impressed. "He has brought a fair-sized force into the field. And is that Bonny Joe with a quarterstaff?"

"I think so. I hope he guards that fair face well."

I heard shouts and whistles from the Jolly Fisher, and a mass of men began to pour out of the gates. It seems that Wakelyn had provided himself with a bodyguard, and they were armed mostly with staves, though I saw a few with sword and buckler. I thought they were not actors but hard-bitten men from the Ramscallions and other such districts, hired for their ability to crack skulls.

"Fetch the footmen from the carriage," I said to Kevin, "and tell them to bring their weapons."

He turned and began to run as the two partisan mobs collided. Blackwell's tall form was visible above the heads of the others, and I saw he did not hesitate for an instant but strode directly at the foe, his bludgeon raised. The club came down, and one of Wakelyn's cullions fell with a broken crown.

After that the action became general. Carts and stalls fell, customers screamed, and fish sprawled on the cobbles. Wakelyn's ruffians were more inured to violence, and the Roundsilver Troupe began to give way before them. I saw Bonny Joe leap over a fish cart as he was pursued by a pair of loutish swashers who knocked the cart aside as they chased after him. I felt I could not let the city's most popular boy actor have his ribs crushed by a pair of grown men, and so I moved toward them, arming myself along the way with a codfish plucked from a stall. This I swung like an axe for the nearest of the rudesbys, and I hit him full in the face and knocked him down. I was able to manage a kick in his courting tackle and another in his ribs before his friend came to his aid, brandishing his staff. Again I swung the cod, but my target stepped back out of range, and so I threw it at him. The fish hit him and knocked him a step back, but he came forward again, by which time I had armed myself with a turbot a yard across. This I let fly at his face and it struck him cleanly, the flat fish wrapping around his head on impact. By the time he'd got clear of it, I'd armed myself with his comrade's staff, which I drove like a spear for his midsection—I caught him by surprise and bent him over, after which I hit him full force in the back of the head and sent him senseless to the pavement.

I tried skipping out of the fight, but the brawl pursued me, and I was driven back against a stall selling live octopus. These had been captured in the traditional manner, in clay pots lowered into the sea by fishermen. The octopus viewed these pots as fine homes and took up residence, after which the fishers pulled the pots from the bottom and capped them with a paper and twine, preserving the octopus alive.

I picked up one of the pots, found one of Wakelyn's men in front of me, and threw the pot at him. It shattered on his skull and opened a gash, but worse than being struck by the pot was the damage inflicted by the enraged octopus, which clutched at the man and flowed into his shirt, where it began biting him with its beak. The ruffian's eyes went wide and he gave a shriek, hopping and dancing as he tried to reach into his shirt to pluck the octopus out. Its suckers firmly adhered to the man's flesh, and the octopus refused to be dislodged, even after the cullion tore off his shirt and started rolling on the ground.

I threw another pot with a like success before another mob intervened, for the brawl took place amid fishmongers who all possessed cleavers and large sharp knives, and who soon overcame their surprise and marshaled themselves to defend their livelihood. I am not abashed to say that I fled before the sharp steel of these seething stallholders, and so did everyone else.

In my flight I encountered Kevin and my two footmen, both in my livery and armed with whinyards and blunderbusses. I halted my retreat and told one of the footmen to discharge his weapon into the air, and the great boom echoing from the surrounding buildings served to accelerate the retreat of the brawlers, and stunned the fishmongers into halting their pursuit. I stepped forward to address them.

"Friends," said I, "I am Quillifer, Lord Selford, and I am here to aid you."

And so I gave silver to those whose carts or goods were damaged, or who had been hurt in the fight. I paid generously enough that they gave me three cheers. I examined those brawlers who lay unconscious or wounded on the cobbles, and if I recognized them as players, I paid the fishmongers to carry them home on their carts. If they lay among fish and woke stinking of sea-slime, I reckoned it the least of their problems.

I advanced into the Jolly Fisher and asked the landlord to take me to Wakelyn's room. This I found deserted, and I searched it for Blackwell's foul papers and found none.

I returned to my carriage, and there I found Blackwell himself leaning against the back wheel, holding a handkerchief to his bleeding forehead.

"Who told you that Wakelyn was at the Jolly Fisher?" I asked him. "That fellow meant to lead you into an ambush."

"Did you find my papers?" he asked.

"Nay. I don't think they were ever here, and very likely Wakelyn left before you ever arrived."

"Well," said he, "I now must write very fast, from memory, for we must put on these plays before Wakelyn can."

"I wish you good fortune and a ready supply of quills," said I. I offered him a ride to the Dead Vile, after which we joined the queue to cross the bridge into Selford. Kevin gave me a searching look.

"Is your life always this hazardous?" he said.

"Only in the last week," said I.

"I am suddenly very glad that my life is a dull one."

I smiled. "May it ever remain thus, if you so wish it."

CHAPTER EIGHT

I have come quite to love my apartment in the castle. I know that it was built for our late king's mistresses, and furnished with items that might be supposed to delight a woman. A pink marble fireplace carved with gloxinia and camellia, which in the language of flowers means both love at first sight and a gift to man. My large bed was carved with climbing roses and arbutus, both symbols of love; and the crown molding featured day lilies, a symbol of coquetry. The brilliant tapestries are a lavish extravagance of flowers, fruits, animals, and birds, each a door into paradise.

It is not a room where a martial nobleman would normally find himself, let alone one with my firebrand reputation: He would rather be discovered, I suppose, with a cask of brandy, the portrait of an ancestor, and a suit of armor standing in the corner. But in this extravagant room I discover a license to play, to let my mind run to fancies and phantoms, to disport and delight and dance. To lie in my lover's arms, bask in her love, and let my thoughts run free.

"Lo, thus I live twixt fear and comfort tossed," quoth I,
"With least abode where best I feel content;
That rare resort where I should settle most;

My gliding times too soon with thee are spent;
I hover high, and soar where hope doth tower,
Yet froward fate defers my happy hour."

"If this last hour were not happy," said Floria, "I much mistook you."

"If happiness came," said I, "then it will not come. And if it not be now, yet it may come. And if—"

"I think you should avoid this froward fate and this deferring," said Floria, "and be content with what is."

"Only if content and happiness be the same," I said.

"You have never been content in your life," said Floria. "For you have always some emprise in store, to import the finest gems or make up all the ink in the kingdom, to beat the enemy at sea and build Fornland's finest canal."

"Indeed," I sighed, "there is much to do." I turned to Floria in that great carven bed, and buried my face in her untidy galbanum-scented curls. "Yet I will try to be content, at least for tonight."

There was a moment of deep silence, then a log cracked in the pink fireplace, and through a screen of Floria's hair I saw light dance on the underside of the bed's canopy.

"I think," said Floria.

"Ay?"

"I think you take too limited a view of this quarrel between Catsgore and Pontkyles," Floria said. "For remember that Pontkyles has a son he wishes to become king, and Catsgore does not."

"Your fancy flies in a narrower channel than mine," I said.

"Were there a poem about Pontkyles," said she, "I would quote it."

"Pontkyles of the Isles," I said.

"Whose smiles, like crocodiles',
Reviles but not beguiles."

"You did not just compose that verse," she said.

"I have been crafting it awhile," I said, "but I own it has not yet achieved perfection."

She laughed. "Now find me rhymes for 'Sandicup.'"

"Sandicup," I began, "that wretched pup—"

"Give it up, buttercup," she cried. "I surrender."

"Floria," said I, "euphoria, gloria, victoria."

"Dysphoria," said she. "I know my own rhymes, you see. So many of my subjects address me in bad verse."

But now my own mind was engaged. "So you suspect," said I, "that the Pontkyles-Catsgore quarrel is not about them, or me, but about you."

"About my marriage, ay."

"If so," I said, "then I should join this quarrel, for I too have strong opinions on this matter."

"Pray leave the subject," Floria said, "for I hear enough about marriage during the course of my day. Even my ladies campaign for their favorites."

"I did not raise the issue at all," I reminded.

"Yet you and every miserable subject in the realm," she said, "feel free to stick their noses in the business."

I inhaled the perfumed fragrance of her hair. "And where is my nose now?" I asked.

"Just where it ought to be," said she as she touched my cheek. She turned to kiss me. "Forget the rhymes until tomorrow. For I have another project in mind that will fully engage, for the next hour, both your wit and your tongue."

I recognized Freothulaf Post the moment I saw him, even though he stood miserably in the dock, his long hair hanging in his face, chains on his ankles. He was dressed only in his shirt, and his face was covered with bruises. There was blood in his hair and on his collar.

He had been caught the previous night as I quoted poetry to Floria in my chamber. He had hired a waterman to take him out of town, but the waterman and his fellows had thrashed him with their oars and taken him to the Hall of Justice. Even though the hundred-royal reward had to be split between eight of them, they were probably now the richest watermen in the history of the River Saelle.

"Goodman Post," said I. "I am heartily glad to welcome you to this court."

Trials in the Court of the Siege Royal took place in a small room somber with dark wood and filled with flickering shadows, lit only by tall black candles on the judge's bench. The judge was Sir Richard Taylor, a distinguished lawyer and member of the Burgesses who had been knighted and appointed by Floria to the treason court, and who so far had been very exacting in performing his duty, which was to send to the scaffold any person the monarch, often through me, thought worthy of prompt despatch.

The prosecutor of record was the assistant attorney general, a tenacious bulldog of a man called Hunter, though I would share the duty with him as I knew the case better.

A scrivener and couple of bailiffs made the court complete. Post did not have a lawyer to defend him, and would not be allowed one. Only the most distinguished of the accused were permitted lawyers, and Post was hardly distinguished. The purpose of criminal trials in Duisland was to send the accused to his reward in the swiftest and most efficient manner, a fact that acted to make civil trials, where both sides argued, more interesting to watch.

I think I was the only prosecutor in the court's history who had also appeared before the same bench as the accused. I had once been dragged into this court as disheveled and bloody as Post, only to face the black round spectacles, fur-trimmed silk robe, and sallow face of the judge. A note testifying in my favor from Floria, then fifteen years old, had resulted in my release, but Post could not expect any such favor from the royal family. Other courts would cry their cases as "the Crown versus John Guiltyman," or whatever the unfortunate's name might be. The Crown in such a case was considered in law a "corporation sole" and taken in some ill-defined way to encompass the entire state, but in the Siege Royal the monarch herself was listed as the plaintiff. And so I stood while the bailiff cried the case of "Her Sovereign Majesty Floria the First, Queen and Sole Monarch of the Commonwealth of Duisland, Sovereign of the Most Excellent Orders of the Red Horse, the Triton, and the Hippogriff, Grand Collar of the Order of the Seven Words, versus the prisoner, Freothulaf Post." Spoken in declamatory tones, the accusation seemed very personal.

Judge Taylor turned to one of the bailiffs. "Has the accused been shown the instruments?"

"Yes, my lord."

Which meant that Post had been taken to the undercroft below the courtroom, shown the painful devices kept there, and had their use explained to him.

I had always imagined that torture would take place in a deep dungeon, inflicted perhaps by gross, greasy fellows with hairy shoulders, hangman's masks, and branding irons. But in truth it was far worse than that, for an interrogation of that sort was a formal legal proceeding, with a judge always present, a lawyer to conduct the case against the accused, and with scribes to record every gasp and utterance. Every finicking nicety of legal procedure was followed, and the proceedings were conducted in an atmosphere of perverse tranquility, with the lawyers debating fine points of law while the accused was having his joints racked apart.

We were at war, and though few Duislanders wanted Viceroy Fosco back, any number thought Fosco's money as good as any man's. At times some miching mercenary was caught, and I had to act quickly to find the man's confederates before they could enact some atrocity. There had been a plot to burn the royal dockyard with a fireship, and another to set Selford itself ablaze. And of course the enemy believed that Oliver Birdseye was ready to raise a rebellion in Aguila's name, for all they failed to realize that Birdseye in fact worked for me.

In all cases, the proceedings had not lasted long before the required information was obtained—not long, just long enough for me to despise myself.

The building shook to a distant thud. The salute of gunfire was beginning, in honor of the *Duque* de Gandorim, who was making his formal entrance into the castle in order to present his credentials to the Queen.

Taylor turned to the assistant attorney general. "Sir, you may begin."

Hunter outbrayed the cannon. "You filthy dog!" he began. "You wretch, you villainous whoreson, you foolish recreant jackanapes!"

Having thus established his theme, Hunter enlarged upon it for a while as the distant cannon boomed away, and then concluded by explaining which of Post's organs he wished to tear from his body with red-hot pincers.

This sort of opening was normal for a criminal court, though it had to be said that Hunter had perfected his delivery, and that his opening rants had become a species of art.

"In the name of Her Majesty," Hunter concluded, "I demand that you confess your foul crimes at once, that you name your vile accomplices and tell us who hired you to perform this infamous deed."

Post swayed a little in the dock, then looked out from beneath his straggling hair. He seemed a little surprised that he would not be abused all the morning long, and that it was now his turn to speak. He cleared his throat, and his bruised hands clenched and declenched on the rail of the dock.

"You are going to kill me, are you not?" he said. "What is the purpose of my saying anything?"

"Ay, it is our duty to see you turned off to Hell!" Hunter's roars echoed off the beams of the small room. "Just as it is your duty to furnish us the information we demand!"

"Then what is the benefit to me?" asked Post. "You are going to kill me no matter what I say."

I answered the question before Hunter could unleash another storm. "Answering the questions truly may save you a good deal of inconvenience when you are taken below to be racked," said I. "Also his lordship the judge may impose whatever penalty is consistent with the law. If he finds you testifying in an accommodating spirit, he may be accommodating himself, in the manner of sentencing."

Taylor himself raised a skeptical eyebrow at this, but I continued.

"Furthermore, Her Majesty has the power of pardon, and if one of us carries to her ears the news that you were cooperative, she may be inclined to exercise mercy."

"Mercy!" roared Hunter in outrage. "For an *assassin*!"

I ignored Hunter and continued to gaze at Freothulaf Post. "This man is not an assassin," I pointed out. "His attack failed in its object, and I am alive to stand as his accuser. He may be convicted only of attempted murder of an individual living under the Queen's Peace." I looked at Post and nodded. "You may cooperate, and hope," I told him. "Or you may refuse to speak, and be racked and killed."

I saw the surrender in the slump of Post's shoulders before he spoke.

"So, excellencies," he said, "what do you wish to know?"

"Who recruited you for this dastardly work?" Hunter demanded.

"My friend Tim Hewes," Post said. "He accepted the commission, but he was not a man accustomed to violent deeds, and wanted to find someone with experience in battle to carry the enterprise to its conclusion."

"Who hired Hewes?"

"That person was an intermediary, acting on behalf of someone else. An apprentice lawyer named Brian Gordon, who has never qualified to stand before the bar but lives writing briefs and petitions for lawyers."

Judge Taylor seemed surprised, and looked at Hunter. "I know the man," he said.

"I have met him also," Hunter said briefly, then returned his fierce gaze to Post. "Who hired Gordon?" he asked.

"I know not her name, sir," said Post.

"A woman?" Hunter cried. "You met her?"

"In a manner of speaking, sir," he said. "We met with Gordon at Philpott Square, and he arrived in a carriage. He gave us our instructions and some money, and he pointed out the house of the courtesan Mistress Ford, and suggested that Lord Selford might visit there."

"And the woman?" Hunter said.

"She remained in the carriage, and I could see her silhouette against the windows on the far side. I couldn't see her face, but I could tell she wore a lace bonnet and a cartoose collar."

"You lie, you dog!" Again Hunter banged the table with his fist. "Name her, or I will burn out your eyes!"

"Sir—I cannot." For the first time, defiance entered Post's expression.

"Name her! Else I will crush your bones!"

Post stood silent but made a gesture of helplessness with his hands.

I had been distracted since I heard that a woman was behind the ambush, and my head spun as I tried to imagine how I had offended a woman so badly that she would be willing to encompass my death. But since Hunter and Post seemed at an impasse, I drew my mind to the present and asked a question.

"Can you describe this carriage?" I said.

Post directed at me a look of relief. "A light carriage, with two horses, both bays. It was painted a dark green, with trim in yellow paint, and yellow wheels. The rear wheels were larger than the wheels in front."

That was a very complete description, and I thought it might serve to show that Post was willing to cooperate, and was a good observer.

"Who drove the coach?" I asked.

"A ban-dog of a man, sir," said Post. "Broad and powerful, with grizzled hair and an overcoat with the collar turned up over his face. I thought him a guard, and I wished not to make any over-hasty moves in his presence."

"Was there anyone else on or in the carriage?"

"Not that I saw, sir."

"Was there a badge on the carriage, or anything that might identify it?"

"Nay, sir."

I turned to Hunter. His grim mouth had set in a cold smile.

"Very well, Post," he said. "Now tell us how you planned to accomplish this villainous crime, and how it came about that you failed."

I was surprised to discover that Post and Hewes had followed me for nearly three weeks, but discovered that my errands in the city were nearly haphazard and hardly ever repeated, and so they determined to watch Lottie Ford's house and wait for me to arrive at her door. By the end of their vigil, their financial situation had grown so desperate that they maintained their watch even during the great storm. They were delighted to see Greenaway's carriage turn into Mistress Ford's lane, and immediately took their own carriage to the place of their ambuscade.

From that point I knew what happened, though I hadn't realized that Post hadn't understood that I was riding atop the carriage when it crashed. He had been so occupied with trying to get Hewes to re-acquire control of the carriage that he hadn't noticed me crouching mere feet away.

"I shall postpone the sentence on the accused," Taylor ruled, when we had run out of questions, "until the worth of his confession can be assessed."

"We hope your lordship will give us a warrant for this Brian Gordon," Hunter said.

"I shall grant it at once."

The warrant delivered and Post dragged off to his cell, as we walked out of court, I turned to Hunter.

"Do you know any of Gordon's friends?"

"I do not know that he has friends," Hunter said. "But he has worked for many of the lawyers in many of the Moots, and I will inquire among them."

"Thank you. And I shall send thief-takers to find his door and break it down." I reflected on the morning's events. "I am deeply offended," said I, "to discover that my life was worth only an hundred crowns, to be divided between the two accomplices."

"You may be thankful," said Hunter, "that better assassins were not hired, for more money."

"I am thankful," said I, "but not comforted. For some woman wants me dead, and I cannot think who it might be."

He raised an eyebrow. "Your lordship has some history with women, I think."

"A *cordial* relationship, I hope."

Again that eyebrow rose. "Apparently not, my lord."

I sighed. "Ay," I said. "Apparently not."

Prince Amadeu rode into Selford in great state, preceded by heralds with trumpets, and escorted by forty of his gentlemen riding hobbies, the nimble light coursers of the western valleys. Amadeu's hobby was iron gray with silver bells braided into its black mane and tail. Silver decorated the black leather of the bridle and the saddle, and the hobby's iron shoes were blazoned with silver.

I had supposed that Albiz were too short to ride anything but a pony, but it seems I was mistaken, even though they wore their stirrup-leathers well shortened, their knees tucked high.

Amadeu wore his black hair long, and his chin bore a well-groomed black goatee. The prince wore a silver chain, silver rings set with precious stones; the scabbard of his sword was mounted with silver; on his head he wore a gold coronet spiky with silver stars, and with a wide band of ermine supporting the circlet. He had a pale brown complexion like that of our late King Priscus.

It had always been said that the Albiz knew the location of hidden mines in the Minnith Peaks and the West Range, and Amadeu dressed as if he wished to confirm that rumor. Of course, all silver and gold mines in the kingdom belonged by law to the crown, even those that had not yet been discovered, so if the prince's precious metal had been stolen from the Queen, he had chosen to boast of it.

People crowded Chancellery Road to see him, and palace workers lined his path to the throne.

Amadeu rode through the great gate of the castle and there met the Duke of Roundsilver in his role as Lord Chamberlain and master of the royal household. Roundsilver greeted the prince, helped him dismount, and escorted him to the Inner Ward and the vast dim space of the Great Reception Room, which remained chill despite its brilliant tapestries and a hearth large enough to burn a log six yards long.

Floria sat in state at the far end of the room, beneath the red-and-gold royal canopy. I, as a member of the court, stood with others in a half-circle behind the throne. I could see Catsgore grinding his teeth as Amadeu entered with a clank of spurs, strode to the throne, and knelt, his head bowed.

"Please rise, Serene Highness," said the Queen, and left the throne to take Amadeu's hand, help him rise, and kiss him on the cheek. Catsgore seemed about to suffer an apoplexy, one hand clenching and unclenching a brooch he wore pinning his cloak. The other courtiers watched with frank curiosity, for most of them had never seen an Albiz before, let alone a royal one in glittering raiment.

Floria and Amadeu were the same height, I observed, and both wore tall heels.

Roundsilver introduced the courtiers present. When my name was mentioned, Amadeu gave me a quick glance from beneath his dark brows, and I could see he reached a swift judgment, but I could not tell what it was.

When Amadeu was introduced to Catsgore, the prince offered a thin-lipped smile. "His lordship and I are already acquainted," he said.

This was the second great occasion of the day. The first, which took up the morning, was the presentation of his credentials by the *Duque* de Gandorim as Ambassador of King Anibal of Varcellos. While that great occasion went on, with salutes and trumpet-cries, I had been at the Siege Royal interrogating Freothulaf Post.

I was inclined to think this encounter with the Albiz prince more interesting than the credentials of any ambassador. Amadeu and his troop were like figures out of some misty legend, and the conflict with Catsgore brought the conflict into the heart of Her Majesty's government. Gandorim brought no such strife with him but only subtle proposals wrapped in honeyed words.

I spoke but briefly to Amadeu that afternoon, for the reception for the prince was large and the conversation was general. I approached Gandorim while he was speaking with Floria, and as I bowed and removed my cap, he looked at me approvingly.

"My lord of Selford comes in triumph," he said, "and I doubt not that he comes to report to you of some matter of great importance."

"I can be of little importance only," said I, "for only the other day, a great lord told told me that anyone could have done what I have done."

Gandorim smiled. "Surely we may all hope for such a world," he said.

Floria gave me a sidelong look. "Now I wonder who that great lord might have been," she said.

"One who confuses dignity with vanity," said I.

Floria sighed. "That leaves still too many possibilities."

"*The scion of an ancient house,*" I offered.

"*His greatness did announce*
Despite a wit that better fit
The brain-pan of a mouse."

Gandorim affected amusement. Floria deployed her ostrich-feather fan before her lips to conceal her indiscreet smile.

"Take care, Quillifer," she said. "Imagine what rhymes others could make on you."

"They could make damn few on 'Selford,'" I said. "And scarce any on 'Quillifer.'"

"That is a specialty of your Master Knott."

"It is all in the way he sings it." I turned to Gandorim. "You were correct that I have come to report," I said. "I hope you will excuse us for a moment."

He bowed graciously. "Of course."

I managed a brief conversation, behind Floria's fan, telling her of the discoveries at Post's trial. Floria gave me a sharp look. "Have you known so many women that you've forgotten this female in a green carriage?"

"Apparently I have," said I, unhappily. For while not every one of my amours ended in perfect amity, I had not thought there any deep-dyed rancor, let alone a cause to murder.

The only woman who has proclaimed herself my foe is you, my Orlanda. And you have said that you would remain neutral for the present.

Yet you must admit that the attempted assassination was very much your style. Just two years ago you sent three of your puppets to kill me, not because you wanted me dead—at least, not then—but because you wished to distract me from another of your schemes.

Remembering this, for a moment I wondered if Post had been sent to distract me from whoever intended to employ the poison, but that made no sense, for the poison had only been discovered a few days ago, and Post and Hewes had been about their business for weeks.

Post's information had only made the situation more confounding.

I spoke that afternoon to the Steward of the Castle, and asked him if he knew of any recent card game between Pontkyles and Catsgore. It was not implausible that the Steward would know, for certain parlors in the castle were reserved for gaming, and these were in the Steward's domain. The Steward said that he did not know, but he summoned to his office the gentleman usher who had charge of the gaming rooms. The usher was an older man with a paunch, a forked gray beard, and a cynical glean in his eye. I guessed that in his gaming rooms he saw more folly and vice in a week than most people in a year.

"Oh, ay, my lord," said he. "That game was—what?—eight days ago. A Monday."

"Monday?" asked I.

The usher took a moment to reckon on his fingers. "Ay," said he. "For it was two nights before the meeting of the Privy Council, and Catsgore had just moved into his apartment, and complained that he had ordered the rushes changed, and that it had not been done." He turned to the Steward. "That was Monday, I'm sure."

"Indeed it was," said the Steward. "I remember all that business."

"That was why Lord Catsgore was in the gaming rooms at all," said the gentleman usher. "He was waiting for his room to be made ready."

"And he played against Pontkyles?"

The usher seemed surprised. "Nay, sir. They were partners in a game of rentoy."

I paused a moment, for now I understood even less than I had, especially why Catsgore regretted a partnership with Pontkyles that won them twenty royals.

"Because of the problems with his apartment," the usher

remembered, "Lord Catsgore arrived late. He was very drunk when he came, and drank more as the evening waxed on."

But Pontkyles, apparently, had not taken advantage of his drunkenness, at least where the game was concerned. I could not imagine why Catsgore had been so offended.

"Who played against them?" I asked.

"His Grace of Waitstill was present," the usher said, "along with his sons. I think they were all playing spoil-five with Lord Pontkyles before Lord Catsgore arrived, and then two of them joined the game of rentoy once it began."

"Which two?"

"I think all three of them played at different times," the usher said, "but I was in and out of the room, overseeing the other gaming rooms and making certain that refreshment was brought, and I can't be certain."

"Do you recall who won the game?"

"Lord Pontkyles and Lord Catsgore," said the usher. "For I remember being surprised that someone as intoxicated as Catsgore would win." He looked as if he had surprised himself, and his cynical eye opened wide. "Now I recollect, my lord! For they won because the two brothers had got their signals confused and made a series of errors."

"So it was Brighthelm and Lord Hunstan who played?"

"Their father played as well, my lord. I remember him sitting at the table and speaking to Pontkyles. But the great coup was against the two brothers, and Lord Brighthelm was furious against Lord Hunstan for making a shambles of the signals."

I reflected that the game seemed to have caused ill-will all around.

"Were there other signs of rancor that you saw?" asked I.

"At that table? Nay."

"Other tables?"

The cynical eye glimmered. "Some folk fail to enjoy losing large sums, my lord. I know not why."

Keeping a list of those who lost money on that night seemed without profit, so I asked no further questions, and I thanked the Steward and the gentleman usher for their time, and left with no fewer questions than I had an hour before.

"Knott reported this afternoon that Gordon's fled," I told Floria that evening, as I poured her a glass of her favorite sloe-flavored cordial. "His landlord said he left in haste yesterday morning."

"He took no chances," Floria said. "He waited only long enough to know the attempt was unsuccessful."

"We'll find him," I said as I poured brandy for myself. "This only delays matters."

"Others have not delayed," Floria said. "Only this afternoon Scarnside told me that he was in favor of the Varcellos match. Even Gandorim has not yet raised the matter."

Floria's brocade dressing gown crackled as I sat next to her on my settee. "I suppose a gift from His Majesty of Varcellos has won Scarnside's heart? For I know that many chests were carried ashore by that embassy, and many were too heavy for clothing."

Floria smiled to herself. "Let him try to bribe *me*," she said.

"He will," said I. "Not with money, but with guns and soldiers. He will say that the moment you are wed to a Varcellan prince, thirty thousand men will advance over the Mendoa into Loretto."

The smile still touched Floria's lips. "Fifty thousand," she said, "at least."

I touched my glass to hers and raised the brandy to my lips. Pleasing fire trailed its way down my throat, and I felt the iron muscles in my back and shoulders begin to melt.

"Varcellos lost its last war with Loretto," I said. "They want their conquered provinces back. By the time they negotiate a marriage contract, let alone carry it out, the campaigning season will be over, and their chance for surprise will be lost. Those fifty or thirty thousand troops should march now, when Loretto is engaged on other fronts. What does your marital status matter to their larger ambitions?"

"I believe my marital status is of first concern of the entire world," said Floria. "It seems all anyone talks of." She sipped her cordial, and the scent of sweet sloes rose into the room.

"The Varcellos offer is only good for this year," I said, "while we are vulnerable to attack. By next year we'll have achieved equal or better numbers against the enemy, and we won't need Anibal's assistance. The year following we'll have an even greater superiority, and Varcellos will have to put most of their royal family on offer at bargain prices to get anyone to pay attention at all."

Floria contemplated her glass against the light of the candles. Darkling reflections shimmered in her eyes. "So you advise me to tell Varcellos they should attack Loretto first, and then we can talk about a long-term alliance afterward."

I smiled. "I advise Your Majesty to say no such thing. I think you should tell Thistlegorm to say it."

Floria laughed. "By the Pilgrim's teeth, I believe I will!"

I took a burning sip of brandy. "Have I told you that my ship *Sea-Drake* came into Innismore this morning?"

"I knew you were expecting it."

"Captain Oakeshott brought my coffer up by water this morning," I said.

Floria gave me an interested look. "From Tabarzam?"

"From far Sarafsham, from the Street of the Shining Stones itself. I will offer the gems to my friends first, and to you first of all."

"Ah!" An expression of delight crossed her face. "You bring such wonderful things, Quillifer!"

"I do."

"And where are they now?"

I indicated a direction with my cup of brandy. "The coffer sits in the corner, my all."

"Let us see what the chest contains," Floria said.

I rose from the settee. "I shall light more candles so you can properly view the contents."

Sea-Drake was a ship I owned along with my friend Kevin Spellman and his family. But the gems brought from Tabarzam were entirely my own venture, bought with my own funds, and if there were profits to be made, I would have them all to myself.

I lit candles and a pair of lanterns, and put another log on the fire. I moved the coffer before the pink marble fireplace and unlocked it, and the two of us knelt before it like children before a box of toys, and with such the same sense of anticipation.

I have mentioned my delight in my apartment, a spur to my fancy with its phantasia of carved flowers and the tapestries brilliant with animals and birds. Gems were another such spur, ruby and diamond and sapphire, cabochon and rosette and pear-shaped, all sparkling in the shimmering light. At one time I had invented stories for my gems, and used them to drive the imagination of my buyers. Now Floria and I invented stories together, of gems pried from the crowns of Kangavid kings, of an egg-shaped emerald held in the navel of a courtesan, or of stones inset on the toe-rings of a dancing girl spelling out a secret message to spies sent from Imperial Grindomahl.

Thus did we spend our time in mirth, fancy, and delight, while the clock ticked on, and the guard changed, and the firelight caressed our faces. All care vanished, all the responsibilities of the kingdom and the world, and we laughed like those imaginary children with their toys, and sheer pleasure filled my apartment during the course of those night watches, in the great lacy castle glowing in the light of the moon.

The next three days were uneventful, and were intended to be so, for the entire court journeyed to the Path of the Pilgrim Monastery for a retreat lasting three days. We were the guest of the Abbot Ambrosius, who had been Berlauda's Philosopher Transterrene in the early days of her reign before being dismissed for his reluctance to cast deadly spells on her half-brother Clayborne. Since his dismissal he seemed hardly to have given up the world. He was often in Selford, a guest at the house of some great lord, or attending some conference of prelates. To judge by the meals he served his guests those three days, neither was he immune to the worldly pleasures of the table.

I considered him a nod-crafty fraud, but for the most part a harmless one.

We slept in rooms intended for monks, where incense lingered in the air. I was given a bed of my own, while the two knights who shared my cell were obliged to sleep on the floor. Our days were spent listening to homilies from our host, or eating at his vast table, or adopting uncomfortable postures while we chanted for the health of the monarch and the spiritual advancement of the kingdom. I felt that the message of the Pilgrim Eidrich was reasonable but incomplete, and so participated not out of conviction but out of politeness.

Of course, there was no secret passage enabling me to attend Floria in her own apartment, which in any case was shared with a number of her ladies. I strove to keep our reunion in my hopes.

I was supposed to keep my mind and being firmly and consciously on my assigned meditations, for a moment's distraction, or wavering of purpose, might well ruin a spell which had been wound up for days; but I'm afraid that I was an amateur where this sort of sorcery was concerned, and I am also certain that I was not the first person to yawn, or to think of something pleasant while mouthing the words.

If the chant's affect had been already thus ruined, I reasoned, there was little point in keeping my mind on the spell, and so I allowed my thoughts to abandon their omphaloskepsis and wander, disembodied as any spirit, through the complex events of the last ten days. I reviewed the case of the poisoner and found nothing new, and I sorted again through Post's revelations. I endeavored to puzzle out the mystery of Catsgore's anger at Pontkyles, and wondered if it were relevant to anything at all but a nobleman's fit of pique. I paged through a mental ledger of women, nearly every woman I could recollect, to find anyone so offended at my actions that she would resort to violence; and though I knew one immortal being who answered that description, I could think of no one earthly who would go to such extremes to seek my end.

But toward the end of the second day of chanting, it occurred to me that the woman, like her own instrument Post, might not be acting on her own behalf—and that, I realized, was my answer.

After our meditations for the day were ended, I sent a messenger to Selford to initiate an inquiry, and the answer came the next day that the green carriage had been found. I spoke to Thistlegorm, who said he would procure the warrant next morning, and I returned to Selford in a long train of carriages along with the rest of the court, and made my way to my apartment, and my reunion with Floria, in a thankful spirit.

CHAPTER NINE

Well, Lord Edevane," said I. "You seem not as surprised to see me as on the last occasion."

"I have had some time to get used to the idea that you might visit," Edevane said. "Has another poisoner been found?"

He sat in an armchair in his cell, his delicate frame wrapped in a cloak against the morning chill. Reflected sunlight glimmered on his gold-rimmed spectacles. The remains of his breakfast were neatly arranged on a small table, and the woody scent of a tisane still lingered in the room. A book lay on his lap.

"No poisoner, my lord, but an assassin," said Judge Travers. "A revengeful vixen who, through a corrupt lawyer, hired men to murder a minister of state and a peer of the realm."

Edevane was motionless for a few seconds, and then the fingers of his right hand began to tap the fingers of his left. "I expect," he said in his soft voice, "that someone has tried to buy his way out of a sentence by laying some information against me, and that this information is most certainly a lie. For that informer believes that no one would defend me, knowing my situation."

"Your wife is under arrest," said I. "Her carriage driver tried to fight, but was run through by a half-pike and lies now at death's door. Lady Edevane's papers have been taken, and it seems she wrote down your instructions very carefully, and took care also to write down the names of her accomplices."

"In her own hand!" said Travers. He seemed caught between anger and indignation. "What spirit possessed you?" he demanded. "How could you involve your own wife in this sordid business?"

Edevane's eyes closed behind his spectacles, then opened again. "It was not precisely my idea," said he. "I think that miching lawyer Gordon had a malign influence on her. But seeing that she was determined, I offered her such advice as I could."

I could not tell if he were sincere, or if he were trying to mitigate Lady Edevane's crimes by foisting them on Gordon and, to a degree, on himself. In the event, it hardly mattered.

Travers presented Edevane with a paper. "If you would sign this confession," said he, "it would spare your lady an interrogation."

Edevane took the paper and signed without reading it. I remembered the look of astonishment on his face on our last meeting, as if I were the last person on earth he had expected to walk through the door. Now I understood the look was as much horror as surprise, for the assassination was to take place that very night, and his first thought must have been that I had discovered the plot and its origins, and had come for revenge. Instead I was the source of relief, for I had only come to ask him about the poison ring.

After Travers and I left Edevane's cell, the judge frowned and looked at me. "I think it is Edevane, and not his lady, behind this plot. Though I am sure he hates you, I believe he did not pursue vengeance so much as opportunity—for look, with you dead, there would be a need for someone to fill your office, someone with experience and a subtle mind, and so amid the chaos Edevane might hope for a recall."

"And he would, I suppose, find the perpetrators," said I. "Not his own agents but innocent folk discovered at the end of carefully laid false trails."

"Ay. That seems likely."

I turned to Travers. "Well, your lordship, this brings an end to your special commission."

"Ay," said he. "I will write a final report, then submit it to your lordship."

"You have worked long on this task," said I, "and I will speak to Her Majesty about an appropriate reward."

"Let Her Majesty not send me back on the circuit, I beg you," Travers said. "Holding the quarterly assizes in one town after another is a younger man's profession."

"I had in mind a knighthood," said I. "But if you wish an appointment to the bench in the capital, I will see what is available."

"I thank your lordship," Travers said. "That would be right good of you."

I wondered if it were possible to have imagined, when Travers and I first met in looted Ethlebight, that only a few years later I would be in a position to recommend a knighthood to Travers or to anyone, or an appointment to a high court, and expect to be taken seriously.

In truth, I sometimes wonder at myself.

I recommended Travers for a knighthood and a judgeship that afternoon, when I reported to Floria in her cabinet, with a goblet of sauternes in my hand and two of her ladies viewing us through the hagioscope. By that point Lady Edevane had been tried and found guilty, and condemned to suffer the noble traitor's fate of beheading. Lord Edevane needed no such trial, only Travers's word that he had violated his parole, and his own execution was assured. Then Post was sentenced to be hanged, along with Lady Edevane's carriage driver, though it would be a race to see whether the hangman or his wounds would carry him off first.

Justice in Duisland is swift, deadly, brutal, and often arbitrary. At least in this case I had the satisfaction of knowing that the condemned were truly guilty.

Only the half-attorney Brian Gordon remained at large, and as there was a two-hundred-royal reward for him, he would not stay free for long. People would cut out their dear mother's beating heart for such a sum.

Not being required as a witness, I was not present at sessions of the Siege Royal, but the reports came to me that afternoon, before I had my interview with Floria.

"It occurs to me that I have never met Lady Edevane, nor even seen her," I said. "And now I play a part in her death."

"I thank the stars that she did not play a part in yours," Floria said. "But sure, it seems she was a fit partner for her homicide of a husband."

"The warrants for the executions will come to you this afternoon," I said. "It is your prerogative to offer mercy."

Floria gave a derisory laugh. "Your gallant and sentimental view of my sex does you credit," said she, "but I know better than to let some hydrophobic female run mad in my country. The wench shall die."

"As Your Majesty wishes," I said. In truth I would not mourn Lady Edevane, and I wondered if anyone would.

I finished the last of my sauternes and bowed in my armchair. "With your permission, I will depart now for Haysfield Grange, the better to welcome you to my home tomorrow."

"You may go," said Floria, "and I will look forward to seeing your house."

I ordered up my carriage, collected Rufino Knott and my gem-coffer, and set out for my estate. It was five leagues west of the capital on the south bank of the Saelle, and the road was good. The views from the carriage windows were a great pleasure on a sun-filled spring day, the river a blue shimmer the color of my watered-silk doublet, the surface speckled with the white sails of pleasure boats and the brown sails of working craft. Cherry and apple blossoms striped the orchards with pink and white, and sheep floated over verdant pasture like little clouds. Rye, barley, and wheat rose in the fields, each a different shade of green, and hops were beginning to climb their gray, weathered stakes. Crocus, hellebore, and white anemone grew alongside the carriage road, and elm seedlings stormed through the air like falling snow.

Moored alongside the river were at least two dozen barges, each painted in bright colors. Each barge dangled into the current a water wheel to power its mill, and each mill made paper from linen and other fabrics bought from ragpickers in the district. The paper mills fed the insatiable appetite of the government in Selford, which ran on paper and ink and windy speeches—and while I made few speeches and even less paper, the ink at least was mine, and every document put money in my purse.

My carriage made good speed and we reached the gate to Haysfield Grange in two and a half hours, and so we turned into the old avenue of towering plane trees, each hundreds of years old, while sheep cropped grass on either side and the dogs barked out a warning, or a welcome.

Of the old castle only the gatehouse survives, a massy rectangular block with a round turret on each of its four corners. It is used now as an entrance to the two wings, which do not match as they were built at different times and for different purposes, one for entertainment, the other for living. Stables, a dairy, kennels, a brewhouse, a malt house, a smokehouse, and a bath-house were clustered behind the main building, which rather spoiled the vista along the long back lawn. I had built a tennis court against the east wing, on the far end.

The Grange was built of the same white sandstone as the castle in Selford, but a hundred years of weather and chimney smoke had stained the stone and left it unlovely. Unlike the royal family, who had a battalion of laborers to polish their palace, the last several generations of the Grange's tenants had not cleaned the outside of the building.

When I rebuilt the house, I would face it with particolored Ethlebight brick, which would solve the problem.

In the morning, on the day of my feast, I would cover the discolored front of the house with banners, the flags of Duisland, the red horse of the Emelins, Floria's double white impatiens, and my own blue-and-white banner. Already the lawn had blossomed with white canvas tents sheltering tables and equipment for sport. There would be outdoor games tomorrow if the weather suited, and I thought it would, for there were no aches in my crooked little finger to signal the onset of storm.

Once at home I inspected the kitchen and the pantry in the company of my cook Harry Noach, and my steward, Master Stiver. Stiver was more properly the steward of Rackheath House, the small palace I leased in the winter capital of Howel, but as I only used the place for half the year, I left it in the hands of the housekeeper and brought Stiver with me to Fornland to bring the Grange's staff up to his unremitting standard.

As I was the son of a butcher, I knew good flesh when I saw it; I could see that Noach had bought—or butchered—only the best. Laid out on the countertops were capons, pigeons, pheasant, rabbits, suckling pig, great chines of beef, and Ethlebight lamb grazed on salt grass, which gave it unique and unparalleled flavor. Barrels of seawater held hundreds of live oysters and mussels. Pike, trout, tench, grayling, and sturgeon lay on beds of snow brought down on barges from the Minnith Peaks. I delighted in the scent and appearance of spring vegetables fresh from the fields: peas and pea greens, morels, leeks, artichokes, rocket, fiddleheads, radishes, leeks, parsley, and cardoons, all at the peak of flavor and waiting to be savored. I had not seen all these vegetables even on Floria's table, and felt pleased with myself that I had managed to take such advantage of the advancing spring.

My chill fruit-room had preserved over the winter pears and apples—pearmains, my mother's favorite—and these would be sliced into elaborate shapes and served with the dessert.

Since the days were lengthening and the cows were giving milk once more, I had told Harry Noach to take full advantage of this springtime dispensation, and to use as much fresh butter, cream, and milk as he could. The butter and cream waited now in the cool cellars, and would be used to provide a lavish enhancement to the next day's meals.

I inspected as well the barrels of wine from Loretto, Varcellos, and southern Bonille. There were also barrels of beer, and the brewhouse had produced fresh ale for the company. For those who preferred not to risk intoxication, there was rose and lavender water, almond milk, soft cider, sage water, and shrub.

After taking pleasure in viewing all this, I enjoyed my own simple supper along with my house guests, Alaron and Edith Mountmirail, beginning with a vegetable pottage, moving on to roast chicken, then roast pork, all served with white manchet-bread, sweet butter, and a selection of the fine spring vegetables. As might be expected with so learnèd a couple, the conversation ranged widely and took in methods of navigation at sea, theories concerning the Land of Chimerae, the casting of artillery, and (from Madame Mountmirail) denunciation of the followers of the Compassionate Pilgrim, denunciation of astrologers and necromancers, and denunciation of physicians in general.

After supper I went to my bath, and opened the tap that emptied the copper reservoir of hot water, which had been heating since my arrival. I delight in hot baths, and in older buildings like the castle such baths could only be obtained at great inconvenience, with a tub of copper or canvas brought to my apartment, then filled by servants bringing up hot water from the kitchens. I drowsed in my bath for half an hour, then took myself to bed with a copy of Rudland's comic verse.

It might serve, I thought, to view tomorrow's feast through the mirror of Rudland, for he viewed people as quintessences or distillations of certain characteristics: He wrote of clever servants, for example, or lecherous lords, pragmatic wives, braggart knights, comely maidens, and reckless lovers. To view my morrow's guests as being composed of these quintessences might greatly enhance my enjoyment, for I could see them all as comic types set up for my own amusement.

But of what quintessence is a poisoner? I wondered, and then felt my analogy fall to pieces.

From that moment the verse failed to charm me, and I put out the light, burrowed into my warm bed, and hoped that anxiety would not rob me entirely of sleep.

"I congratulate you," said the *Duque* de Gandorim, "on uncovering the source of that conspiracy against you, and to reveal that pair of vipers who had so enriched themselves by coiling themselves about the late queen and her viceroy."

"Duisland will be cleaner without such vipers, Your Grace," said I.

"And of course you first rescued Her Majesty from that Edevane," said Gandorim. "A brilliant feat, even if Master Blackwell's play was somewhat exaggerated."

"I thank you," I said. "Exaggerated or not, I am fully prepared to believe in my own genius."

We stood together before the old castle gatehouse, Gandorim in a suit of silver tissue, his mild brown eyes fixed on my face. He had been one of the very first guests to arrive, and must have left Selford before dawn.

The sun was brilliant on the green lawn, and on the white canvas of the tents. Across the front of the Grange my banners flapped idly in the gentle breeze. Servants in my blue-and-white livery bustled about their preparations, or stood waiting for guests—I had hired many of my tenants, and half the local village, for the day. The scent of cooking meat floated in the air.

The only blight on the day was Gandorim's relentless flattery. I wondered if he would continue this for the rest of the day, or if I could divert him into some other topic.

His policy was clear enough. He understood my position as favorite, and knew that whatever he hoped to achieve could be best accomplished with my cooperation. He would not oppose me unless he was forced to it, for that course would be perilous if I proved the stronger.

"It seems to me that your contributions to the realm may not be rewarded as you deserve," Gandorim said.

"How so?" asked I. "The Queen has been most generous, and given me more property than I could visit in a year. I have a title, and I have money. What do I lack?"

The ambassador spread his hands. "It seems to me," he said, "that you lack a wife, as well as a child to carry on your name, your property, and your title."

Ah, I thought. "I have lately met with men offering me their daughters," I said.

Gandorim smiled. "I have no daughters but three fine, strong sons."

"You offer them to Her Majesty?" I asked, but only because I couldn't resist.

Gandorim seemed amused. "I think we stray from the topic," he said.

I affected to consider the matter. "Perhaps, then, the subject of our discourse should be made more explicit."

"We were speaking of your marriage," Gandorim said.

"You spoke of marriage, Your Grace, but I remind you that I did not."

Gandorim gave me an inquiring look. "Have you objections to a widow young and beautiful?"

I smiled at him. "I haven't in the past."

He returned my smile. "Donna Arianna, Marquesa dels Altimirs, is the lady that comes to my mind. She is twenty and was widowed just last year when the Marques was felled by an apoplexy."

"Apoplexy? She was not, I take it, his first wife?"

Gandorim paused for a moment's calculation. "His fourth," he said finally.

"Well." I waved a hand. "The Marques is with his first three wives now."

"She comes with an extraordinary dowry," Gandorim said. "For she fell heir to the vineyards of the Valle de Saude. Because these fields face the rising sun every morning, they produce the finest wines in our kingdom. These vintages are unknown here, and whoever imported them would make a great fortune with very little effort."

A beautiful well-born widow, I thought, and money, too. Gandorim was determined to make me the luckiest man in Duisland, if only I surrendered the one thing in the world that I loved above all else.

"I have the marquesa's portrait in miniature," he said, "if you would care to see it."

"Perhaps later," said I. "For now it seems I must offer my respects to the unmarried daughters of an important man."

For I recognized Thistlegorm's carriage coming down the avenue, and I presumed that Candice and Emily were aboard, and they would have been instructed to make themselves pleasant to me. I strolled from the gatehouse to the drive, and was able to hand both of the ladies from the carriage, and to greet their father when he appeared.

"I wish to thank you for your cooperation in helping to apprehend Edevane and his assassins," I told him. "This business is concluded with far more speed than I had imagined."

"You are most welcome, my lord. I am very pleased that this unhappy chapter has been brought to an end." He leaned closer to me and spoke in a low voice. "Her Majesty has signed the death warrants, and now the matter rests with the executioner. There will have to be a few days' advance warning; otherwise there will be insufficient crowds for the pie-vendors and ballad-sellers to make a profit."

"Ay," said I, "there must be time for all the crows to gather."

Emily stood nearby, looking at the range of entertainments available. The glossy bowling greens awaited only players, and elsewhere there was palle-malle, lawn billiards, quoits, shovel-board, lawn darts, and battledores-and-shuttlecocks.

"Is there a game that would please you, mistress?" asked I.

"Quoits, please," said Emily, and then added, "I have a good backhand."

We walked toward the quoits pitch. Emily looked at me. "Will Bonny Joe be here?"

"He is still at the Dead Vile, so far as I know," said I. "But Master Blackwell will be here today, and you may inquire of him."

Emily's face confided that she was not interested in Blackwell. Instead she bounded ahead to the quoits pitch and equipped herself with a flight of metal rings.

She did in fact have a good backhand, and managed to flip her rings so that they floated like an inverted saucer toward the targets, then came to a gentle landing. "Very good, mistress!" I said, and then turned to her older sister, who hadn't said a word since thanking me for helping her out of the carriage.

"Is there any amusement you desire, Mistress Candice?"

"I might take a drink of cider," she said.

I took her arm in mine and walked her to the refreshment tent, where drinks and light collation were available for those unwilling to wait for dinner. "Have you seen Lord Hunstan since the other night?"

She was expressionless. "Nay," she said. "I have not."

I signaled for two cups of cider. "Your concern for his injury did you credit," I said. "How long have you known him?"

"All my life," she said. "Our house in Howel stands next to the duke's, and we see each other every winter. Sometimes we shared a tutor or a dancing master."

"That accounts for his great regard for you," said I.

She blinked and looked at me in surprise. "Great regard?" she said.

"He has spoken to me of his esteem," said I. "He admires you."

I had to trust that my plan, which might as well have come from one of Blackwell's plays, was not utterly transparent. I hoped that Candice was not yet inured to the relentless flattery and duplicity of the court and was thus unable to see through my honeyed scheme.

I was about to enlarge on Lord Hunstan's admiration when out of the corner of my eye I saw Alaron Mountmirail jumping and waving a handkerchief in my direction. "I apologize, Mistress Thistlegorm," I said, "but I am now obliged to fire a cannon."

I hastened out onto the sward, where the Mountmirails and Edith's brother, the gunfounder Ransome, stood about a small cannon, which was manned by a journeyman and two apprentices from the Loyall and Worshipfull Companie of Cannoneers. The journeyman handed me the linstock and said, "We are primed and ready, my lord. You may begin whenever you like."

"Thank you, goodman." I made sure everyone was standing clear, and then I set the burning match to the touch hole. The cannon let out a great crash and spat a smoking rope wad a hundred yards down the lawn. Birds rose shrieking from the trees in black clouds.

The cannoneers busied themselves with reloading. Mountmirail shook red hair from his eyes and watched them critically. Ransome preened his mustaches and padded around the gun to view it from a different angle. "I cast this gun myself, two weeks ago," he said, as corned powder was poured into the touch hole. "And I pride myself that—"

I applied the linstock, and the gun boomed, cutting off Ransome's words.

We were firing one of the small new leather guns, conceived by my friend William Lipton, Lieutenant-General of Artillery, and brought into being through Mountmirail's engineering skill. The gun fired a six-pound shot, like a saker, but a saker was over three yards long, and this gun barely over a yard. The barrel was brass and quite thin, but wrapped in thick suede secured by iron bands.

The early versions of this weapon had all burst, but Mountmirail had solved that problem by increasing the width of the brass on the breech, then again wrapped everything in suede. The result was a gun that no longer burst—or at any rate, burst no more than any other kind of gun.

I dipped the linstock toward the touch hole, and the leather gun spat thunder. There was no danger whatever of its bursting, for we loaded with no ammunition, only a rope wad to hold the powder in place.

By the time I completed the royal salute of twenty-three guns, white smoke drifted in thick banks along the avenue, and the air had turned bracing with the tang of burnt powder. Floria's carriage, with its footmen in red and gold livery and its escort of officers in the black leather jerkins of the Yeoman Archers, had drawn up before my house. I hastened to where the carriage waited.

"Welcome to Haysfield Grange, Your Majesty," I said, and with a bow helped her from her carriage.

"We are pleased to see it at last," Floria said, "though for a proper view we shall have to wait for the smoke to clear."

She wore a gown of stiff black silk spangled with beads of jet, with sleeves, collar, kirtle, and partlet of bright yellow dotted with black sarcenet puffs. Her points were tipped with gold, and she wore a belt of gold links over her hips, with a lacy pomander ornamented with a star sapphire that I had sold her years ago, when we barely knew one another. A hat embroidered with gold lace was tipped over one ear, with three plumes and an enameled gold pin. She had brought all twelve of her ladies, and this required a convoy of three carriages, so it was a large party of glittering women that I escorted through and about my manor.

"And now I show you the least impressive library in the realm," I said, and showed Floria into an elegant room, with a range of windows bringing in the northern light, and shelves, still wafting an odor of varnish, that held mementoes of my life and voyages: ivory carvings from North Fornland, shadow-puppets acquired on the Candara Coast, a selection of my guitars, a great many maps, and a flag from the *Royal Stilwell,* which Kevin Spellman and I had captured from Clayborne's rebels off Longfirth, in Bonille.

There were few books, and these were worn volumes I had carried with me for years. I hadn't the time to haunt bookstalls in town, and while I could employ some agent or other to stock my library, something in me rebelled at this idea. I wanted books that I could love, not fashionable volumes selected from a list by a self-appointed arbiter of taste.

"Are all your books in Howel?" asked Lady Mellender.

"Alas," said I, "I haven't had time to finish this room. I find that libraries require special attention, don't you? After all, they are where our real treasures are stored."

"And we had thought you stored your treasures on your fingers," said Floria.

I waved a jewel-bedecked hand. "Those are but frivolous tokens of the realm of the profane," said I, and donned my pious anchorite face, "whereas true wisdom consists in the contemplation of the eternal things."

"And here we thought you had not read Abbot Fulvius's book," Floria said.

"Every word was a gem," I said. "And now, perhaps Your Majesty would welcome refreshment?"

At one of the refreshment tables I encountered the Chancellor of the Exchequer, Sir Merriman Sandicup. He wore the ribbon of the Red Horse, which matched his red hair, and in his hand he held a pie.

"Your cook makes an excellent venison pie, Selford," he said. "But are you really taking deer out of season?"

"I will pass your compliments on to the pastry cook, Sir Merriman," I said. "But that pie is beef."

A look of disbelief crossed his face. "I know venison when I taste it, Selford!" he said. "You're taking deer in April, and even though you come from some barbaric corner of the realm, you should know that this is not proper!"

"It is a recipe of my mother's," I said, "a trick to make beef taste like red deer. First, you slice your beef very thin." I illustrated this with motions of my hands. "Then you shred suet and beat it in a mortar, and in a pan you lay a row of suet, a row of beef, and so on, and with each layer you strew cloves and mace, nutmegs and pepper and salt, with just a little sugar, and you add also good wine vinegar. Then you beat it flat with a rolling pin, and press it under a weight for a day before putting it in the pie, which when it is cooked, will taste like the finest venison."

"This is not a recipe; it is a ragbag of nonsense," said Sandicup.

"I will send the recipe to your cook, if you like."

"He will not use it."

I shrugged. "A pity, then, that he has not tasted my mother's cooking."

"I daresay we will all taste it at dinner this afternoon."

I laughed. "If you like not my mother's cooking, I will have Noach make something else for you."

He smiled. "Nay, I will suffer with the others."

"I commend your courage, then."

I saw that Her Majesty, a goblet of wine in one hand, had gone to the quoits pitch, and that she and some of her ladies had joined Emily

Thistlegorm in a game. I observed Lord Hunstan Wilmot at one of the bowling greens, warming before bowling by rotating his throwing arm, and I made my excuses to Sandicup and joined Hunstan on the green.

"I hope I might join you in a game of bowls without your brother dragging you away," said I.

"Oh, Brighthelm?" Hunstan rotated his arm in the other direction. "He didn't come."

I was not surprised. I bent and picked up the kitty. "Would you like to throw the kitty, or shall I?"

"Go ahead."

I placed the mat on the green, and standing thereon I tossed the white kitty, where it inscribed a gentle arc over the grass before stopping. "Your throw, my lord."

Hunstan picked up a yellow bowl, put his feet on the mat, and threw with a kind of lunging step. He threw too hard, and his bowl ended in the ditch.

I chose a blue bowl and managed to get it behind the kitty, where it was a little protected.

"I heard that Catsgore was wroth with Pontkyles over the card game you played with him the week before last," I said. "Do you know why?"

Hunstan seemed puzzled. "I don't know why Catsgore would be upset, since he and Pontkyles won forty royals off us."

"Forty? I'd heard it was twenty."

"Twenty each." Hunstan did his lunging step again, but this time he mastered it, and his bowl fell within inches of the kitty.

"Very good!" I said.

"I know that my brother was very angry with me," Hunstan said. "He said that I'd got the signals tangled, but he was the tangled one, not me."

"Brothers are often like that, I understand," I said. I threw my bowl in hopes of getting it between the kitty and Hunstan's last throw, but I misjudged and my bowl crept up to Hunstan's, then toppled over partly atop it.

"Ay," I muttered. "There's the rub!"

"Unfortunate," Hunstan commented. He picked up a yellow bowl and stepped to the mat. He paused a moment, then rolled it perfectly, so that it dropped a few feet in front of the kitty, thus guarding it from any attempt by me to knock the kitty away from Hunstan's shots.

I picked up a blue bowl and frowned down the rink. "What were Pontkyles and Catsgore talking about that night? Were any kind of insults exchanged?"

Hunstan considered the question. "Catsgore was very drunk. He seemed very pleased with himself, and kept trying to explain why, but I made no sense out of it. There was talk of silver mines, and ships, and some Albiz that were making trouble, and he kept going on about some other fellow lodged in Mossthorpe, but I could not follow it." Another thought occurred to him. "I suppose Catsgore was so drunk that he might have heard an insult where none was intended."

"That might be the most sensible explanation," I said.

I looked down the rink and saw that I must break up the rub, knock my last bowl free from Hunstan's, and with luck move the kitty as well, to a place less well protected. In order for this to occur, I needed to apply more force to my bowl, and I threw with too much power. My blue bowl struck my previous bowl and bounded over it, ending in the ditch.

Hunstan's last bowl fell just before the rub, which guarded it against any more interference from me. I tried to get my final bowl on an arc between the two yellow guards, in hopes it would fall close to the kitty, but I failed, and Hunstan won the end, one shot to naught.

As I picked up the mat to carry it down the rink, I noticed Hunstan limping slightly. "Is your leg still bothering you, Hunstan? Should we give up the game?"

"I think I shall be all right," he said.

"I hope Candice Thistlegorm wasn't right to be so worried for you," said I. "I think the concern did her great credit."

"That was right good of her," said Hunstan. "Though her distress was unwarranted."

"She holds you in high esteem," said I. "I gather you have known her all your life?"

"I have," said he. "It's my turn to set the kitty, ay?"

I set the mat down for him and he rolled the kitty to the far end of the rink. I gathered up my blue bowls and chose one for my first shot.

"Candice seems a most accomplished young lady," I said. "Educated, unspoiled by the court. An ornament to her family, and to any gentleman lucky enough to attract her affections."

Hunstan gave me a speculative look. I sent my first bowl down the rink, and managed again to roll it behind the kitty, eight or ten inches away.

"I beg your pardon, Lord Selford," Hunstan said. "But does Lord Thistlegorm not intend that you will be that gentleman?"

I straightened and looked at Hunstan with my noble martyr face. "I should not care to engage myself to anyone whose sentiments so clearly lie with another," I said.

I let him absorb this, and then he picked up his first bowl. When he sent it down the rink, it was clear that his concentration was no longer on the game, and I won the end by two shots.

If my scheme worked, I thought, I would give the story to Blackwell for a play.

During the third end, Hunstan slowly recovered his wits, and eventually he won the game eleven shots to nine. I offered him my congratulations. "It's a pity we forgot to wager," I said, "you might have won some of your twenty royals back."

"At court there is no lack of occasions to lay a wager," he said.

"True enough." And then I saw Lord Catsgore making angry gestures at me from the end of the bowling green. I made my excuses to Hunstan, and walked to where Catsgore waited.

"Catsgore," said I, "your choler is such that I fear you will have an apoplexy."

"The false prince is here!" he said. "Did you invite him?"

"Amadeu?" asked I. "He is a guest of Her Majesty, so I was obliged to send him an invitation."

Catsgore's teeth ground together so hard that I fancied I could hear his molars shatter. "He came galloping up on his hobby with half a dozen armed retainers!"

"An inadequate number to storm my fortress, Catsgore," said I.

Catsgore took my arm and marched me in the direction of the stables. "I will tell you what he is going to do, Selford," he said. "You have seen how he is dressed, all shining in silver gauds, silver even to the shoes of his horse!" He leaned close and hissed in my ear. "He will imply that he knows the location of a secret silver mine, or more than one. Even that admission is illegal—all silver in the ground belongs to Her Majesty!"

" 'All mines of gold and silver within the realm,' " I quoted, " 'whether they be in the lands of the Queen, or of subjects, belong to the Queen by prerogative.' A principle in law established by the Exchequer Court more than a hundred years ago."

"Precisely!" said Catsgore. "Amadeu will hint and insinuate and signal that he knows where such mines will be found, and that he will offer to help Her Majesty's servants 'locate' these mines, and in exchange Her Majesty will be asked to give him title to *my* lands! And in the end, the mines will prove old and exhausted and not worth the finding."

"I will report your sentiment to Her Majesty," I said. "But do not fear losing your land—the law forbids the monarch to give away land that belongs to her subjects."

"Ah, but how do I prove such an old title," said he, "and in such wild country? It could be claimed that I never owned the land at all."

I rather thought he hadn't, but of course it was possible that Amadeu hadn't, either.

"Her Majesty can hardly make a capricious decision in anyone's favor," I said. "If Amadeu presses his suit against you, it will have to be in the courts, and it will go on for years."

He snarled. "And I am to hope for *that*? Years in the courts instead of an arbitrary ruling against me?"

"Alas," said I, "we are ruled by laws, even the monarch."

At that moment the dinner bell rang, and I hastened to my house, for as host I had to take Floria in to dinner. As I walked with the Queen through the screening passage and into the hall, trumpets played a sennet, one that called my name in three descending tones: *Quil-li-fer Quil-li-fer Quil-li-fer.*

Haysfield Grange had two wings spreading from the old gatehouse, one for lodging, and the other consisting almost entirely of the great hall, an oak-beamed chamber, brilliant with window-glass and varnish, that rose to a peak overhead. My arms were blazoned over the fireplace, and the walls were decorated with old hunting trophies and new tapestries that depicted a miscellaneous collection of scenes— there had not been time for newly commissioned tapestries to have been woven, so I had acquired tapestries I happened to like, and for good or ill my own deeds and those of my ancestors were not glorified in wall hangings, as were found on most houses of the nobility.

The floors displayed gold and brown tiles painted with woodbine and flower-de-luces. A dais stood at the far end of the room, to hold the high table, and above it a portrait of Floria gazed down in full, stern majesty. She was dressed as Dame Justice, with white robes, a sword in one hand, and the red rose of mercy in the other. By this I hoped to contrast her reign with that of Priscus and Fosco, who with Edevane had made of justice a travesty.

Against the far wall was another, smaller portrait of Floria, this one less recognizable. This showed Floria with cropped curling hair and boy's clothing, the Floria I had known when I smuggled her across Bonille in the guise of my page. It was a furious, frantic, frozen journey in the dead of winter, and after I had finally got her safely onto my privateer *Able*, we had kissed, and embraced, and spent together our first night of love.

Floria looked nothing like that young boy now, but whenever I saw the portrait, I felt a swell of love and sweet happiness. Those hours on *Able* were a private treasure we had created between the two of us, for ourselves alone. Now we were compelled to share our time with scores of other people, and though we guarded our time together, we know that just the other side of the door there might be a guard, or one of Floria's ladies, or someone with an urgent message from Bonille, enough to take us back into the world outside one another's arms.

I took Floria in through the screening passage from the outside, then down the length of the room to the dais. I helped her to sit in her chair, then stood behind her while the other guests filed into their places. Floria had Ambassador Gandorim on her right, and Roundsilver on her left. My own place was across the table from her, but that put my back to most of my guests, and I wished to formally welcome them, and for that it was only polite to face them.

The tables were crowned by great centerpieces of marchpane, either the tritons of Fornland, the hippogriffs of Bonille, or the Red Horse of the Emelins, the horses and hippogriffs the size of hounds cantering over a sward of lifelike green grasses, with rabbits and foxes and birds frolicking at their feet. The tritons were half-submerged in an ocean of blue sugar glass, with dolphins and cuttlefish visible through the transparent surface of the sea. Every piece, the tritons' beards, the green grass, the hippogriffs' fierce beaks, the blue ocean, was edible. Noach and a small legion of sub-cooks had spent the last week painstakingly assembling these masterpieces, then carrying them with great care into the hall and setting them on the tables.

I waited for my guests to find their seats, and then I looked to the gallery above the screening passage, and gave a signal to Rufino Knott, where he waited with his small orchestra. Knott in turn signaled the trumpeter, who played another brief sennet that sang from the varnished roof-beams. The echoes of the last flourish died away, and left the hall silent.

"Your Majesty," I said, with a bow to Floria, "and my lords, ladies, and gentlemen—I am honored that you join me at my first savory dinner here at Haysfield Grange. I hope you will have a fine day, and that you will take home pleasant memories of your time here."

Again I turned to the Queen. "Haysfield Grange is mine only through the generosity of Her Majesty the Queen, who offered me this reward far above my deserving. Though it is impossible for me to repay her truly, I nevertheless wish to offer Her Majesty a token of my esteem, a token which has just arrived on my ship *Sea-Drake* from Tabarzam." I looked at my shoulder at my steward Master Stiver, and he stepped forward carrying a box clad in green leather. I opened the brass lock, opened the box, and took out the necklace of gold and rubies, then paused as the entire room gasped.

Scarlet and gold were the royal colors, and for that reason Floria owned many gold and ruby baubles. I am proud to say that this outshone them all. There were no less than three different ropes of rubies joined by gold links, a hundred and forty rubies altogether surrounded by ruby chips, with the largest, a pear-shaped stone weighing fifty-two *karatioi*, dropping like a bloody raindrop from the lowest strand.

I had commissioned the necklace a year and a half before. It had taken nearly a year for the stones to be cut and assembled on the Street of the Shining Stones in Sarafsham, and the assembly had barely made it to *Sea-Drake* in time.

My guests burst into a thunderstorm of applause. "Pilgrim's toes, Quillifer!" Floria muttered. "You could have bought a galleon with those stones!"

"A small one only," said I in her ear. "With everyone these days spending their money on wars, the price of gems is depressed, and this necklace was a bargain." I smiled. "If Your Majesty would care to wear my gift, perhaps Her Grace of Roundsilver could help you remove that unfortunate necklace of jet with its vulgar festoons."

The duchess and a marchioness were recruited to help Floria keep her hair clear of the unfastening and fastening of the jewelry, and in the end there was another round of applause as the gold and rubies glittered around Floria's throat.

"If you would add to this your ruby carcanet," I said, "you would be the most glittering queen in all history."

"Should this fashion advice continue," Floria said, "I will appoint you Mistress of the Wardrobe and let you piece together all of my gowns."

When the applause again died away, I wished my guests a good appetite, and then walked around the high table to my seat. Along the way I passed Ambassador Gandorim, whose brown eyes, I thought, betrayed a degree of pique.

Yes, I thought, a mere marquesa will not buy me.

Knott's orchestra began to play. I took my seat across from Floria, who sat framed by a marchpane hippogriff on one side and a triton on the other. Prince Amadeu sat on my left, glittering in silk and silver; and Her Grace of Chelmy, wife to the former partisan of Clayborne, was on my right. Chelmy himself was on her other hand.

Indeed, were I not the host, I would not be at the high table, for the seating was by right of precedence, and I would normally be lounging farther down the room with the other counts.

"That was a right noble gift," said Amadeu. He laughed. "And people imagine that *I* am rich!"

"I venture to say that people imagine all sorts of things about you," said I. "That you own secret mines, that you and your people live in beautiful underground cities sculpted from the native rock, while you dwell among them in a palace carved from a single great jewel."

"I have more than one underground palace," Amadeu said, "but they aren't very gemlike, and I don't live in them."

"Does anyone live there? And if not, why were they built?"

"They are not cities so much as refuges. When my neighbors invade, my people take shelter underground."

"That can't be very pleasant for them," said I.

Amadeu waved a hand. "Oh, these hidden cities are tolerable enough, and quite large. The upper floors are for cattle, sheep, and horses, and below there are many rooms, some for supplies, some for the people. There are water wells, shafts for air, kitchens, and chapels to our gods."

"These cities sound most complete," said I. "Do you keep them always ready?"

"Of necessity," Amadeu said.

"Your neighbors attack you so often? We don't hear in Selford of wars in the West."

He gave me a narrow-eyed look. "Nay," he said. "You never do."

"Are you at war now?"

"In the present circumstances, 'war' is an overused word," said Amadeu. "Say rather that we are under attack."

"And who attacks you?"

His dark eyes narrowed further. "I hazard your lordship can guess."

"I suppose that I can."

While Amadeu and I spoke, I remained alert as service began. The yeoman of the ewer poured scented water into bowls so that we might wash our hands, and the yeoman of the buttery arrived with wines for the high table. Their deputies served the other guests. Footman rolled in wheeled serving tables loaded with the first remove of pottage.

In the last few years, I had grown famous for my savory dinners. The fashion in cooking was for the meat to be sweetened with sugar or honey or dried fruit, and I felt that this treatment was an insult to meat of any true quality. My boyhood as a butcher's son had taught me to know fine flesh from foul, and I served the meat cooked simply, in gravies or in its own juices, the sauces lightly enhanced by wine or spices.

For those who thought such fare too common, I served a deal of the over-sweetened dishes, though for myself I did not care for them.

A pair of footmen, both servers of long experience, had been assigned to serve Floria, one to carry a tray with a selection of bowls and dishes, and the other to serve the article that she chose.

"Her Majesty is capricious," I had told them, "and will want to choose from a variety of dishes."

She would want the dish without poison, I thought.

Three soups had been brought forth: a bread soup with garlic and new spring onions, a pottage of veal with cinnamon, and a saffron stew of fish and mussels served with toast. Floria chose the last.

"We hear of no great battles in your district," I said to the prince.

"Nor are they," said Amadeu. "They come in small parties to raid, burn, and slay. They do not settle and occupy the land; they seek only to drive us out."

Catsgore, I suppose, would condemn the country's banditry and lawlessness, and seek to put his own companies in place to enforce the peace. A peace entirely of his own design.

"Of course we don't make it easy for them," Amadeu continued. "We know the country better than they do, and often we can ambush them, kill a few, and send the rest flying home. But that only serves as an excuse for the sheriff to cry the Act Against Tumult, and under its protection ride in with a company of horse to hang anyone he finds with a weapon."

"Perhaps you need a sheriff of your own."

"Should Her Majesty send a sheriff to defend me," said Amadeu, "I will bless her for it. I hope to move my suit tomorrow, for I have an audience with the Queen, and I hope you may attend."

"Of course I will attend, Highness."

Her Grace of Chelmy turned to me. "Which jeweler made that necklace for you, Selford?"

I had neglected her since I had sat at the table, but I saw no need to apologize, for apparently she'd been staring at Floria's necklace the entire time, and mentally recording the price of each and every stone.

"I employed the artisans at the House of Sohrab, in Sarafsham, Your Grace."

Her Grace seemed disappointed that she could not send for a jeweler from Lapidary Street in the city. Nevertheless she offered me a sweet smile. "I was told that in the past you have made stones available to your friends."

"I have," I said, "and to such a friend as Your Grace, I will be more than pleased to show you a selection of stones myself."

"Why, thank you, Selford."

I thought it possible that Duke Chelmy would not thank me for selling gems to his wife, since I was confident that his finances were in shambles after his return from exile, with some of his property sold while he was away, and the rest of it only having recently been returned to his family.

Yet even if he were in funds, he would write me a note for any purchases, and redeem his note whenever he pleased, which might be never. I was not in a position to chase down a duke, and a fellow councillor, for a few hundred royals.

So perhaps he would be in a position to thank me after all.

The rolling tables moved in and out of the room, carrying one remove after another: trout and tench cooked in a broth of butter and wine, pike boiled in wine and then turned crisp with vinegar, a pottage of green peas and bacon, capon larded with lemons, a pigeon fricassee, all served with the new vegetables of the season and a specially chosen wine.

Then came the coqz heaumez, roast chickens equipped with a lance and a cardboard helmet and shield, riding astride crackling brown roast pigs. The helmets were ornamented with tin leaf, and the shield of each was painted with one of the badges of our orders of chivalry. The guests laughed and cheered at the spectacle, and carvers offered each their choice of pork or chicken along with the cracklings.

The coqz heaumez was intended to be an interval, as in a play. The guests might stand and stretch, or pay a discreet call upon the jakes. Floria herself, out of compassion for her subjects, stood and left the hall with some of her ladies, which permitted everyone else to stand.

As Floria returned, the trumpet played another sennet, to let everyone know it was time to once again find their seats. When the rolling tables came in, they bore roast Ethlebight salt-grass lamb, roasted whole. I rose from my seat and took the knife and fork from the carver.

"Your Majesty, my lords and ladies," I said, "I hope you will savor this taste of my home country."

I carved the lamb, and as I delicately separated the legs from the body of the lamb, I looked up to see Boatswain Lepalik standing in one of the doorways beneath the screening passage.

Lepalik stood high in my household, a prime sailor who commanded my racing galley in my absence. He hailed from a small island thousands of leagues southeast of the Candara Coast, on the far side of the equator and well beyond the scope of any map I had ever seen. His skin was black, and in accordance with the custom of his people he shaved his head and let his gray curling beard grow long.

He had spent half his life at sea, wandering far from his home, and had been rewarded with the silver whistle of a boatswain.

He had been in my service for some years, and had expressed a desire to sail home, to an island so far over the horizon that I was afraid he would never find it. I was prepared to do what I could to help him, but then he had fallen in love with a woman of Duisland and changed his plans. Her name was Agatha, and she worked as a baker in my kitchen.

Lepalik had the lithe, clean frame and whipcord muscles of an ancient god, which he told me was common for the men of his home island; but he had often complained to me that the women of Duisland were too thin for his taste, starvelings almost. Agatha was a woman of considerable girth, and that girth had a pillowy appearance, as if she were stuffed with down. She was his ideal, and I think he had fallen in love at first sight. She was now expecting their first child.

Lepalik held up dispatches, and I signed for him to wait. If Lepalik had come at all, if he had ordered out my galley and raced up the Saelle right on the lip of the tide, that meant the dispatches were urgent.

But not so urgent as to disturb my guests at their meat. If they saw me rush away from my carving, they would wonder why. They would soon conclude that something had driven me into a panic, and this they would take as permission for themselves to panic, and ere long they would be seeing the smoke of burning Selford on the horizon.

I gave Floria the lamb tenderloin, a small, delicate, and delicious morsel, then sauced the meat, and surrounded it with radishes, parsley, and pea greens cooked with leeks and salt pork. Other cuts were given to my other guests, and I awarded myself some chops.

"If you will excuse me, Majesty," I said to Floria, and her darting eyes saw Lepalik at once, and she nodded.

"You and the crew should find food and drink at the tents outside," I told Lepalik. "I may need you to carry messages back to the capital."

I examined the three dispatches he had just handed me and recognized the hands of Lipton and Barkin, respectively the Lieutenants-Generals of Artillery and Cavalry, and I recognized also the seal of the Constable, Scutterfield known as Drumforce.

The Constable would have composed an official record of whatever action had taken place, I thought, and the others had writ privately to me in order to make certain I understood what had truly occurred. I put the dispatches inside my doublet and returned to the high table, where I approached Floria and spoke into her ear.

"Dispatches from Drumforce and two of his officers," I said. "I cannot imagine that all three would write unless the matter was urgent. After dinner, we should retire to the library and try to make sense of the reports."

"The least impressive library in the realm?" she asked.

"It has maps."

"Excellent well." Her hazel eyes flashed from one guest to the other. "Bring Thistlegorm also, and Sandicup and the privy seal."

"Very good, Majesty."

I passed the news to Thistlegorm, Sandicup, and Waitstill, then returned to my seat. Prince Amadeu gave me a look from half-lidded eyes. "Important news, Lord Selford?"

"It can wait," I said, then took up my knife and addressed my chops. The taste brought memories of my boyhood, when the salt-grass lamb was served often on my mother's table. I was half-lost in reverie when I saw Floria's eyes on me, a half-smile playing on her lips, and I knew that she was aware that through the special taste of the lamb, I had been possessed by some pleasing childhood memory, and she had been enjoying it at second hand. When she saw that I was aware of her observation, she gave me a sympathetic private smile and turned toward Roundsilver.

The wheeled carts came in and out, and at last brought the final removes: fruit, custards, clotted cream, trifles, egg pies, fools, puddings, and snow, which is cream beaten with the whites of eggs, then strewn like fine winter flakes on a sweet loaf. Floria rose to make a gracious speech of thanks, and raised a toast to me; and then she and her ladies withdrew while the trumpet played yet another sennet.

I thanked my guests, hastened to visit the close-stool in my bedroom, then made my way to the library. By the time the others arrived, I had read the dispatches, and had maps laid out on a long table.

"I have read them all," said I, when we were all seated. "From the Constable, Lipton, and Barkin; and though they differ somewhat in detail and interpretation, they all agree that we have been defeated in the field, and that Melcaster is, or shortly will be, under siege."

"When?" demanded Floria.

"Marshal Rutilan began landing his soldiers on the coast between Castras and Melcaster on the twenty-second of April. The Constable wrote that he was worried that the enemy were astride his lines of communications, and so he marched his forces out of—"

"Pilgrim blast him!" Floria cried. "He had ten months' supply in the city! He could have held Castras without a battle!"

"Ay," I said. "You positively ordered him not to engage."

The Queen's nostrils flared in anger as she glared her fury in every direction. "You warned me," she said. "You reminded me that Drumforce had no military experience, that he hated the enemy so much that he was bound to attack even at a disadvantage."

Sandicup gave me a resentful look, as if he loathed me for being such a good augur.

"Ay, well, the Constable attacked five days ago," said I, "and Rutilan marched a modest number of soldiers out to meet him. According both to Lipton and Barkin, the Constable could see nothing but those soldiers, a lure to draw him into an engagement, and he ignored the woods that overhung our right, even after Barkin drew his attention to them. The Constable maintained the woods were too thick and tangled to hold any great number of men, but of course he had never been in those woods and could not know for certain. So as soon as our army were engaged, half of Rutilan's army charged out of that wood and shattered our forces in minutes."

"The Constable must be replaced," said Waitstill. "I could leave in two days, an Your Majesty's choice falls upon me."

I could see derision dancing in Floria's eyes at this attempted self-advancement, but she responded in reasonable terms. "Let us hear the news to the end."

"Lord Barkin writes that the Constable behaved well in the face of disaster," I said. "He put himself at the head of the Queen's Own Regiment of Horse and the other cavalry reserves, and charged the flanking force with such fury that he drove them back and saved the balance of the army."

Floria sighed. "Of what does this balance now consist?"

"The Constable led eight thousand soldiers into the fight, and escaped with somewhat over five thousand. He also lost all the artillery save for a few leather guns that Lipton was able to drag off the field."

Which, I knew, was the fault of the Guild of Carters and Haulers, who brought our artillery to the battlefield, and then—not being soldiers—withdrew out of danger and awaited the conclusion of the battle. If the fight were a victory, all would be well; but if a defeat, the Carters and Haulers were positioned to flee the field with admirable dispatch and leave the guns behind.

I drew my finger across the map north of Melcaster. "Rutilan did not march on Castras, but turned east and north toward Melcaster. I venture to predict that they were able to get across the fords north of the city and are now setting up their siege camps, with their navy in support."

"We must remove the Constable," Waitstill said.

"If he is to be replaced," said I, "replace him with Lord Barkin, a tried and experienced soldier." Waitstill held his peace, but his lips pressed into a thin white line. "But I think it matters not who commands that army," I added, "for it will be shut up in Castras until Rutilan is defeated by another force."

Waitstill seemed thoughtful, for there was little glory in commanding an army that would be sheltering up behind city walls for the next year.

"And who shall raise this new force?" asked Thistlegorm. "And what will we do with it?"

"If the enemy's dispositions permit," I said, "we must throw defenders into Melcaster to hold the city. But I think this will not be possible, and Melcaster must hold as best it can, while we do our utmost to build up a relieving army at Bretlynton Head."

"Who commands there?"

"The lord lieutenant is Benning," said Floria. "Supported, I hope, by the sea-consuls."

"If we are to raise a new army," said Sandicup, "we must pay for it, and that I suppose is up to me."

"I hope it will not *tax* your ingenuity," said I. And then, seeing Floria's exasperated look, cast her an apologetic glance.

Floria's face turned grave. "Gentlemen," she said. "We have been defeated, and we must form a response to this disaster without wrangling among ourselves." She gazed down at the map before her. "Lord Coneygrave has been holding the fleet ready to sail at a few hours' notice," she said. "Now he must sail to discover what may be done against the enemy. Unless Rutilan captures Castras and the border forts, he can only draw support by water, and we may hope that Coneygrave may raise some mischief among the enemy shipping."

"We should not throw the axe after the helve," said Thistlegorm. "Dare we send Coneygrave to sea without knowing the location of Admiral Mola's northern squadrons? Once our navy has gone to the south coast of Bonille, all Fornland lies open."

I looked at the map. "I think Fornland knows well how to receive Admiral Mola," I said. "I fear not for Fornland."

"I fear for Fornland," said Thistlegorm, "once Fornland sends its every trained soldier over the sea to fight Marshal Rutilan."

Sandicup picked up a pen and waved it over the map, as if it were a magic wand. "I think we stand in better straits than you imagine," he said. "We raise new companies of soldiers every day. Dozens of ships will be launched in the next twelvemonth. We have greater reserves than the enemy, who fights on too many fronts. The worst we can do is act in haste and waste our resources in order to repair a battle we have already lost."

I was surprised to find these ideas sound. "I agree with this counsel," I said. "But I think we must make some answer to this Rutilan lest half the country fall into despair. As many cities have fallen through loss of heart as to superiority of numbers."

The debate went on for another half hour, and then Floria rose. "We shall take this up again tomorrow afternoon," she said. "More news may come in, and once we are in the castle, we will have a complete record of all our forces and where we might find them." She looked at me. "Quillifer, I would speak with you briefly."

The others made their way out. I walked to Floria's side, so that we could speak in low tones and foil any of the Council who lingered with their ears to the door.

"I will have to forsake your hospitality," she said, "and will depart in an hour or so. I know you must entertain your guests until after supper, but I trust you will sleep in the castle tonight."

"Of course, Your Majesty," I said.

"Then anything remaining," she said, "may be said then, and with greater freedom."

The tide shifted mid-afternoon, and with the tide I sent Boatswain Lepalik with a letter to the Lord Admiral instructing him to take the fleet to sea the next afternoon, but on all accounts to wait for me. Before I returned to my guests, I sought Rufino Knott, who I found in the garden, strolling with his guitar and singing a ballad, "The Two Great Lords of Ethlebight," which extolled my adventures, and those of Roundsilver, in the galley races held in Howel.

Originally there had been three lords in the song, but one of them had tried to murder me, so I thought he should no longer be so commemorated. If he missed being the subject of a ballad, he could write one himself.

I waited for Knott to finish the song and collect whatever silver his audience was willing to offer him, and then I took him aside.

"We are for the sea, Master Knott," I said. "I wish you to pack me a trunk, and one for you besides."

"At once, sir?"

"At once, ay. We shall take them on the carriage tonight. And pack as well my armor."

Knott left on his errand. I looked for the Roundsilvers and found them, for they outshone everyone, dressed alike in black silk sewn with verdant green foliage and bright red fruit, which I recognized as the Cornelian cherry. I approached and bowed.

"I am sure you understood," said I, "when I presented Her Majesty with her necklace, that I have some gems just ashore. I would be happy to show you my coffer, but if you wish any stones, you will have to take them home with you today. After today I might not be available for some time."

Her Grace looked at me with bright sapphire eyes. "Does this have aught to do with those dispatches brought by your boatswain?"

"Your Grace is observant."

The duke frowned. "Am I not to be informed?"

"Her Majesty will call the Council for tomorrow afternoon," I said. "Until then, she wishes the information kept close."

Roundsilver's frown deepened. "Perhaps," I said, "we should talk about my beautiful gems."

I took them into my study and opened my coffer for them. I sent a footman for Their Graces of Chelmy, to tell them that my gems were now available for viewing. I invited as well Ambassador Gandorim, my friend and partner Kevin Spellman, and then I thought of Prince Amadeu and laughed. Perhaps this would tell me whether he was as wealthy as he seemed.

Roundsilver purchased several of my best stones. From Gandorim I asked more than the gems were worth, but he happily signed his note, probably under the impression he gave me a bribe. Her Grace of Chelmy coerced her husband into buying some fine sapphires, and Amadeu purchased a single large emerald for his wife—and perhaps that money was also intended as a bribe. Kevin Spellman bought some diamonds to ornament a pomander.

I was locking my coffer in my study when word was brought to me that the Queen was leaving. I went downstairs to help Floria into her carriage and kiss her hand, and then I made a calculation concerning how many of my guests would leave in the next hour, having come to pay court to the monarch and not to me.

Indeed, half my guests took their leave, though I would like to think that those remaining were the merriest of the lot, and the best company. For the rest of the afternoon there were games, wine, and music, while the staff drifted one by one to their hall to dine on the remains of the great feast. At the end of the day, I served my guests a supper rather simpler than the grand dinner held at noontide.

As soon as the supper was over, I was in my carriage for the capital, with Rufino Knott across from me. My casket of gems sat on the seat next to me, and our sea-chests were roped to the roof, along with trunks that held my weapons and armor. I drowsed throughout most of the journey, and was awakened by the sound of the castle bell ringing nine thirty, and the horses' iron shoes echoing an answer on the cobbles of the Outer Ward.

———

"What is it," Floria demanded, "that compels great lords to treat me like a disobedient child? For half the day, I was being lectured about marriage, beginning with my ladies on the drive to your house. Then Waitstill and Pontkyles separately urged their sons upon me, and Thistlegorm and Catsgrove together argued for a candidate from Duisland, though they recommended no one in particular. Sandicup and Scarnside spoke for the Varcellos match, and because of those two, Gandorim didn't have to say a word."

"He spoke to me," said I, "and he offered me a twenty-year-old marquesa with a dowry the size of the sea."

A dark look crossed her face. "This will grow worse when news of the Constable's defeat becomes known. Then I will be urged to make the Varcellos alliance, or marry some great man who can command the armies and reverse our fortunes."

"Why," said I, "that man stands before you now."

"That supposition may be tested sooner rather than later," Floria said, "if you have your way." Her tone was resentful, and I could not blame her, for she was being battered back and forth like a shuttlecock, not only by the hectoring of the lords but by the fortunes of war, and by my own ambitions, which I own are not small.

We stood in my apartment. Floria had just come down the passage with her candle, and I had just pulled off my jerkin. I reached into the jerkin's pockets and pulled out some pies wrapped in a napkin.

"I come also equipped to supply our armies," I said, "for I brought mince pies in case you missed your supper."

"I did not," said she, "and it was a pleasant repast, for I forbade the topic of marriage. For too many of my ladies, marriage—either mine or their own—is their only topic of conversation, and so the meal was restful, and I supped content."

"I am sorry that you have been so abused," I said. "In tender regard for your sensibilities, I will avoid pressing my own suit."

"The Pilgrim make me thankful for all such small mercies." Floria dropped onto the settee and kicked off her slippers. Her galbanum scent floated gently in the air. I put the pies on a table and coiled myself at her feet like a faithful hound, then took her feet in my lap and began to knead them. She sighed in pleasure, then looked at me from under her lashes and took a document from her dressing gown. "I have writ the commission you requested," she said, "but I am half-minded not to give it thee."

"I am confident in Robertson's advice," I said, "and I have seen those islands myself, from my tower, with the water calm as a mill-pond."

"Yet I cannot spare you," said she. "Your work here is too important."

"The work may be indispensable," said I, "but I need not be the one who performs it. Put Judge Travers in my place until I return—I will not be gone long."

"Have you forgot there is a poisoner at large?" Floria said. "Will you abandon me to his mercies?"

My hands ceased their kneading of her feet, and I looked at the floor, almost afraid to meet her eyes. "In truth, my conscience is tender on this point," I said. "Yet you are well-guarded, even unto your quandias ring, and you have not been careless at mealtimes, and have chosen your dishes from an array laid before you. Never was caprice turned to so good an account."

And now I did turn to her, and gave her an imploring look. "Did you not tell me, just a few days ago, that a victory would give you freedom? I desire that you have that freedom, my darling."

Her hazel eyes held mine for a moment, so that I could feel a taut invisible line drawn between us, and then that line evaporated, and she held out the paper.

"Take my commission, then," she said. "And let us now forget all discord between us and the world, for I would have no strife enter this chamber tonight, our last before you go to the war."

CHAPTER TEN

My boat's crew waited at the docks to take me to Admiral Coneygrave and the fleet, but there was one task remaining, and that was to attend the morning's audience, when Floria would hear Prince Amadeu's petition. For this the Starry Drawing Room was reserved, a less formal setting than the Great Reception Room, and plagued by fewer drafts and chills. The ceiling of the chamber was the deep blue of the sky at twilight, with six- and seven-pointed gilded stars, and the rest of the room echoed that starry sky. Gilded capitals sat on pillars of blue chrysoprase, and the cushions were blue with stars of gold thread. The blue carpets were woven with vines and florets of gold, and the furniture was inlaid with lapis and turquoise, and stood on gilded legs.

Floria sat behind a table that had been surfaced with chips of water-sapphire polished smooth as glass. The three strands of her gold-and-ruby necklace were draped across the white partlet she wore over her russet gown, and she wore matching rubies on her fingers and dangling from her ears. She sat not on a throne but on a stately, imposing chair adorned with a rayed sun, and she had foregone the canopy of state and any of the other symbols of her majesty. Flanking her on either side were Thistlegorm and Waitstill, and I sat outside of the Chancellor, while on the far side of Waitstill was Catsgore, present both to represent his own person and also in his office as Minister of State for Fornland. The Abbot Fulvius sat somewhat apart, beneath a window, and was there I suppose to restore civility if there were too much shouting.

Also present were a secretary and the Assistant Attorney General, the ferocious Hunter, who, having no one to abuse, remained silent.

The Steward of the Castle entered and announced Amadeu, and the prince entered, flanked by two of his gentlemen. One of the men carried a casket mounted in silver, and I wondered if it contained a gift for the Queen. As if to echo the room's colors, Amadeu wore deep blue silk woven with fantastic beasts in silver thread, and wore as well the silver jewelry that had caused such a sensation on his first arrival.

Amadeu and his gentlemen knelt before the Queen, and rose at her command.

"Your Majesty," he said, "I wish to bring before you a petition for the relief of my people from oppression."

Catsgore shifted in his chair, and I could see red anger send blotches of scarlet into his cheeks.

"How may we be of service to Your Serene Highness?" asked Floria formally, and Amadeu spoke of the attacks against his people, the burnings and harryings, all clearly designed to drive the Albiz from their homes.

"The matter was referred to the sheriff," said Catsgore, interrupting. "And also to the lord lieutenant. The bandits were caught and executed."

"And yet," Amadeu said, "the attacks continue. Perhaps the sheriff killed the wrong bandits, or invented some where none existed." Catsgore's lipless mouth snarled, but before he could speak Amadeu continued. "I implore Her Majesty to send a royal officer and some men into these disputed districts, to protect the people."

"The sheriff *is* a royal officer, as is the lord lieutenant," Catsgore said. "If violence continues, it is because those who dwell in those dark coombs have long borne violent grudges against one another. Those districts are not settled at all, and though my family has long held title there, we have not been able to impose order."

I could see cold satisfaction lodge somewhere behind Amadeu's eyes, and still gazing at Floria he said, "The issue of title, Majesty, was settled by your great ancestor Emelin the First, he whose conquering hand reunited the broken realm of Duisland, and who also conferred upon my family the grant of our property." He gestured to the man bearing the casket. "I have brought the charter, complete with His Majesty's seal."

The casket was opened, and a great parchment was unrolled before the Queen. Attached to it by faded grosgrain ribbon were two wax seals, one large and the other small. The Keeper of the Seal, Waitstill, examined the larger of the two. "It is the Great Seal, Your Majesty," he pronounced.

"And the other," she said, "would seem to be King Emelin's personal seal." She peered at the letters of faded brown. "The handwriting is difficult to make out," she said.

Thistlegorm had perched a pair of spectacles on his nose, but even so had to bring his face close to the parchment to make anything of it. "It is a court hand," said he. "But a version so old I know it not."

"With your permission, Majesty," I said. I slid out of my chair to look at the document.

Court hand, used at court and by the nobility, was a version of chancery hand, a cursive once employed by lawyers. Over the centuries, chancery hand had grown more and more elaborate, until documents began to resemble serpentine puzzles or the complex knots woven by sailors, impossible to read without special training. A few generations ago, the reigning monarch had grown tired of being handed one unreadable writ after another, and had decreed that henceforth all legal and court documents were to be written in secretary hand, which could be written and understood by anyone who could read and write. The decree met with rejoicing of all save for a generation of scribes, who had spent years in training and had now lost their occupation.

I had trained as a lawyer and of necessity had learned how to read the old documents, though I had never learned to write in that convoluted fashion. Fortunately Amadeu's charter was in an early version of chancery hand, and ere long I was able to make sense of it.

"*We, Emelinn, Kinge and Sole Monarch of all Fornlonde,*" I read, "*son of the royall King Eggwine on whom bee pece, in considderation of the manie aides given unto Mee by My trustie servaunt Satordus, Prynce of the Albeez, againste the foul enemie Cay of Blaenarth, doo award to sayd Satordus and his heirs and successours in fee simple absolute the dayles or coombes of Potsalawa, Oorkiola, Iszkoria also called Brenmore, Aecora, und Hurrius, all to bee found inn the Westerne Range of My realme of Fornlonde. In return, said Satordus pledges to bee a trew, sinceere, and faithfull servant unto Us, and unto our heirs, successoures, and assignes. Signed by Mee, on the viij daie of Septembre, in My Year VIII.*"

King Cay, as we had all read in Cantwell's *History*, had his realm around Inchmaden, and was the last of the independent kings of Fornland to fall before Emelin's conquering hand. With Cay killed and Fornland thus under his sway, Emelin had begun to formulate his plan to travel over the sea to Bonille and unite the old kingdom of Duisland that had been sundered by the many incursions of the Osby Lords.

Catsgore waved a dismissive hand. "Brenmore and the Coomb of Hario are long settled by my family," he said. "Our tenants have been plowing the soil in peace for many generations. As for these other vales, they lie within my claim, though I regret to say that the inhabitants live lawless and savage lives, and scorn Your Majesty's good laws."

Amadeu did not so much as glance as Catsgore. "He claims the land where my own homes stand, and where my tenants live. Where my own palace stands. Where my ancestors have lived since the mountains were formed."

Floria's glance darted to Catsgore and remained fixed there. "If our great and royal ancestor gave these lands to this Satordus in recognition of his achievements against this King Cay, then the honor of our house demands that we discover fully what has become of King Emelin's grant."

"It may be that the heirs of Satordus sold their inheritance bit by bit," said Catsgore. "But in my opinion, that document is a forgery."

"The seals . . ." Waitstill began.

"Over the centuries, there have been many documents signed with the Great Seal," said Catsgore. "A copy may have been plundered from an old archive, and King Emelin's seal likewise." He offered a scornful laugh. "A bit of melted wax, and the seal is fixed to the document by its ribbon, and the forgery is made perfect."

"The forger would require a fluency in writing three-hundred-year-old court hand," I said, "which is not easily come by."

"A good forger can make this document and a hundred like it," said Lord Thistlegorm. "That is why the penalties against forgery are so severe." He removed his spectacles and turned his eyes to me. "There would have been more than one copy of this document," he said. "Think you it might be found in the Archives?"

"A few crowns might have assured that a copy would be planted there!" cried Catsgore.

"I will have it sent for," said I, "and if it exists, it will be found."

I wrote a note to Bledso asking him to find the document and bring it, and to bring himself if it could not be found. I then sent the note with a page, and returned to my seat just as Floria looked up from the document to regard Amadeu.

"Good prince," said she, "setting aside for the moment of this grant, what would you have us do to assure peace in your lands?"

"A royal officer," said Amadeu, "and not a man from the West but someone who does not belong to any of the factions from the Western Range. He and a score of good men, with a warrant to seek out those miserable hirelings who trouble the peace there, along with those who pay them."

Catsgore purpled with rage. "You say I hire murderers?" he demanded.

Amadeu looked at him sidelong, and contempt touched the corner of his mouth. "I have mentioned no names, and made no accusation. Let an investigation be mounted. I'll warrant that every one of those brawlers and burners may be found in their local alehouses, boasting of their deeds, and it would be easy to discover who paid them."

"If there is trouble in our realm," said Floria, "then it is our plain duty to see it quelled."

"I have been trying to quell it since I was a boy," said Catsgrove. "And I have more followers than a score."

The Queen adjourned the meeting then and rose to join her ladies in her quarters. I approached Catsgore.

"You leashed your temper admirably," I said. "I was afraid you would burst out in anger and ruin your cause before Her Majesty."

Catsgore snarled. "As soon as he pulled out that nonsensical document," he said, "I knew I had won. There was never any such charter, and I very much doubt that ever there was a Prince Satordus."

"Well," said I, "rest you merry, my lord."

I knew that Catsgore was behind the violence in those western dales—everyone in the room knew it—but I knew also that he was a great and powerful lord, that his ancestors had been taking land from Amadeu's people for generations, and that in his own country he was accustomed to doing as he liked. I doubted there was aught Floria could do to stop his campaign, not without turning half the House of Peers against her.

How many of the folk of Duisland, I wondered, had ever met an Albiz? How many cared what became of them? They were half-mythical beings who lived underground, cousins-german to the Fairies, and of no concern to Floria's stolid subjects.

After leaving Catsgore I walked out into the corridor to see if Bledso was coming with a copy of the charter, but Bledso was not to be seen, so I returned to the Starry Drawing Room, where I found Prince Amadeu and his gentlemen standing by the door.

"You presented your case well, Highness," I said. "And that is a very interesting charter you gave us."

"I hope it will have some effect," Amadeu said, with a glance over his shoulder at Catsgore.

"It must, I think," said I, "if an archived copy can be found."

His glance was sharp. "And if not?"

"Further examination, I suppose," I said. "We may have the charter, I hope?"

"We will not leave the charter here," said Amadeu. "If you wish to bring men to examine it, they must come to my lodgings and do the work there. We will not have the charter out of our sight lest some mischief befall it."

I looked down at him and smiled. A prankish thought had occurred to me. "I wonder, Highness," I said, "if you have ever considered taking your seat in the House of Peers?"

Amadeu was surprised by the notion, and for a moment lacked words. "It is not our custom to take part in the doings of other tribes," he said finally.

"Her Majesty has just recognized your title of prince," I said. "You are her subject and have a title and lands, and there is no impairment under Duisland law to prevent you taking your seat. And once you take your seat in Howel, perhaps those fabled mines of yours can be opened, and your largesse spread to the politicians, who may sponsor legislation that will benefit your cause."

"If those mines"—he gave an annoyed jerk of his chin—"those *supposed* mines—were opened, the Queen would help herself to the contents, and never would I, or the legislators, see a penny."

"Entering Selford, you as much as wore silver plate," said I. "It would be hard to deny the existence of mines now."

He only gave me a sardonic look.

"Ay, well, let me think, Highness," I said. "For silver finds its own way through the world, I find."

I quickly wrote another note, this to the engineer Mountmirail, asking him to discover what he could about silver mining, and have the information ready when I returned to Selford in just a few weeks. I sent the letter to where the Mountmirails were staying at Haysfield Grange, and after I sent the message away, I found Bledso returning, his hands empty.

"I'm afraid I found no such charter, my lord," he said. "But it may have been misfiled, and I will search for it."

"If you find it not, you may begin another search," I said. "This for archivists who have in the last months come into money, or who have unexpectedly retired to some ancestral land in the west country."

Bledso's eyebrows crawled in surprise up his balding forehead. "I shall, my lord."

"Find anything relating to Prince Satordus and his heirs, and any grants to any Albiz by King Emelin in the West Ranges."

"Yes, my lord."

I found myself admiring Catsgore's scheme, for accusing Amadeu in advance of planting a forged copy of the grant in the archives, a feint to cover the probable fact that he himself had paid to have the copy stolen.

I returned to the drawing room, gave Amadeu a look that told him my news before I opened my mouth, and then reported that no copy of the charter had been found in the archives, but that my deputy would continue his search.

"There!" Catsgore proclaimed. "I hope that puts an end to the pretensions of this imp!"

Amadeu shot him a look that would have knocked a songbird stone dead off his branch. Floria looked at him in fury. "No more of this incivil language, my lord!" she said. "When you do such a discourtesy as to insult a guest in my home, it is I you insult!"

Catsgore bowed with reluctant grace. "I beg your pardon, Your Majesty."

Floria turned to the others. "We declare this audience at an end. We shall look forward to seeing most of you this afternoon, at the meeting of the Council." Then her glance darted to me, and she made a snapping motion with her fan, to bring me toward her. We walked a little apart from the others.

"Is the injustice to my subjects as apparent to everyone as it is to me?" Floria asked.

"I think so," I said.

"Yet I need Catsgore," she said. "He carries with him the votes of all the nobility and burgesses of the West Range."

"And he considers it his prerogative to hunt Albiz out of their holes," said I. "And so does every gentleman in the county, I imagine."

"I am half-minded to give Amadeu the commission he asks for," Floria said, "but if I do, Catsgore may carry away half the Peers."

"That is a calculation that every monarch for the last few centuries has made," said I, "and always Catsgore's house has prevailed."

She gave me a look. "And now you desert me, when this weighty matter has arisen."

"This business will not be settled overnight," said I. "And I shall not be gone for long."

"See that you are not," said my Queen, and I bowed in obedience.

CHAPTER ELEVEN

he sea rose beneath *King Emmius*, and I felt the deck slowly rock beneath me as the wave swept us toward the white clouds that sailed the blue sky overhead. Admiral Coneygrave's banner snapped overhead in the fresh breeze. The brisk air bore the scents of the sea, of tar, and of the burning slow-matches waiting by the leashed cannon.

Nearly above our heads, hidden in the sun's dazzle, was a new moon.

The Queen's Navy was on a quarter reach heading into the Bay of Melcaster. Lost in a green haze off our starboard beam was the battlefield where the Constable's army had been set to flight, and off the larboard bow were the rocks and islets of the Races, bearded with white foam as the incoming tide dashed itself against the black stone fangs.

Off the starboard bow were the sails of the fleet of Loretto, coming out to meet us.

Lord High Admiral Coneygrave, decked in steel armor ornamented with elaborate, shining brass inlay, walked the poop up and down with a concentrated air, as if he were determined to show confidence but had to suppress his own awareness that he had never before commanded ships in battle. His undershot lower teeth gnawed his upper lip. He held his baton in one fist and otherwise carried no weapon.

I wore armor as well, a fine set of proof I had looted from Sir Basil of the Heugh, the bandit. The cuirass, worn over thick suede buff coat, showed dimples inflicted by enemy handgunners at Exton Scales, and I derived a certain amount of confidence from the knowledge that my breast would not be pierced by anything smaller than a cannonball.

I carried also a pair of pistols and a broadsword with a gold-wire inlay, also courtesy of that incourteous knight Sir Basil, though if the day went utterly wrong and I found myself having to fight at close quarters, I would use for preference a boarding pike, as the closest thing to a pollaxe on the ship. If I were handy with any weapon whatever, it was a pollaxe.

In truth there was a deal of armor on the poop deck, for the ship carried a hundred soldiers borrowed from the army, and those assigned to the poop deck stood impassively and rather stupidly on the lee side, weapons grounded on the deck while the soldiers waited for a chance to be useful. Most of them had been very sick on the voyage out, making of the ship an infernal scene of sounds and stinks, but by now most had recovered, and the soldiers merely looked glum and out of place.

The soldiers, sailors, and I congregated on the lee side of the poop because Coneygrave continued his pacing up and down the weather side. The weather poop belonged to the commander, and he had the right to walk there alone unless he desired company. Just below, on the quarterdeck, *Emmius*'s captain also paced the weather deck in sole majesty.

Floria's navy was composed of over a hundred and eighty ships, but most of these were small vessels used to carry dispatches or bring supply to the ships that mattered, which were those galleons of over two hundred tons, large enough to stand in battle against the great ships of the enemy. Of these there were forty-two, and every single one of them now sailed under Coneygrave's flag.

Only a minority of these ships were actually owned by the crown. The rest were private vessels hired by the admiralty for the duration of the war, and some were ships owned by prominent men, who out-fitted them at their own expense and loaned them to the crown. One such ship in our line, the *Sovereign* of eight hundred tons, was jointly owned by me and by the Spellman family. She was commanded by the veteran Captain Gaunt, who had survived with me the wreck of the *Royal Stilwell* on Gannett Island a few years before, and I was sorry not to have joined him on this voyage, and regretted that I was obliged to remain on the flagship.

Our forty-two ships were outnumbered by the enemy, who had something like seventy great ships. We had not achieved anything like surprise, for the enemy had scout ships out, and men with spy-glasses on the headlands, and these would have seen us at a distance of fifteen or twenty miles. Yet on our reach we were making good progress into the bay, while the enemy were forced to come out close-hauled on their slowest point of sailing. If I were a certain kind of sea-captain, I thought, I would cut across the bay and engage the enemy van, and hope we could defeat them before the rest of their fleet intervened.

But, I thought, they would be expecting that. All the enemy van had to do was reduce sail and allow the ships in the rear to come up with them, and then we would be engaging superior numbers again.

It was in its way like a game of chess. Certain moves were known, and predictable.

Duisland had always been, of necessity, a naval nation. Fornland is an island and Bonille is surrounded on three sides by water, and we are safe from invasion so long as our navy is superior to that of any enemy. Were our navy at full strength, the enemy would never have dared to invade our coasts; but Berlauda and her husband Priscus had cut the naval funds, for Berlauda had married Loretto's heir and believed that never again would there be war between the nations. Lord High Admiral Mardall, who objected to being deprived of half his fleet, was beheaded after Lord Edevane's professional perjurers had provided evidence against him.

Geography dictated as well the deployment of Loretto's resources. They have a long eastern border with rivals like Thurnmark and Sélange, and are subject to invasion by land, so their energies are directed more toward maintaining armies than in building warships. Geography also forces them to maintain not one but three separate fleets of ships.

Loretto is a nation more or less rectangular, longer north-to-south than east-to-west. Adhering to the northwest corner is Bonille, separating Loretto's northern and western seacoasts. On the southwest corner lies another peninsula, the sun-kissed Kingdom of Varcellos. Loretto thus has a northern, western, and southern seacoast, held apart by other nations. In order to maintain a proper defense of their entire seaboard, Loretto maintains three different fleets, each to guard its own particular stretch of coast. The fleets had poetical names: In the north was La Flota Boreal, the western was the Occidental, and the southern La Flota Austral.

At the beginning of the war the Austral Fleet rounded Varcellos to join forces with the Occidental, and so in the Bay of Melcaster we faced two-thirds of Loretto's naval strength. I took a telescope from the rack and watched as that combined fleet came toward us, banners waving brave in the sun, buff-colored sails painted with bright heraldic beasts, the ships heeled hard over on their close-hauled tack, spindrift flying over their starboard bows as they shouldered into each wave. Sunlight reflected off the waves and dappled the sails with dancing light. This was a brave and beautiful sight, and my heart rose as I viewed those lovely ships, then sank again as I remembered that

I had come to sink every one of them and do my best to drown every jack aboard.

I was thus in a fey mood as I returned the telescope to the rack and viewed the enemy in a more dispassionate light. Our own fleet was traveling into the bay with good speed, while the enemy were clawing their way out. If we got much farther into the bay, the enemy could come about and block our exit, which I thought we should strive to prevent. I was about to speak to Lord Coneygrave on the matter when the Admiral walked to the break in the poop and called down to his flag captain.

"Will you join me, Captain Naylor?"

Ginger-haired Sir Roger Naylor came up the companionway to the poop, and the two conferred together while gazing at the enemy fleet. I longed to join that conversation, for I knew that neither of them were sailors, but had achieved their appointments because of Coneygrave's following in the Estates, and Naylor's being the second son of a count.

Yet neither of them were dull-witted, and they had exerted themselves to learn their new trade. They had done their best to drill the fleet—and themselves—in routine maneuvers on our way to Melcaster, but very little could be done during our eight days' passage. As they gazed at the enemy, Naylor and the Admiral knew enough to realize that a moment of decision had come but were a little unsure of their proper response. I waited for them to ask my opinion, but they paid me no attention.

"Master Gladwell," Naylor called. "Will you join us?"

A quartermaster rang the first bell of the forenoon watch as Gladwell came up the companion, and I was glad to see him, for Gladwell was an experienced sailor and held the rank of sailing master. He was notable in that his dark beard had two white stripes falling from the corners of his mouth, as if he had been careless drinking cream. His low birth had barred him from commissioned rank, but he had faced a board of examiners in order to be awarded his warrant officer's certificate, and those placed over him had not.

Still, I would rather they had asked me.

Gladwell spoke but briefly with his superiors, and then answered in his lilting baritone. "Sirs, I advise you wear the fleet around onto the starboard tack."

"See to it, then, Master Gladwell," said Coneygrave.

This would turn the ships, our sterns passing right across the wind, until we ended close-hauled on the starboard tack, parallel to the enemy and sailing in the same direction. We did not wear around right away, for organizing a maneuver for forty-two ships was not an easy thing. We could signal by trumpet calls, or by hoisting flags and firing guns to windward or leeward, but it was possible that the trumpet calls would not be heard by all, and unless the wind was kind enough to stream the flags out where they could be seen, other captains were apt to misunderstand what was expected of them.

So, very soon a trumpet sang out from the poop, and the call was repeated by other trumpets up and down the fleet. A blue flag went up to the maintop, and soon blue flags were streaming from every maintop we could see. In the meantime Gladwell walked to the break in the poop and was shouting through cupped hands at the crew.

"Stand by to wear ship! Man the clew-garnets and buntlines! Lateen brails! Bonaventure brails!"

Bare feet tramped on the deck as the sail-trimmers took their stations. I saw white teeth grinning in sun-browned faces, and I realized that the crew were happy that action was coming on. They were tired of waiting, and I realized that I was tired as well—tired of the shadows and vipers of the court, tired of a place where uncertainty and ceremony went hand-in-hand, and happy of a brisk sea-change in my life.

Of course I and the crew would probably change our minds the first moment the cannons boomed, and soon I might well long for my rose-carved bed in my apartment, with its merry fire, Floria in my arms, and her galbanum scent swimming through my senses.

Gladwell peered fore and aft, and walked to the Admiral and saluted. "My lord, have I your permission to wear ship?"

"Ay," said Coneygrave. "Let us bring her 'round."

Gladwell practically skipped back to the break in the poop. "Down the signal! Fire a gun to windward! Haul taut—up mains'l! Brail in the lateen and bonaventure!"

The blue flag came down on the run as the trumpet sang and the signal gun boomed. Powder smoke trailed out over the bow. The huge lateen and the smaller bonaventure were brailed up to the yard, so that they wouldn't steal too much air from the main topsail when our stern crossed the wind. *King Emmius* seemed to pause for a long suspenseful instant, and then Gladwell brought the moment to an end with a cry.

"Put up the helm!" The timoneers leaned on the whipstaff and the rudder was slowly pushed to leeward. *Emmius* began to swing off, a slow turn to starboard, lumbering through the water.

"Weather main braces! Haul taut! Keep the spritsail full!"

Blue flags were coming down every mainmast as the Admiral's signal was acknowledged, and the other ships, some quick and some slow, began to make their turns.

"Fore braces! Clew-garnets! Rise fore tack and sheet!"

Emmius pitched into the trough of a wave, and I felt the breeze shift on the back of my neck as the wind started coming in over the starboard quarter. The crew dragged the fore- and mainyards slowly around to keep as many sails full as possible.

"Shift over the spritsail! Lateen outhaul! Bonaventure outhaul!"

The lateen and bonaventure were run out from the yards. The lateen flapped with large, lazy ripples, like a sun-browned mirror of the sea, and then suddenly the wind filled the canvas with a rumbling boom, the sound of listless summer thunder right overhead, and then the taut lateen pushed the stern downwind and helped *King Emmius* onto its new heading.

"Haul taut!" Gladwell's singing baritone filled with triumph. "Brace up—gather aft!"

"Full an' bye, sir!" called the quartermaster.

"Give her a good full."

The crew busied themselves with coiling line and otherwise putting the ship in perfect order. I peered out over the taffrail to see how the other ships were managing the maneuver, and saw that some had been less expert than others and ended up far to leeward—but worse even than these were the pair of ships who had apparently never noticed nor heard any of the signals, and continued to blithely sail along on their old course.

"I want the names of those ships!" snarled the Admiral.

"Ay, my lord," said Naylor.

"*Triumph* and *Tiger*, Lord Coneygrave," said I. The ships were distinctive, one with green-and-white dicing on its aftercastle, and the other an elderly razee with the top deck cut away to extend the ship's life. I was surprised that Coneygrave didn't know them by sight.

The Admiral gave me a searching look. Perhaps he had forgot I was present.

"Thank you, Selford," he said. He looked out over his self-scattered fleet. "Signal for all ships to enter the flagship's wake or grain."

This would put the entire fleet into a long line, the ships bow to stern. Since most guns were to be found on a ship's broadside, this line made perfect sense, for it allowed every ship to fire its broadside guns at the enemy without friendly vessels getting in the way. So again signal flags went up, trumpets blared, a couple of guns were fired, and the fleet began to edge its way into formation.

I kept my eye on the enemy fleet, which maintained far better order than our own. Occasionally I took a glass and looked to windward, to the water boiling around the rocks and islets of the Races.

Above those broken black teeth I could see the white gleam of the tower I had built on my estate at Dunnock, on the cliff overlooking the sea. I knew not whether my little manor still existed, for it was but a few days' march from the enemy camps at Melcaster, and if Marshal Rutilan had been foraging to the west, they might have stolen everything and left nothing but fire and corpses behind. I did not imagine the enemy would spare the property of the man who had crowned Floria queen.

But if my house survived, I hope my steward and the staff were in the tower, watching as the ships maneuvered in their deadly dance.

"We shall bear down on the enemy," the Admiral said, when *Triumph* and *Tiger* had rejoined and the fleet was finally disposed to his liking. "Signal that we shall come down all together." He looked at Gladwell. "Master Gladwell, please put me alongside the enemy flagship."

Gladwell looked out over the enemy array and hesitated. The enemy flagship, the famous *Imperial* of nine hundred tons, was easily distinguished, for it was the largest vessel in either fleet, with a vermilion hull, gold leaf gleaming glistening on its fore- and aftercastles, and flags that streamed from every mast.

"My Lord Admiral," Gladwell said, and then spoke with slow deliberation. "The enemy flagship is in the middle of their line."

"Ay," Coneygrave said. "Let us go there and fight him."

"We are outnumbered," Gladwell said. "If we go right into the middle of them, they will overlap us on either end."

Coneygrave's face contorted with thwarted fury. The teeth in his underslung jaw flashed. "Since this war began, I have ever been accused of a want of courage," he said, "because I have followed Her Majesty's commands and not engaged the enemy. And now that the enemy finally lies under our lee, I cannot seek out my foe and destroy him in a fair fight?"

"If your lordship will remember," said I, "our plan is not to—"

"Oh, ay," Coneygrave snarled. "There is to be cunning, yes, but no unnecessary valor!"

I thought that valor was necessary only when cunning failed, but clearly the Admiral did not share my philosophy.

"You might instead engage the vice-admiral commanding the van squadron," suggested Captain Naylor. "His is a formidable ship and must carry fifty guns at least, and two hundred soldiers."

Coneygrave showed his teeth again, and waved his baton in frustration. "As you will," he said. "Just give me something worth shooting at."

Again trumpets rang out, and flags went up the masts. Three guns were fired to windward, and as the smoke was carried back over the ship, I smelled gunpowder for the first time, and felt the tremor of rising excitement. Either it beckoned me to battle or urged me to run away, and I knew not which.

King Emmius slowly turned its bow toward the enemy, and around me I could feel the soldiers stir. Armor and weapons rattled as they checked their hackbuts, made certain their slow-matches were lit, and loosened swords in scabbards.

I did not wish to tell them that, if the battle went as planned, they would never have a chance to fire those hackbuts or to draw those swords. They would spend the day being targets but never have the opportunity to return fire and harm the enemy. I chose not to enlighten the soldiers on this point, for I feared the knowledge might discourage them.

The fleet bore down more or less together, and the only disorder was caused by the flagship, as Coneygrave insisted on fighting Loretto's vice-admiral and had to jockey through his own fleet in order to come up to the place in line he wanted.

Maneuvers under sail are slow and deliberate, at least to landsmen. If it could move over the surface of the water, a cavalry regiment could trot right past a fleet approaching battle, and probably maintain better order. Yet I found our approach of intense interest, and I watched with great attentiveness as we crept closer to the enemy. For one thing, I knew that Coneygrave badly wanted to engage the enemy closely, and my plan instead called for a rather distant bombardment. For another, I knew that though Coneygrave treated me with civility, he nevertheless resented Floria's command that had placed her favorite aboard his flagship to dictate this engagement—just as I would have resented anyone that Floria placed over me. It may as well be admitted that Coneygrave's resentment had a solid foundation.

But yet Floria's warrant gave me some authority here, and I would use every ounce of that authority if it were needful, and suffer the consequences of that resentment later.

I had made a point, on joining the fleet, to meet as many of the captains—and their sailing masters—as possible, and to explain what was wanted. My guide Robertson had spread his fellows through the fleets and placed them aboard the commanders of the van and rear squadrons. Given the few days since our departure from Selford, we were as prepared as we could be.

"My Lord Admiral," said the sailing master Gladwell. "We should bear up, for we must leave the ships room to wear around."

Coneygrave waved his baton listlessly. "If we must," he said.

King Emmius turned to windward, the rest of the ships conforming, until we were parallel again to the enemy at a distance of about five hundred yards. The flagship of the enemy van was directly across from us, its hull painted with yellow ochre, with stripes of scarlet over the gunports. The painted head of a wolf snarled on its main topsail. There was a great silence on the water, for it seemed as if all the world held its breath, and I heard only the splash of the waves against the hull, the creak of the masts and yards, and the voice of an enemy talking, the sound carrying all the way from the Loretto ships.

The Admiral turned to Captain Naylor. "Captain," he said, "you may open fire."

I looked at the nearest of the ship's guns, and made sure I stood clear of the recoil.

Naylor saluted. "Ay, Lord Coneygrave." He went to the break of the poop and gave his orders. "Ready, my bullies!" he said. "Take good aim, and give three cheers for Duisland!"

The cheers roared out, and then Naylor shouted *"Fire!"* and our broadside went off all in one great salvo. The sound seemed to snatch the breath from my lungs, and my heart gave a great leap. The ship shuddered as the great bronze weapons hurled themselves back upon their tackles, and rivers of white gunsmoke flooded between me and the enemy.

The other ships of the fleet now fired, and thousands of pounds of solid iron was hurled at the ships of Loretto. The wind tore the smoke into long streamers. From the direction of the enemy we could hear the sounds of iron balls cracking wooden timbers.

King Emmius was designed to carry forty-eight great guns, though more had been crammed in wherever there was room. On the lower deck were cannons, firing forty-two-pound shot; culverins on the maindeck, firing iron shot weighing seventeen and a half pounds, and smaller weapons in the castles, demiculverins and sakers firing balls of eight and five and a half pounds, along with the swivel guns and other close-range weapons known collectively as "murderers."

My ears rang, but not loudly enough to obscure the shouts of the ship's cannoneers, who were reloading in a frenzy. Some of the sakers—very long guns, and consequently accurate ones—had not sufficient room to recoil, and had to be reloaded by men hanging outboard the ship.

It was possible for a commander to order gun drill even while the fleet was in port—at least so long as the firing of cannon were mimed—and *Emmius's* crew were fast enough reloading so that we got off another salvo before the enemy made up their minds to respond. I think it likely that the enemy were disappointed that we had chosen to engage at such long range, for we could hardly have a decisive battle unless we narrowed the distance between the fleets. We would not close, and the enemy *could* not, for we held what is called the weather gage, with the wind behind us blowing toward the enemy. The Lorettans were already pinched up as close to the wind as possible, and if they tried to sail directly at us, the wind would push them stern-first away, possibly with their masts crashing about their ears. Likewise the ships in their rear were completely out of the fight, for they could not get any closer to us, and confined themselves to firing a few chase guns in our direction.

The first enemy broadside thundered out, and then came a howling overhead, the eerie shriek and moan and shudder of hot iron tearing apart the air. I suppressed the impulse to duck into my cuirass like a turtle into his shell. I heard a lone crash forward, where a ball lodged in the hull, but the rest flew over us. Some lines parted, and Gladwell sent men aloft to splice cordage.

I felt heartened. A very large galleon had unloaded its broadside at me, and it had missed.

The enemy were lying on the starboard tack, thought I, and the pressure of the wind heeled their ships over to larboard, which tipped up the muzzles of the guns so that they fired high. Our own ship was likewise heeled over, which pointed our guns into the water, but they could be elevated to fire right above the wavetops. The sakers and demiculverins, both long-range weapons, were intended to skip shot along the surface of the water to crash into the enemy hull, and I supposed that was what the gun captains were attempting.

More broadsides were exchanged, though the drifting wall of smoke between us, and the smoke that filled the gun decks, so obscured the enemy that we fired almost blind. Since the smoke streamed into the faces of our enemies, they likely could see nothing at all. The Lorettans continued to fire high, though some shot lodged in the hull, and one roundshot cleared a bloody path right across the poop, hurling bodies, armor, splinters, and sharp spinning weapons into the packed soldiers and crew. Something—someone's arm perhaps—struck my helmet a ringing blow, spattered me with gore, and left me half stunned.

I shook my head to clear it. I did not care to view the tangle of dead, and so I stepped with care over the carnage and went down the companion to the quarterdeck, and there encountered Goodman Robertson, a fisherman from a village near my Dunnock manor who I had brought with me onto the flagship. He was a man of thirty with the hard hands and sun-browned face of his profession, and one of his eyes was set in a permanent squint.

"Well, goodman," I said. "I hope you have been keeping an eye out to windward."

"Ay, sir," said he. "The tide is flooding in brisk-like, and we should have slack tide by four bells."

I looked up and tilted the visor of my helmet back in hopes of seeing the new moon, but of course saw nothing. "What time is it now?" asked I. "I haven't heard the bell over the sound of the guns."

"It just struck three bells of the forenoon watch, sir."

"Thank you, goodman," said I. I stood aside as some of the wounded were carried down the companionway, and I saw Boatswain Lepalik, of my galley's crew, stood on the quarterdeck near the mainmast, and I walked over to greet him.

"Maybe you wish you had gone home when you had the chance," I said.

He grinned at me, and shook his head. "You fellows fight very noisy battles," he said.

The rest of my boat's crew were serving here and there as volunteers, either handling sail or crewing a gun as their talents permitted. Rufino Knott, whose nautical skills were of modest dimensions, was assisting the surgeon on the orlop deck.

By now the guns were no longer being fired in great salvos, but each as fast as it could be loaded and run out, and so there was a continuous drumroll of guns firing, and my nerves leaped with every discharge. The great banks of smoke made it impossible to see the enemy at all, though I knew they were there because of the uncanny wail of return fire arcing overhead.

I returned to the poop, where severed limbs and the bodies of the slain were being thrown overboard. I approached Gladwell, the sailing master, and leaned toward him so that he could hear me over the din. "Half an hour to slack tide, Master Gladwell."

He gave me a startled look as if I were a specter emerged from the smoke, but then he nodded. "Thank you, Lord Selford."

I made my way to where Coneygrave and Captain Naylor stood by the weather rail, and approached and saluted. The Admiral grinned at me, and with his underslung lower jaw looked like a badger laughing at a dog barking at him from the far side of a fence.

"Does *Emmius* not fight bravely?" he asked.

"Ay," said I. "We do the enemy more harm than they do us."

"That we do!" He slapped the rail with his hand. "Never shall they beat us! Never!" He peered at me. "Are you wounded, Selford? There is blood on your face."

"It is not mine," said I. "I wished to tell you that there is less than a half hour to slack tide, and so perhaps—"

"Ay, ay," he said, and waved a hand in a dismissive way. A solid shot struck *Emmius* just below the poop, and I could hear it carom through the space just below us, striking the deckhead such a knock that the planks below my feet leaped. There followed the screams of wounded, and I tried not to shudder at the sound. Coneygrave grinned again.

"That has made a shambles of my cabin, ha?" he said. For indeed his great cabin, where he held feasts for his officers, was just under the poop deck. Though he traveled with all the finery expected of a great lord and commander, he lost nothing but some sailors to the enemy shot, for all his belongings, the fine furniture and silver plate, had been carried to the hold when the ship readied for action.

"I hope their gunnery is not improving," said I.

"They know not where we are in all this smoke," said Coneygrave. "That shot was merest luck on their part."

As if to put a period to this pronouncement, two more shot struck us amidships, one on the maindeck, and the other tearing across the quarterdeck and killing a half-dozen soldiers.

"Hang me!" Coneygrave said in surprise.

"My lord," said I, "they have learned not to fire high, and this is turning too quickly into a fair fight. Let us get onto the other tack, and—"

Master Gladwell appeared, saluted, and spoke quickly. "Best signal for wearing, my lord," he said. "We have a tide to catch."

Another shot went low over our heads, and I ducked. Any inclination to embarrassment evaporated when I saw that Coneygrave and Naylor had crouched as well.

"Ay," said the Admiral as he straightened. "Let us get the blue signal aloft."

The blue flag went to the maintop, and trumpets brayed out over the sound of the guns. There would be a deal of uncertainty whether the entire fleet would see the signal, and so the trumpets called out again and again for five minutes or more, the ship shuddering every so often as enemy shot lodged home, before the flag was run down to begin the maneuver, and Gladwell called out, "Haul taut—up mains'l! Brail in the lateen and bonaventure!"

The helm was put up, and *King Emmius* began its curve in the direction of the enemy line. I looked at the ships before and astern to see if they were following the maneuver, and I saw blue flags coming down to signal they were beginning their turn. A few last shots were fired in the direction of the enemy, and then Naylor was calling down, "Gun crews to the starboard battery. Run out!" and then the ship rumbled like a growling lion as the starboard guns were dragged up to the ports.

"Weather main braces! Haul taut! Keep the sprits'l full!"

Thick clouds of smoke darkened our decks. Our guns had fallen silent while the enemy continued to fire, and one large shot struck the bow low down, while others parted lines or tore gaps in the sails. I felt the wind shift on my cheek, and knew the wind was now coming over the larboard quarter.

"Shift over the sprits'l! Lateen outhaul! Bonaventure outhaul!"

Emmius rolled in the trough of a wave, then steadied as the lateen thundered into life. I was peering out over the starboard bow, for I knew there was an enemy fleet to be found there, but in the smoke and murk I knew not how close they were.

Then a dark shadow loomed up ahead, and as *Emmius* continued its turn we saw a great high-charged galleon of Loretto about to pass us close along the starboard side. Though there were shouts of surprise and warning from the enemy vessel, I am sure they knew not who we were, whether enemy or a friend that had got lost in the smoke.

"Fire as you bear!" Gladwell cried in his singing baritone, and as we came abreast of the enemy the guns began to go off, and from the enemy ship I heard the simultaneous groan of six or seven hundred men as they realized they were about to receive an entire broadside at close range, with little chance to respond. If the enemy fired a single shot, I marked it not. On the enemy ship I could see pieces of the enemy bulwark dissolve, and men blown to pieces, and then something spun through the air toward me, and instinctively I ducked my chin—and a yard-long oak splinter, blown from the enemy ship, bounded off my burgonet and set my skull ringing like a monastery bell.

As the last of the great guns went off, the soldiers flocked to the rail and let fly with their firelocks and murderers into the astonished faces gaping at them from the enemy aftercastle. And then our great curve continued, and Gladwell's baritone sang out in triumph.

"Haul taut! Brace up—gather aft!"

"Full and bye!" called the quartermaster.

"Keep her full. Let her go through the water."

As Gladwell gave his commands, there were a series of great concussive bursts out in the murk, and I thought that others of our fleet were unloading their broadsides. Then came another series of warning shouts, and my heart leaped as I realized that the cries were coming from all around me. I turned and saw a sprit topsail looming through the smoke above the poop, and then I was almost flung off my feet by a massive lurch, followed by a hideous din as another ship rammed us on the starboard quarter and carried away the Admiral's quarter gallery, the gilded, ornamented balcony that stretched across the broad stern of the ship.

"Damn you, sir!" shouted Coneygrave. "What ship are you?"

We had been struck by one of our own vessels that had been blinded by the great gunsmoke. But there was little damage done, and we soon parted without the Admiral ever discovering who had torn away his balcony. In moments, we broke out of the clouds of gunsmoke, and I laughed at the brilliance of the sun and the light sparkling on the deep blue water. Emerging behind us came a cloud of ships, each flaunting the colors of Duisland, and my heart lifted at the sight. It seemed we had won our first throw of the dice.

Now, you may know that there would have been a different way to have brought our ships to the other tack, which is to get on a good burst of speed, turn the ship upwind until it crosses the wind entirely, then falls off onto its new heading. There is more to it than that, a lot of shouting and hauling of yards and hauling the mainsail, but that is the substance of it.

If the fleet had successfully performed this maneuver, we would all have got onto our new heading without danger of colliding with our own ships or with the enemy. But the maneuver has its own dangers, for not every ship can get across the wind easily, and may end up in irons, being driven stern-foremost with the sails aback and the crew scrambling to put things to rights. Or, alternatively, some ships may have suffered damage aloft in the fighting and been left unable to tack at all. I had not wanted any such strays to be left behind, where they could be gobbled up by the entire enemy fleet.

I decided, therefore, to wear the whole fleet sharp around, to serve the enemy with a few close-range broadsides, and then make our escape in the smoke, and that was exactly what we seemed to have done.

I went to the break of the poop and called down. "Goodman Robertson!" I said. "Now is your time!"

Robertson came up onto the poop and saluted the Admiral. Coneygrave frowned at him—perhaps he did not like his squint—but then he nodded.

"You shall be our pilot, goodman," he said.

"Thank you, my lord," said Robertson. He plucked a telescope from the rack, and trained it forward. "Too many damn' sails," he muttered, and walked to the lee rail, where he leaned over the rail and gazed out. "Now that is Martin's Foot," he said to himself. "And over there, that is Groaning Myrtle all a-blossom, and I see the holm oak atop the peak of the Saddle." He lowered the telescope and gave me a confiding look. "I know where we are, my lord, and just where to con her."

"Splendid!" said I, for Robertson had relieved a deal of my anxiety.

"I think a point to starboard would be best."

"Quartermaster!" called Gladwell. "A point to starboard!"

"Raise the orange pennants!" said the Admiral. Long fork-tailed pendants rose to the mastheads and trailed out in the wind. This was the prearranged signal for "Follow me," and soon other ships of the fleet began to shuffle into our wake.

I turned to look over the taffrail to see more of our ships emerge from the murk. As the smoke thinned I could see beyond them to the enemy, and the damage we had done to their upper masts and rigging was plain to see: yards shot away and hanging in the slings, sails punctured, parted lines that left the rigging askew. The enemy still fired, but with the smoke blowing back into their faces, they succeeded only in blinding themselves. As we sailed gracefully away from them, the enemy gradually ceased fire, and then I imagine they stared in consternation at the Duisland fleet sailing blithely on to ruin.

For we were headed directly for the Races, the cluster of black, stony, tide-racked islets that stretched west from the Bay of Melcaster, and that had destroyed more ships than all the naval battles in history.

A few years ago I had watched from the shore as a galleon blundered into the Races in the fog, and I saw the tide boil against the isles, rocks, and stony ledges, while the ship spun helpless in the grip of whirlpools, or was dashed upon the rocks. At the end of an hour, the ship was naught but wreckage, and most of the crew drowned or swept out to sea while clinging to flotsam. Seven men survived out of a crew of sixty, by managing to climb onto one of the islands.

But in the time since that agonizing hour, I had learned more about the Races, and about a species of fishermen who sailed there in perfect safety. They came at high water, and while the tide was slack checked their traps—for the islets were an ideal place for catching lobster or octopus, and low tide revealed mussels, cockles, and seaweed that clung to the islets' stony flanks.

On some of the larger islands a small boat might be drawn up safely, and there the fisherfolk had built drystone huts so that they could spend the night, or cook some of their catch over a smoky seaweed fire.

So the enemy now beheld our fleet, scattered and in apparent flight, abandoning the battle and fleeing toward the most dangerous feature marked on their charts. If they wished to completely secure their victory, they should go about now, pin us against the Races, and cut us off from any escape to the open sea.

But now, as the smoke cleared, I saw they had another choice, for not all our ships had managed to escape. One—the *Trefoil* galleon of three hundred tons—had lost her mizzenmast, and had been unable to come up onto the larboard tack. Instead she took advantage of the smoke and had run clean through the enemy formation, and was now flying before the wind with as much sail as she could raise. Ahead of her, *Triumph* and *Tiger* sailed on in line abreast. The two had again missed a signal, or had taken too long to wear around, and so sailed through the enemy and away.

"Those two again!" Coneygrave snarled. "I shall send those captains home in irons!"

Because of those three fugitive ships, the enemy now had another choice. They could put up their helms and capture the three ships downwind of them, and this would enable their commander to report that he had driven off an enemy fleet and taken three prizes in a victory that was absolutely certain and that entailed no risk whatever.

Or, if their admiral were spirited, he would bring his entire force about and pursue us, and have the kind of victory that admirals could only dream of.

Signal flags went up the masts of the vermilion-hulled *Imperial*, and were soon being repeated by the other ships. We could hear trumpet calls clearly. But if it took a long while to pass commands to our forty-two ships, it took even longer for each of the seventy-odd enemy to repeat the signal, and so several minutes ticked by in suspense before the flagship's signals ran down, two signal guns were fired to windward, and the entire fleet tacked—or tried to, since some were slow in stays and failed, and others had been damaged aloft and had to wear around. But soon they were all on our trail, and I felt a wild exultation rise in me. The enemy had taken the bait, and we had won the second cast of the dice.

"Might we take in some sail?" Robertson asked. "It is hard to see our course with so much canvas in the way, and I don't want to bring us into the Races at a rate too reckless."

Gladwell gave the order to clew up the fore- and mainsail, and we proceeded under topsails alone. Five other ships in our fleet had raised orange pendants, for they carried Robertson's fellow-fishers, who knew the Races as well as he. We would not have to sail through the Races in one long line, and risk the rear being cut off by the enemy, but by half a dozen different paths.

The silence was startling after the clangor of battle. *King Emmius* hissed through the water, its timbers creaked, and the sea chuckled beneath the transom. Sea-birds called. A captain of the soldiers, balancing back and forth as the waves lifted and dropped the ship, wore a boot that squeaked with every wave. When the quartermaster struck four bells, the bright peals seemed to chime down from the heavens.

"Half a point to starboard," said Robertson. "Ready to put the helm down."

He went to the starboard side of the poop, peered forward, then went to the larboard side and peered again. My heart gave a startled leap as I saw a jagged rock slide past close along the larboard side—I had no idea we were already in the Races.

"Put the helm down," Robertson said. "Handsomely, now."

"Handsomely," repeated Gladwell. "Keep her full."

Slowly we eased into the wind, and the fore topsail rattled as the wind no longer filled it.

"Brace up!" called Gladwell. Then, the sail filling again, "Reeve and haul the bowlines!"

"Helm amidships," said Robertson.

A black island loomed on our starboard bow like an unwelcome shadow, then moved past in stately silence. The waves burst white against it, but I saw nothing like the raging seas and spreading foam that marked the Races when the tide began to run.

It had of course occurred to me that the depth of water safe for a fishing smack might not be suitable for a high-charged man of war drawing three fathoms, and I had carefully questioned Robertson on the matter. "A high tide will put another fifteen feet of water on them rocks," said he, "and a spring tide another five or six. Your ships will be safe as a babe in its cradle."

The new moon, trending to the west though invisible, guaranteed a spring tide, and Robertson's prediction held. Coneygrave paced on the weather deck, gnawing his upper lip with anxiety. A tall spike of an island passed by, its top crowned by the pink flowers of crape myrtle—I assumed this island was the Groaning Myrtle that Robertson had mentioned, though perhaps I would have to wait for a running tide to hear it groan. I was surprised that the myrtle would flower this early in the year, and thought perhaps the sea air was salubrious.

We sailed on in near-silence, the stillness interrupted only by the sound of water and the cries of birds, the wind sighing through the rigging, the sound of the ship's bell every half hour, and Robertson's mutterings as he conned us through the rocky maze. Behind us, a line of ships plodded in our wake, and behind them, on the open sea, was the great advancing crescent of the enemy, *Imperial* in the lead.

The quartermaster struck five bells, then six. The bright sun on my armor baked me like a lobster in coals, and sweat trickled down my forehead.

"The enemy signals, my lord!" cried a lookout. Telescopes were trained over the taffrail. The enemy fleet was still outside the Races, and was nearing the point where they were going to have to decide whether or not to follow us. We knew the enemy commander was a bold man, but was he a reckless one? He had, after all, seen our entire fleet sail into the Races without harm. Time itself seemed to tick by at a decreasing rate, treacle-slow, and every second seemed a lifetime.

"Come. Come," I urged. "Do you not boast that Loretto has an excess of courage? Come, let us all see that courage now."

Then the signal was hauled down, a gun boomed, and the great vermilion galleon kept on, while the other ships began to form a long column behind it.

I believe I laughed aloud. I took my burgonet off my head and waved it.

"A fig for thee," I cried, "you fat-kidneyed fashion-mongers in your noxious cheap perfume and your red leather dancing shoes! Your dances are over, and I will trip the last caper ere this day is done!"

The officers seemed startled, and Coneygrave favored me with a thoughtful look, but the sailors and soldiers laughed.

Seven bells rang. Jagged islands passed by in silence. As eight bells approached, the navigator appeared on the poop with his back-staff, to gauge the sun's altitude and determine when the captain could declare it noon. I smiled at this, for Alaron Mountmirail had invented that backstaff, a great improvement on the cross-staff that had preceded it, and I had manufactured that new instrument in a workshop I had built in Selford. Floria had seen to it that every ship in the navy had at least one such engine aboard, and I'd had to expand my workshop to accommodate the demand.

The navigator reported to Captain Naylor. "Make it noon," the captain said, and eight bells was struck.

Robertson came over to me and spoke in a low voice. "Slack tide is ending," he said. "I had thought to have us out by now."

"How much longer?" I asked.

"Half an hour, may be. If longer, the tide will take us out whether we want it or no."

The invisible moon sailed toward the horizon and drew the water west, and we would go with it.

"Should we put on more sail?" I asked.

"I dare not put on more."

I looked at him. "Then we must trust you, and you must trust Pastas the Netweaver."

Robertson made the sign of the god, and returned to the break in the poop.

As the minutes passed, I fancied that the islets were moving past us with growing speed. I looked closely at the islands and saw that, judging by the high-tide mark on the stone, the level of the water seemed to have fallen by two feet. But the current had not yet begun to roar, and the water had not turned white. We had time yet.

In another fifteen minutes we were tearing through the water as if we galloped on a race course, and the timoneers had to throw themselves hard on the whipstaff to persuade the galleon to obey Robertson's instructions. Streaks of white appeared on the water, and little whirlpools, and my heart leaped into my mouth.

I stood on the deck with cold fear prickling along the back of my neck, but I saw a smile come to Robertson's face, and I gazed ahead to see only a few small islets between us and the open sea, and my apprehension turned to joy, then laughter. I clapped Robertson on the shoulder, and then as we came near an island a tremor ran through the ship, and then I heard a grating, rumbling sound as the keel struck a ledge and ground along it. The ship pitched over to larboard. I know that everyone on the ship was struck frozen with terror, but the shudder lasted only a few seconds, and then *Emmius* was free, the ship was righting itself, and we were rushing for safety as fast as the boiling tide could carry us.

Gladwell snatched a speaking trumpet from the rack and ran aft to the taffrail. "Ledge!" He pointed and called to the ship astern of us. "Ledge off that island! Steer clear!"

That ship heard and obeyed, and word of the danger was passed along the line from one ship to another, so that no vessel in our column touched bottom. We passed—or rather, were hurled—from the Races like an arrow fired from a bow, and it was some time before we could do anything but run before that tide.

"Thank you, Goodman Robertson," said the Admiral. "Master

Gladwell, please put us on the starboard tack. Signal for the fleet to form in our wake or grain."

Our column of eleven ships was spat out of the Races like orange pips squeezed between thumb and finger, and none suffered any damage but the last, which had been caught in a whirlpool and spun around, glanced off a stony islet, and came out of the Races stern-first, every sail aback, with the fore topmast broken at the cap and toppled into the mainmast, so that it was impossible to control the sails. The tide carried her past us, but her hull seemed sound, and after repairs were made to her masts, she would join us or make for the shipyards of Bretlynton Head.

Not all our ships were as lucky. Two were lost before they could escape the roaring tide—one flew spinning out of the Races with its pumps clanking, the sound of hammering rising from the hold as the carpenter and his assistants repaired damage, and the sailing master baying orders as he tried to fother a sail over a hole punched in the hull by a stony dagger. The ship floated long enough to be run aground, and all aboard were saved.

The last ship, *Champion* of four hundred tons, failed to escape the Races entirely, being caught in a whirlpool, battered to bits on the rocks, and sunk. A few crew came out clinging to scraps of wreckage, and these were saved; but nearly five hundred men perished.

But many more died than those five hundred. I had come to lure the enemy onto the rocks, and I had succeeded. I watched with a telescope as our pursuers were caught, spun, toppled, and raked over the rocks. Masts pitched over, ships listed as their sides were stove in, and some were shattered into kindling. My feelings of triumph faded, and I felt only a cold, creeping sense of horror as one ship after another was destroyed. There were, I calculated, twenty-five or thirty thousand crew and soldiers aboard those ships. Only a hand-ful would survive, and the rest would suffer the worst death the sea could offer them—hearing first the growing roar of the waters, then knowing that the tide had taken their ship and it was no longer under command, after which they would experience the grind and shudder as their ships were hurled upon the islands or dragged over rocks, followed by the rending of timbers and the sound of the cold sea pouring into the ship; and lastly, as the ship went down, having to strike out into the foaming tide, only to feel the water close over their heads.

The bodies, I thought, would be washing up for days. I would have to send word to Dunnock to burn them on the beach so that they would not carry disease to our landsmen.

"Well, Lord Selford," said Coneygrave quietly. "It is a sad and glorious thing you have done."

"I cannot disagree, Lord Admiral." Yet, a short while later, he decided that not enough sad and glorious acts had taken place that day, for the enemy flagship *Imperial*, its vermilion sides streaked from collision with the rocks, was hurled from the Races. We could hear its pumps clanking. Four other ships followed, two in sinking condition. Coneygrave gave a barking laugh, and turned to the sailing master.

"Gladwell," said he, "put me alongside their flagship."

It was all I could do not to stare, and yet somehow I managed to hold both my peace and my patience. Coneygrave wanted a fight, toe-to-toe, with the enemy commander, and though he'd failed in that ambition a few hours ago, now there was nothing that could stop him. My commission from the Queen ended when the enemy fleet went onto the rocks, and now I was a mere passenger, while Coneygrave had resumed his place as the absolute master of the Queen's Navy.

If I had been in his place, I would have surrounded the enemy flagship with a dozen ships of my own, then asked politely for their surrender. If they hadn't given it, I would have finished what the Races had begun, and pounded them to bits from a position of relative safety. But Coneygrave was filled with visions of carrying his country's flag over the ramparts of his enemy's aftercastle, receiving his enemy's surrender in person, and then perhaps giving him a good dinner and engaging him in a gentlemanly conversation about wine.

So *King Emmius* left our own line, went about, and shaped a course for the *Imperial*. Our captains waited for some signal, saw none, then did as they pleased. I was myself very happy that a goodly number of them chose to support their admiral.

I was near astonished when the Loretto admiral accepted the challenge to combat, threw up his helm, and bore down on us. He was no less willing to fight than Coneygrave—though when I considered the matter, I supposed that death at the hands of the enemy was a kinder fate than that awaiting him back home, after losing seventy ships to rocks that had been marked on every chart drawn for the last two hundred years.

We approached one another on converging courses. *Emmius* fired first, into the enemy's starboard bow as she approached, but then the enemy hauled her wind and gave us a broadside that made our ship shudder, sent splinters flying about our ears, and killed twenty crew outright. Then the action became general, each gun firing as fast as it could be loaded and run out, and as the enemy drew near our ship became a hot, torn, bloody slaughterhouse. I suspect we had the worst of it, for now the powder smoke was blowing into our faces and blinding us and not the enemy.

I had nothing to do, and no men to command, but I was obliged to stand under the enemy fire anyway, I suppose to set an example to the ordinary sailors. I could not still my feelings of resentment. I had given Coneygrave the most complete victory in history, but here he was determined to throw both our lives away in a pointless fight, out of what he might well have called *unnecessary valor*.

As for Coneygrave, he was delighted. He paced madly back and forth, gesturing with his baton and laughing. "Bravely, bravely!" he kept repeating, and he cheered the firing of every gun.

Imperial grew closer, and now the thunder of the great guns was joined by the bark of swivel guns and the rattle of firelocks. Bullets pelted the poop deck and spattered off the armor of the soldiers. I realized that *Imperial* overtopped us, and that the soldiers on her poop could fire right down into us while sheltering behind the ship's bulwarks.

As we grew close, *Imperial* did not haul her wind to ride alongside us, but kept straight on, as if she intended to collide. Suddenly Gladwell was shouting orders for us to put up our helm, but the enemy's sails had blanketed our own, and *Emmius* lost way and did not answer the rudder.

"Collision! 'Ware collision!" I bawled, and then *Imperial*'s bow crashed into ours, and there was a tortured shriek of timber and half the men on deck were thrown off their feet. Coneygrave and Captain Naylor tumbled to the planks in a clatter of armor. Grapnels flashed in the air as *Imperial* tried to lash itself to *Emmius*. "Cut those away!" I shouted. "Cut away those lines!"

I don't know if anyone heard me, but the ships drew apart anyway, as *Emmius*'s bow rebounded from the collision. But this threw our stern up into *Imperial*, and there was another groan of timber, less shattering this time. I looked up at the enemy ship, and my heart sank.

Imperial had been carrying a kedge anchor on her aftercastle, and one of its flukes was now planted in our bulwark. The ships' aftercastles were locked together, and we were doomed to fight the battle against an enemy who could fire down into us at will.

Bullets rained down on us. Our own soldiers fired back, but the enemy were protected by their own bulwark and exposed only their heads and shoulders for a brief instant as they fired.

"Axes to the poop!" I called. Perhaps we might cut the gunwale away and part the ships.

I saw that the gangs of the enemy were hauling on the grapnel lines, trying to bring the ships together broadside-to-broadside. I saw swords flash as some of our crew hacked at the lines. To protect the grapnels, hackbuts and swivel guns fired from *Imperial*'s forecastle down onto *Emmius*'s maindeck. The cannonade continued, our guns so close to the enemy hull that their blasts scorched the vermilion paint.

Haul though the enemy might, they did not draw the fore part of our ship any closer. The kedge anchor had locked our ships together in a certain configuration, and it would not be altered. Neither ship was under control, and we were spinning slowly downwind, the sails crashing overhead as the wind took them aback.

I ran to the crews of the sakers that lined the poop. "Elevate your guns!" I shouted. "Fire up into the enemy soldiers!" That would involve firing through the side of *Imperial* and then through the poop deck, and I was not a sufficient expert cannoneer to know how possible it was, but I thought it might help keep that deadly fire off our decks.

Admiral Coneygrave was on his feet again, and with Captain Naylor paced the deck and cried encouragement to the soldiers and sailors. I approached the Admiral and shouted into his ear.

"They will clear our decks and board us!" I told him, and then I realized what the enemy actually intended. "They will board us and *sail away*. Our own ships might not know to stop them."

Comprehension dawned in the Admiral's eyes. An enemy bullet shattered on my cuirass and shards of lead pierced my buff coat and bit into my arm.

"I think they have trained for boarding," I said. "They have more soldiers than we, and—"

At that moment a downward-directed bullet plunged through Captain Naylor's neck and into his body, and he fell stone dead at my feet. Coneygrave and I leaped away in surprise, but then I returned and knelt by the body. I had barely assured myself of Naylor's fate before three sailors picked up the corpse and rolled it over the side. I stood.

"Where is the first lieutenant?" I asked the Admiral. "Someone needs to tell him he now commands the ship."

The Admiral clearly did not know. At the moment, a great shout came from *Imperial*'s crew, and I saw that their gunports were closing. They were giving up the fight with artillery, and marshaling their entire compliment to swarm across to our ship and take it. Our own crew bellowed their scorn at the enemy's abandoning their batteries, then busied themselves with loading their guns now they could take aim and fire without danger of return fire.

Even with their advantage in position and numbers, I felt we had a chance of withstanding the enemy, for it is harder to fight your way aboard an enemy ship than you might think. People seem to have this absurd notion that boarding parties swing from one ship to another on ropes, but they do not take into account the fact that all the lines on a ship are meant to hoist or control the sails, and that if you throw a line off a pinrail and use it to swing to another ship, you are depriving your own ship of the ability to sail properly.

And of course once you launch yourself on a rope's end toward your enemy, you are committed; you cannot alter your course even when you see an enemy level a boarding pike at your navel and wait for you to impale yourself on it.

It is possible to board by crawling out of a gunport and then through the enemy's port, which is why *Imperial*'s crew closed their own ports to keep us from crossing to their ship, but it is wise to make sure the enemy have deserted their stations before attempting it, lest someone pick up a cannonball and drop it on your head.

No, the best way to board an enemy ship is over the bow or the stern, which is one reason why we build fore- and aftercastles in those vulnerable places. I could see enemy sailors racing aft, brandishing weapons as they surged toward the poop. I thought we could expect a rain of enemy fighters landing on our deck at any moment.

Then a horrifying thought occurred to me, and I ran aft to peer out over the taffrail, only to see a gang of enemy crowding *Imperial's* stern and quarter galleries. These ornamented balconies built out over the stern were intended as a private and pleasurable place for high-ranking officers to take their exercise, but now they proved ready-made boarding bridges to enable the enemy to climb onto *King Emmius* unopposed.

They could not climb onto the Admiral's stern gallery, for it had been torn away in the collision with our own ship, but they could clamber over Captain Naylor's gallery on the maindeck, and that was exactly what the first of their party was doing, a nimble sailor with a baggy knit cap and a whinyard in his fist.

Mind whirling, I jumped back from the taffrail and ran to the Admiral. "They come over the stern galleries onto the maindeck!" I shouted. "I will try to keep them off!"

Without waiting for an answer from the Admiral, I flung myself down the companion to the quarterdeck, and amid the firing of guns and firelocks I found a lieutenant of the soldiers. "They're crossing onto the maindeck!" said I. "I need you and your men!"

He was a young man overwhelmed with the clamor and slaughter of his first battle, and he goggled at me. "Sir?" he said.

I had no time for another explanation. "You and your men follow me!" I said, and then dashed for the companionway to the maindeck. I looked over my shoulder as I descended, and saw the lieutenant rallying his troops and sending them toward the companion. Once my feet landed on the maindeck, I looked about for Boatswain Lepalik, and found him serving a culverin with a rag tied around his shaved head. I touched his shoulder and shouted into his ear.

"The enemy boards aft!" I said. "Gather together a party of armed men and follow me!"

"Ay, sir!" His broad smile told me that he approved more of hand-to-hand fighting than this business of shooting great guns at one another.

I returned to where the soldiers were assembling near the companionway. In modest surprise I realized that I had volunteered to do something other than to stand in the open and be shot at. I had not precisely intended to cast myself in the part of a valiant man of action, and I would happily have left the task to another, but there seemed no one else willing or able to do the act.

I stared down the length of the deck. The maindeck was a long unbroken platform stretching the length of the ship, pitched upward fore and aft, dark and pungent with gunsmoke. A line of culverins, each bronze barrel as hot as a griddle, were being worked by toiling, sweating crew that looked as if they were demons drawn up from Hell. Two of the culverins had been dismounted, and two of the gunports had been beaten into one by enemy fire. With no one to tend them, powder-stained bodies lay stretched on the deck in pools of blood.

Peering aft, the light from the stern windows could be seen only dimly through the smoke. The soldiers, no more than a dozen, gathered around me, and their lieutenant came up and saluted. "My lord," he said.

"They're coming aboard over the stern gallery." I drew my broadsword in my right hand, and a pistol in my left, and perhaps to that young lieutenant I looked a seasoned veteran, but I knew that I was a poor swordsman and a worse shot. Though I donned my fire-eating warrior face, I felt far from invincible as I led my party aft at a brisk walk, hopping over training tackles and the shattered, blackened debris strewn over the deck.

We had gone no more than twenty feet before we were rushed by a mass of dimly seen figures, all running as fast as their feet could carry them. Despair filled me from my brains to my boots. They so outnumbered us that any battle was hopeless, yet if I ran I would be cut down from behind, and so I crouched, my sword cocked to hack at anyone who dared to approach me—and then I saw the mob were *Emmius*'s own jacks, the unarmed gun crew fleeing from the boarders. Relief so unstrung me that my knees sagged halfway to the deck.

"Come back!" I shouted as they passed. "Arm yourselves and return!"

They ran on, and I resumed my advance. The deck's upward curve grew more pronounced, and I saw the enemy silhouetted in the light of the stern windows. There were a score of them, some soldiers but most seamen.

"Shoot!" I cried. "Shoot them now!"

The soldiers with firelocks took aim, and I thrust out my pistol and fired at the armored man who loomed in front of me. My bullet struck him in the cuirass, and for a moment I cursed myself for shooting him exactly where he was best armored, but then he clutched his face and staggered. My bullet had rebounded from his cuirass and come up under his chin, breaking his jaw and shattering teeth.

Hackbuts flared in the darkness and a few enemy fell. I hurled my empty pistol at a seaman, then brandished my sword. "Charge!" I bellowed. "Charge them!"

A part of me remained astonished at this behavior. I had led a charge at Exton Scales, but I'd had the excuse then of being young and ignorant of war, and afterward I'd sworn never to be found again on a battlefield. Yet here again I was, swinging a blade through air heavy with powder smoke, and doing my best to hack an enemy to pieces.

My first cut missed, because the blade struck the deckhead above me, and I realized there was no room for swashing overhead cuts, and instead I jabbed out with my point. The soldier I'd shot parried my first blows with his own broadsword, but he was wounded and unable to fully defend himself, and I got past his guard with a short backhand cut to his face, and he fell. A sailor thrust at me with a pike, and I leaped away from the point and then slashed out blindly in the direction of an enemy I sensed looming up on my right. My blade struck sparks from his armor.

Around me in the dim light I could sense men fighting and falling, and through the diamond panes of the stern windows I could see more enemy packing the gallery. I thrust and hacked and felt enemy weapons grate against my armor. Then the darkened maindeck turned even darker as something eclipsed the stern windows, and I saw a ship with a gilded forecastle crossing *Emmius*'s stern. I blinked sweat from my eyes and recognized *Regal* of four hundred tons.

"*Regal!*" I cried. "*Regal* joins the fight!"

And then the diamond-paned stern windows blew to pieces as *Regal*'s guns began to go off, and the low, broad space of the maindeck filled with the shriek of iron. I threw myself to the deck. Blood, bone, and sharp steel flew through the air while bodies dropped all around me. Splinters whirred overhead. The raking roundshot, coming right through our stern, had nothing to stop them, and they traveled the length of the deck, killing men and dismounting guns.

The cannonade seemed to go on forever, and when the thunder ceased, I remained prone on the deck for a few moments, in case a belated gun chose that moment to go off. Then I took a firm grip on my sword and staggered to my feet.

My ears rang, and I spat gunpowder from my lips. Blood dripped down my face and from the visor of my helmet. Wreckage, human and otherwise, was scattered over the scarred planks. A few stunned scarecrow figures rose from the deck, so ragged and stained with powder and blood that I could not tell to which ship they belonged, or to which nation. With great effort I drew out my second pistol, and pointing it vaguely at them I said, "Gentlemen, be at peace. This war is over for us." And then I repeated my words in the language of Loretto.

At that moment a group of sailors came rushing up, led by Lepalik, a party he had gathered and armed from the weapons chests. He and his men secured the prisoners from Loretto and gave succor to our own injured men. He looked at me and nodded.

"Too noisy, this fight," he said.

Regal, as it happened, had not intended to fire into us, but instead to rake the enemy—but some of their gun captains were too eager, and others were unable to get a proper view through their narrow gunports, and fired at the first thing they saw. Most of their ordnance was however discharged as intended into *Imperial*, and devastating as their attack was upon *King Emmius*, it was far worse on the enemy flagship. The large boarding party that had concentrated on their stern was shot to pieces and dispersed, and never could the officers assemble it again. *Regal* hauled its wind to swing alongside *Imperial*, lost way, and fell back, its stern coming aboard the enemy's aftercastle, where brave men lashed the ships together. *Regal*'s captain led boarders over the enemy's bulwarks and nearly captured the aftercastle before being mortally wounded, after which the boarders were driven back.

For myself I was renewing my vows never to again find myself on a bloody field. I put my sword in its scabbard, put away my pistol, and wandered forward to see what was afoot, and so I missed the intervention of *Epic*, Captain Elstree, a galleon of seven hundred tons, which shouldered its way into the fight, first scraping along *Emmius*'s stern, then *Imperial*'s, and then lodged its cathead into *Regal*'s quarter gallery, locking the ships together. Miraculously they did not fire a gun into us, or indeed into anyone.

What I felt was a lurch that almost knocked me off my feet, and then I heard sails booming overhead as they filled. In fair amazement I ran past the break of the quarterdeck into the light, looked up, and saw we were under way, plain sail filled. I made my way to back to the poop, where I found Coneygrave standing in a towering rage amid a vast litter of corpses and dismounted guns. *Imperial*, *Epic*, and *Regal*, viewed over the transom, were growing ever distant. A piece of our bulwark had ripped away, leaving jagged splinters, and it seemed that

Epic had delivered us a hard-enough blow that it had torn *Imperial*'s kedge anchor out of our side, and let us run free before the wind.

"Bring me back!" the Admiral shouted down to the quartermaster. He threw out his arm and pointed his baton in the direction of *Imperial*. "Bring me back to the enemy!"

"Helm won't answer, my lord!" called the quartermaster. I looked about for someone to interpret the Admiral's wishes, for Coneygrave's knowledge of seamanship was limited, Naylor was dead, and I did not see the sailing master, for Gladwell had been wounded and carried below, and even now was dying in the orlop.

"What's the matter with the helm?" I asked.

The quartermaster looked up at me. "I think the whipstaff is shot away below deck."

"Do we have a spare?"

"I believe we do, my lord, but I know not where the boatswain has stowed it."

"Send one of the timoneers to the boatswain and ask. In the meantime send a party to rig relieving tackles to the tiller head."

The timoneer was sent away, and I turned toward the Admiral and stepped toward him over the dead bodies lolling on the deck. Not all the bodies were from Duisland, and I concluded that the enemy had tried to board us but were beaten back, possibly with the aid of *Regal*'s broadside.

Coneygrave was in a tearing rage, storming up and down the deck, flailing his baton as if he were cudgeling an underling.

"Just when I had them!" he barked. "Just when we were going to board!"

I looked at the men standing on the poop, far too few to make up a boarding party, and wondered whether Coneygrave had lost his mind.

"The whipstaff is shot away," said I. "We can only run before the wind."

"Damn! Damn!" Coneygrave stamped on the deck in his fury.

"With your permission," said I, "I'll shorten sail, so we won't leave the battle entirely."

"They're going to say again that I'm craven!" stormed the Admiral. "They're going to say I ran away!"

"They shall not," said I. "When I report to the Queen, I shall make your courage clear."

For the first time he seemed to master his rage, and he turned to me and stared. "By the stones of the Pilgrim, Selford, you're covered in blood!" he said. "Where are you injured?"

"None of the blood is mine," said I. "It came to hand-strokes on the maindeck, but we drove them back."

"Good man," said he, and put a hand on my shoulder. "You will tell them I didn't run away? Truly?"

"I'll tell them you bore down on the enemy with a furious courage both mad and reckless," said I. Which was not precisely a compliment, but he beamed at me.

"Mightily do I thank you, Selford," said he.

"And in the meantime, rejoice," said I. "For you have won the most complete victory in the history of war."

I walked back to the break in the poop and considered the situation of the ship. Sails were punctured, and lines hung useless from the yards. I knew not how many of the topmen or the mast captains survived, so rather than reef the topsails, which would have sent parties aloft, I shortened sail without anyone leaving the deck, and so brailed in the lateen and bonaventure, and clewed up the topsails, which left us sailing under the spritsail alone. After that I sent all hands to mend and splice.

Once the relieving tackles were rove to the tiller-head, I was able to shift the rudder, and we came up onto a broad reach but could get no farther into the wind. It was then that I heard a rumble of gunfire, and turned to see the old *Princess Royal*, a veteran ship cut down into a razee, sailing up alongside *Imperial* and firing a salvo into her unengaged side, where *King Emmius* had lain twenty minutes before. *Princess Royal* lashed herself onto the three-ship platform, and sent her own men over the side.

By now *Imperial* was beaten half to pieces, its crew scattered and outnumbered, and in a hopeless situation. Yet its admiral fought on, and drove off three more attempts to board before some practical soul, seeing the source of the problem, fired a swivel gun at the enemy admiral and cut him in half, after which the survivors gave up the ship.

The other Lorettan ships had surrendered after token resistance, so we captured four warships. This put Coneygrave in a far better mood, as he would get one-eighth of the prize money, and with his share of the head money for the thousands of enemy lost in the Races, he would become fabulously wealthy.

The enemy commander was discovered to be the Conte de Cuerzy, a man with about as much experience of the sea as Coneygrave. Cuerzy's body was put in a cask of brandy, and he was taken to Bretlynton Head and buried there until the war's end, when his family could come to fetch him home.

King Emmius was too battered to stay with the fleet, and so it and other damaged ships would convoy our prizes to Bretlynton Head. With them went Robertson and the other pilot-fishermen, with more silver in their pockets than they would have earned in three years of plundering the Races for lobster and seaweed.

I offered Coneygrave the hospitality of my ship *Sovereign*. *Sovereign* was a high-charged galleon of eight hundred tons, grand enough for an admiral, and Coneygrave shifted his flag along with what was left of his staff. After our losses and detachments, we had thirty ships remaining, and these sailed around the Races at night, and arrived in the Bay of Melcaster at dawn, where we made a brave sight sailing to the relief of the besieged city. We anchored on the friendly side of the bay, away from Marshal Rutilan and his siege guns.

Rutilan knew of de Cuerzy's defeat, of course, for some of his outposts overlooked the Races and had seen the destruction of their fleet. Now it was clear that our ships had not been destroyed along with our enemies. Our arrival meant the end of Rutilan's campaign, for he was entirely supplied by sea, and now we had him blockaded. He had no choice but to burn his supply ships, abandon his heavy guns, and march east, toward his own country, and this he did at dawn the next day.

He would not have an easy march, for he would have to detour around Castras, still held by the Constable, and then attempt the mountain passes between Duisland and Loretto. He could not take the coast road, for he had not cleared the forts that barred his way, but would have to blaze his own road over the mountains, with the Constable's army harrying him the entire distance. He would be lucky to return with half his men.

I did not stay for the end of that campaign but sailed for Selford the next day in *Sovereign*. Coneygrave shifted his flag again and sailed on to Castras to consult with the Constable.

With me I carried Coneygrave's official dispatch and the tattered flag that had flown over *Imperial*'s poop. I had achieved the victory that Floria so badly needed to re-establish her supremacy in her own capital, and to drive off those irritants who would not cease their harping on the matter of marriage. For I intended that I should be the only man to ask for her hand, a hand I would set a-glitter with gems from my own coffers.

CHAPTER TWELVE

T he fine May weather ended a few days after the battle, and so we endured squalls and drenching as we fought headwinds in the Sea of Duisland, then at last came up the Saelle on a dark, rainswept afternoon, icy water sluicing in torrents from the sails, until we found our mooring off the royal dockyards at Innismore. My crooked little finger had ached for days.

Though the afternoon was miserable we did not go unnoticed, for we flew the flag of Duisland over the enemy banner taken from *Imperial*, and we fired signal guns as soon as we came within sight of the forts guarding the river's mouth. Word of a victory passed swiftly up the banks of the river, and when we arrived in Innismore the wharves were crowded with hopeful denizens of the town, all awaiting news of the victory.

"Well," said I, "if they are willing to come out in this weather, then let us tell them."

I stuffed the captured banner under my oilskins, and because my own galley had been shot to bits in the battle, we lowered a whaleboat, and I stepped into it along with Rufino Knott, Captain Gaunt of the

Sovereign, some of Gaunt's own men, the ship's trumpeter, and my boat's crew under Boatswain Lepalik. We rowed adjacent to one of the crowded wharves, and the trumpeter played my sennet before I rose from the stern sheets and spoke.

"Victory!" I called. "The enemy fleet of seventy ships was lured into the Races, caught in the great whirlpools, and destroyed, while their crews were drowned. Four ships escaped but were captured, including the enemy flagship! Three cheers for Her Majesty!"

I was startled by the thunderous rapture of the crowd, the three great roars that went out across the river to the opposite bank, and then reflected back so that I heard them, faintly, again.

"Marshal Rutilan is in retreat, pursued by the Constable!" I cried, for though I did not know for certain that this was true, I was confident that I did not lie. "More victories will come!" I promised, and then I signaled the boat to go on.

"Three cheers for Sir Quillifer!" called someone in the crowd, and the cheers roared out again. I rose again and waved my oilskin hat in answer.

I delivered the same message at each pier in Innismore, and though not all my listeners offered me three cheers, I did not hold it against them. Guns began to boom from Innismore's towers as the cannoneers announced the good news.

The boat's crew stretched out on their oars, and we shot upstream toward the capital while rain drummed on our oilskins. Just short of the great bridge to Mossthorpe I directed the boat to the Marygold Stairs on the Selford side of the river, and then blinked up in surprise as I saw a glittering assembly waiting for me, officers of the Yeoman Archers on horseback, lords and ladies of the court, and an ornamented carriage, half-covered in gold leaf, with the royal cipher on its mirror-polished door.

Guns were still booming as I disembarked, along with Captain Gaunt and Rufino Knott, and came up the broad wet stair. A footman opened the carriage door, and as Floria stepped out of her carriage I felt the blood rise hot in my veins. She had thrown back her cloak to reveal the ruby necklace of three strands that I had presented to her, and she wore a matching ruby carcanet about her throat. More gems winked from a tiara atop her unruly hair.

I bowed, and doffed my hat. Rain promptly pasted my hair to my forehead.

"Well met, my lord," said Floria. Her eyes were bright. "The sound of guns precedes you and tells me you have good news."

I took *Imperial*'s flag from beneath my oilskins and laid the great banner, ten yards long, at Floria's feet. The cobbles seemed to rise and pitch beneath me, for I had not yet recovered my land legs, and I hoped people would not think I was drunk.

"Admiral de Cuerzy's entire fleet is destroyed or taken, Majesty, every ship," said I. "Cuerzy died in the fighting, along with thirty thousand of the enemy. Melcaster is saved and Marshal Rutilan's army is in full retreat, with the Constable in pursuit."

A stir rustled through the crowd like a wind through autumn leaves. Floria's chin lifted as a triumphant smile played about her lips. She indicated her carriage. "Will you join me, Lord Selford?" she asked. "I would hear more of this."

"Of course, Majesty," said I. "But may I first introduce Captain Gaunt of Your Majesty's ship *Sovereign*?"

Gaunt bowed and snatched off his hat with a big hand, and otherwise stared dumbstruck. Floria nodded graciously at him. "We are always pleased to meet one of our brave officers," she said, and then she turned to enter her carriage. I walked across Loretto's fallen banner, leaving dark footprints, then entered the carriage and sat next to her. Raindrops hung in her hair like gems, and her galbanum scent drifted in the brisk air. A footman picked up de Cuerzy's flag and bundled it into the boot. A trumpet brayed, and someone called out, "Her Majesty goes forth!" which signaled the head of the column to ride on.

The carriage lurched into motion, and its iron-shod wheels thundered on the cobbles. "This news of yours is well timed, Quillifer," Floria said. "For it falls on the heels of a disaster."

"Admiral Mola?" I asked. "He's landed?"

"Ay," said she. "And in brief, Ferrick is lost, the Knight Marshal is killed, and Stanport is under siege, and is not like to hold out for long."

I took a long breath.

"Well," said I, "we need not concern ourselves with Rutilan and south Bonille till next year. All reinforcements intended for Melcaster and Bretlynton Head can be sent north, along with Coneygrave and the fleet—"

"Let us leave Mola and Stanport till tomorrow," Floria said. "I desire no serious business tonight, but only your company, and a joyous reunion."

I took her hand and kissed the soft slink lambskin gloves, then peeled the glove from her hand, turned it, and kissed her palm, and heard her sharp intake of breath. She drew the fingers of her other hand down my cheek, and I felt my body give a shudder all the way to my boots. She laid her head against mine, and I felt her warm breath on my ear.

"We must not go much farther along this path," said she, "for we are surrounded by half the court, and—"

"The curtains are drawn against the rain," said I, "and we are alone together, and together I think we might dare anything. But all I desire is to kiss your lips."

She gave me her lips, and the kiss went on for many minutes, as the carriage toiled up the bluff and turned onto Chancellery Road. The next few minutes were spent in arranging our clothing and hair and making ourselves presentable for the court.

"You smell much of tar," Floria observed.

"We saucy sailors do," I said. "I will have a bath brought up to my apartment before supper, and arrange a sweeter fragrance."

"The scent of tar is sweet enough," said she. "But I will not deprive you of a bath, if you have been so long without one."

The cavalcade passed through the gate and to the Outer Ward of the Castle, and servants with umbrellas flocked around us. Floria and I left the carriage, and I made sure to fetch de Cuerzy's flag from the boot. I thought if Floria didn't want it, I might display it at Haysfield Grange.

We led the procession to the Inner Ward, where Floria bade the Castle's guns fire a salute, and its bell rung, to alert the town to our victory. She arranged also for heralds to be sent to all the town's squares and parks to announce the victory of the Races.

"For Loretto's triumphs have made it hard here," Floria said, as we walked along the gallery above the courtyard, "and all the court thinks that if I only marry, the war will somehow be won. All I hear is wed, wed, wed, like a flock of popinjays calling one after the next."

"You should marry the author of a victory," said I.

"The author should not smell of tar," said Floria. "I will leave you to your bath, and see you at supper."

I went to my apartment and sent for a portable canvas bathtub and buckets of hot water brought up from the kitchen. Maidservants with those buckets were waiting their turn in the corridor when Rufino Knott arrived with porters who carried my sea-chest, my weapons and armor, and my guitar. In short order my apartment became very crowded, and after Knott had stowed my clothes and armor in the wardrobe, I gave the porters their fee and told Knott he was free till the morning.

"You may premiere your ballad if you are so inclined," I said. "And before you go, lay out a suit for the evening."

Then, after the maidservants walked in one after the next to fill the bathtub, I gave them some silver, poured lilac-scented oil into the bathwater, and fetched some soap. I treated myself to a long soak, and then did my best to scrub the sea from my skin, and to don the manners of a courtier.

I dressed in the russet suit that Knott had laid out for me, then summoned the maidservants to carry away the water and the folding tub. At least they didn't need to carry the water back to the kitchen, but hurled it from the gallery into the courtyard, where it joined the rainwater in forming the small lakes that shimmered over the cobbles.

I noticed that my little silver clock had run down, and I wound it again and set it by the chimes of the great castle clock. I put on my rings and my chain of office, then made my way to the lobby outside the banqueting hall, where courtiers waited for the Queen to arrive for her supper. I saw Lord Hunstan Wilmot loitering just outside the door, his head bowed deep in thought, and I approached him. So deep were his introspections that he gave a start as he saw me, and then bowed.

"My lord," he said. "Please accept my congratulations on the great victory in the Races."

"I thank you," said I. "Though I must give due credit to the tide, which performed as anticipated."

He offered a laugh. "A half hour ago I heard your Master Knott sing a ballad about the battle."

"Did you?" I affected surprise. "Was I featured in the song?"

Hunstan laughed again. "I believe I heard your name once or twice."

Knott had writ the ballad on the journey home, and I helped now and again with the text. I wished my part in the battle known, since full credit might fall entirely on the Lord Admiral, who after all commanded the fleet. Yet I did not wish to offend Coneygrave by praising myself overmuch, and so I commended the Admiral's courage in charging the *Imperial* with his own flagship, and managed to imply that he had boarded *Imperial* and captured it himself. I had promised Coneygrave that I would testify to his bravery, and so I had.

Within the next few days, the text would be sent to a printer's, and it would be available as a broadsheet ballad. The tune was an old favorite known to all, "The Fragrance of the Roses, O," and so folk would be able to learn it quickly, and I trusted that ere long the entire kingdom would be singing the praises of Coneygrave, of myself, and of the Queen, who had the wisdom to send me forth with my special commission.

The song would brighten and cheer the entire nation, or so I surmised.

"And you, Lord Hunstan?" I asked. "Will we soon be making ballads about your adventures?"

He shook his blond head. "I have had no adventures."

"Fie, you disappoint me. You have had Mistress Candice to yourself while I was away, and you have not taken advantage of my absence?"

He reddened, then looked up at me. "You truly have no interest in this lady?"

"I have great regard for her," said I, "but I would not stand in the way of her happiness."

Hunstan looked over his shoulder to make certain no one overheard. "Ay, well," said he. "We wish to marry, but her father intends her for you, and would never give his permission."

"Then you must fly together," I said. "But if you are to elope, you must do it in accordance with the law, to make certain that what is done may not be undone."

He spread his hands. "What must we do, then? One hears stories of matches made and broken, but they are mere stories, and I dare not consult a lawyer, not when her father is head of the judiciary."

"It is fortunate then that I trained as a lawyer," said I. I leaned close and spoke privately into his ear. "Candice is not yet twenty-one, and may not marry without her father's permission. Yet these stric- tures are broken often enough, and matter less if everything else is done according to form."

He regarded me with great seriousness. "You must give her a ring," said I. "There is a tradition that a straw ring will do, but I think one less ephemeral is better in law."

"I can afford a golden ring," he muttered.

"Of course," said I. "You must plight your troth to one another, promise to love and honor and so on—simple language is best—and you must do these things before witnesses—at least two. You may bring friends to witness for you. And the wedding should then be recorded in the ledgers of a magistrate."

"Where do I find such a magistrate?"

"You hunt a magistrate with baits of silver. When I was in Blacksykes with Utterback's Troop, I was given to understand that many in that vicinity of Blacksykes are amenable. Some even hang out signs."

Again Hunstan cast a look over his shoulder. "And the anvil priests of which I hear?"

I was amused. "It is a quaint belief in the country that blacksmiths may perform marriages, for through their art they are able to forge the links of love. You may be surprised to discover that this is true, for in law blacksmiths *can* perform marriages—but then so can any- one regardless of profession. The law is most liberal in this regard, though I would advise finding a justice of the peace or a county clerk, and have the ceremony properly recorded."

"And then?"

"And then you spend a blissful night in each other's arms, after which you beg forgiveness from your parents."

"Ay, well." His eyebrows went up. "My own father may forgive me, I hope, for failing to marry the Queen, but Thistlegorm has a sterner spirit."

"Yet he loves his daughter dearly," said I, though privately I added, *though not as much as thirty thousand royals.*

"There is a man named Greenaway," I said, "who owns a stables over the bridge in Mossthorpe, and he is most discreet. He will rent you a carriage with a good team, and you will be away to Blacksykes to make your escape before you are missed in Selford."

Hunstan's eyes tracked over my shoulder. "Ah. Here is the great lord himself."

A party all in white had appeared, Thistlegorm and his two daughters. "I must offer my respects," said I. "But remember Greenaway's stables in Mossthorpe." I then went to greet the great Retriever.

Thistlegorm was in a merry, bustling mood. "Lord and Lady Edevane are dead, hanged along with their accomplices," said he. "Travers had the trials finished before your ship left port."

"There was little to do but put the confessions in the record," said I.

"Edevane's was a popular hanging." Warm satisfaction rose from Thistlegorm. "Thousands came to watch him twitch at the end of the silken cord. He tried to make a final address, but the crowd jeered so loudly that he could not be heard."

"I can guess what he said," said I. "Treachery justified by the necessities of state. It was ever his refrain."

"He will commit no more treacheries," Thistlegorm said. "It was a good day's work for the hangman. And—oh, have you heard?—we have laid hands on Brian Gordon, the apprentice lawyer who served as an agent for Lady Edevane in hiring the assassins. He had fled to Aberuvon, where he tried to get a ship to take him abroad, but the captain was suspicious and turned him over to the bailiffs."

Edevane could hardly expect mercy from the man from whom he had extorted thirty thousand royals, but I thought Thistlegorm's gloating was not edifying for the two ladies. I turned to the younger of the two.

"And how fares Mistress Emily?" I asked.

"Excellent well!" said she in a shrill burst of happiness. "There will be a play at court tomorrow!"

"The Roundsilver Company?"

"Yes. *Two Gentlemen of the North*, a comedy."

"Ah yes. I remember Master Blackwell mentioned the play."

"I hope you will arrange for me to speak to Bonny Joe again."

"I will do my best." I turned to Candice. "I hope you are enjoying the season, mistress."

"I have taken pleasure in the company of my friends," said she, and I guessed that most of the pleasure came from one friend in particular. And then she exchanged a look with her father, and I suppose received her cue, so she looked back at me and recited the lines he had doubtless prepared for her. "We were surprised at your absence, my lord. You had not warned us that you would join Admiral Coneygrave in pursuit of the enemy."

"We had only just discovered where that enemy was," said I. "And once the enemy was discovered, we had to sail at once. Yet I apologize for not sending you a note before I left."

"Yet you have brought us a victory!" Thistlegorm said. "That is the best message we could expect!"

"I trust this victory is the first of many," said I, hardly for the last time. "Once we are secure in our naval superiority, Admiral Mola can hardly keep his forces in our country."

Doors boomed open, and Floria entered, followed by a wedge of her ladies all in purfles, petticoats, and lace. She stopped to speak with a group of gentlemen, and then I noticed the tall figure of the Marquess of Morestanton stroll past me in a velvet suit of buttercup yellow that made him look like a walking aspen tree. He was intent on worming himself as near to the Queen as possible, and now that I had returned to Selford, I intended to maintain that position for myself.

"Morestanton!" said I. He turned in some surprise.

"Selford!" said he. "Welcome again to the capital."

"I thank you," said I, "but I am surprised to see you here. I had thought your troop would have departed for Bonille."

"Sadly," said he, "we have not yet made up our numbers."

"You can make up your numbers in Bonille as well as here," said I. "And the need for your demilances there is greater."

"It is not for me to decide," he said. And at that point Lady Holdsworth, one of the Queen's ladies, came up to me and spoke in my ear. "Her Majesty invites you to take her in to supper," she said.

"I would be honored to do so," I said. I bade farewell to Morestanton and the Thistlegorm family, and followed Lady Holdsworth to Floria's side.

Suppers in the Castle were less formal than dinners, for there was no audience of gawpers in the gallery, and thus less need to display magnificence. But still there was magnificence in plenty, and a good deal of jostling as the nobility sorted themselves out in order of precedence. I never understood why this always took so long, since they all had such practice at it.

During supper I did most of the talking, which perhaps was not unusual, but the novelty was that no one seemed to resent it. I gave a report verbal on the Battle of the Races, and besides a few questions and some exclamations and sighs of pity for the wounded or slain, I held center stage as if I were an actor delivering a soliloquy.

"I wonder, Selford," the Queen said at the end. "Was Coneygrave's attack upon the enemy flagship entirely necessary?"

"His blood was up," I said. "And I think he was too sensitive to the accusations that have been made against him, claiming an absence of courage when he was only obeying Your Majesty's commands not to risk his ships."

She frowned at me. "Your answer is judicious, Selford."

I reached for a glass of wine. "I have had time to consider it. The Lord Admiral is a brave commander, and you will find no one braver."

"But wiser?"

I offered a smile. "No wise man goes to war," said I.

Because I had done so much talking, I'd had very little time for eating, which I found a shame, because it had been a long time since breakfast and my stomach was growling like a battery of cannon-drakes. When the meal ended I put a lamb pie in one of my pockets, some sausages in another, and carried away an almond tart in a napkin.

I did not stay for the usual castle entertainments of cards and dice but went to my apartment, where I lit a fire, ate my cold supper, drank a cup of wine, and changed into my dressing gown. The air still wafted a memory of my lilac-scented bath. I made myself comfortable on the settee and closed my eyes, and immediately felt the deck rise and fall below me. I think I probably drowsed a little, and I remember with great clarity that I felt the castle swing to a shifting tide. Then I heard Floria's dressing gown rustle in the secret corridor, and I opened my eyes to see the door swing noiselessly open, and Her Majesty enter. I rose to greet her.

"The tide just changed," I said, "and the weather will be fair tomorrow."

"I suppose you are expert on the subject of tides," said Floria. "But how do you know the weather will change? It's still beating down rain."

I held up my crooked little finger. "My finger has stopped aching."

"Ah," she said. "Your finger of divination. I had forgot."

She stepped into the circle of my arms, and I kissed her warm lips for a long, exalted moment. "I was wrong," said I, "for the weather has turned fair sooner than I predicted."

"Then I will hardly need this," Floria said, and let her dressing gown fall from her shoulders, revealing herself clad only in her stockings, high-heeled slippers with bows, and my three-strand ruby necklace.

For a long moment I stared, overcome, and then she gave me a challenging look.

"Well, Quillifer," said she. "Don't you know how to keep your Queen warm?"

"I believe I do," said I, and swept her up in my arms.

CHAPTER THIRTEEN

I n the morning I gave Coneygrave's official report to Floria, after I had unpacked it from my sea-chest. I asked her for the reports made of Mola's fight for Ferrick and the siege of Stanport, and she said she would send them. Then I kissed her in such a way, I hoped, that implies many more such kisses would be forthcoming, after which she went up the passage to her room.

The reports came as I was putting on the clothes that Rufino Knott had just laid out for me. I read them over breakfast, and learned of the catastrophe that had befallen Knight Marshal Emerick and his army.

Admiral Mola had landed his army on the coast between Ferrick and Stanport, and Emerick, who, like Constable Scutterfield, did not want an enemy army in his rear, at once marched his forces over the Long Bridge from Ferrick and toward the landing-grounds. He reasoned that Mola, with the ships available to him, couldn't possibly have landed all his eighteen thousand soldiers in the time allotted, and that Emerick with his eleven thousand had a chance of an engagement on equal terms. Nor did he, like the Constable, fall into any trap—in fact his calculations proved correct, and he successfully brought Mola to battle on equal terms.

The left of our army was commanded by my old enemy the Marquess of Stayne, and he successfully routed Mola's right after a ferocious charge. He pursued the fleeing enemy as far as the enemy camp, which he then stormed and looted.

The other two-thirds of our army was thrown back and routed in its turn, and streamed back to Ferrick, where they crowded onto the Long Bridge only to discover that the city's leaders had locked the gates against them. The result was a slaughter, six or eight thousand helpless men crowded together on the bridge and butchered. A few saved themselves by leaping into the river, but hundreds more leaped only to drown. The Knight Marshal was hacked down with the rest.

As far as the invaders were concerned, we were a nation of traitors to our rightful King Aguila, and our soldiers deserved nothing but a traitor's death.

Ferrick's mayor and council, having doomed their defenders, then sent an emissary to Admiral Mola and offered to surrender the city on terms, terms which the admiral happily accepted. The gates that had stood firm against our own army were opened to the invader.

I thought that there had been a good deal of silver distributed among the aldermen of Ferrick in order to procure this result, and I swore an oath to myself that there would be a reckoning.

After some hours of looting and debauch at the enemy camp, the Marquess of Stayne bethought himself to wonder what had become of the rest of our army, and discovered that we had suffered a massive defeat. Though it took him an hour or two to get his drunken soldiery under orders again—Mola was busy with his massacre and gave him the time—Stayne, perceiving the day was lost, formed up his command and marched them off to Stanport along with their loot.

Stayne placed himself in command in that city, and busied himself with its defenses. Mola's army did not appear for five days, and his siege guns for another three; but now all were present, and Stayne was calling for aid.

I reckoned Mola was more hindered by the country than by Stayne. I had been to Stanport and knew that, like most towns on the north coast of Bonille, it was built on the largest piece of solid land in the district, and was surrounded by rivers, marshes, runlets, and canals. Mola would have to find solid ground to mount his siege guns, or build it somehow. He had not managed to encircle the city, but kept his forces on the firmer ground to the east, with the soldiers on his left creeping around the city from one watercourse to the next while building causeways to march upon. In the meantime we could move supplies and reinforcements into the city by boat, and carry out those who could not fight.

But still Mola had superior guns and superior numbers, and however hampered he was by the country, he would sooner or later bring his forces to bear, and then the enemy works would grow closer to the defenses hour by hour, while the siege gun pounded the city walls to rubble.

Later that morning, at ten o'clock, was a meeting of the Privy Council. Floria had transformed into that semi-divine embodiment of Monarchy, her gown and jewels a-shine in the light of the clerestory, her face and hands an opalescent shimmer beneath the arms of Duisland. She wore the three-strand ruby necklace, and I sat next to her, the better to make my report of the Battle of the Races. But first she handed Admiral Coneygrave's report to me, and asked me to read it aloud.

This I did, and I found the report more flattering to me than I had expected. Not only did the Admiral credit me with the plan for drawing the enemy fleet onto the rocks, but also praised my courage in fighting the enemy's attempt to board *Emmius* over the stern gallery. Coneygrave might have had just cause to resent my presence on his flagship, but victory had made him generous—and it is more than possible that he calculated that flattering the royal favorite might win him some royal favor for himself.

Coneygrave dwelled overmuch on those elements of the battle that involved fighting and which reflected well on his courage, but he praised others as well, and his list of officers deserving of commendation was a long one.

I put the report on the table. "I feel now that my own report would be superfluous," I said.

"And most of us heard it yesterday," said Sandicup, the Exchequer.

Roundsilver raised a gemmed, glittering hand. "Where is the fleet now?"

"Admiral Coneygrave intended to work with the Constable to savage Rutilan's retreating army. He told me that if circumstances then permitted, he would embark as many soldiers as he could and make an attempt to take Perpizon by storm."

Perpizon was the harbor and storehouse of the Occidental Fleet, and to pillage the place would supply our own fleet for a year.

"What do you reckon are his chances?" asked Duke Chelmy.

"The enemy are overstrained everywhere," said I. "Perpizon is well fortified, but the defenders are not of the best quality, and if we are in luck the city may fall."

Sandicup stroked his red beard. "Should the fleet not be deployed north, against Mola?"

Floria answered him. "That is what this council must decide."

It did not surprise that the council decided nothing. Baron Berardinis of Longfirth, who had held that city against Clayborne's rebels, was ordered to the winter capital of Howel to hold it against Mola. Orders were given to send reinforcements to Stanport, but no one knew whether the city might fall before they arrived. A message would be sent to the Lord Admiral telling him that if the Perpizon expedition proved impractical, he was to take the fleet to Selford for resupply, and then prepare to sail north to confront Mola.

Even these vague commands were argued back and forth by all the members in council. The only thing on which we could all agree was that a commendation should be sent to Coneygrave and the fleet, and that bells should be rung throughout the kingdom in celebration of the victory at the Races, and Coneygrave's report published and sent to every town in the realm. Floria announced her decision to raise Coneygrave from baron to the rank of count, and this was well received by all save by Scarnside, for whom his own rank of baron was the epitome of all splendor.

There followed dinner, where all our differences of opinion were given another airing, after which I crossed to the Secretariat with the intention of reviewing the last weeks' correspondence. Outside my door I found my old schoolfriend Theophrastus Hastings reclining on a bench, his blond head pillowed on his hands, his eyes closed. As I approached I kicked his boots off the bench and waited for him to come to his senses.

He slowly opened his eyes and blinked at me. "Ah," he said. "I heard you were back."

"And you have returned as well," said I. "Assuming of course that you ever reached Basilicotto."

"Ay, I traveled there, and I ordered your fricandoes for you." He shook his handsome head. "Yet I am blest if I understand what any of that was about."

"Did you deliver my message?"

He yawned. "Oh ay, a fellow came up to me on the street and asked me what I wanted, so I reckoned he was the man I was supposed to meet, and I gave him your letter. He seemed a little surprised to receive anything in writing, but he carried away the letter, and I waited another two nights to see if there was a reply, and then came home. We made good time until we met those squalls, and then I was sick as a dog until I arrived two days ago."

"You and your bilious stomach have my sympathy," said I. "I hope to hear more of your journey, but I have other business now. You may go to the house of your mistress, and sleep in a real bed."

Again he yawned. "We do not do much sleeping in that bed. When all is said, Elsie is a demanding woman."

"Go then and submit to her demands. I have work to do."

I went into my office and asked for Jeronimy Bledso. Bledso arrived half a minute later, with arms full of papers.

"Have you found the charter from King Emelin to Prince Amadeu?" asked I.

"Nay," said he. "If we ever had it, it's gone or has been so mislaid that it will never be found. But I have found much else concerning those coombs, and I have the files here."

The files went back generations, correspondence written on old, crumbling paper, the seals fallen away or illegible, but over the decades the substance followed more or less the same form. One or another of Amadeu's ancestors complained to the crown of their lands being raided and plundered by their human neighbors. Some of them accused Catsgore's ancestors as the inciters of these attacks, and some were more discreet.

Always the monarch did his duty, and wrote to the lord lieutenant or the sheriff asking for an investigation—and always the lord lieutenant or the sheriff would respond, writing that the malefactors had been caught and hanged. But over time the boundaries of the disputes seemed to creep from one green valley to the next—in the early days the dispute was over the Vale of Brenmore, and then Brenmore and the Coomb of Hario, and then Hario alone, until it became Hario and Aekora, and now Aekora and Orkiola. I remembered Catsgore saying that Brenmore and Hario had been in possession of his family for generations, and now it was clear how he had obtained that possession, and how the course of justice in the Western Range had been corrupted.

I wondered if anyone had ever examined this entire correspondence in this way, and I thought no one had. Taken together, they formed a convincing indictment.

"Master Bledso," I said, "have you found any archivist who has discovered an unexpected trove of money?"

"Nay, I have not."

"There is no scrivener who has come into an inheritance from an uncle, or a librarian who's become lucky at dice?"

"Nay, my lord. And I have made it my business to look."

I considered the files before me. "It concerns me that one of my underlings is corruptible," said I, "and that documents may vanish to the benefit of some courtier or other."

"Truly it is distressing, my lord."

I closed the files. "Well, Master Bledso, I hope we may howster this fellow out."

I put the files into the strongbox built into my office wall, then applied myself to more of my correspondence. There was an invitation to a gathering at His Grace of Pontkyles's country house, which was not surprising even though Pontkyles hated me. The entire court would be invited whether Pontkyles hated them or not. The invitation was dated a week earlier, and the party would be the day after tomorrow. I wrote a message accepting, and sent it to Pontkyles by a page.

I then applied myself to the report I had asked Alaron Mountmirail to deliver to me on the subject of mining silver. I read this with interest, then crossed to the castle again to view *Two Gentlemen of the North*.

In the courtyard of the Inner Ward, Rufino Knott entertained people with his ballad of the Battle of the Races. As I walked beneath the bright May sun and entered the Great Reception Room, the drop in temperature was immediate, and I do not speak figuratively, for the Reception Room was always chill, even in midsummer. The presence of Ambassador Gandorim did not warm my heart, though I bowed when he smiled and approached me.

"It was a brilliant victory at the Races, my lord," said the *duque* in his pleasant voice. "And I understand that you had a great part in it, and that the Lord Admiral himself acknowledged both your contribution and your valor."

"The Lord Admiral was very kind," said I. "And now, should your King Anibal find himself at war with our ancient enemy, he will find that his navy may plunder the enemy's coasts without opposition."

"For that I thank you," said Gandorim. "And—should His Majesty enter the war—some suitable reward might be found for you. His Majesty might find for you a peerage, and an estate of a size and income to support the dignity of a peer."

He had progressed beyond offering me women, it seemed.

"His Majesty has the reputation of a generous prince," said I.

Which, for all I knew, might be true.

"King Anibal knows the hearts of men," said Gandorim, "and is clear-sighted in matters of statecraft. He knows that it is unwise to enter a military alliance without certain guarantees."

"Ay," said I, "that is wisdom truly." I waved a hand in the direction of the gilded chair from which Queen Floria would view the play. "But what guarantees are necessary beyond the word of another monarch, one stainless, without reproach, and equally farsighted?"

I enlarged upon my theme. "Does King Anibal fear we will leave the war and leave him to fight on alone? Nay—it cannot happen. For there will be war between Her Majesty and King Aguila forever. I can imagine Loretto giving up a city, or three cities, or six, but I cannot imagine Loretto forsaking their claim upon Duisland as long as Aguila and his heirs draw breath." I turned to Gandorim.

"Come," I said. "Let us make our alliance now. You say that Anibal will bring fifty thousand valiant men of Varcellos into the field. Loretto has stripped the garrisons on your frontier in order to fight us, and those soldiers will not be coming back, for they drowned in the Races. The cities are open to you. Your fleet will sail unopposed. Surely such a wise king as Anibal will not let this moment pass."

I saw a flicker in his brown eyes, as he considered a reasoned response; but there was no reasoned response that would achieve his objective, and so he bowed. "I must write to my king for instructions."

I bowed in my turn. "We shall await His Majesty's reply."

At this point Thistlegorm and his daughters appeared at my side, and I welcomed them as a relief from Gandorim. Thistlegorm was avuncular, Emily was ecstatic at the prospect of again meeting Bonny Joe Webb, and Candice spoke hardly at all. Clearly nothing had changed in my absence. I wished to get Candice alone in order to encourage her to elope with Lord Hunstan Wilmot, but I was unable to think of a way to separate her from her family.

A sennet sang out from the gallery, and Floria entered at the head of a brilliant, glittering wedge of her ladies. I excused myself and went to stand by the platform on which Her Majesty would sit, and as she approached I bowed and helped her rise to her gilded chair. She asked me to sit on her right hand, and Roundsilver and his lady sat on her left. On my own right was Fulvius, the Philosopher Transterrene.

In a low voice I related the substance of my conversation with Gandorim. "Now we shall see what Anibal really wants," said I. "If it is the lost cities back, they will strike now. If an alliance in which we agree to do all the fighting while they reap the rewards, Anibal will not budge."

She raised an eyebrow. "And if they want their provinces above everything else, they may not want my hand?"

"All worthy men do," said I. "I thought that went without saying."

Floria tapped her chin with the tip of her fan. "We know exactly what Varcellos wants," said Floria. "The question is whether to give it to them."

"If Varcellos does not attack," said I, "then they are worthless, and they may be left out of our calculations entirely. It is too reminiscent of how Prince Priscus promised your sister to bring soldiers over the mountains to fight against Clayborne's rebellion, and then did nothing—but she married him anyway, and laid the foundations for our present conflict."

"I am sick of this matter being hashed and chopped about," Floria said. "The argument is not between kings; it is between your Varcellos, Scarnside's Varcellos, Gandorim's Varcellos, and Sandicup's Varcellos, all of which are at quarrel with one another, and none of which exist."

"My apologies, Majesty."

"Pray find a more agreeable topic of conversation."

"As Your Majesty pleases," said I. "Do you think there will be sufficient diverting pastimes at Pontkyles's gathering?"

"There will be a fox hunt. That is sufficiently diverting."

"Dare I ride with the hunt?" I asked. "Or will Pontkyles try to run me down again?"

Vexation tugged at the corners of her mouth. "Quillifer," she said, "I have made my feelings known to him."

"Well," I said, "I shall ride, and take my chances."

It seemed impossible to please Floria this afternoon, and so I turned to Abbot Fulvius and asked if he was working on a new book. He replied that he was, and that it would be titled *Exegeses on Certain Aspects of the Doctrine of the Compassionate Pilgrim, with Reference to Noted Philosophers of All Times and All Places.*

"It sounds fascinating," said I. "I hope you will send me a copy."

"I will be delighted to do so," he said. He began by way of demonstration to offer his opinion on the Fiat of Abbot Reynaldo, but thankfully this and his other *Exegeses* remained unrevealed, for at that moment the trumpet played another sennet, and Master Blackwell stepped onto the stage to offer Floria the usual laudatory prologue. In addition to enumerating the Queen's virtues, I was pleased that the prologue mentioned the great victory at the Races, and that this generated great applause, though I was to a degree disappointed that my name was not mentioned.

The play went forward, and I was not surprised that it involved two gentlemen of the north, neither of whom was played by Wakelyn. The northern worthies traveled to Selford to seek their fortunes, and instead encountered two ladies from Selford, along with comic misunderstandings and misadventure. Lexter, who for so long had played second to Wakelyn, was now lead ingenue, and raised more than his share of laughter. He was seconded by Blackwell himself in the role of the second ingenue, and Blackwell acquitted himself well, though his northern accent was wont to stray into more familiar channels.

Bonny Joe Webb played of course the lead female ingenue, who pleased his audience by disguising himself as a boy for much of the play, for singing a song, and leading the others in a dance. Blackwell knew to give his most popular actor a stellar scene in his every play, for he knew that many patrons parted with their pennies in order to watch Bonny Joe work his magic.

The story featured a love letter that went astray and was passed to a different wrong person in scene after scene, wafting its way through every act until it finally lodged with the right recipient, after which the plot was resolved with some affecting love poetry and a pair of weddings.

I watched as the letter passed from hand to hand, and of a sudden I experienced a revelation fully as astonishing as that of the Pilgrim.

Ah, thought I, *now I know.*

But now that I knew, I had to work out what to do, and how to do it.

After the performance I complimented Blackwell on the success of his play. "Fortunately it was at the copyist's when Wakelyn stole my papers," he said, "otherwise the play would be his triumph, and not mine."

"Has Master Wakelyn yet formed his company?"

"Oh, ay." Blackwell snarled. "He has found a rich patron, and his company will be known as Sandicup's Players."

I considered this development. "Does Sandicup know that Wakelyn is presenting stolen work?"

"His Grace of Roundsilver so informed him, but Sandicup says he knows nothing of it. Next week his players will present *Ethlebight Aveng'd* at the Old Mill in Mossthorpe."

"I have heard you speak of that play for years," said I. "Everyone knows it is yours." For I had inadvertently inspired the play on the first occasion I met Blackwell, when I had told him of Ethlebight's sack, and of my hope for somehow avenging myself on the reivers. But I was not a spy or an assassin, and had few skills likely to harm ravagers who lived far away. Ere long I was caught up in the doings of the court and proved myself a poor avenger in the years since, but Blackwell's hero would succeed in assassinating the reivers' admiral before dying in a blizzard of pentameter.

"I think Wakelyn's premiere should meet with the reception it deserves," said I, "and perhaps the two of us can work out how to do it."

CHAPTER FOURTEEN

"The Council meeting this morning was tedious as ever," said Floria.

"The meeting sufficed to point out the necessity of trusting the management of the war to a single person," I said.

"I thought *I* was that single person," said Floria.

"Your Majesty has much other business to distract you."

She held out her crystal goblet. "Pour me more distraction, then."

I reached for the flagon and filled Floria's goblet with golden moscato. She drank, then regarded me with narrowed eyes.

"You seek another office, Quillifer?" asked she. "The Queen's Captain-General?"

"I already have all the necessary information," said I. "It is a matter of bringing it all together and taking action."

She sighed. "I suppose your success in the Races has given you visions of commanding in the field and driving Mola from his siege camps."

"I have no wish to command an army," I said. "The action at the Races reminded me how unpleasant a battle can be. I understand ships and cargoes. Were I to receive the commission, I would occupy myself with sending troops, supplies, ships, and guns to where they are most needed. Let those who desire glory on the battlefield have that glory, for I desire never to leave your side again."

"I prefer you in your current office."

I shook my head. "It is discouraging to deal daily with treachery, double-dealing, conspiracy, and the sweet rosy arbors built to conceal the cesspits of ambition. I prefer to leave before I lose every last happy illusion."

"Treachery, double-dealing, and conspiracy," Floria said. "Welcome to life at court, Quillifer. Did you think you can escape any of that by changing office?"

We were in my apartment, Floria on the settee, and I sitting on cushions at her feet. She wore her satin dressing gown open to reveal a gown of sarcenet fine as spider-silk and pale and transparent as a wisp of morning mist, embroidered at neck and hem by seed-pearls. Her galbanum scent mingled with the sweet bouquet of the moscato and the earthy odors of our mutual pleasure. We had already engaged in a rather complicated embrace that evening (I know how interested you are in these things), and now we talked and sipped moscato while readying ourselves for another engagement.

You might find this an unusual conversation for a tryst. Yet you have not lived at court, where politicians find the subject of office the most stimulating of all.

"This matter of Catsgore, for example," said I. "It is as clear a case of robbery with violence and murder as can be made, yet Catsgore is entitled to a trial by the Peers, and never will Peers find Peers guilty if they can help it."

Her birdlike glance darted to me. "Have you found King Emelin's charter?"

"I have not. I think it was stolen. But I have read correspondence dating nearly three hundred years showing a pattern of usurpation and corruption of justice as plain as the back of my hand, more than enough to hang them all, back twelve generations or more—if only they were not members of the peerage."

A frown furrowed her brows. "How many votes does Catsgore command?"

"In the Peers and Burgesses both? Enough to make him necessary. I might suggest buying his friends away from him, but those western men are clannish and not so easily swayed."

"What would you suggest, then?"

"Let me speak to Prince Amadeu," said I, "and then I will see if my solution is even possible."

I took her feet, placed them in my lap, and began to stroke her legs. Floria took a sip of wine, then tilted her head back and sighed.

"This is why I need you in your current office," said the Queen. "You find things out, and you offer remedies. For most, the only remedy they can suggest is that they be appointed to some bureau with a fine salary and a thousand perquisites."

I kissed her knee. "You are the only perquisite I desire," I said.

"Ah," said she, and gave me such a direct look from those hazel eyes as to bring a shiver up my back. She raised her glass goblet and swirled the golden liquid within. "I am inclined to grant you this perquisite," she smiled, "so you fill my cup again, and slowly, that not an ounce of its gratifying savor escapes me."

First thing the next morning I wrote to Prince Amadeu, asking leave to call upon him, then went to the Secretariat to hear a report from Judge Travers, who had taken my place in the time I was away. I made him comfortable in a leather armchair, and sent away for sauternes.

"There was one matter only worthy of your lordship's attention," said he. "Customs arrested a man at the Innismore docks with two large trunks full of pamphlets blackguarding the Queen—and yourself, of course."

"Her Majesty and I seem fated to be blackguarded together. Who is this man?"

"He is from Durba, and so far has refused to name the person to whom he was supposed to deliver the papers. I have put him in a cell at Hall of Justice, and I've put one of my own men in the next cell, supposedly on a similar charge. There is a chink through which they may communicate, and I hope my man will convince the messenger from Durba to talk freely to his new friend, and confide the information we want."

I was impressed by this stratagem, and was relieved that the instruments in the undercroft of the Siege Royal would not be called upon.

"Very ingenious," said I. "Would you like to remain in charge of this investigation, or shall I have your fellow report to me?"

"I am willing to continue," Travers said. "I seem to have no other occupation at present."

Which meant, I imagine, that he still hoped for appointment. "I have recommended you to Her Majesty," said I, "and now I will have another reason to bring you to Her Majesty's attention."

Travers bowed his venerable head. "I thank your lordship."

"Do you have copies of these pamphlets?"

He handed them to me. One branded me a sorcerer who had bewitched the Queen into treason against the lawful king, and the other referred to Floria as a depraved vixen infamous for her licentiousness, while I served as her lover and procurer.

"Perhaps we are fortunate that our enemies lack imagination," I said. "I could have libeled myself much more effectively."

Travers departed, and I occupied myself with correspondence until a note came from Amadeu inviting me to his lodging at midafternoon. After another of those castle dinners, with a gallery of gawkers watching my every mouthful, I called for my carriage.

Amadeu had taken a large brick house across the park from the much larger palace of the Duke of Roundsilver. The house had octagonal turrets on each corner, and terra-cotta busts of gods and heroes inset into the facade. The weathered shield of a half-forgotten noble family perched over the entrance. A pair of Amadeu's gentlemen waited outside for me, and very civilly conducted me to the prince's study. High windows of painted glass bathed the room in bright hues. I crossed the creaking herringbone floor and bowed to His Serene Highness, then was asked to sit. I was offered food and wine, but I'd just had dinner, so I accepted only a glass of stepony. We both sat on straight-backed armchairs, with a small round marble-topped table between us. Several of his gentlemen loitered in the corners and pretended they weren't listening.

"Congratulations, Lord Selford, on your part in the Battle of the Races," Amadeu began. "I am not a sailor, but I understand you did something remarkable."

"It was a miracle brought about by a handful of fishermen from Dunnock," said I, "and their names will never appear in any history."

"Insofar as I understand history," said the prince, "it exists to glorify great men, and occasionally women, and to exalt the nation while explaining away its faults and failures. Which accounts for the difference between your people's history and mine."

I sipped my stepony, and let the tang of lemon freshen my palate. "I have found some of your history in the Archives," said I, "and it supports your own narrative."

"You found the charter?"

"Nay," said I, "I believe someone has taken it. But I have seen correspondence between the crown, your ancestors, and royal servants, and it is clear that a subversion of justice has taken place."

"Ah." His dark eyes glittered, and he leaned toward me. "Tell me, what will be done about that?"

"Most of the usurpations occurred before either of us were born. It is impossible to prosecute people who are dead."

"But my land," said he, "and that of my people. Can it be returned?"

"Ay, but you will have to make use of the courts, and it will take many years, and cost a deal of money. Fortunately the Lord Chamberlain is in need of funds."

"Cannot the other side bribe as well?"

I smiled at Amadeu's pragmatic approach to justice. "It may be that Her Majesty will advise Lord Thistlegorm which bribes are acceptable."

Again his dark eyes glittered. "The Queen concerns herself with my case?"

"She cannot commit herself in public," said I, "for that would be seen as a perversion of justice. But it is possible to maneuver, as it were, behind the arras."

He tilted his head and frowned. "Yet I sense that these delays and evasions may not end favorably for me."

"I have a proposal," said I. "But I would put it to you privately, without witnesses."

Prince Amadeu seemed surprised, but he looked up at the others in the room, and said, "Gentlemen, if you please."

I sipped my stepony as the others left the room. When the door slid shut behind them, Amadeu turned to me. "Well, my lord," he said. "What is it you have come to say?"

"Much depends on whether there is a silver mine, or mines," said I. "That is why I wished us to be alone, to discuss the matter without your having to make an admission in front of witnesses."

"And if there is a mine?" Amadeu asked. "Why should we reveal these supposed diggings, if the Queen will take them away and leave us with even fewer resources to defend ourselves?"

I recalled the relevant section of Mountmirail's report. "It is my understanding that silver is found in conjunction with other metals, such as lead or copper."

"And sometimes gold," Amadeu said.

"That is impertinent, for gold is also an element of Her Majesty's oredelf," said I. "My point, Highness, is that while silver belongs to the crown, the lead or copper does not."

"Ah." I could see the flurry of calculation behind Amadeu's impassive face. "So if this supposed mine exists, the lead and any other metals may be retained by the miners, and sold on in the usual way?"

"There is nothing in law against it, Highness."

He offered a tight-lipped smile. "But after extracting the silver, the lead is in the form of litharge, which is poisonous and has only a few uses, in dyes and such."

I thought that for a member of the landed nobility, Prince Amadeu had a very thorough knowledge of mining, and that perhaps more of this knowledge was firsthand than he was willing to admit. Though fortunately Mountmirail had consulted an authority who knew more even than Amadeu.

"I am told there is a process for extracting the lead," said I, "involving comminution, some manner of leaching to remove the extraneous waste, and then a precipitation that produces a very pure form of lead."

The prince frowned. "I know of no such process."

"It is used in alchemy. You will find that alchemists are always trying to transform one thing into another, and sometimes succeed. You should speak to Master Ransome, the Queen's Gunfounder, and see if he will give you a demonstration."

His frown deepened. "Alchemists may conduct investigations in their cabinets, but works must be large to support a large mine."

I waved a hand. "Any small experiment can be made on a larger scale." I reached for my stepony. "Shall I write to Master Ransome and tell him you wish to see him?"

"You may." Amadeu glanced out the painted window while he considered again his situation. "This . . . arrangement of yours may offer a degree of satisfaction to my people. But I think we must have more guarantees before the crown is invited to meddle with any hypothetical mines."

"Indeed," said I. "The mines might employ Albiz in all but a few offices, such as chief engineer and—"

"We have engineers," said Amadeu.

"Do they have experience with large-scale cupellation furnaces and stamping mills? For these will be necessary." I sipped my stepony, then put the cup on the marble table. "More importantly," I said, "there will be royal officials present. They will be charged with collecting, counting, and transporting the silver bullion, and keeping it safe during its journey. For that reason they will have an armed force capable of protecting the silver pigs as they travel, and this force may protect you and your people as well."

"They *may*, certainly," said Amadeu. "But our experience of royal officials is that they are better at predation than protection."

"When you produce wealth for the crown," said I, "you become worthy of the crown's most energetic defense."

Cynical amusement touched Amadeu's lips. "He that hath need of a dog," said he, "calleth him 'Sir Dog.' Or so goes a saying in my country."

"It is a droll saying," I said, "but I see nothing in Your Highness's person that would invite comparison with a cur."

His skeptical look deepened. "You say there will be royal officials, but where will these officials be drawn from? Catsgore's mesnie? Because that will put the fox in the henhouse, sure."

"They will be strangers to the West Range," said I. "And I think the present sheriff and lord lieutenant may be replaced with officials more congenial to Your Highness."

Amadeu raised a hand. "Two points," said he. "First, while you may import an engineer to set up the work, I desire that my own engineers serve as his apprentices and successors."

"I know no reason why this may not be granted."

"And next, I wish all these guarantees to be enumerated in writing, under Queen Floria's seal and sign-manual."

"I think this also could be arranged, though I will have to speak with Her Majesty," said I. "But I remind that the crown insists on one principal condition, and that must be that any mine be very rich indeed. We will not go to the trouble of sending a swarm of officials to your country, and building works and stamping mills and so forth, for a vein that will fail after a few short years."

Amadeu spoke carefully, as he gazed out the window and toyed with one of the silver rings on his fingers. "I too, would not wish to waste the crown's resources. Were I to offer a vein of silver to Her Majesty, I would first drive test shafts along the line of the vein, to discover its extent, and make a proffer only if the vein would guarantee a rich lode of silver that can be mined for many years to come, and to help pay for this war of yours."

"Of mine? *Ours*, surely."

He turned from the window to look at me. "Yours," said he. "You *did* cause the war, as I understand it. You spirited Floria from Howel and placed her on the throne, and now Loretto wants that throne back."

This had I done, though during the trip Floria had been in agony over the war that would be the inevitable result of her escape, while I had argued that the war had already been started by Fosco, persecuting so many citizens of Duisland, and that very little blood would be spilled throwing him out of the country.

So perhaps it was my war, after all.

"I think sanguine war is not so simple as to be brought about by a single knight," said I hopefully.

He gestured with one hand. "In any case, Queen Floria's war is not my war. I have a war much closer to home."

"Should we reach an agreement, you will have every reason to support Queen Floria in and out of war, for without her, there will be no hope of peace in your own land."

Amadeu raised his eyebrows. "I look forward to that day, Selford."

"As do I, Highness. And now that we have an outline of an agreement, I beg to return to the castle and report to the Queen."

"Of course." The two of us rose, and he held out a hand. "It is good to make a friend in a strange and hostile country."

"The city will never be less strange or hostile, I'm afraid," said I, and took his hand. "But friendship always beings light into darkness—and I hope you will seriously consider taking your seat in the House of Peers. You would make a sensation, and I would be more than happy to introduce you to those who guide the state—and the many others who hope in future to do so."

"I will consider it," said he, "but I have many problems to address before I can meddle in politics not my own."

I reported the substance of this conversation to Floria that evening, as we lay in my great bed carven with arbutus and roses, her small frame curled spoonwise within the half-circle of my own. "Lay it all out in lawyer's language," she said, "and then I will review it and sign."

"You don't wish to consult Thistlegorm or the attorney general?" asked I.

"Nay, not until the thing is agreed. I don't want word of the agreement escaping—it would go through the court like a whirlwind, and reach Catsgore in seconds."

"I will have a draft ready after we return from Pontkyles's party." I sighed. "I wish Pontkyles weren't playing host, not simply because I dislike him, but because I must spend two nights apart from you."

"Two nights is not such a great sacrifice," said Floria.

"But I am only just back from war," said I. "We are barely reacquainted."

"We shall reacquaint again in three nights' time," Floria said. "But now I must leave you." She threw off the satin sheet, and a waft of her galbanum scent tingled along my senses. She reached for her stockings. "I must leave at dawn; otherwise I'll be caught on the bridge and mired amid the handcarts and drays."

"Another reason to dislike Pontkyles," said I. "He disturbeth sleep."

I sat up and watched with indulgent pleasure as she dressed. Once she had put on her slippers and made some attempt to make her hair tidy, she reached for the candle to light her way to her room.

"Will Your Majesty condescend to favor this unworthy wretch with a kiss?" I asked, and she laughed, took my head in her hands, and obliged. The kiss went on for several long, languorous moments, and then, just as the moments began to mount up to something greater, and my blood turned scalding, she broke away and ran for the secret passage with a laugh, and with a wave over her shoulder.

Pontkyles's country house was northeast of Selford, a ride of two hours assuming that the long bridge over the Saelle wasn't packed with wagons, carriages, and swarms of hucksters dragging their barrows into town. Rufino Knott knocked on my door before dawn and, once I'd opened the door, brought in my shaving water and began laying out my clothes.

Once I had my breakfast, I set in motion my own plan for avoiding the crowds on the long bridge. I had ordered a haquenai from one of the stables outside the city's gates to be at the castle's gate at dawn. Knott and I strolled out of the castle, boarded the haquenai, and were taken to the Marygold Stairs just downstream from the bridge. From there a waterman rowed us over the river to the Old Mill Stairs, where my carriage, my groom Oscar, and my charger Phrenzy waited. I had sent them, along with my trunk, over the bridge the previous day, and they had lodged in Mossthorpe overnight.

The dawn chorus of birds was in full cry as we stepped off our boat, and I recognized the calls of chaffinch, goldfinch, robins, chiff-chaffs, and even a pair of tawny howlets calling *who who-o-o* at each other. The air was still, and I could scent the wildflowers just opening at the first breath of sunrise. The river was sheened with silver, and Selford crouched in shadow below its bluff, while above in full sunlight the castle blazed out, its white stone just tinged with the faint pink of dawn. I paused to drink in this sight, and then shook dew from my shoes and climbed into the carriage.

Knott and I had a merry time on our journey, for we had put our guitars in the carriage, and we strummed and sang as the sun rose into a perfect day. We sang "Old Captain Jermain" and "Black are My Lover's Eyes," and "The Fragrance of the Roses, O" in its original version.

For his country residence near Selford, the Duke of Pontkyles had built a great towered prodigy house called the Tiltyard, a name intended to remind everyone that he had once been a great jouster. The tree-lined drive from the gate to the manor was paved with tons of crushed oyster shell. The house crouched in its green park beneath its score of twisting chimneys, its hundreds of panes of window-glass throwing back the sun. Flags flew from the four round towers on the corners, and from the massive gatehouse. Already there was a row of carriages in the drive, and among them I recognized the large gilded carriage that carried the Queen from place to place.

A footman in Pontkyles livery opened the carriage door, and I stepped out into the morning sun and adjusted my hat. Pontkyles's heir, Morestanton, was on hand to greet me, and again I expressed surprise that he and his troop were not yet bound for Bonille.

"We sail for Bretlynton Head next week," he said, "now that you have so efficiently cleared the seas of the enemy."

Bretlynton Head was on the far side of Bonille from the war at Stanport, but it was the fastest way to get to the besieged city. From

Bretlynton Head the troop would go by barge up the Dordelle to the winter capital of Howel, and from there cross by canal to one of several rivers that would bring them nigh the siege. It was much faster than marching them across the Cordillerie from Longfirth, and they would be fresher when they arrived.

"I wish you all success in the field," said I.

I deduced Floria's presence by noting a clump of tall men and assuming that the Queen was in the midst of them. I walked over to bow and pay my respects, and among the men I saw Pontkyles, Thistlegorm, Gandorim, Sandicup, and Lord Hunstan. When the group briefly parted to admit me, Floria seized her chance to break free of the pack. She took Pontkyles's arm.

"Do you have a palle-malle court, Your Grace?" asked she. "I should like to see it, and partake perhaps of a game."

Pontkyles was pleased to have the Queen's full attention, and led her down a gravel path, trailed by a line of courtiers. I wandered in the same direction, hoping to speak with Lord Hunstan, but he was deep in conversation with someone else.

Therefore I wandered over the park and gardens, where flowers and shrubs were arranged in precise geometrical or heraldic designs, until I came to the actual tiltyard in Tiltyard. Pontkyles's tiltyard was built on the same titanic scale as the rest of his establishment, and was about two hundred yards long and nearly as wide. Three stone towers had been built for privileged guests to overlook the jousting.

There would be no tilting during the next few days, for most of the country's great jousters were away at the war, and it was felt that mock combat was indecorous in a time when combat was all too real.

I had seen jousts, but in Ethlebight, when the Court of the Teazel King had one of its celebrations. But the Court were made up of rich merchants who enjoyed pretending they were characters in the Teazel romances, and I didn't know how expert they were at the sport. Certainly in their elaborate armor, flowing colors, and great-shouldered horses they were impressive enough, but I don't know if any of them could have bested Pontkyles in his prime.

Many at court took the jousting very seriously, and I wondered at it, for it was a celebration of an archaic form of warfare no longer practiced in the field. The last of the knightly cavalry, the Gentlemen-at-Arms of the Royal Household, familiarly the Gendarmes, had joined Clayborne's rebellion and been cut down at Exton Scales. They had been replaced by a regiment of modern demilances commanded by my old comrade Lord Barkin, who I supposed was now harrying Marshal Rutilan's retreating army.

As I returned along the boundary of the tiltyard, I encountered a nursemaid herding a pack of five children—obviously from the same family, for they came in five different sizes, the oldest a boy of six or seven, and the others fair-haired girls. The boy, dressed in blue satin, gave me a haughty look as I passed, before turning to his sisters and exclaiming.

"When I am older, I will joust here!" said he. "I shall enjoy knocking recreant knights off their horses and breaking their necks."

I thought the bloodthirsty child would fit very well with Pontkyles and his family. I left him and his suite, and entered the gardens. Just ahead of me a woman lingered, and something in the languid way her hips swayed back and forth struck a memory of someone I had not seen for nearly seven years. I hastened over the oyster-shell walk and caught up to her.

"My lady," I bowed, "perhaps you will remember me."

Amalie, the Marchioness of Stayne, stared at me with something like horror.

"Quillifer!" she said. "What are you doing here?"

"I am here at His Grace's invitation. As are you, I surmise."

At the tender age of sixteen, Amalie had been married to the Marquess of Stayne, a man three times her age, for the express purpose of breeding an heir, a task he had failed to accomplish to that point. She was carrying that heir when I met her. I was newly arrived in Selford, an eighteen-year-old refugee from the sack of Ethlebight, and she was seventeen and, in the absence of her husband, ready to embark on an adventure.

And so we adventured together for some months in perfect contentment, until her time drew near and her husband returned. He never imagined that the wife of someone as great as himself would become the lover of an obscure provincial like me; but he did suspect me of improperly pursuing her, and so he did what a nobleman of his particular stripe would do, which was to hire a gang of swashers to murder me.

That did not go as he hoped, and Stayne was exiled to his manor at Allingham. Amalie he carried away with him, and I understood that he had kept her with child more or less continually in all the years since.

I then realized that the pack of children with the nursemaid were Stayne's heir and his sisters. That bellicose boy who spoke so pleasantly of breaking necks, I thought, was certainly his father's son.

Amalie was not quite the smooth-skinned, bright-eyed girleen I remembered. Her mane of tawny hair, dressed with strands of pearls, was as I remembered, as were her small, chisel-shaped teeth, which I had once found strangely entrancing. But her face was lined, cosmetic had failed to entirely conceal her blotchy complexion, and over all there seemed an attitude of despair.

The parade of children in her womb—or perhaps seven years in the close company of her husband—had aged her at least a dozen years.

"Quillifer!" she said. "You've got to leave. We can't be seen together."

I looked about. No one was in sight—they were probably clustered around the great hall, waiting for the dinner bell.

"We are alone, my lady," I said.

She leaned closer to me and hissed through half-closed lips. "Get away. If we're seen together, my husband will hear of it!"

He would send out the assassins again, I suppose. There were already too many assassins about the court.

I bowed. "Your servant." And I sped away.

I wandered back to the manor in time to hear the dinner bell, after which we all found our places in the Great Hall, and the servants brought us one remove after another for the next two and a half hours. The great marchpane centerpieces all featured a dumbshow of one or another of Pontkyles's ancestors performing a service before an approving monarch, and I think were intended to suggest that the Queen's gratitude to the Pontkyles family would best be expressed by plighting her troth to Lord Morestanton.

Amalie came in late, and sat at the bottom of the hall, far away from me.

After the vast meal we retired to one or another drawing room, where cards or chess or skittles were played. Thistlegorm made sure that Candice was placed at my table, and I did my best to be pleasant to her, though she was so modest and withdrawn that it was difficult to draw her into conversation. Her father filled the silence by asking her about her accomplishments, in hopes that I would be impressed.

Her younger sister I saw in the train of one of the entertainers, for Bonny Joe Webb had been hired as a performer, and wandered from room to room singing and playing on his lute. The boyish soprano that had so enchanted the public a few years ago was gone, and Bonny Joe sang in a fine, sweet tenor that held Emily enraptured, along with the other admirers in his train.

I looked at Thistlegorm and wondered if he was going to permit his lovesick youngest daughter to trail after an actor, who in the eyes of the world was ranked with swashbucklers, pimps, and cutpurses; but he seemed only to be paying attention to Candice and myself.

We played cacho, which is a simple card game that requires players to either make a series of ever-larger bets, or to fold. Money changes hands, and I suppose that is the point.

I took note that the strict Retriever Thistlegorm had no philosophical objection to gambling, and that he encouraged his daughter to play as well. Of course, he was after more than what he could win at cards, and at times I thought I saw his thirty thousand royals glittering in his eyes.

After cards there was supper served under tents in Pontkyles's park, and then music and fireworks viewed from the formal gardens. Floria presided from a gilded chair, and Morestanton served her in the role of page.

The next morning featured a fox hunt in the park, and I rode Phrenzy in the chase, and managed to avoid being either trampled by Pontkyles or falling and breaking my neck. Floria and Morestanton rode together, she on her dapple gray, and the young heir on his giant black, Dickon. Afterward I detected a glint of satisfaction in Pontkyles's swinish eyes at how well the two were getting on together.

As we rode back to the stables I tried to talk to Lord Hunstan to discover when he planned to elope with Candice, but his brother Brighthelm scowled at me and fetched him away. After dinner I played a game of tennis with Roundsilver, which I lost because I lobbed the ball so high it struck the roof of the tennis court and dropped right in front of the duke, who promptly smashed the ball into the dedans to win both the set and the match. It was a foolish mistake, and I lost ten royals to His Grace, but was happy to pay the price for not having to spend the afternoon with the silent Candice or her insinuant father.

I washed and dressed for supper. The bell had not yet rung, and the guests were still in the drawing rooms, being served by grooms in livery. A groom in Pontkyles livery approached me, and I saw that he carried cakes on a tray, each on a plate made of sugar. "By your leave, my lord," said he, "would you enjoy a cake? One is made special for each guest."

I looked at the tray, and saw that each ginger cake was decorated with a sugar-icing escutcheon, and that the pastry chef had very carefully marked one with my arms, the galleon and the three pens on the white chief.

"Ah," I said. "Very good."

I took the ginger cake on its sugar tray and looked about me, failed to see who I was looking for, and then moved on to the next room, where I found the two tallest men in the room, Pontkyles in royal scarlet and gold, and Morestanton in a silver tunic, standing together, engaged in conversation with Scarnside and Her Grace of Roundsilver. I approached Morestanton and donned my smiling hearty-lad face.

"My lord," said I. "Have you seen these cunning cakes?"

Pontkyles glowered at me, but Morestanton was more civil. "Those are your arms, Selford?" he said.

"They are, and I regret to say that by accident I ate the cake intended for you. I apologize for my thoughtlessness, but I offer you my own cake in recompense."

Pontkyles's scowl deepened, and Scarnside sniffed. Morestanton considered the cake offered him, then picked it up from the sugar plate and—more out of politeness than hunger, I suppose—opened his mouth to bite into the cake. I slapped it out of his hand.

Morestanton stepped back in shock, but Pontkyles gave an angry bellow while Scarnside and the duchess stared in surprise.

Pontkyles advanced on me, one huge hand reaching to his belt for a knife that wasn't there, and in sudden alarm I realized just how big the man was. "Quillifer, you cullion!" he said, "I'll—"

"The cake was poisoned," said I, "and now I know who the poisoner was. Your Grace—" This to Pontkyles, whose advance toward me had stuttered to a halt. "I think you should have your grooms shut the doors of the house and prevent anyone from leaving." I turned to his son. "Morestanton, go to the Queen and make sure she does not come down from her rooms. If you could also send me some of the Yeoman Archers and one of their officers, we could end this matter within the hour."

Morestanton, delighted for a chance to play the hero before the Queen, raced to do my bidding. Pontkyles redirected his fury and began bellowing orders. I bent to retrieve the cake from the floor, and wrapped it in a handkerchief, which I gave to the duchess.

"Keep this safe, for now," said I. "I suppose we'll have to give it to a dog to prove it's poison."

The duchess blinked up at me with her blue eyes. "Quillifer," she said. "Who is—"

"Not now, Your Grace."

I soon acquired a cornet of the Archers and two of his men, and began sweeping through the building, and I found the Marquess of Brighthelm on the terrace overlooking the formal gardens, talking to two of his friends.

"My lord," said I, as I approached. "You may consider yourself under arrest. Please hand over that little cuttle on your waist."

Brighthelm gave me a look of purest hatred from beneath his shock of blond hair, and gave his eating-knife to the cornet. I searched him for other weapons, and found none. I took him into a drawing room, sent everyone else away, and bade Brighthelm to sit in a chair by the window, with one of the Yeoman Archers as guard. Then I took the cornet and his man and went in search of the footman who had been serving the cakes, and found him in the kitchens, loading more cakes onto his platter. He protested as we hauled him up the stair, and I think I frightened him enough so that he told the truth when he said that he was being paid by Brighthelm, and that no one else was involved. We put him into the butler's pantry, with a guard on the door.

When we returned to Brighthelm I found his father stamping outside the door and demanding to be let inside.

"Selford!" he said. "What is the meaning of this? What is this nonsense about my son?"

I looked at the Duke of Waitstill in his colors of white and green and shook my head. "I'm afraid Brighthelm has brought poison into the court," said I. "He wished vengeance against me for the fatal outcome of my duel with Sir Brynley, and possibly also to put me out of the way and let Hunstan have a clear path at Her Majesty."

"This is absurd!" cried Waitstill. "Where would my son get poison?"

"I'm sure that you remember the poisoner who was thrown off the battlements of the Castle," said I. "Brighthelm and his minions were responsible."

Waitstill ground his teeth at me. "This is madness."

"Your Grace," said I, "this business has put poison in the same house as the Queen. It is a very serious matter."

"I wish to see my son."

"That will not be possible at present." He looked at me in a sudden rage, and for a moment I thought he would try to knock me aside and force the door, but at that moment both his wife and Brighthelm's arrived weeping, and with these two ladies Chancellor Thistlegorm, the Roundsilvers (Her Grace still carrying the cake in its handkerchief), Pontkyles, Catsgore, and Sandicup. A captain of the Yeoman Archers followed tramping in heavy boots.

So many explanations were required that it was several minutes before I entered the room, along with the Chancellor and the captain of Archers. Brighthelm's lip twisted in contempt as I entered. A half hour of sitting in the sun beneath the window had raised dots of sweat across his brow, and the sour scent of failure hung about him. Nevertheless his angry spirit had not been quelled.

"You killed my brother, you cur," he said.

"It was a duel he forced upon me," said I. "But you wished no honorable encounter on me but used foul poison."

"It is all you deserve," said he. "I am heartily sorry it went amiss."

"Hah!" said Thistlegorm. "Is that a confession, then?"

Brighthelm gave a sullen look to the Chancellor but offered no reply. I took Thistlegorm aside.

"Brighthelm and his minion must be delivered to the Hall of Justice," said I. "I would take them in my carriage, but I must report to Her Majesty."

"I'll carry them in mine," Thistlegorm said. "I'll take a guard of Archers, and then send the carriage back for Candice and Emily tomorrow."

"That is good of you, my lord," said I.

He sent for his carriage to be readied. I called Pontkyles into the room, and asked if he would prevent anyone leaving Tiltyard for at least an hour after the Chancellor's departure. He said that he would, and his swine's eyes moved from me to Brighthelm and back.

"You thought I was the poisoner," he said.

"You are the host," I said, "and the cakes were passed around by a man in your livery."

"I have hired so many for this event that the house is full of strangers, all in my livery."

"Ay," said I. "Your livery gave him permission to go anywhere. I am sorry, Pontkyles, that I offered a poisoned cake to your heir, but I thought that if you were the real poisoner, you would hardly allow Morestanton to eat it."

His eyes narrowed. "That was insolence."

"It was insolence that proved you weren't the poisoner, and that Brighthelm was. Rejoice that you don't sit where Brighthelm sits now."

"How did you know it was Brighthelm, then?"

"I'll leave you to work it out," said I. "Now I hope you will oblige me in the matter of keeping your gates closed for the next hour or more."

He nodded with his accustomed ill grace, and made his way out. I turned to Brighthelm, and I said, "We shall have to bind your hands, my lord. Your feet will remain free, for you will need them for the long walk to your cell."

An hour later, as the long shadows were creeping over the tree-lined drive between Tiltyard and the imposing front gate, Floria and I walked together down the lane while I gave my report. We were alone but scarcely unobserved, for at least fifty people watched us from the lawn at the front of the manor, and probably more viewed us from the windows. Yeoman Archers, posted at either end of the drive, assured that we would not be interrupted.

The approach of twilight seemed to have caused the entire world to make a slow exhalation. Even though the gardens were on the other side of the manor, their sweet scent seemed to flood the air. The plane trees that lined the drive were overspread by spherical blossoms with their delicate scarlet tentacles, and the odor of the pollen was an astringent contrast to the air's sweetness. Night-birds were beginning to flit through the trees.

"It was *Two Gentlemen of the North* that suggested how the dose of poison passed through the court," said I.

"As the love letter passed from hand to hand in the play."

"Indeed." Our shoes ground the oyster-shell paving beneath our feet. "Brighthelm learned of the existence of this man-bane, then lured the poisoner into the castle—I presume he pretended to be Luzi's employer—and then threw Luzi off the battlements and carried away the toxicant."

"Toxicant?"

"A new word. I made it up."

Floria's eyes lifted to the horizon as she gave the matter thought. A nightjar trilled overhead. "Brighthelm must have had helpers on the battlements."

"We will interview members of his household, and will start with the footmen and varlets he has here. We'll find the accomplices and convince them to testify against him."

Floria did not ask how these men would be convinced, for we both knew, but instead leaped straight to her next thought.

"So you were Brighthelm's target. I presume Luzi's employer had another victim in mind."

I looked at her sidelong. "Would it offend your vanity to know that you were never the target?"

"Ha! It would surprise me."

I told her the name of the man who had brought Luzi to Duisland, and who he intended Luzi to kill.

"Well," Floria said, "perhaps I am not surprised after all."

CHAPTER FIFTEEN

I took my carriage to Selford the next morning, to see how the prisoners and their warders fared, and in the lobby of the Hall of Justice I found Waitstill in conference with Judge Taylor.

"It is not my decision," said Taylor. "I do not determine where prosecution is to be brought. But here is Lord Selford, who may be able to answer your lordship."

I understood at once that Waitstill had come to find out what court had jurisdiction in the matter of his son. If the Siege Royal, the trial would be swift and the sentence certain. If Brighthelm was tried before a jury, however, there would be a chance of his son's living to a ripe age.

"Lord Waitstill, I have not an answer for you," said I. "The matter is not yet decided. I haven't had a chance to speak with the Chancellor or the Attorney General." And of course the Queen would make the final decision, but I didn't want Waitstill harassing her on this business.

"Yet surely the Marquess of Brighthelm should be entitled to a trial before the House of Peers," said Waitstill. He was in wretched condition, and probably hadn't slept: His eyes were shot with blood, and his blond hair and beard had lost their glossy sheen.

"Brighthelm as the son of a peer has a courtesy title only," said I. "It does not entitle him to be tried by the Peers, but by a judge, or a jury chosen in the normal way."

Waitstill would have known this if he hadn't been so distracted by grief and anxiety. I felt sorrow for him, because none of this had been his fault, and the worst that could be said for him was that he wanted his third son to be King.

"I regret this extremely, Your Grace," said I. "You have always treated me with fairness and decency, which must at times have been difficult for you. But Brighthelm as much as confessed to me and to Chancellor Thistlegorm, and I am very sorry to say that you and your family must ready yourselves for grievous sorrow."

He made no answer to this, but only shook his head. I bade him farewell and I went to my office in the Secretariat, where I busied myself with correspondence until an usher came in to announce Lord Catsgore.

Catsgore rivaled Waitstill in disorder: His hair hung lank about his shoulders, and there was a strong smell of brandy. I rose.

"You're very welcome, Catsgore," I said. "Sit down. How may I help you?"

Catsgore slumped into a chair. "It's that damned dwarf," he said. "He's driving me mad."

"What has Amadeu done now?"

Catsgore's lipless mouth drew into a snarl. "He's traducing me all over town! I fear his slanders will reach the ears of the Queen, and she will rule against me in the matter of Amadeu's petition."

I viewed him with interest. The previous day, at Tiltyard, he had been a model courtier in glittering raiment and shining gems, and now it seemed he had overnight taken counsel of his fears and ridden home with a bottle of brandy for company.

"I may offer you some small consolation," I said. "I know that the

Queen has no intention of depriving you of the valleys of Brenmore and Hario."

His lower lip sagged open with relief. "Ah," said he. "You have no idea how that comforts me, Selford."

"I hope I have relieved your anxiety on one score, at least."

I steered him toward the door and worked for another half hour on my correspondence, and then I was told that Lord Thistlegorm hoped to speak with me. I was prepared for a discussion of jurisdiction in the matter of Lord Brighthelm, but to my surprise he practically leaped into my office.

"Selford!" he cried. "My daughters are gone! Missing!"

"Both of them?" said I in surprise. I rejoiced at the disappearance of Candice, since I hoped she was even now enjoying her first taste of matrimony with Lord Hunstan, but I couldn't imagine her eloping both with her lover and her sister.

"I sent my carriage to Tiltyard for them," said Thistlegorm, "but neither could be found. Candice hasn't been seen since yesterday, and Emily took a pony from the stables this morning and rode away. The pony was found near the gatehouse, but Emily hasn't been seen since she first left the stables."

I rose from my seat. "Is Pontkyles searching for them?"

"His messenger said yes."

"Are their maidservants gone as well?"

Thistlegorm's blue eyes blinked at me. "I do not know," he said. "Pontkyles's messenger did not say."

"That would tell us much." I walked around my desk and put a hand on Thistlegorm's arm. "Go home," said I. "You must be there in case any message comes. I will begin a search immediately."

"Where?"

I hesitated. "At the moment I have only half-notions."

I escorted him out of the building and to his carriage. I went to the castle and had my carriage readied, and I told my footmen to bring truncheons in addition to their swords and blunderbusses.

"The Dead Vile," I told the driver. "In Mossthorpe."

The tide of traffic on the long bridge was at an ebb, and we crossed with good speed. As the good burgesses of Selford preferred not to have such depraved villains as actors lodge in their town, the theater companies performed their plays in Mossthorpe, usually in the courtyards of inns, and I saw pasted on walls several notices for *Two Gentlemen of the North*.

The Dead Vile was in a lane overlooking a small river that had become a drain, particularly noxious at high tide when the sewage could not get out. The half-timber building itself presented a respectable-enough front, the common room seemed to have been swept in the last month, and the air still held a little savor for whatever had been cooked on the hearth for dinner. Some men and women sat at the trestle tables with their cups of ale, and when I and the footmen stepped into the room, the landlady came bustling up, wiping her hands on her apron.

"May I help you, Lord Quillifer?"

At another time I might have been pleased that she recognized me, even if she hadn't quite got my title right.

"Bonny Joe Webb," said I.

She seemed surprised at the question. "Why, he is at the theater, sir."

I lashed myself for forgetting that the troupe's plays would be performed outdoors in the light of the sun, unless they were performed at court, where the costs of the candles were borne by the Queen.

"Has Bonny Joe a young lady with him today?" I asked.

She shrugged. "He always has somebody, sir. I no longer bother to tell one from another."

"The play's at the Barley Mow?" asked I.

"Yes, Lord Quillifer."

"Thank you." I touched my hat, as if the landlady was some grande dame I saw every day, and then I gestured to the footmen and went back to my coach.

The Barley Mow was a large inn on the main road that ran between Innismore and Blacksykes. A flag with the Roundsilver shield flew overhead to let the world know a play was intended for the afternoon. Several burly men stood by the entrance, in case Wakelyn and Scarnside's Company tried to interrupt the performance.

The clowns were performing and the laughter of the audience boomed up into the bright blue sky. I paid for seats in the gallery for myself and my footmen, but rather than take my place I worked my way around the inn-yard until I had a view behind the stage. Actors waited to go on, and I recognized Lexter, the new lead ingenue, preparing to burst onto the scene. I edged my way behind the stage, and as Lexter bounded onstage I took his place, and glided through the people waiting in the near darkness. I did not see Emily, even after I bent down to look below the stage.

Behind the center of the stage a curtained tiring-house had been built, where the actors could change their costumes, and I could not see around it. So with a degree of caution I parted the curtains and looked inside, and there I saw the Honorable Emily Wilmot, her eyes aglow, adjusting a golden-haired wig atop Bonny Joe's head.

Emily was still in the riding clothes she had worn to Pontkyles's stables that morning, and I reached out to seize the collar of her leather riding jerkin and pull her away.

"I am heartily sorry to interrupt your interlude, Mistress Emily," said I, "but it is time to see your father."

She kicked me on the shin with her boot, and I hastened to hand her to my footmen before she remembered to make use of the long spur on her left boot, intended for those riding sidesaddle and designed to prick a horse even through layers of petticoats and a stout woolen skirt.

Bonny Joe viewed the scene as if something like it took place every day, and perhaps it did. I stepped close to him, then leaned over to whisper in his ear.

"Tell me," said I, "have you interfered with this lady in any way? It is best to tell me now, so that we may know how to proceed."

He waved a languid hand, and I recognized that gesture as belonging not to him but to the character he played onstage. "I but gave her a ride to town," said he. "We have shared a few kisses at my lodging. It is nothing."

I took ahold of his collar and drew him closer. "Toying with a daughter of the high nobility, Bonny Joe, is to bring high danger on yourself."

"It is they who toy with me." He looked at me down his nose "You have slept with their wives, Sir Quillifer, and you have suffered no damage."

"Yet I fought three duels, and killed one man and crippled another. Are you prepared to do the same?"

His pupils widened. "It will never come to that."

I snarled. "Nay, it will not, for no one will deign to duel with an actor. They will pay half a crown to some runagate to stick a dag in your kidney and leave you to die in the dust."

I released him and returned to Emily and my footmen, who had taken a firm grip on her arms and thus far avoided her kicks. "Come," said I, and I followed as the footmen carried struggling Emily through the crowd. Those who saw us thought we were providing mighty entertainment, and laughed.

Finally we threw her into my carriage, and put one of the footmen beside her. "Cause any more trouble," I told her, "and I'll have him sit on you."

"You have no business giving orders to me!" she cried.

I gave her a handkerchief. "You might wipe Bonny Joe's paint off your lips before your father sees you," I said.

Reluctantly she swabbed at herself, and as traffic had thickened, we joined the throng waiting to cross the bridge. It took half an hour in the company of a sulking child before we entered the city, and shortly thereafter the carriage pulled up in front of Thistlegorm's house. His was a modest town dwelling, for his financial condition had forced him to rent out his palace to a fashionable architect, who was increasing its value by adding a new facade in the current vogue.

We marched Emily into the lobby, and there her father came roaring down the stair, his face blotched red with passion.

"By heaven!" said he. "This is too much!"

"I have not found Candice," said I, "and it is too late to start today. Folk should inquire up and down the road past Tiltyard, and find if anyone has seen her. Pontkyles's staff know the country and are probably best for this, but I will send men if you think it best."

"I'll dispatch a rider to Pontkyles at once," said he. "And I thank you for the return of Emily. Where did you find her?"

"Back of the stage at the Barley Mow," said I. "She thought to join Roundsilver's Company. If you will take my advice, you will send her to her mother before she takes it into her head to join a circus."

Emily gave me a ferocious glare. I left them to their reunion, and gladly, for I had a reunion of my own to plan. I supped at the castle, but the Queen did not appear at the table, and left word that she had retired early. I went to my apartment, lit scented candles, put on a dressing gown, and read some of Erpingham's *Tales* until Floria, refreshed by a nap, came ghosting down the passage. Then I told her of my day's adventures, and we shared our tender ardor till midnight, when at last we fell asleep, content, in one another's arms.

Four days after Brighthelm's arrest, we met again in the Starry Drawing Room, Floria in her chair with the rayed back. Before her was the table of water-sapphire, and she was flanked by Thistlegorm and Roundsilver. Waitstill, after the indictment of his son Brighthelm, had resigned the office of privy seal, and had not yet been replaced, so Roundsilver served as temporary privy seal. Catsgore was present, for the matter concerned him, and there was also Hunter, the assistant attorney general, and a recording secretary. I sat across the room from Catsgore. He was in a much better state than when I had last seen him, but his lipless mouth was drawn in a grim line, and there was a tight wariness about his eyes. He seemed as if he had spent many anxious hours in these last days.

My crooked little finger ached, for it had rained for two days, and was going to continue for at least a third. Rain drummed on the roof and spattered the windows. It was chill, and a fire burned in the hearth. The pointed gold stars on the ceiling gleamed dully in the subdued light.

"Good afternoon, gentlemen," Floria said. "We have invited you to witness our hand and seal to an agreement between the crown and His Serene Highness Amadeu, to establish a silver mine and works in his domain."

Catsgore's mouth dropped open, and then his rage puffed up his neck like that of a frog. "Your Majesty, there is no silver mine!" he said. "This false prince but gulls you and leads you down paths paved with false hopes—he is nothing but a brazen-faced coney-catcher!"

Amadeu gave Catsgore a disdainful look and raised a pomander to his nose as if to ward off a great stink, so it was I who answered the charge.

"The document offers many guarantees to the contracting parties," I said. "There will be silver, or the agreement is void."

"There will be just enough silver to enrich your hopes without ever enriching the treasury," Catsgore said. "This lust for silver is a species of madness."

Thistlegorm was weary of this carping. "Her Majesty has not

invited comment," he said. "Catsgore, you are here to be informed, not consulted."

Water spattered the window-glass. The fire on the hearth crackled and popped. Catsgore's face turned scarlet with anger, and his fingers clawed at the arms of his chair. A coffer of beaten copper was placed on the table and opened, and pens, ink, and several parchment copies of the document were placed on the table. Amadeu edged his chair closer to the table, and then he and the Queen applied themselves to signing and sealing the documents. Roundsilver produced the privy seal when required.

When the business was finished, Thistlegorm rolled a copy of the document, secured it with a ribbon, and formally presented it to me. "For the Archives," he said.

I bowed and accepted the parchment. Amadeu left his chair and knelt before the Queen. "Please rise, cousin," she said, and then she stood, everyone else rising with her.

"Gentlemen," said she, "we wish you all a good afternoon."

We bowed as she swept from through the south door in a rustle of petticoats, and then we straightened and looked at each other as a bolt of lightning seared across the heavens and thunder rattled the casements.

Amadeu regarded us for a moment, then bowed. "Gentlemen, I am obliged to you," he said. "I hope you will visit me in my own country."

He and his gentlemen left by the gilded double doors on the west side of the room. Catsgore glared after him, and his lipless mouth twisted in a snarl. Then he walked swiftly to the small south door that Floria had used, and for a moment I was alarmed that he might pursue the Queen down the corridor to argue with her, or even to assault her. But then I remembered that two of the Yeoman Archers had been stationed outside that door, and that they would accompany the Queen to her private apartments, and I did not think Catsgore would be able to fight his way through them.

Thistlegorm approached me, carrying the coffer in his hands. There was a tentative look in his blue eyes.

"Have you heard, Selford?" he said.

"That Candice has married Waitstill's son? Ay." I made an equivocal gesture with one hand. "If she is happy, then they have my blessing."

"That is very generous of you, Selford." He hesitated. "I do not suppose you would consider Emily?"

"I think she is a little young," said I.

"Too young to marry, perhaps," said Thistlegorm, "but not too young for a betrothal."

I put on my dutiful apprentice face. "My lord, I am not insensible of the fact that the young lady hates me."

"At her age these passions come and go," said he.

"Perhaps we should wait a little longer for her temper to fade."

With a sigh, Thistlegorm surrendered the idea of a son-in-law who would pay off his debts with interest-free loans.

I left the room with a light heart, and then I encountered Catsgore waiting for me in the corridor, and my heart descended to its usual realm. He seized my arm.

"What is this, Selford?" he demanded. "Did you not assure me that this matter would have a happy outcome?"

"Has it not?" said I. "The vales of Brenmore and Hario remain in your family. I thought that was your chief concern. After all, what is the silver mine to you, or you to the silver?"

"This silver is on my land!" he hissed. Spittle sprayed my cheek, and I detached his hand from my arm and stepped away.

"You might claim the land," I said, "but you cannot claim the silver. The oredelf belongs to Her Majesty."

"This is beyond outrage!" Catsgore said. "Her Majesty even called him 'cousin'!"

"Come with me," said I. I led Catsgore to the ornamented stone gallery overlooking the Inner Ward. Rain poured off the gallery roof in sheets. The air was chill and carried a pleasing scent. I looked at Catsgore narrowly.

"Have you known of the existence of this mine for some time?"

I saw that this question staggered him, but his belligerence was unquenched. "There is no mine!" he declared. "There never was a mine!"

"If you knew of the mine," said I, "that might explain the violence that has been convulsing the dales these last years. Perhaps you hoped to seize the diggings and profit in secret."

His mouth worked wordlessly for a moment, and then he spoke. "That is a villainous accusation, Selford."

"I have not yet exhausted my stock of villainous accusations," said I, "for I know that it was you who brought the poisoner from Basilicotto, with the intention of making away with Amadeu."

"What is this?" he demanded. He struck the gallery wall with a fist. "What madness vexes your brain?"

"Then you made the mistake of getting drunk in the company of Brighthelm and Pontkyles, both of whom have reason to hate me. One of them took the poison off your hireling, and it was only five days ago that my experiment discovered which of them had done it."

Catsgore seemed to stagger, and then put a hand to the wall to steady himself. He gazed at me with a kind of pleading.

"Has Brighthelm made a denunciation?" he said. "I tell you now that he lies."

"He is not talking yet, but he will have every reason to speak when the time comes. No—I heard you accuse Pontkyles of the theft, and I worked out the reason."

"Yours wits are disordered," Catsgore said. "Who would believe this?"

"I," I responded. "The Queen. One or two others to whom I have confided the matter." I donned my solemn bailiff face. "Were I you, Catsgore, I would support this settlement with a full and grateful heart, and devote yourself to pleasing the Queen with every atom of your being. Otherwise you may find yourself exposed, and losing Brenmore and Hario may be the least of your punishments."

He gasped at me, his lips moving noiselessly while his eyes bulged from his head. His countenance was a brilliant scarlet. "I," he began, and then he put a hand to his throat and tore at his collar. "I. I."

And then his lungs gave a wrenching heave, and Catsgore fell dead at my feet.

CHAPTER SIXTEEN

I once told Castgore that he should take care to avoid an apoplexy," said I. "He failed to take my advice."

Rain tapped on the window of Floria's cabinet. She frowned at me. "What became of that poisoned cake you acquired the other day?"

"It was fed to a dog—an old, sickly dog with little time remaining on this earth—and the dog died. Three witnesses have signed a document to that effect. One of them is the assistant attorney general."

"Was the entire cake eaten up?" Floria asked.

"I hardly think anyone could have got Catsgore to somehow eat half a poisoned cake," said I. "If he were poisoned, it wasn't by me— though now that I think on it, I may nevertheless be at fault."

Floria raised an eyebrow. I considered my response while I looked through the hagioscope at the two ladies who, from the next room, were guarding the Queen's virtue. Both were engaged in embroidery, and I thought that on such a cloudy day there was not enough light in their room to accomplish their tasks without straining their eyes. I hoped they were not straining their ears as well.

"I wrote to that guild of poisoners in Basilicotto," I admitted. "I told them their man Luzi had been murdered, probably by the person who hired him—in my defense, I believed this to be true. If they were inclined to revenge—and the entire literature of their country insists that they are—they may have sent someone to finish Catsgore."

"Let there be no inquiry into the manner of Catsgore's death," Floria said.

"As you wish, Majesty," said I. "I will prevent any necropsy."

"Necropsy?"

"A new word. I made it up."

"Of course," she murmured.

"Catsgore's body will be sealed in its casket and sent it to the halls of his ancestors. By the time it arrives, weeks from now, no one will be able to read the cause of death from the remains."

She nodded. "Let this be done." She tapped the helve of her fan against her chin. "How old is Catsgore's heir?"

"He is nine, and has two younger sisters."

She smiled. "They shall be made wards of the crown. I will take tender care of them, and foster them to members of the high nobility—in Bonille, perhaps, where they will not be exposed to the clannish ways of the west."

"And their mother?"

"May return to her family, with the assurance that her children will become the special charge of their loving monarch."

"When those children are grown, they will have become strangers to their old home."

She smiled. "The daughters may not ever see their old home again, if I can arrange good marriages for them."

I nodded. "And of course Your Majesty must appoint a steward to sit in that old flint castle and manage Catsgore's property until the oldest reaches maturity."

Her smile broadened. "That steward should be a resolute gentleman, unwilling to put up with violence or disorder. Perhaps with his own mesnie, so that he need not depend on local resources."

"He must be steadfast indeed," said I. "He will be unable to rely on normal administration of the county, for it may be in flux. The lord lieutenant, for example, may be ordered to take the soldiers he has been raising, and bring them in person to Bonille and the battlefield."

"The sheriff might also be moved to a new post," Floria said. "Though I do not at present have an office available for a corrupt sheriff."

"You need not employ him at all," said I. "He serves at your pleasure, does he not? You may dismiss him and not give a reason."

She looked to the rain-spattered window. "His older brother is a loyal member of the Burgesses," she mused "I will have to give him something."

"You need not give it immediately."

"I suppose not."

"And before it escapes my mind, I should advise you to tell your administrator in charge of the new silver mine that he should pay no attention to any sign that the mine has been worked recently."

Floria smiled. "I shall so charge him."

"But with Catsgore dead, someone must be appointed Minister of State for Fornland."

Floria seemed to weary of the subject, and turned her quick glance to me. "Go and see to the matter of Catsgore's body, and make certain no one meddles with it."

"I obey, Majesty." I rose, bowed, and turned for the door.

Through the hagioscope, I could see the two ladies still busy with their embroidery.

The crown was invoiced for a fine coffin lined with satin, which sat—with Catsgore sealed inside—in the Great Reception Room for five full days, so that any mourner could pay appropriate respects. Abbot Fulvius led a memorial for the court, and praised Catsgore as a loyal subject and a paragon of nobility. We all attended, even Prince Amadeu, who watched the proceedings with a mordant expression on his dark face. I did not see any great display of sorrow even among Catsgore's followers.

After the scent of decay began to waft from the bier, the wooden coffin was placed in a lead outer coffin, the lid soldered on, and the late Baron Catsgore was carried off to his palace to be sent home at his own expense.

Later that day I received word that one of my houses had been burned—the manor called Winegrove, in the vine country of south-west Bonille. Her Majesty had given it to me, but I had never seen it. It had been burned by a mob come out from the nearest town, a place with the inviting name of Pleasanton. The mob denounced me as a sorcerer who had bewitched the Queen, and burned me in effigy along with my house, after which they became drunk on wine looted from my winery and staggered home spewing.

I had heard from the lord sheriff of the county, who said that he would round up the malefactors, then asked what I wanted done with them.

"You are growing dangerous, Quillifer, to those near you," Floria said. "Of the three murder plots discovered in the Castle, two were against you, not me. Now they burn your house, and that is only one step removed from burning mine."

"I will send my own men to Pleasanton," I said, "and find out who is spreading these dangerous ideas."

"Loretto slanders the both of us," said she, "and now I fear those slanders are taking root."

The next day word came from Constable Scutterfield that the last of Rutilan's men had been driven back over the border. Two thousand at least had been slain in the pursuit, and nearly five thousand captured, including many nobles and other men of note. Thirty standards had been taken. The remnants of Rutilan's forces were scattered, having found their own way over the mountains, and come starving into their own country.

Admiral Coneygrave had offered the Constable what assistance he could, and now had embarked some of Scutterfield's men to attempt the capture of Perpizon.

The heralds rode forth from the castle with the news of Rutilan's rout, and soon the air was torn by the clamor of bells and the booming of guns as the city went mad with celebration.

Within days news from north Bonille came, and that news was less worthy of celebration. Admiral Mola's siege of Stanport had begun in the thunder of guns. A reconnaissance-in-force of a thousand men led by Lord Gadsby, the lord lieutenant of a neighboring county, was caught by surprise at Stanport Levels and killed or captured, after which the captives had been herded to Stanport and killed as traitors before the town walls.

Mola hoped thereby to sow terror among the defenders, but instead he inspired defiance in them. Lord Stayne, bent on revenge, led out a sortie in the dead of night, captured a few dozen careless cannoneers, then bound them and hung them in wicker baskets from the city walls targeted by Mola's cannonade. Mola called a halt to the bombardment for only an hour or two, after which he ordered the guns to open fire, doing execution among his own men. In anger he then fired into the town the incendiaries called carcases, and Stanport burned for two nights and a day, leaving only half the town standing.

Lord Stayne reported that Mola's cruelty had only inspired the defenders to greater determination. They were rebuilding the broken walls by night, or digging trenches behind the breaches to trap the storming parties, or laying powder charges to blow them up. At night they would creep into the enemy works to slay the enemy sappers, or to destroy the trenches creeping ever closer to Stanport's walls.

"This barbarity must cease," Floria said at a meeting of the Council.

"There is nothing so barbarous and woeful as a siege," said Thistlegorm. "I remember when your royal father took Avevic in the last war, we broke into a city inhabited only by walking skeletons, the inhabitants so starved and ill-used that even our most heartless soldiery were moved to pity."

"Mola is emboldened in his savagery because we could not retaliate," said I. "Save for those few captured by Stayne's sortie, we could not treat the enemy as he treated the Knight Marshal's army. But now the Constable has captured thousands of Rutilan's forces, and this may check Mola's outrages. I suggest we have the captives draw lots, starting with the nobles and the officers, and that Mola be informed that if he executes any more of his prisoners, we will retaliate against our own captives."

"Oh, so we must now threaten butcheries of our own?" Floria said. She snarled and waved a hand. "Oh ay, if we must, though I like it not."

Instructions were sent to the Constable to begin the sortilege, marking which prisoners would die and in what order. He was to send one of the prisoners to Mola along with an officer to confirm that Rutilan's army had been defeated and largely captured, and to give Mola a list of those whose lives would be forfeit. On this list would be a great many captives with the noble "de" in their name, and if they died, it would be for Mola to explain to their kin and to the Regency Council why these deaths were to Loretto's benefit.

I thought that those Lorettan kin were not the only folk to be sorry if those prisoners were executed—for if they were nobles, they would be worth a ransom, and no one was worth a ransom dead.

So the Council's orders went out and we awaited news, for we expected that Mola might take Stanport before the message could even reach him. Yet the city held, and word came of Stayne's deeds of courage and skill in the holding of it. As the Marquess of Stayne was a man I hated, I resented having to admire him, and I wished to have the liberty to doubt the accounts in the dispatches that arrived under his seal; but there were other messages as well, written by such notables as Stanport's mayor and the captain of the city's Trained Bands, that confirmed Stayne's reputation as a commander of great resource and daring.

While savage war was fought in the siege lines and beneath the walls of Stanport, the court continued its accustomed activities. There were balls, hunts, plays, masques, and entertainments of all sorts; there were great occasions on the estates of the high nobility, there were galleys raced on the great river, and choral works presented in honor of the Queen.

So advanced the calendar of the court, stately as a pavane, and as the season advanced the war seemed remote indeed, like a dream fading in the sun of high summer.

The Old Mill Inn sat next to the Slake, a small river emptying into the Saelle in Mossthorpe. Sandicup's flag flew from its pole above the inn, and every so often someone fired off a blunderbuss to attract attention. Placards announced the new play *Ethlebight Aveng'd*, to be performed by a new company led by the great actor Wakelyn.

Rogues and ruffians lounged by the gate, there to crack the crowns of any of Blackwell's partisans who threatened to interrupt the performance. They paid no particular attention to me, for I was no brawler or swashbuckler but a well-dressed courtier who paid a half-crown for a seat in the galleries that had been built in the inn-yard. I attended with Kevin Spellman, who I thought might enjoy the sequel to our adventure in the fish market.

"Will there be fish?" he asked as we took our seats.

"Players deserve a more varied diet," said I. I saw Sandicup sitting nearby in the gallery, and I nodded at him politely. He gave me a suspicious look from beneath his red eyebrows as he offered me a gracious wave.

The winter capital of Howel had an old stone Aekoi theater that could seat thousands, but Mossthorpe had to make do with the yards of inns. A stage was built against one wing of the Old Mill, with a tiring-house behind, and across from the stage, against the stables, was the elevated three-storey gallery for the viewers who could afford a half-crown. Those unable to afford seats in the gallery paid a penny to stand in the yard. The stage, which thrust out into the midst of these groundlings, was currently occupied by a group of musicians playing popular tunes. The songs included "The Fragrance of the Roses, O," newly revised by Knott and myself as "The Battle of the Races, O." I hummed along with the melody.

Kevin and I regarded the other spectators. In the gallery I saw Duke Chelmy and his duchess, and Ambrosius, the former Philosopher Transterrene, with a group of well-bred worldly acolytes, for the most part older ladies who glittered in satins and jewels. He wore a benign expression as he spoke to them, and they seemed to marvel at his every word.

I paid particular attention to a number of young women who sat in the gallery, each escorted by a young gentleman. These women were heavily painted, and like all fashionable gentlewomen wore petticoats atop farthingales and bumrolls that broadened their hips, so that below the waist their clothing tented about their legs. In outline they resembled handbells, and their clothing seemed designed to hold the world at a distance. They stayed generally behind their fans, and spoke only to their gentlemen.

The play began with a trumpet fanfare, and then an actor playing a character named Prologue came out to offer an introduction to the play. This managed not only to market the play itself, but to flatter the audience and to praise the company's patron, Sir Merriman Sandicup, who acknowledged the flattery with a graceful wave of his hand.

It was wretched verse, and I rather thought Blackwell hadn't written it.

There followed a scene of Aekoi captains discussing their planned raid on Ethlebight, after which they marched off to assemble their troops. Then the play's central character arrived, played by Wakelyn.

He was Kit, a man of humble origins in love with the virginal Dahlia, whose rich father had forbidden them to meet. His posture as he walked onstage made it clear that he was deeply troubled, and he gazed soulfully in the direction of the gallery for several long moments before he opened his mouth. He was intended to speak at length about his dilemma, but managed only part of the first line— "Oh, woe that I"—before the theater exploded into chaos.

As soon as Wakelyn came into sight, the young ladies in their tentlike skirts bent forward to hike up their farthingales, revealing the cloth bags concealed beneath their skirts. These their escorts detached, and handed to certain youths loitering among the groundlings.

The bags were filled with eggs, overripe fruit, and old mince pies already "on the turn," as the saying is. All these were soon pelting Wakelyn, while his attackers cried out their accusations. *"Thief!" "Play-stealer!" "Speak your own words!"*

I spoke into Kevin's ear. "You see what I meant about a more varied diet? Wakelyn may find himself enlarged by this fare."

The hired rampallions at the gate charged into the crowd to put a stop to the barrage, but first had to struggle through members of the audience who fled at the first hint of a riot. Most did not flee, however. The groundlings had paid a penny apiece for their entertainment, and when the fruit began to fly they were mightily entertained, so when Wakelyn's defenders got into the crowd, the groundlings got in their way, tripped them, or sometimes clouted them on the head.

In mere seconds Wakelyn was covered in slime and refuse, then was half-stunned by a turnip that knocked his hat askew. Louting back, he stepped on a broken egg and slipped, then fell sprawling on the stage, his costume in ruins. Having brought down the actor, the young tearaways dropped their bags and fruit and disappeared into the crowd.

As for the young ladies, they hid behind their fans and squeaked in terror, while their gentlemen tried to protect them from flying debris. It now seemed that spirit of misrule had got among the audience, and in the pit there was general combat with whatever missiles could be found, reused, or improvised.

I decided to leave before I was caught up in the action. Kevin and I made our way to the exit, and found ourselves amid a troop of the well-dressed ladies and their escorts.

"You see," I told Kevin, "Bonny Joe is not the only young actor in the city. If you look about, you will see the future heroines of the Duisland stage."

The painted ladies were all boys outfitted in costumes from the Roundsilver Company, and their gentleman escorts were either actors or were drawn from one of the city's choral societies that often performed at the same holidays and festivals as the actors.

They, and the groundling boys, would be well paid for their efforts, and the ambitious would-be actors among them might well be satisfied with their audition.

As the inn-yard emptied and everyone dispersed into their carriages, Sandicup stormed up to me.

"Selford!" he said. "You were behind this; I know you were!"

"I?" I put my hand over my heart. "I threw not a single particle of food tonight."

His eyes narrowed. "This is exactly your style, Selford. You amuse yourself with this sort of disgraceful buffoonery."

"You shock me, Sir Merriman," said I. "But I was shocked also by the accusations that came from the crowd tonight. Does your company actually intend to mount stolen plays?"

"I know nothing of it," he said.

"It seems to me, sir, that you do not want your name connected with any sort of thievery at all—remember that you are in charge of the Exchequer. *Theft* is a word that must never attach to you."

He snarled. "I will complain to the Master of the Revels!"

"You may complain all you like," I said, "but I have nothing to do with the Master of the Revels one way or another. I have no troupe of players, and I do not mount entertainments for the public."

"I will have my revenge for this!"

"Be careful of revenge," I said piously. "For a man who seeks revenge must first dig two graves, one for his victim, and the other for himself."

Which proverb Abbot Ambrosius had quoted to me at our first meeting, when I had expressed my wish to have revenge for ravaged Ethlebight. I was happy to invoke the reverend abbot at such an occasion.

"You are impossible!" Sandicup cried, and stormed away. I turned to Kevin.

"I hope you've found this night's diversion worth your half crown."

"Oh, indeed," said he. "And I was right glad that the missiles flew only in one direction, and not toward me."

"Well," said Floria, "it seems that I must now intervene in the matter of riots in the theaters."

"In only one theater, Majesty," said I.

"A theater, a fish market, and who knows where else? All these brawls over plays that Roundsilver claims Wakelyn stole from Blackwell."

"*Ethlebight Reveng'd* is Blackwell's. I was with him when he conceived it."

"I will tell Sandicup that Wakelyn must return Blackwell's papers. If not, his company will have no license to play in Howel, Mossthorpe, or at the court."

I kissed her lips. "That is justice, my darling."

Floria's eyes sparkled in candlelight, and her sweet breath was scented with her sloe cordial. We lay on the great bed in my apartment, and she was turned toward me, her head pillowed by her arm. My eyes roamed over the outline of her body, the curve of hip and breast, the sharp outline of a clavicle, the mischievous smile. I kissed her lips again. She sighed.

"You have done the realm service, Quillifer," said the Queen, "but you have done yourself an injury. For you have deprived yourself of allies: Catsgrove was your friend on the Council, Waitstill treated you with courtesy, and Thistlegorm was your ally so long as he had hope of your marrying his daughter. Now Thistlegorm has joined the Varcellos faction, and torments me with praising the virtues of this Oriol that Gandorim has decided is the best prince for me, and Roundsilver is your only remaining friend. Only Pontkyles holds out for a Duisland match, for he has not lost hope that his son Morestanton will return from war and win my affections."

"Gandorim has relieved some of Thistlegorm's debt," said I. "Is it not alarming that so many of your trusted councillors are in the pay of a foreign power?"

"Gandorim throws sacks of money about the court," Floria said. "Should we wonder that some pick it up?"

"I wonder that they flaunt it openly and show not more discretion. Why do they not kneel and swear their loyalty to King Anibal, and have done with it?"

I stroked her cheek, and again kissed her lips.

"There is a straightforward solution to all these problems," I said. "It will win me an endless number of friends, and will dispose of this Prince Oriol."

"And this solution?"

"Marry me," said I. "And then all the court will smile at me, for they will try to use me to influence you. And the golden prince may remain over the horizon forever." "Oriol" was "golden" in the language of Varcellos, and certainly he had been worth gold to several of the Council.

Floria's look turned solemn. She reached out and touched my shoulder, the merest caress.

"Quillifer," she said, "I must ask you to help me."

I looked at her in surprise. "Help you? Of course."

Again her fingers brushed my shoulder. The gesture was, I realized, intended to be comforting. "You must help me to understand how a sovereign prince can marry the son of a butcher. I cannot think it has ever happened in all the ages of the world. I have even consulted histories. If we married, I would lose the support of all the Peers and half the Burgesses, and we both might lose our lives."

I was so surprised that my mind clattered for a moment like the broken gears of a water mill, but after a moment I recovered my wits and began to assemble my arguments, one after the next.

"Do you know what else has never happened in all the ages of the world?" asked I. "Duisland has never before had a Queen regnant, and now it has had two in a row."

"Only because there was not an heir male," said Floria. "The alternative was civil war among the high nobility to see which of my cousins would reign, and fortunately none of them were mad enough to want that."

"Except for Clayborne, and all his noble supporters."

"Well. Ay."

"Also, consider that I am the Count of Selford," said I. "If a count has not enough rank to marry a Queen, you may make me a marquess or a duke, and I will bear it somehow."

"But *I* made you a peer, Quillifer," Floria said. "They will say you influenced me unfairly—by the Pilgrim, they say it *now*. They say the Order of the Red Horse should be enough for you, or at most a baronetcy, but making you a count was the result of my woman's weakness and a misplaced affection."

"I cannot agree that your affection is misplaced," said I.

"Nor can I," said she. "But a mob burnt your house, and two nobles tried to murder you. That is how your popularity stands now."

I waved a hand. "Everyone loves a good story," said I. "How many tales exist of a young man overcoming obstacles and being rewarded with a princess and half the kingdom? And I remind you that I am not even asking for half the kingdom."

"Some folk may enjoy these fantasies," said Floria. "But I think the nobility tell each other different sorts of stories—stories of their own lineage, and the greatness that descends to them, and how it must be hoarded and never shared outside their own circle."

By now I was growing a little angry. "I have saved you from Fosco's plotting," said I. "I have brought you the victory of the Races, with the whole of the enemy's campaign destroyed, their navy sunk and their army scattered and starving in the mountains."

Fury flashed in Floria's eyes. "And none of that matters!" she said. "That is what is so maddening! There has never been anyone like you, and people don't know how to think about you! They don't see you as a great man; they see you as a freak, one of nature's monstrosities."

"You said you would be free if you had victories," I said. "I have given you victories."

"I feel I am not free at all!" Floria cried. "I am as besieged as the city of Stanport!" She brandished a fist. "They *surround* me, Quillifer— even my own ladies. They never cease their barrage. They wear down my defenses."

To my astonishment I felt warm tears fall onto my chest. I put my arm around her shoulders, and I kissed her temple.

"Then marry me not," I whispered into her ear. "Let us go on as we do now, for all that matters is that we love each other."

"I love you truly," said she, "but I am also Queen, and I owe a debt to my country. I must secure the throne by having a child, and for that I must be married."

"We are both young. We can afford a few years before the question of children becomes so important it cannot be ignored."

I could tell that she was not entirely persuaded by this argument, but she made up her mind to be content, and laid her head on my shoulder. More tears dropped upon my chest.

"And as for those ladies of yours," I said, "why do you not recall Edith Mountmirail? She has the sharpest tongue in the kingdom, and cares not who she offends—and if you instruct her to prevent those bitches from besieging their Queen, she will do it in a way they will not soon forget."

That brought a gasp of laughter from Floria. "Pilgrim's toes," she said, "I will do it."

"Leave it to Mistress Edith," said I. "She will bring you peace in the daytime, and I will do my best to give you rest at night."

But though my speech remained blithe, I began to suspect that at that moment a shadow had fallen across me and Floria, and that from this moment it would not all be joy and delight, but that now there would be no sweet moment of happiness without the bitter aftertaste of sorrow.

Life at court continued its dreaming dance, with hunts and horse races and balls. Edith Mountmirail brought order to the royal household while her husband returned to his work on the Ethlebight canal. Lord Thistlegorm and I disagreed on how and where Brighthelm's trial would be held. Thistlegorm was confident he could manage a jury here in Selford. Even though Brighthelm's was a courtesy title and he was not entitled to a jury of peers, out of courtesy to his family Thistlegorm seemed inclined to choose jurors from among those with titles and escutcheons, a preference I misliked. I was not sanguine that a group of peers would consider it a capital offense to murder a foreigner and try to poison a butcher's son. I wanted the trial before the Siege Royal, with the verdict sure and the end as brisk and final as that of Edevane. Thistlegorm replied that the treason court had been overused of late, and that he wished to shield Her Majesty from a charge of tyranny. I pointed out that bringing poison into the proximity of the Queen was treason enough for the accused to be hauled up before Judge Taylor.

The final decision was Floria's, however, and she delayed. I imagined that Waitstill's family was exerting itself behind the scenes.

In Bonille, Lord Stayne continued to hold Stanport against one savage attack after another. The bombardment of the town ceased only when a truce was called to drag the bodies out of the trenches. The left wing of Mola's army continued its creeping movement around the city, leveling woods and groves to provide the timber necessary to build up causeways across the boggy country.

Word came from the fleet that Coneygrave had made his assault on Perpizon and had failed to take the city by storm, but nevertheless had managed to seize the port, take some prize ships, and burn the warehouses that held the supplies for the enemy's Occidental Fleet. Thousands of tons of seasoned wood, cordage, victuals, canvas, paint, masts and yards, and barrel staves went up in flames. Half-built ships were destroyed on the ways while cannons and hackbuts were carried away. At the last, slow-matches were lit in the powder store, and the resulting explosion shattered windows for leagues around.

The attack on Perpizon was a cause for celebration in Selford, for more bonfires and bell-ringing, and the air was again scented with powder from the gunfire salutes. There was even more celebration a week later when Coneygrave and the fleet sailed into Innismore. The four galleons captured at the Races were in company, the flag of Duisland flying over the banner of Loretto. Coneygrave had even brought the *Imperial* with him, the enemy flagship that had been so battered in the fight that it could barely float, but now after repairs in

Bretlynton Head made a brave sight in its renewed vermilion paint and gold leaf.

Coneygrave flew his flag again in *King Emmius*, which after intervention by those same dockworkers at Bretlynton Head was now fit once more to carry the High Admiral.

The Queen took her barge down the river to meet him, and I joined her along with most of the Council. Coneygrave welcomed Floria onto his quarterdeck, and as he knelt before her, she made him a Knight of the Red Horse, then greeted him by his new title, Viscount Coneygrave of the Races. He gave his guests a dinner in his great cabin in which the pease porridge, salt beef, and plum duff of the sailor was mixed with fish from the local market, and lamb and fowl cooked in an Innismore tavern and rushed to the flagship in a whaleboat.

Floria repaid Coneygrave's hospitality three days later, when he, his officers, and many sailors and soldiers made a procession through the city while bells rang, guns fired, and the people waved their handkerchiefs and cheered till their voices failed. Coneygrave and the officers enjoyed a dinner in their honor in the Great Reception Room, while the ordinary soldiers and sailors feasted on trestle tables set up in the Middle Ward. After many speeches in his honor, Coneygrave rose from the seat of honor to proclaim that as soon as the fleet finished a refit, he would lead them to Stanport and "see what can be done about that great manslayer, Admiral Mola." The cheers echoed from the roof-beams.

"Did all that make you wish to go back to sea, Quillifer?" Floria asked me that night, after we were alone in my apartment.

"I have no clever scheme to defeat Admiral Mola," said I, "and so I would as lief stay in bed, as always with present company. In fact I think very little will come of Coneygrave's expedition—the fleets are too evenly matched, so if it comes to battle, they will batter each other until their stores of powder and shot are exhausted, and then our fleet will return to Selford for another refit."

"You don't think Coneygrave could win the fight, and blockade the enemy on shore?"

"He would have to be very lucky. Though the sight of *Imperial*—the largest and most celebrated warship in the world—sailing among our fleet might drive Mola into a rage, and cause him to do something foolish." I sighed. "Well, we can but hope."

"If only it were possible to dine on hope," Floria said, "I would have a feast every night. But I must remind myself that hope must be rationed, like provisions in a besieged town, and that I must dine sparingly, lest I consume every last bit of my hope, wander into the desolate ground between the lines, and there perish."

I felt astonishment at this, and at the bleak look in her hazel eyes. "There is no cause for such despair, Majesty," said I. "The enemy laid their plans well, but one of their armies is come to grief, and the other is dying by inches in a siege."

"Dying by inches, ay, along with my besieged city hammered into the dirt," said she. "And another city freely opened its gates to the enemy that had just cut thousands to pieces before their eyes. How many more such cities do I have in my kingdom? How many traitors? And how many butcheries before it is over?"

"You must trust those who love you," said I—a hopeless statement, for it answered none of her questions.

"Love," said she, "is another thing to be rationed. For I may indulge only here, and at night, and in hopes that all but we two are a-slumber."

Coneygrave was feasted all over the town, at one or another of the guild halls, or toasted by lawyers at the Treasury Moot, or praised at a dinner given by the *Duque* de Gandorim at the Goldsmiths' Hall. I own that I became a little jealous, for though my part in the battle was known, no one had carried me around town on their shoulders, recited a complimentary ode in my honor, or flattered me with an address at the theater. If I were the subject of a ballad, it was because I wrote the ballad myself.

I wondered if Coneygrave were finding it so pleasant in Selford that his fleet would not sail till the next age, and indeed he seemed not to be in such a hurry to find Mola's ships and bring them to battle.

The fleet was still anchored off Innismore on a hot July afternoon when a message from Floria brought me from the Secretariat to the castle, where the servants loitered in the shade, the Yeoman Archers drowsed over their halberds, and folk sought out the Great Reception Room because the perpetual chill and the bracing drafts were so refreshing. When I came into the Starry Drawing Room I saw Floria with the Count de Coots, the ambassador from Thurnmark, who was accompanied by another gentleman dressed in gray velvet. Roundsilver, standing by the Queen, glittered in a shimmering silk doublet that matched the deep blue of the cushions.

The casements were open to allow fresh air to blow in, but the air drifting through the windows seemed as sultry as the air already in the room. A flagon of golden Varcellos wine was laid on the water-sapphire table, alongside a silver-gilt bowl of peaches that offered their soft scent to the air. Floria was delicately slicing a peach with a small knife, and looked up as I entered and bowed.

"Ah, Selford," said she. "Have some wine, and a peach if you desire. We wait only on Coneygrave, and as I had to send to his flagship, he may be some time."

"Is something afoot, Majesty?" asked I. For as there were no servants in the room to pour the wine or to slice the fruit, I knew we would be discussing matters of state, to be held closely by only a few people.

Floria concentrated on the peach in her hand. "Allow me to introduce the Count de Coots," she said.

I bowed. "Of course we are already acquainted." De Coots was a stout man with small dark eyes and broken veins in his face. A lace handkerchief dangled from one hand, to blot the sweat from his forehead.

Floria indicated the man in gray. "This is Master Teunissen," she said. "He is a special messenger just arrived from the court of the Hogen-Mogen."

"Ah." I bowed. "Honored to make your acquaintance."

Teunissen made a sweeping bow. He was a man my own age with the kind of dark brown hair that develops a red tint in the sun. He wore his hair long, had a pointed beard, and he carried himself with the poised posture of an actor, or a swordsman.

"I am delighted to know the man the Loretto court calls the Demon Dom Keely-Fay."

I was amused. "Do they truly call me that?"

"Since the Battle of the Races, yes," said Teunissen. "They think you are a sorcerer of some sort, who bewitched Admiral de Cuerzy into sailing his fleet onto the rocks."

I smiled. "True, I work what magic I can."

"Keely-Fay" was the nearest those of Loretto could come to pronouncing my name, as they have no letter Q in their alphabet. Since so many of their pamphlets and broadsides against me claimed I was a sorcerer who had bewitched the Queen, I wondered if they had decided to believe their own absurdities and now credited me with preternatural powers.

"Please, gentlemen," Floria said. "Sit. There is no need to stand on such a hot afternoon."

I gave myself a cup of wine and chose an armchair. The wine was a white gouais still cool from the cellars, and on tasting I kindled a memory of honey made from apricot blossoms, with the tiniest tart essence of lemon.

We watched while Floria ate her peach, and then dabbed the juice from her fingers with a napkin.

"We may as well begin," said she, "and we can catch Coneygrave up when he arrives." She turned to Teunissen. "Sir, if you would be so good . . . ?"

Teunissen bowed. "Thank you, Your Majesty." He turned toward me and Roundsilver, who sat on my right. "We have located Priscus's Army of Duisland. They are brigaded together, lying in garrison near our borders, and we think it might be possible to retrieve them."

Roundsilver gave a little intake of breath, and I felt my heart speed a little at this news. When Priscus of Loretto had been our King, he had brought Duisland into his father's war with Thurnmark, even though we had no quarrel with that country. He had also demanded twenty thousand soldiers for the war, which the Estates voted him with reluctance. He hoped to lead this corps personally into battle, but the war had widened by the time the men began to arrive, and they were fed piecemeal into the conflict and suffered accordingly.

The next year, Priscus had demanded twenty-five thousand more soldiers, which the Estates, intimidated by Viceroy Fosco's tyranny, had voted under compulsion. Most of these soldiers never went to Loretto, as the success of Floria's revolt kept them in the country, where they formed the core of those forces led by the Constable and the Knight Marshal; but an unlucky few thousands of our soldiers found themselves in Loretto when their homeland changed sides.

We had heard little of the Duisland troops in the last year and a half, but assumed that they had been eaten up by war and contagion.

"How many are there?" asked I.

"We have spies not among those soldiers," said Teunissen, "but in Prince Tiburcio's headquarters, and these say that these troops are issued almost nine thousand rations."

"I had not expected there would be so many," said I.

Roundsilver's eyes were alight with calculation. "Do they know that Floria is Queen, and that we now fight Loretto in alliance with Thurnmark?"

I looked at Roundsilver in surprise, for I had not considered that this information could be kept from our soldiers.

"Nay," said Teunissen. "We think they know not the true situation, and that they are stationed on a fortified island in order to be kept in ignorance."

"Who commands there?" Roundsilver asked.

"A man named Sir Cadwal Campion."

Roundsilver nodded. "Cadwal is Lord Campion's younger son."

"Is Lord Campion in Selford?" I asked. "Perhaps he should write a letter to his son, with his hand and seal."

Floria frowned. "I have not seen his lordship of late."

"He suffers much from gout," said Roundsilver, "but I saw him the other day, being carried in a chair about the park."

The Queen offered me a level gaze. "Nine thousand troops," she said. "If we could carry them over to Bonille, that would prove a fine stroke against the enemy, and might be what we need to save Stanport."

"Indeed," said I. I had an idea what Floria's gaze might mean for me, and I did not care for it.

The ambassador spoke for the first time. "We have not only to get a message to this Campion," he said, "but somehow get these soldiers off the island and onto ships. We can provide some ships but not all."

"Have you tried getting a message to Campion yourselves?" asked I.

"It has been attempted," Teunissen said, "but we don't know what became of the messengers."

"And your messengers know the country," said I. "If any of our countrymen tried to blunder their way onto that island, they would find themselves at the end of a rope."

"We would provide expert guides," said de Coots.

"Those men you lost? Were they not expert?"

At this point Coneygrave entered, and had to have everything explained to him. "Nine thousand men?" he said. "It would take at least twenty large ships to transport so many, and that is half my fleet. The craft would be so crowded that we would have to dismount the guns, and there would be no possibility of my engaging Admiral Mola."

"Baron de Coots has said that Thurnmark would provide some ships," said Floria.

"How many are reserved for that business?" asked I.

Teunissen offered a cheerful grin. "None yet," he admitted. "When your emissary comes to our country, we will begin assembling those ships. We have a substantial merchant fleet, and a very efficient navy, though not as large as yours. We can carry a few thousand at least."

Coneygrave and I shared skeptical looks. Floria saw the looks and frowned at us. "Gentlemen," she said. "We need those men at Stanport."

"We have ships that even now carry soldiers to Bonille," said Roundsilver. "We could send the ships to Thurnmark instead."

"But to send them to Thurnmark," said Coneygrave, "means our soldiers will no longer be carried to Bonille, where they are so desperately needed."

"Say that we send ten or a dozen ships to Thurnmark," Floria said. "Building new ships, we can replace them while they are away."

"Where is this island?" I asked. "Is it on the coast so that we can easily carry the men away?"

"Nay, nay," said Teunissen. "It is Briese Island in the Linye Delta, and there are other islands to seaward of it, and one large island between it and our fortifications on the mainland. Those islands are garrisoned."

"Then how do we get these men off, even if we persuade them to change sides?" asked I.

"We could slip them away in small boats," said Teunissen. "It would take several nights, but these garrisons don't keep good watch."

I did not find this plausible. "I suppose they would have to fight their way to friendly territory," said I. "What forces stand between them and your own side of the river?"

"There is a company of mercenaries on Gravelinye Island. About four thousand, but well fortified, and commanding the bridges and the high ground."

"And to seaward?"

"Also mercenaries, in a fort commanding the main channel, but there are fewer of them. It would be less trouble to take the island, but the problem then becomes how to evacuate your people over the tidal flats to the ships, especially when there would almost certainly be counterattacks."

"Large ships can't get up the Linye?"

"Elsewhere, but not there."

"Yet those small boats you mentioned?"

"Yes. Certainly. We would need more of them, that's all."

I looked at Coneygrave again. He was in a study, his chin on his chest, his eyes fixed on the floor. I turned again to Teunissen.

"You have set us quite the puzzle, Master Teunissen. One misstep and the emissary and all Campion's command would be killed."

"Quillifer," Floria said. "That is why you should be my messenger to Cadwal Campion."

This was what I had dreaded from the moment I had understood why Teunissen had come to Duisland. "Majesty," said I, "I hardly think I'm the best candidate for the task."

"Yes, you are," said the Queen. "It's exactly the line of business that has won your reputation. And I want those nine thousand men."

"And I wish more information," said I. "Have we a map?"

Floria and I sat on the settee in my apartment. The day's heat lingered in the room, and I wore only a fine lawn shirt that pooled in my lap, while Floria had taken off her dressing gown to reveal a silk gown of golden sarcenet that shimmered over her body like the light of a rising sun. I had fetched a bucket of snow from the cold cellar, and plunged into it a flask of hock, which I had then poured into chilled goblets.

The hock danced on my tongue and cooled my throat. I had thought that tonight's conversation might be eased by a degree of relaxation that stopped just short of intoxication, and so I refilled our goblets earlier than I might have, and drank mine off. Eventually I felt emboldened enough to voice the thoughts that had been churning in my mind since the meeting that afternoon.

"You wish me to undertake this quest to find a lost army in Thurnmark," I said. "I worry that I might find it, then be ushered to the nearest noose. Campion might be loyal to little King Aguila."

"You need but deliver some letters," said Floria. "Everything else will be arranged by others."

"If I am captured by the enemy," said I, "they will have special treatment for Demon Dom Keely-Fay who not only put you on your throne and drove off the Viceroy, but who wrecked the enemy's fleet on the Races. They despise me as the son of a butcher, and they fear me as a great necromancer. They might hang me, burn me, or cut me to bits, but they would be certain to finish me off." I ventured a laugh. "Why don't you send Scarnside?" I said. "He and Campion both belong to noble houses, and if Scarnside's captured, he and Campion could have a long discussion about the glories of their ancestors, and then Scarnside would have a pleasant holiday in some castle or other until his friends raise his ransom."

Golden candle-glints reflected in Floria's eyes. "You have been in many perils, and with great success."

"I have generally chosen those perils for myself," said I. "I prefer not to let others send me into danger, especially into a situation in which previous envoys simply vanished."

Vexation spread lines from the corners of her mouth and eyes. "If the cause is hopeless," said she, "you need not make the attempt. But you will not know what is possible until you arrive in Thurnmark."

I nodded. "Very well," said I. "I will imperil myself out of love for you. But I have a condition or two."

Floria raised one eyebrow. "This is a new custom, is it not? When was it ever necessary for us to bargain?"

"From today," I said. "For I must send a message ere I leave Selford."

She waved a hand. "Very well. What is it?"

"I want Brighthelm dead before I go."

Her eyes deepened to blackness, and even the light of the candles guttered out in her wide pupils. "That is not your province, Quillifer," she said. "That is Thistlegorm's business, and the attorney general's."

"And thine," I said, "for the decision has always been yours. The case against Brighthelm has been ready for weeks. His cake-passer has confessed along with the two brutes he employed to throw Luzi off the battlements. But Thistlegorm will put men of rank on the jury who will see nothing very wrong with Brighthelm's actions, and Brighthelm will be released to disturb the Queen's peace again and again, because he's as mad as his younger brother Brynley."

"I can speak to Thistlegorm about the jury."

"Speak to Thistlegorm if you will, and tell him to send Brighthelm to the Siege Royal to have his head topped." She opened her mouth to speak, but I interrupted. "Nay, madame, I am tired of being made into a mark for every well-born malt-horse in the kingdom. When Sir Edelmir Westley first challenged me, I half-drowned him in Lake Howel, but I dragged him out once he learned his lesson. When mad Brynley Wilmot insisted we fight, I took care to preserve his life, but I failed and he died. The next man I planned only to wound, but he fell three storeys and broke his back, though yet he lives.

"But these lessons were insufficient, for Edevane tried to kill me and died for it. Even a lord dangling from a silk cord proved an insufficient lesson for Brighthelm, but perhaps Brighthelm dangling next to Edevane will bring home the lesson that I am not a play-toy to be smashed by wanton children."

Floria's mouth had tightened into a grim line. "Very well," she said, "I will send Brighthelm to the treason court."

"I thank Your Majesty." I raised my goblet and tasted the hock, but it had grown warm, and I felt it would no longer cool the heat that blazed in me, so I put the goblet down.

The Queen surveyed me from the other end of the settee. "You said you might have more than one condition," said she.

"I have two more, now I think on it," said I. "First, I will need several chests filled with silver."

"I suppose I can guess why."

"Second," said I, "I would like to know why you are trying to get me out of the way."

I watched as her face turned to stone. I waited a few seconds, and then I spoke.

"I have wit enough to understand what is happening," I said. "But I would like to know why. I assume it has something to do with negotiations with Ambassador Gandorim, presumably about this Prince Oriol he has settled upon, but if it is something else, then I should like to know."

Her glance fell to her hands, to the fingers wrapped around her glass goblet. "Ay," said she. "Negotiations with Gandorim have reached a critical stage. You would be an unnecessary complication."

"You have benefitted from my complications in the past."

She shook her head. "Yet you do not bring fifty thousand soldiers into the war."

"Nor will King Anibal, I'll warrant." I shook my head. "You know that I think the Varcellos alliance is hedged with unnecessary conditions. You know that I told Gandorim that Varcellos should attack now while the enemy are on their heels. Has Gandorim even answered my observation?"

"He says he is not authorized to negotiate on those terms."

"Of course he would say such a thing. His king wishes to gain a daughter-in-law for nothing."

"I think Anibal wants a war and an ally both," Floria said.

"I believe you should place a clause in the marriage contract that guarantees a Varcellan army. If Anibal does not attack with every one of those fifty thousand men, and do so within six weeks of the marriage, you should have the right to ship this Oriol home aboard the meanest flyboat on the ocean."

I believe Floria almost smiled. "You seem to think that I have decided to accept this marriage."

My heart gave a leap. "You have today given me every reason to think so. I rejoice if that is not the case."

"The case is that I consider carefully my options."

"As you should, for I fear the court tries to bully you into marriage." I nodded. "And you should consider your choices not only in your role as Queen, but as a woman with a right to her own desires."

A skeptical look invaded her eyes. "What do you know of a woman's desires?"

"Perhaps only a little. Yet I venture to claim that I know the woman in question better than anyone on Earth." I gestured toward Floria with my glass goblet. "The world knows you as Queen, brilliant in silks and gems, an icon for secular worship and a virtuous embodiment of the state. And indeed you *are* that, whenever you sit in royal state, or rule the Council, or accept the praises of the world at some court masque. But *that* lady—that lady is an idol, flawless perhaps but made of stone or maybe brass, and not a living being.

"But I—" I raised a finger. "I know a somewhat different lady, and I know her only here in this room and a very few other places. Together we plotted to free the nation from tyranny, to return justice to the land, and to bring about victory in war. That lady has laughed with me, and schemed, and shared her mind with me, and shared as well a thousand kisses. And this lady is not an idol of brass or stone, but a breathing woman, full of sweetness and honey, copious of wit and generous of soul, precious as a newborn flower.

"That lady I have loved with all my heart, and I have labored to keep her safe in her person and triumphant in all things. That lady has unburdened her mind to me, and I have tried to help her grapple with the perils that beset her."

I looked soberly at Floria, and I saw her return that look, her eyes deep and dark, her face planes and shadows in the light of the candles.

"If this Oriol—or Morestanton, or some other young fool—stands between us," said I, "you will lose what we have together. The young lady that I love will perish for want of that love, smothered as if locked up in a chest and forgotten, and you will have to be that stone idol forever. And that, my only darling, is what I most fear, that you will become the loneliest being in the kingdom, surrounded by flattery and lies and the measured dances of court, but unable to speak your heart to anyone."

I waved a hand at the room, at the carved bed, the hangings with their bright colors half-subdued by darkness, the settee where we had so often spoken late into the night. "How can you replace this?" asked I. "Here there is safety, here there is love, here we speak the truth. Where else at court will you find such honesty as we practice here?"

Floria's glance dropped to her listless hands that half embraced her goblet. I saw the tears coursing down her cheeks like falling stars.

"I desire—" she began. "I desire—"

"And you have a right to your desires," said I. "You have a right to happiness."

She took my hand and kissed it, and then she rose and reached for her dressing gown. "I must go," she said. "It is too hot, and I am too unhappy."

I rose. "I'm sorry if I have made you miserable."

She gave a little shake of her head. "Not you. The world."

She took her candle and left through the secret door, and I stood for a long while staring at that door, and feeling the long, slow beat of sorrow throb through my heart.

CHAPTER SEVENTEEN

I cannot eat but little meat
My stomach is not good
But sure I think that I can drink
With him that wears a hood.

Though I go bare, take ye no care,
I nothing am a-cold
I stuff my skin so full within
Of jolly good ale and old.

About six weeks later, near the end of August, I cast my serenade on the wind as I sat with my guitar near the military camp on Briese Island in the Linye Delta. Above, gray cloud streamed in the firmament, clawing stripes across the distant, brittle-seeming stars. Reeds rattled against one another by the water, and gusts rolled across the river's surface.

Back and side go bare, go bare;
Both foot and hands go cold;

But belly, God send thee good ale enough
Whether it be new or old.

I had taken leave of Selford with reluctance, and only when I had no business there remaining. Floria had been merciful to the Marquess of Brighthelm, and ordered him beheaded instead of hanged like a pickpocket or a thief. But the day did not go without hanging, for Brighthelm's three accomplices met the executioner an hour before his lordship breathed his last.

I had purchased tickets to the event, and witnessed it from a gable overlooking the place of execution. I had little stomach for it, but I felt that as I'd insisted on Brighthelm's death, I should condemn myself to witness it.

The crowd was merry and sang songs that taunted the condemned, or related celebrated executions of the past. There were barrows selling gingerbread, sausages, oysters, and cakes. Acrobats performed, folk walked on stilts, and monks and prophets offered moralizing homilies. It was like a fair.

Lord Waitstill and his son Hunstan watched from a carriage. Their wives were not present. They had brought a dozen or so footmen to keep the crowds at bay, and to help carry away the body afterward.

The second Brighthelm's head fell from his shoulders, the courtesy title would shift to Hunstan. If it were not for the unfortunate means of his brother's death, the style of marchioness would have made a fine gift to his new bride Candice.

The event itself, when it came, was almost an anticlimax. Brighthelm made some speech to the crowd which I could not hear, though this did not matter, for the writers of broadsides and ballads had already invented Brighthelm's last words, and had them for sale well before the execution.

The headsman placed Brighthelm on the block, and then let the axe fall. It was neatly done, and the crowd gave an enormous cheer that must have been heard for miles. Then the cries of the gingerbread-sellers and the oyster-mongers rose again, and the heart of the city beat on, minus a few corpuscles that stood as a lesson to those able to hear.

> *I love no roast but a nut-brown toast*
> *And a crab laid in the fire;*
> *A little bread shall do me stead;*
> *Much bread I not desire.*
> *No frost, nor snow, no wind, I trow*
> *Can hurt me if I would;*
> *I am so wrapped and thoroughly lapped*
> *Of jolly good ale and old.*

> *Back and side go bare, go bare;*
> *Both foot and hands go cold;*
> *But belly, God send thee good ale enough*
> *Whether it be new or old.*

A few nights after the execution I took Greenaway's haquenai to Philpott Square to visit Lottie Forde. Her house was scented with rose oil, as always, and I kissed her cheek fondly. We supped together, and afterward my spy Barbosa arrived, and the two of us went upstairs to lay out plans.

Barbosa had been staying in Innismore with his lugger and his crew since the spring, when he had reported on Admiral Mola's movements. Until now I had not decided how best to employ him, but now I told him that I was sending him to Ferrick. He was surprised.

"Not Avevic again? Not Stanport?"

"I would not send you into that pestilential hell of Stanport," said I, "and I expect no surprises from Avevic. But I am interested in Ferrick, and who rules there, and with what force."

"Ay," he said. "I understand."

"But bring no reports to me here," said I. "I shall be in Thurnmark. I will give you the address."

> *And Tib, my wife, that as her life*
> *Loveth well good ale to seek,*
> *Full oft drinks she, still you may see*
> *The tears run down her cheek:*
> *Then doth she troll to me the bowl*
> *Even as a maltworm should,*
> *And saith, "Sweetheart, I took my part*
> *Of this jolly good ale and old."*

> *Back and side go bare, go bare;*
> *Both foot and hands go cold;*
> *But belly, God send thee good ale enough*
> *Whether it be new or old.*

Floria continued to visit my apartment most nights. There was delight, there was wit and banter, there was all the appearance of love; but too much was left unsaid, our conversation had lost some of its candor, and I knew not how to recover it. It was as if I were already embarked, drifting away on a sluggish tide, and I had no anchor.

The barbarous siege of Stanport continued. Only a few buildings still retained four walls and a roof, and the population dug into their cellars like rats. Mola's army continued its slow creeping to the left, and hoped to encircle the city within the month.

Lord Savidge, His Grace of Roundsilver's father-in-law, followed Waitstill as privy seal. Catsgore's replacement as Minister of State for Fornland was Rothwell, another man of the west from Aberuvon, at the foot of the Minnith Peaks.

Neither of these two were hostile to me, which I counted a blessing, and I was pleased also that Rothwell was another westerner, and we could league together to protect one another's interests.

There was difficulty in making up sufficient transport to carry the Duisland army home, and so with Rufino Knott I went ahead with Captain Gaunt in *Sovereign,* taking Teunissen as a passenger. We left a few days after Coneygrave took his fleet to seek out Admiral Mola, and we encountered that same fleet on its return journey. There had been a battle, which Coneygrave claimed as a victory because on the way he had captured a few shallops and a transport vessel filled with salt beef and cheese. He had not taken any of Mola's warships, nor had he lost any of his own, so I thought any claim of outright victory would not go far. He was returning to Selford for ammunition and a refit, after which he would have another try at Mola. The war at sea was beginning to seem as brutal and futile as the siege at Stanport.

As soon as Fornland fell below the western horizon, and I felt the deck roll beneath me, I sensed my anxiety begin to ebb. It was not that my problems had vanished—my leaving Selford only compounded them—but once I was committed to the voyage, it was impossible to me to affect the greater world in any way. The dance of the court was proceeding without me, and where the courtiers trod a measure, or with whom, no longer had anything to do with me.

Teunissen was pleasant company, always smiling, always confiding. He was, I decided, an excellent spy, though I declined to furnish him with very much information. He played the fipple flute, and joined in making music with me and Master Knott.

Sovereign swung far north to avoid the coast and Mola's fleet, and arrived at the Hook of Zomer on the twelfth of August. The navy of Thurnmark was in the anchorage, but the great ships carried only anchor watches, for most of the crews had been marched off by the Hogen-Mogen for the season's campaign against Prince Tiburcio.

My boat's crew and Boatswain Lepalik took us up the Senagne to Houbek, the port town on the north coast that had served as

Thurnmark's capital since its true capital had been occupied by the enemy. Here we paused a few days while Teunissen contacted friends and members of the government to discover what had taken place while he was away, and I amused myself by attending meetings of the Assembly of Notables, which has only a single chamber, nobles and commons mingled on the benches. The proceedings were conducted in a language I did not comprehend, but I understood the goings-on well enough, as they were identical to the dull, droning pageant enacted in the Estates of Duisland.

I traveled incognito, as a merchant named Herbert Rothwell, for if Lord Selford turned up in Houbek, any spies of Loretto would take note, and alarms rung from there to Longres Regius.

I paid my respects to Floria's ambassador, Sir Harley Warriner, and showed him my commission from the Queen, which focused his attention wonderfully. He arranged for carriages to carry me and my dunnage south to my meeting with the Army of Duisland, and we drank together to Floria's health.

I met the Hogen-Mogen, the Graaf de Hendricks, who had been installed after the previous Hogen-Mogen had lost half the country in the Loretto invasion. The constitution of Thurnmark permits the Assembly to dismiss their head of state, by a three-fifths majority, then appoint another, which I thought was a useful innovation that other nations might well consider.

The Hogen-Mogen was a thin, pale man, with sunken dark eyes and a bright yellow beard swiftly going gray. He moved with a degree of care, as if he were an invalid, but Warriner told me he was tireless in combat. He was not a brilliant commander, but he was a thorough one who made few mistakes, and was utterly without fear. He and had met Prince Tiburcio in several titanic, hard-fought battles that had shifted the lines at least a few leagues in the direction of the old Loretto frontier. He was not in Houbek to see me but to persuade the Notables to give him more money and soldiers, and in this he was successful.

De Hendricks and I drank brandy and conversed in the only language we had in common, that of our enemy Loretto. I congratulated him on the brave fight he was making against the enemy, and he was equally complimentary about the victory in the Races. He seemed to know a great deal about that encounter, and about the siege of Stanport as well, and I concluded that Ambassador de Coots was very thorough in submitting his reports.

"You are very good even to take notice of our trouble at Stanport," said I, "for your country has borne many grievous sieges in the last few years, and will endure many more before it is over."

"If the badger will not come out of his den, we must dig him out," said de Hendricks. "Yet I will take my country back, ditch by ditch if I must." He looked at me, and his sunken eyes brightened as he scrutinized me. "That is where the garrison at Briese Island might prove useful. If we can persuade those men to change sides and hand Briese to us, then we could outflank the enemy river line on the Linye."

"Your lordship will have an army ready for that?"

"Ay, unless Tiburcio attacks somewhere else. But I think he has exhausted his resources for this year, and stands now on the defensive everywhere."

"But is there not this island of Gravelinye between Briese and your troops?"

De Hendricks nodded, and spoke in an offhand way that I instantly mistrusted. "We would have to storm that island," he said.

"And the other occupied islands?"

"The ones downstream would be cut off and would have to surrender. The garrisons upstream would be flanked once we get over the Linye, and forced to withdraw."

"Your lordship has laid his plans well." The scheme was so nicely and plausibly developed that it would be difficult for me to escape its coils, and I preferred to allow myself, like Floria, to consider carefully my options. The Hogen-Mogen's plans all hinged on whether I could persuade my countrymen to change sides, and the disappearance of previous messengers was not encouraging.

De Hendricks and Teunissen probably thought they had me trapped in this hazardous enterprise. Yet I hoped I would squirm and thrash free enough to meet this adventure on terms more acceptable to me, and perhaps keep my neck free of the noose.

> *Now let them drink till they nod and wink,*
> *Even as good fellows should do;*
> *They shall not miss to have the bliss*
> *Good ale doth bring men to.*
> *And all poor souls that have scoured bowls*
> *Or have them lustily trolled,*
> *God save the lives of them and their wives,*
> *Whether they be young or old.*
>
> *Back and side go bare, go bare;*
> *Both foot and hands go cold;*
> *But belly, God send thee good ale enough*
> *Whether it be new or old.*

Knott and I held the last note, then let it die in a gust of wind that rattled the reeds down by the river. Our audience of half a dozen soldiers bawled their appreciation and slapped their thighs by way of applause.

"Do you know 'The Female Saylor'?" asked one.

"Ay," said I. "But singing is thirsty work. Where is that cask, friend?"

We had come to Briese to make friends, and for that we did not rely entirely on song. We had brought a small barrel of apple brandy, and it assured that within less than half an hour we had acquired six boon companions.

We sheltered from the wind in a little dell near the camp. Even in the dark I could see that our new comrades were not far removed from destitution. Their clothing was in tatters, and their shoes were held together with patches and leather scraps. Most huddled in blankets for warmth, and their lean bodies showed they were frequently hungry. Two of the men had bad coughs.

The cask rolled toward me across the grass, and a soldier tossed me the polished copper jigger with its graceful little handle. I removed the bung, filled the jigger, and drank, and then passed the cask and the jigger to Knott.

"Whose company are you?" asked one of the soldiers.

"Hughes's Company, from Ethlebight," said I.

"I have never heard of no Hughes's Company," said another.

"Nor should you," I responded. "Coronel Hughes sent twenty of us ahead under his nephew Conrad, and we arrived two summers ago. But the rest of Hughes's Company never came, and we were put into garrison in Sélange. There we have been these two years, never seeing any of our countrymen or receiving news from home, until the Emperor attacked with his allied army. We were thrown into the fight like grain before the harrow, and Knott and I are the only two left. Someone heard others from Duisland were in garrison here, and so here we were sent."

"Grain before the harrow, ay," said a soldier. "That is how Loretto treats us. And now we are so sick and shot to pieces that we are only good to garrison this wretched island."

"Let us have another song!" said another, and then burst into a frenzy of coughing.

Knott and I sang "The Female Saylor," and others joined in. The cask was passed from hand to hand.

"Ay, thirsty work," said I, as the cask came again to me. I drank and passed it on.

"How is Campion, your commander?" asked I. "A good soldier?"

"A brave gentleman," I was told. "Though in him, the bravery makes good for some other flaws."

"Is he cruel? A despot? Will he hang a man for drinking with new friends beneath the light of the stars?"

"He cares not about such things," said one soldier. "Nay, discipline is relaxed here, for there is no fighting, and we are on an island and cannot escape. They count us every morning, we drill twice a week, and we have sown crops so that we are not dependent on the Loretto commissary, which steals half our food. The rest of the time is our own."

"Campion is in thrall to his Loretto whore," said another. "He keeps a red-haired doxy in his quarters, and she rules him with a fist of iron."

"And there is also that Conte Aspasio," said a third, "who is King Aguila's governor on this island. He is a grim swag-bellied fellow, with a little troupe of executioners, and Campion must dance to his tune."

"Aspasio is the cruel one," the first soldier affirmed.

"Surely Campion doesn't allow him to discipline Duisland men," said I.

"Nay," said one, "but all others are his to whip or hang as he will. He has strung up men he said were spies, and he is the terror of the camp-followers, for he squeezes silver from them, and if they cannot pay, he sends his men to beat them, or to steal their wares."

So this Aspasio had disposed of Thurnmark's messengers. I thought that where Aspasio was concerned I had best keep the weather gage and stay well upwind of him.

"Have any messages come from Duisland?" asked I. "I have received not a word from my family in all this time, and the rest of Hughes's Company never marched."

"If any dispatch comes from Duisland, word of it never reaches us," said a soldier. "Some of us are dying for want of news about our wives and families, and that news never comes."

"I think something must have happened in Duisland," said I. "Some great change, to keep the rest of our army from coming."

"Could Duisland be invaded?" someone asked.

"But who would do it?" said I. "We share a border with no one but Loretto."

"I grow melancholy at this futile refrain," said another soldier. "We know nothing, we do nothing, we are forgotten on this barren island, which might be Hell. For all the Pilgrim's sake, let us have a merry song."

Knott and I obliged him, and then we passed the keg around again, and said that we would be back the next night, after sunset.

The north coast of Alford is low, filled with salt-marsh and islets, with great mud flats and sand banks that reach out from the coast at low tide to strand unwary ships. The rivers spread out their fingers in search of the sea, and often shift their banks in floods and storms. Towns perch atop the firm land and are surrounded by bogs and peat-colored water.

Moving in near-perfect silence through the dark water, taking care not to be silhouetted against open water, Teunissen had brought Knott and me on the water the night before. We worried that guard boats might be on patrol, but we saw none. When we arrived on the island of Briese we found a place in the reeds where we might hide the boat. That day we had studied the Duisland camp with the aid of a child's toy that Teunissen had bought in the market in Houbek. This device was called a polemoscope, and consisted of a cardboard tube with a mirror set at each end, so that you could look into the lower aperture and view the world from the top of the tube. Thus we could raise the polemoscope and view the camp without sticking our heads above the level of the reeds.

The polemoscope was a very useful device, I thought, particularly I supposed in sieges, and I thought that when I returned home, I'd establish a workshop to manufacture them.

The soldiers had been on the island for over a year, and they had made themselves as comfortable as they could. They had made dugouts for themselves, burrowing a yard or so into the soil, then raising wattle walls with roofs of canvas or reed thatch. Peat smoke rose from mud-and-wattle chimneys. Gardens had been planted and fenced against wandering livestock. A tattered flag with the quartered hippogriffs and tritons flew over a substantial farm building, and I assumed this was Campion's headquarters. Half-starved cattle, driven I imagine onto the island to serve as food for the soldiers, grazed on the rich grass.

For the most part the soldiers seemed to have little to do. They worked their garden plots, or played at dice, or fished for their dinner, or simply lay in the summer sun.

When night fell Knott and I took our guitars and the keg of apple brandy to a little dell near the camp, and then began to play, and soon men from the camp wandered out to join us. After that first meeting ended, we returned to the boat, wrapped ourselves in blankets, and took our rest.

The next day we ventured further afield with the polemoscope, staying always in cover of the reeds that surrounded the island. We paid careful attention to the bridge from Briese to Gravelinye, a wooden structure two hundred yards long built on piles driven into the river bottom. The mercenaries on Gravelinye had built a large wooden tower on the far side, with wooden stockade walls stretched left and right, and a drawbridge that raised the span nearest the tower. Cannon were aimed from the battlements toward Briese. Gravelinye was higher than Briese, and those on that island looked down on the Duisland camp.

It was as if Briese were a prison, and the mercenaries the warders.

> *Wines indeed and girls are good,*
> *But brave victuals feast the blood;*

> *For wenches, wine, and lusty cheer,*
> *Gods would leap down to surfeit here.*

The little dell filled with our song, and our audience—those who knew the words—sang along. To these starvelings, our song offered a bounty of capons, pigs, and mutton, solid food for the imagination to feast upon.

We had brought another cask of apple brandy, and the little copper jigger, and we passed it about.

"Where did you get the brandy?" asked a soldier. We had met him only tonight, for this evening our audience was twice the size of the night previous.

"We brought it with us," said I.

"Here we have only small beer," the soldier said. "Poor stuff, well watered, and we get it only rarely. Otherwise we take water from the river."

"Well," said I, "you are welcome to our keg until we run out, and then it will be small beer for us as well."

The keg came back to me, and I filled the jigger and drank. Brandy fumes went up my nose, and I sneezed.

Knott strummed a few idle chords. "I delight in fishing," he said. "Are there boats I might use?"

"Nay," said a man, "all boats were taken to the west side of the river, so the enemy could not find or use them. You will have to fish from the shore."

"That is sad," said Knott. "There is nothing like a fine boat."

"No boats," I said. "And I have seen that bridge built between here and that other island, guarded by a tower and guns. It is as if you are being confined here."

"We are so confined," said the first soldier. "But what can we do about it?"

"And not even your commander gets word from home?" said I. "Has he complained, do you know?"

A new voice spoke, measured and thoughtful. "There is no one to complain to but Conte Aspasio," said he. "And Campion complains to that gross man, and he also writes dispatches to Prince Tiburcio and to Longres Regius, but he must send them through Aspasio, so the messages never leave the island and nothing is ever done."

The speaker, I saw, wore an officer's sash, and also had one sleeve of his doublet pinned up. His face was long and melancholy, and there was a plume in his hat, so tattered it all but looked like a twig.

"Welcome, sir," said I. "Are you in Sir Cadwal's confidence?"

"I will not claim intimacy," said he. "Yet as I have lost my sword arm, I endeavor to make myself useful in the headquarters."

"I applaud your sentiment, sir," said I. "It is clear that some attempt is being made to break our spirit, and you stand resolute against it."

"I do not know if I would commend myself on those terms," said he. "Perhaps I find that mere idleness leads to tedium, and I avoid it."

"That is why we make music," said I. "It lifts the spirits, and keeps idle hands from mischief."

"Ah," said the officer. "Mischief, yes." He regarded me with dark melancholy eyes. "And which company do you belong to?"

I believe I succeeded in keeping my voice level, though my heart fluttered in my chest like a frantic bird.

"We are new to the island," said I. "Our company was in garrison in Sélange, but after the summer's fighting they are dead, and we have been sent here."

"I suppose you have reported to the headquarters?" said the officer. "I did not see you there, but I am not there every minute."

"To speak truth," said I, "we have not reported. For we have brought a certain amount of provision with us"—I indicated the cask of apple brandy—"and we have paid good silver for that provision, and we wish to be assured that our goods will not be confiscated."

The officer tilted his head and regarded me from his sorrow-ful eyes. "Do you intend to sell your provision to the soldiers here? Because they haven't been paid in over a year and have no money. All the camp-followers and sutlers are leaving because they can't sell their wares, and because Conte Aspasio charges them for such of-fenses as breathing and standing upright."

Again I indicated the apple brandy. "We have not asked for a penny. We simply ask not to be robbed."

The officer tilted his head. "I can assure you that Sir Cadwal will not rob you. Of others in the camp, I can make no promises."

"Let's have a song!" said one of the soldiers.

So we sang "Hard Times of Old Duisland," which was sad enough that even the melancholy officer joined in. The keg was passed again. I rose from the damp grass to stretch my legs, and I approached the officer.

"Sir," asked I, "may we speak privately?"

He looked up at me. "Do I know you?" he said. "You seem familiar."

"My name is Herbert Rothwell," said I. "I come from the west, as you can tell by my accent."

"I do not recall a Rothwell from the west," said he, "but I am pleased to meet you."

"And your name, sir?"

"Tate," he said. "From no place in particular."

He rose on his long shanks, and we stepped a little apart. I saw that he had a pronounced limp.

"I wonder," said I, "if you can bring Sir Cadwal Campion to meet me tomorrow, privately in this spot."

He peered at me. "And the purpose of this meeting?"

"I have a letter for him. It is best delivered and read away from any busybodies loitering about the headquarters."

"What sort of letter?"

"Instructions from the Council in Duisland. I have been sent to find this army, which Loretto has been hiding from everyone, and to give Sir Cadwal his instructions."

Tate's lips pursed in an unvoiced whistle. "So, Master Rothwell, you are a spy," he said.

"I am not," said I, with spirit. "I haven't spied on anyone, and don't intend to. I will deliver my letter and go home."

My defense seemed to amuse him. "I don't suppose you can let me see this letter?"

"I must deliver it by hand to Sir Cadwal."

"Well, well." He gazed off toward the camp, his expression thoughtful, and then looked at me and nodded. "It has long been time without word from Duisland," he said. "I will bring Sir Cadwal here tomorrow morning, after the morning roll call. But he may not wish to come, or I may not be able to speak with him privately."

"I would be obliged for any assistance you can offer."

He nodded again. "I will do what I can, Master Rothwell."

With that he limped off into the night. I wondered if he was going to fetch a half-company of soldiers to arrest me, but I reflected that I could always take to my heels, and that I knew where our boat lay and Tate didn't. I returned to the party in the dell, and we sang "Lord Southall," passed the keg about once more, and then said good night and made our way to our rest.

In the morning we made use of the polemoscope to see whether anyone lay in ambush near the dell. We discovered no one. I went to the dell alone, with Teunissen and Knott concealed in the reeds behind, each with a rifled caliver, ready to cover my withdrawal in case an enemy obliged me to fly.

Peat smoke stung the air and hung in drifts over the camp. The drummers beat the long roll, and the soldiers listlessly formed in their lines. When the officers finished the roll call, the drums boomed out again, and the soldiers broke ranks and returned to their idle summer's day.

Within a few minutes I saw two men approach, and I recognized Tate by his limp and one-armed silhouette. The other was shaped like an ashlar tipped on one end, a solid block of man with a full black beard and a black scowl. He walked with one fist clamped on the hilt of a broadsword.

I waited politely, and doffed my cap on their approach. "Gentlemen," said I, "good morning."

"Sir Cadwal," said Tate, "may I present—" He blinked at me. "This is Sir Quillifer of Ethlebight."

My heart gave a leap. "My name is Rothwell," said I.

"That may be," said Tate to Campion, "but I saw Sir Quillifer when he dropped that severed dragon's head at the feet of Queen Berlauda, and I could swear that this is the man."

"Swear not in vain," I advised.

"It matters not the fellow's name," said Campion. His voice was as ill-humored as his visage. "You have something for me, sir?"

"A letter from your father," said I. "And another letter, once you have read the first."

I passed the first letter into Campion's thick-fingered hand. He looked with care at the seal, then opened it.

"It is my father's hand," he said. He held the letter to the morning sun and began to read. As his eyes scanned the page, I could see his neck swelling like that of a great toad, and a purple rage began to spread across his face.

"That rump-fed malmsey-butt!" he snarled. "That lumpish cozening scroyle!"

I hoped he was not referring to his father. He came to the bottom of the page, and then folded the letter and stuffed it into his jerkin. "The next," he said, and held out his hand.

I drew the second letter out of my doublet. A round seal, the size of a small plate, was attached to the letter by a length of red and gold ribbon.

"What is this, sir?" Campion asked.

"The Great Seal of Duisland," said I. "This letter cometh from the Queen and her Privy Council."

He read it quickly, eyes darting from one phrase to the next. He rolled it up and tapped me on the arm with one end.

"Ay, it says I must trust you," he said, "but well I know someone I may not trust, and we should visit him now."

He turned and walked away with such speed that he left Tate and me staring at one another. We pursued the bustling ashlar into the camp, though Tate's limp caused him to fall behind. I caught up with Campion speaking to another officer.

"I want you and half a dozen of your lads," he said. "Bring your swords."

I began to feel that things were swiftly running beyond my ability to influence events. "Sir Cadwal," said I. "What is your intent? If it involves swords, it cannot be discreet."

He turned to me, rage still coloring his face. "That time is past!" he snarled.

I wondered if we were about to have a civil war in the camp. I had no weapon but a dagger tucked into the small of my back, and at that moment I felt the lack of armor intensely.

Tate, breathless, caught up with us. The officer rounded up his men and their swords. Without another word Campion again marched away, his fist still closed around the hilt of his sword, and I saw he was walking toward his headquarters. I followed, torn between pragmatic caution and the impulse to discover what would happen next.

Two guards with helmets and half-pikes flanked the door, and straightened to the salute as Campion marched toward them. "Come," he growled as he passed.

We followed through the entryway and found ourselves in a room with a low ceiling and a desk covered with neat stacks of paper. The bald secretary behind the desk looked up. He did not seem surprised that Campion was in a passion—perhaps choler was not unusual in the commander.

"His lordship?" Campion asked, and the secretary pointed with his quill to the door on his left. Campion gave a brisk nod and strode through the door, the floorboards shifting and creaking beneath his weight.

A gross fat man sat at a table in the room, a wine-cup halfway to his lips. He saw Campion enter and rose to his feet, then smiled and lifted his glass as if about to utter some pleasantry. He was taller and broader even than His Grace of Pontkyles, but had the same small, swinish eyes. Two men were with him, each wearing the badge of a goat, rampant and guardant, with a gold collar and chain. Entering through a door at the back of the room was a young serving-man in livery carrying a decanter.

"*Thou dissembling renegado!*" cried Campion, and then drew his broadsword and drove it point-first into the fat man's chest. The small eyes nearly popped from the bloated face. Campion cleared his blade as the fat man fell with a crash into his seat, and then Campion swung it at the neck of one of the other men. Blood sprayed the table.

The serving-man shrieked and dropped the decanter, then turned and dashed back through the doorway, screaming "*Socorro! Socorro!*" The sweet odor of spilled wine was mingled with the metallic scent of blood.

The second of the men with the goat badge leaped away from Campion's lunge and drew his own blade. He backed into the doorway, and blades clashed as he parried Campion's slashing attacks.

"Kill them all!" Campion shouted. "All Aspasio's men!"

The order was straightforward enough, I thought, and was enough to shock Campion's men out of their surprise. One of the headquarters guards thrust over Campion's shoulder with his half-pike, and the swordsman had to jump back as he made a frantic parry.

I felt I had seen quite enough for an unarmed man and backed into the room with the bald secretary. He looked at me with a raised eyebrow, and I wondered if he had been expecting this sort of broil for some time.

There was a rumble and a clatter on stairs somewhere at the back of the building, and then pouring into the room from a door behind the secretary came men with goat badges and swords in their hands. The secretary covered his head with both arms and dived into a corner of the room. I snatched up the brass inkwell stand from the secretary's desk and threw one of the two cut-glass inkwells at the first of the intruders. The heavy glass bounced off his forehead, and he staggered while ink spattered like blood. I threw the second inkwell at the next swordsman, with less effect, and then hurled the brass inkwell stand itself, which accomplished nothing beyond scattering quills in the air and creating a clang. Lastly I drew my dagger from behind my back and threw that as well. One of the swordsmen did a strange awkward dance as he parried it, like a man with a palsy, but beyond inspiring a lack of coordination in one of Aspasio's followers, my knife did nothing.

"Behind you! Behind you!" I wanted to let the men with Campion know that they had been flanked, and then as the ink-spattered leader lunged at me I made a dive for the outside door. There I encountered Tate, who was tugging a pistol from under his jerkin.

"Help!" I shouted as loud as I could. "Help, ho! Aspasio's men attack our soldiers!" Nearby soldiers stared, then began looking for their blades.

The clatter of weapons came loud from the doorway. Tate's pistol had caught on his clothing, and with only one hand he was helpless to free it. I detached it from his jerkin, and he handed it to me.

"My left hand aims poorly," he said. "You take it."

The pistol was small but had three barrels and a single wheel-lock, ideal for someone with bad aim, such as Tate or myself. I ventured back to the door and saw three of Aspasio's mesnie crowding the doorway as they fought Campion's men, and I thrust out the pistol and squeezed the trigger. I was only two yards distant and couldn't miss, not with three bullets.

One struck a swordsman in the shoulder, and he yelped and leaped back. I missed the second man, but the sound of the three barrels going off so startled him that he went rigid for a second or two, long enough for a soldier to drive a blade through him. The third I shot in the body, but he kept fighting with grim, calculated fury, sword in one hand and dagger in the other, and I wondered if he'd even noticed the lead ball driving between his ribs.

I stepped back into the road and handed the pistol to Tate. From the headquarters I could hear Campion bawling, *"Kill them! Kill them!"* Soldiers appeared outside the headquarters, weapons in their hands, but they were uncertain, and knew not what to do.

"Tate," said I, "you are the officer."

He sighed. "So I am." He gestured the men forward and gave them instructions. They seemed not to resent the fact that he did not lead them but directed them with the spent pistol held in his one hand. They charged into the fight, and at once the tenor of the combat changed. There were shrieks and a bellow of rage followed by the sound of bodies thudding on the floorboards.

I looked down the road and saw a man with a goat badge on his jerkin walking toward me, and as he heard the sounds of combat he stared up at the headquarters, his feet slowing. I pointed at him.

"Take that man!" I cried. "Someone take him!"

There were soldiers enough in the road by that point, but as soon as my shout reached the man, he had spun about and began a dash for his life. The others were slower, and soon Aspasio's man vanished from sight, pursued by half a dozen Duislanders.

The clamor of fighting ceased, and was replaced by the sounds of execution as Campion killed every one of Aspasio's party, a dozen swordsmen and eight or ten manservants. Those not found in the building were hunted through the camp, run down, and killed.

I approached Tate. "A party should be sent to the bridge," I said. "Make certain no one flees to Gravelinye."

"Ay," Tate said. He looked about, found another officer, and gave him instructions to block the bridge.

"If the company on Gravelinye asks why you're there," I said, "tell them you're hunting deserters."

"It would not be the first time," said the officer, and led his party away.

A rumor ran through the camp that Campion had ordered everyone from Loretto killed, which imperiled the sutlers, laundresses, and other camp-followers. Several were cut down before Campion could restore order.

Yet these Lorettans were from an enemy country, and had to be confined somehow. For the present they were put in a pasture and a guard was set about them. An exception was Campion's mistress, whose hair was such a brilliant red that I thought she might be you, my lady, in another guise. She left the room they shared at the head-quarters and helped bind Campion's wound—his sword arm had been run through, though it seemed not to concern him, and instead the ashlar was very pleased that he'd killed Aspasio. He'd been dreaming of driving a sword into the man for months, he said, and he'd finally achieved his wish.

For myself, I was not so pleased. Campion's decision to kill Aspasio and his whole party meant that I had somehow to arrange his army's escape very quickly, before someone managed to alert the enemy forces stationed all around.

I didn't know if the Hogen-Mogen had his army poised to storm Gravelinye, but I doubted it. I had assumed there would be more time for planning, and I'm sure the Hogen-Mogen thought likewise.

I went to where the boat was moored in the reeds, and brought

Teunissen and Rufino Knott to the camp, and then we had a conference with Tate, Campion, and several of his captains. Campion had
been reading Aspasio's correspondence, and this had him again in
a fury, since Aspasio's instructions were filled with the methods by
which Campion would be deceived.

I explained the Hogen-Mogen's plan to use Gravelinye and Briese
as a bridge to cross to the west side of the Linye, and attack into
Loretto itself.

"But events here have been so rapid," said I, "that I know not
whether Thurnmark is ready to attack Gravelinye, and neither do I
know whether you will be able to attack over that bridge, for you have
no boats to carry you over somewhere else."

"Can the Hogen-Mogen not supply us with boats?" asked Tate.

"Yes," said Teunissen, "but these boats must somehow get past
Gravelinye."

I turned to Tate. "Did you not say last night that you have not been
paid for over a year?"

"Ay," he nodded.

"The soldiers on Gravelinye are mercenaries, are they not?"

"Ay."

"How long since *they* have been paid?"

Everyone around the table exchanged thoughtful glances.

"I think I would like to know the details of their contract," I said.

CHAPTER EIGHTEEN

The mercenary force on Gravelinye were made up of several companies, brought together under command of a Coronel Kosma. He was from Radvila, and so originally were his men, but his company had lost soldiers to battle and disease, then recruited everywhere they'd marched, and now his company was brigaded with several others, and together they probably spoke every language beneath the sun.

Kosma was a broad man, with a snub nose and stubby fingers, his fat so dense it seemed as hard as muscle. A fan-shaped chestnut beard spread across his shoulders and chest, and he wore a faded blue velvet gown, with chains of gold around his neck. Sir Cadwal Campion had invited him to sup with us, and there was some frantic effort at the headquarters to remove the bodies and scrub the blood from the floorboards before he arrived. Even so, it was decided to eat out of doors, beneath canvas, so the state of the headquarters would not be remarked on.

"Where's the hedge-pig?" Kosma asked Campion as he dismounted from his large-framed piebald steed.

"Called away," said Campion. "May he never return."

Aspasio and his household had been called away to a local bog, where they had been weighted with stones and sunk into the peat. Kosma, it seemed, would not miss him.

"While Aspasio's away," Campion said, "I thought I might have you to supper, so we may speak our minds without fear of our words being reported to Longres."

"A sound notion," said Kosma. He turned to look at me and Knott. "Who are these gentlemen?"

"My name is Rothwell," said I, "and this is my friend Master Knott. We are soldiers from Duisland, but found our way here only lately."

Kosma nodded, then looked at Teunissen. "And you, sir?"

Teunissen's expression was guileless. "My name is Teunissen. I am a spy, recently crossed over from Thurnmark with intelligence."

Kosma laughed. "I shall look forward to any disclosure," he said.

We spoke in the language of Loretto, for once again the only tongue we shared was that of my country's enemy.

Even in the out-of-doors, beneath our canvas shade, the August day was hot. The wines were good, as they had been plundered from Aspasio's stock. We ate our way through pease porridge, greens picked in the camp's gardens that afternoon, fish caught in the river, pickled vegetables, and a roast cut from a steer butchered that day. I had never before been served a meal cooked over a peat fire, and I cannot say that I recommend it. As we ate, we discussed the course of the war and our expectations for the next campaign.

"Though you have been without pay for as long as we," Campion said. "We are constrained by our oath of allegiance to King Aguila, but your allegiance is to naught but a contract that has been violated by your employer. If I were in your position, I would march away from Gravelinye and find another prince to serve."

Kosma was amused. "I own that notion has crossed my mind," said he. "But who would accept our services? Thurnmark has no money—you can tell easily enough by the quality of the soldiers they send against us—men stout and brave, but half-starved and badly equipped." He laughed. "At least Loretto feeds us."

"Not well." Campion indicated the fare spread on the table. "Pease porridge, salt pork, and rock-hard cheese are the daily fare here—this fresh beef is a special dish, cooked in your honor, and we had to boil it long to make it tender."

"Our commissary is no better supplied," Kosma said.

"So what constrains you?" Campion asked. "Alford is full of warring nations—even your own country is now at war with Littov."

It seemed for a moment that Kosma was going to spit, though in the end he restrained himself. "I would not serve my country's prince," he said, "if that caitiff were the last ruler on earth. The last time I saw him, I said I would someday tread on his grave, and I count that a solemn oath."

Campion shrugged. "The Three Kingdoms, then. Pick any one of 'em; they're all at war with one another. Why should we not go on our own account?"

Kosma's eyes sparkled, and he grinned. "Now you speak of *we*? Are you turned freebooter now?"

Campion glanced left and right, as if making certain those at the table were in his confidence. "In truth," he said, "I think these men would follow me in preference to our infant King and his Regency Council, who wasted us in bloody combat and hold us famished captives on this island."

Kosma looked at Campion, and then Teunissen. "You speak of this in front of the spy?" he said.

Teunissen's grin was white against the growing twilight. "Fie, Coronel," he said, "I did not say I spied for *Loretto*."

Kosma's laughter boomed out from beneath the canvas. "Well, that is devilish interesting!" he said. "Does your master have silver to pay my brigade?"

"He does," said Teunissen, "and you may view the money yourself, if you like."

Kosma was surprised. "The silver is here?"

"Nay, sir," said Teunissen. "It is on the mainland. But you may come over under a flag of truce and view it any time."

The evening ended with Kosma agreeing to view the silver, or to send someone to do this for him. As soon as he climbed heavily onto his piebald horse and rode away into the night, I bade farewell to Campion and hastened with Teunissen and Knott to the boat. If Kosma decided to betray us, I wanted to be on the same side of the river as the Hogen-Mogen and his army, for that army was going to have to storm Gravelinye and rescue the Duisland troops, and I meant to be on hand to make certain it was done.

Kosma chose treachery, but I was not its victim, but rather Loretto. He and several of his officers crossed under a flag of truce, and were taken to the nearest walled town, a place that rejoiced in the sonorous name of Genk, where I had taken the chests of silver that I had asked Floria to provide me. Elements of the Hogen-Mogen's army were brigaded around the town, and within the walls the silver was guarded in the city hall by Lepalik and his boat's crew, all very fierce with short swords and pistols.

"There is enough here to pay your men for two months," said I. "After which, when we go to my country, I will have access to more funds."

"And your country is . . .?" Kosma asked.

"Does it matter?"

"I think Duisland," said Kosma. "For you speak that language with our friend Campion."

"Let us pretend it is Duisland, then," said I.

I was not allowed to sign a contract with Kosma then, for these mercenaries were very meticulous about their contracts, and though there were conditions in his old contract with Prince Tiburcio that allowed him to leave Loretto's employ, these had not been met. If he were mistreated, or pay, fodder, or rations unreasonably withheld, he could write a letter of complaint to his superior, and if the reply was unsatisfactory, he could send a final letter saying that he would leave his employ after a week's grace period. He had made ample complaints to Tiburcio's headquarters, and received no reply, possibly because Aspasio had intercepted the letters. He had yet to write the final letter, granting a week's grace . . . and this he did, and the letter was passed on to Campion, who sent it on only after five of those seven days had already passed, and there was no hope of its reaching Tiburcio in time.

Kosma also insisted that he would not surrender Gravelinye, for such a surrender would be disgraceful. Instead he would abandon the island, and if Thurnmark then occupied the place, it was no business of his.

The seven days' delay was welcome, for the Hogen-Mogen needed time to collect his army, gather a fleet of boats to carry them over the Linye, and to gather supplies for his new allies. I spent the time making music with Knott, or enjoying Teunissen's company. I told him stories of my adventures at sea, and he told me of his career as a confidential agent for one prince or another. I think his stories were probably about as true as mine.

Finally the grace period expired, and on a day of clouds and wind, Kosma and his brigade stepped off onto the bridge to the mainland, drums pounding and trumpets blaring as they marched past the Hogen-Mogen's army drawn up to salute them as they passed. He and his men were dressed in what remained of what must have once been glorious finery—but the slashed doublets revealed faded, patched shirts, the blackened, fluted, and etched armor was battered and worn, and the once-bright banners under which the soldiers marched were faded and much mended.

Campion's army followed and made a less brave show in their tattered clothing and beaten armor, the cavalry mounted on starveling horses, their sick carried in wagons padded with straw, and their commander's red-haired mistress driving her own two-wheel cart. Careworn though the army was, the expressions on their faces were hopeful, for they had been told they were going home.

Last came the supply wagons with the last of Loretto's rations, and herds of sheep and kine to feed the soldiers on their march to Houbek.

After the last of Campion's army passed over the bridge, the regiments of Thurnmark formed and began their march across Gravelinye to Briese. Galleys were taken off carts and carried down to the water, then laden with supplies for de Hendrick's invasion of Loretto. I wished the Hogen-Mogen good fortune, and then turned my borrowed horse and rode to the head of the column.

At Genk the soldiers were brigaded in the encampments the army of Thurnmark had just vacated. I produced my commission from Queen Floria, signed a contract with Kosma, and presented his command with two months' wages in advance.

Shortly thereafter, in Campion's camp, the drums were beat, and the soldiers formed up in a hollow square. Amid those ranks of silent men I brandished my commission, named myself as Sir Quillifer, Lord Selford, then informed the soldiers that Duisland had revolted against Aguila and the tyrant Fosco, and that our country had been at war with Loretto for nearly two years. I promised that if they would throw off their allegiance to Aguila and his Regency Council, I would see them shipped home, where they would have pay and good rations, and might have a chance to fight the true enemies of our country, the same foul foreign measles who wasted them in a pointless war of conquest and kept them penned up on a barren island for more than a year, living on scant rations and broken promises. I asked them then if they would swear a new oath of allegiance to Her Sovereign Majesty of Duisland, Queen Floria the First.

I was then stunned to the core by the sound of thousands of men shouting "*Ay!*" and then the sight of many of the soldiers falling to their knees, tears streaming down their upraised faces, at the realization that they would no longer be starved and abused, and that their country had not abandoned them. Sir Cadwal Campion himself dropped to his knees beside me, along with all his officers, and once the hubbub had died down I administered the oath promptly, and though the words were a simple formula cadged from a hundred swearing-in ceremonies, I felt the tears sting my own eyes.

Afterward there was feasting, for the Hogen-Mogen had left a commissary at the scene, and for the first time in years the Duisland soldiers were given all the food they could eat, along with ale from the town that had been brewed special for this occasion.

Even the horses ate well, for they had eaten nothing but grass for the last year, and they were given a double ration of grain.

I wandered among the soldiers, making sure that each had a fair share of the feast and all the ale he wished, and I felt a mixture of joy and loss, for I wished that Floria had been present in that hollow square and seen the soldiers' display of hope and devotion. For that display was genuine, raw, and unrefined, so unlike the court's elegant and glittering unrealities, and it would have moved Floria's heart, and perhaps by comparison showed the court for what it was, the cockpit of vanity, falsity, and ambition.

I had ridden from Houbek to Genk in one long day, but the return march to Houbek required four days, for the soldiers were weak with undernourishment and were no longer used to marching long distances. More and more dropped out of the march, and were carried in the wagons, but the Hogen-Mogen had arranged rations along the way, and no one starved. Once in Houbek I took myself to see the Ambassador, Sir Harley Warriner, and found there a message from my spy Barbosa, letting me know where he lodged. After discussing with Warriner the difficulties of feeding the army and moving it to Duisland, I went in search of Barbosa and found him by the water-front at a sea-officer's lodge. We went to an alehouse on the far end of a pier, and sat at a table overlooking the Senagne and the busy barge traffic moving up and down. The coriander-infused lemony tang of the ale made fine company with the herring pie we shared.

Barbosa had arrived from Ferrick three days before, and now made a full report of the state of that unhappy town. There was a company of Loretto soldiers occupying the Citadel, he said, and troops in the gatehouses, but the largest force in the town were new companies of the Trained Bands, the Duisland militia that supported the city's new regime.

The city, he said, had for the last generation been torn by a rivalry between two powerful families of wealthy burgesses, the Ropers and the Fernyhaughs. Each family had allies among the lesser burgesses and the nobility, and all attempts to reconcile the factions had failed. In the latest election, a Roper had been elected lord mayor, and held a majority among the aldermen; but a Fernyhaugh held an appointment as lord lieutenant, and commanded the city's defenses, including the Trained Bands—though, since the war's beginning, he was under the orders of Lord Emerick, the Knight Marshal.

When Mola landed his army to the west of the city, Emerick and Fernyhaugh had marshaled their forces to oppose him. After our army was routed, it was the Lord Mayor Roper who ordered the city's gates closed against them, and Roper who then surrendered on terms to Admiral Mola after Emerick and Fernyhaugh were killed. This empowered him to conduct a persecution of the surviving Fernyhaughs and their supporters, along with a confiscation of their property that enabled Roper to buy a degree of popularity, and to raise new companies of Trained Bands under his own loyal officers.

"So the city fell to Loretto not because of hatred for the Queen," said I, "but because of a rivalry between two sets of burgesses who hated each other more than they loved the freedom of their city."

I thought Floria might be relieved to know the true situation, for she had told me she feared traitors might be plotting to hand more cities to the enemy. I thought I should write her to explain that the tragedy of Ferrick was caused by a pair of feuding families, and not by any allegiances that extended beyond the city walls.

I signaled the landlord to bring another pot of ale. "What is the temper of the city?" asked I.

"The people do not like the foreigners perched up in the Citadel," said Barbosa. "Some are angry that their husbands or fathers were slaughtered in order to make the Ropers supreme. But there was no rebellion that I could see, not even slogans daubed on a wall. The city is either afraid, or is waiting for events to make up their minds for them."

"We shall give them events," I said, "never fear. What of the forts on the border?"

"The enemy has cleared all the forts on the road between Ferrick and Loretto. They send supplies that way, when ships are not available."

"And Mola?"

"For the most part he keeps his ships at sea, moving supplies between Loretto and the siege at Stanport."

"And the siege?"

"The enemy claims the city is at last encircled, and that Stayne will soon be starved into surrender."

Then, I thought, we would have to move quickly, perhaps before we were ready.

The landlord brought another pitcher of ale, and I refreshed our cups. "I shall ask you to carry dispatches to Selford," said I. "I wish the Queen to know what I intend."

The spy took a healthy gulp of ale. "I shall do so, my lord."

I had been laying my plans for weeks. Now it was a matter of discovering whether it were possible to carry them out.

Teunissen and Ambassador Warriner proved crucial to my expedition to Duisland. We had to procure ships and supplies, and neither were available in quantities necessary for the scheme I had in mind. I had *Sovereign*, of course, and Thurnmark provided three small galleons out of the dozen or so they had promised. Some other ships I simply hired, the funds coming courtesy of Warriner, who borrowed the money on his own account. But even that was inadequate until, to my immense surprise and gratification, three large warships of Duisland appeared at the Hook of Zomer, detached from Coneygrave's fleet at the Queen's express command.

With these I was able to carry over four thousand men, divided evenly between Campion's men and Kosma's mercenaries. The weak and sick were left behind to be carried home later, and the artillery was broken down and put into the holds of the smaller ships. Those who sailed with me were the best and fittest available.

On the ninth of September the ships were busked and boun, as the saying is. I shook Teunissen's hand on the wharf, and thanked him for his aid.

"I told you I could get you onto that island and off again," he said, "and now Demon Dom Keely-Fay has an army. May your foes ever flee your approach."

"I shall look forward to our next meeting," said I. "And I hope you will find no more errands for me in hostile country."

"I am confident you can find those on your own," said Teunissen. "And while you do, I will try to find you more ships."

We hove up our anchors and set sail from the Hook of Zomer, sailing northwest on a broad reach, the wind brisk, the sea steep. I was delighted and thankful to find myself at sea again, breathing the rich sea air, but *Sovereign* was carrying over five hundred soldiers, most of whom were immediately sick. To avoid the stench I climbed the foremast and viewed the sea from the foretop.

We sailed along a long curve to avoid the coast of Loretto, for I did not want my eleven ships to be intercepted by Mola's forty-odd. On the eighteenth we anchored in the Bay of Basford, a bight indented into the foothills east of Ferrick. This was one of the few places where large ships could come near the coast without danger of being stranded on a mud flat, and soon we had boats in the water and began moving our soldiers to land. My little army was ashore by the morning of the nineteenth and we began our march along the fine Aekoi military road that would take us into Duisland. Kosma sent a messenger ahead to tell Mayor Roper that reinforcements for the siege of Stanport would be arriving that afternoon, and that we would be obliged if he could open the gates for us, and arrange for us to refill our water bottles before we marched away. The messenger returned with Roper's assurance that this would be done.

When we came within sight of the city, we uncased the flags and marched in under the banners flown when the companies had fought for King Priscus. Kosma flew the leopards of Loretto alongside his own personal flag, which featured an armored knight galloping across a field of white roses. Campion, marching next in the column, rode beneath the flag of Duisland with the shield of Loretto inescutcheon at its center. We marched to the beat of drums, and trumpet calls floated high on the breeze.

Wearing my half-armor, a broadsword on its baldric over one shoulder, I rode with Kosma at the head of the column. A pair of horse-pistols were thrust through my sash. Before us Ferrick rose above the flat country, distance turning its roofs and walls blue. Masts in the deep eastern harbor rose above the rooftops, and the silhouette of the Citadel, a wide round tower offset atop a wider round tower, stood brave against a bank of white clouds. Offshore, brown tendrils of silt advanced into the blue of the sea.

We marched around the walls that encompassed the port and east-ern harbor, then approached by way of the south gatehouse. This was part of an old Aekoi fortress, built of gray stone to control the road and access to the harbor, and we could see silhouettes of soldiers passing back and forth amid the battlements.

My heart leaped as a cannon boomed out, and I gave a wild look around me, to meet a few other wild looks and then Kosma's know-ing, superior smile. I realized that we were being honored with a sa-lute, and the others realized it at the same moment, and we shared a moment of shamefaced awkwardness before turning away from each other and gazing on toward the gatehouse.

The gun salute boomed on, white gunsmoke flowering along the battlements. We passed beneath the ancient arch of the gate, and there we saw a welcoming party, all wearing chains of office. I had expected the Lord Mayor to be some foul, mean, grasping, brutal creature, like Conte Aspasio, but Roper was a slim, assured man of sixty, with long white hair and a close-cropped beard. He wore an agate-colored velvet robe trimmed with white fox fur, finery that set off his chain of office. He doffed his cap.

"Coronel Kosma?" he said. "I welcome you to our city."

We drew off to one side, and allowed Kosma's mercenaries to con-tinue their march into the city.

"Coronel Kosma does not speak your language," said I. "I will translate, if you like."

"That would be very good, master—?" He gave me an inquiring look.

"My name is Rothwell."

"Very good." He presented the other members of his commit-tee. Most were aldermen, though there was a grim man of middle age, in armor and burgonet, who was revealed to be his son and the commander of the Trained Bands. Another son was the harbor mas-ter, who had replaced the harbor master I'd known in the past, and who I hoped was still alive. One officer was from Loretto, the captain of the company that occupied the Citadel, a gentleman I was very pleased to encounter.

"The coronel is pleased to meet you," I said. "Coronel Kosma hopes that you will accompany him to the top of the gatehouse, where he hopes to show you a rare sight."

They seemed surprised at this, but Roper graciously agreed, and so we dismounted and let the Lord Mayor lead us up the winding stair to the summit of the gatehouse. With us came a party of dismounted demilances, including a trumpeter.

We were all a little out of breath by the time we achieved the roof, our spurs clattering on the stone flags. My heart was thumping like one of Kosma's drummers, but I could not tell if it was from the climb or from what was to follow.

The scent of gunpowder was strong, for the salutes had been fired from here, and the gunners were swabbing and securing their guns. I stepped to the battlements and saw the small army advancing under its bright banners, the road gently curving as it followed the city wall.

"Now you shall see something fine!" Kosma said in the language of Loretto, and he pointed at his trumpeter. The trumpeter puffed out his cheeks and blew a rousing clarion that echoed back from the rooftops and chimneys. The soldiers answered with the battle cry of Radvina, *"Urra! Urra! Urra!"*, then lurched into a quicker step. The sound of tramping reached us at the top of the tower.

"Are they not brave?" asked I. "Pikes rising like a forest, armor shining in the sun, the banners flying overhead?"

The Lord Mayor viewed the army through the battlements, then turned with a bemused smile on his face. "Your fellows are certainly in a hurry," said he to Coronel Kosma.

"They must have somewhere to go," said I.

"We had a welcome prepared," said Roper. "You asked for water, and—"

"We will have the water later," said I.

Something in my voice brought a slight frown to his lips, and the fine lines around his eyes deepened as he looked at me.

"What do you mean by that?" he asked.

"We are surrounded by water," said I. "It will wait. Now is time for the spectacle set before us. View the men running into your city. See these fine soldiers blazing with eagerness to fight for the rightful monarch."

A gust of wind blew Roper's fine long hair across his face. He swept white strands out of his eyes.

"Where are these men going?" he said. "What is the meaning of this?"

"Ah—the men?" I allowed myself a broad smile. "They set us an example—they go to their duty. If only everyone did their duty, Ferrick and indeed the entire world would be much the better for it."

Roper drew himself up, fine in his velvet and fur. "Master Rothwell," he said, "I must insist that you ask Coronel Kosma the meaning of this action."

"I'm afraid you have the name wrong," said I. "That is, Coronel Kosma is Coronel Kosma, but I am not Rothwell. My name is Selford—well, that is not my name either; that is my *title*." I drew my pistols and pointed them at the collection of dignitaries before me. "My *name*," I said, "is Quillifer. Some have done me the injustice of calling me the Queen's assassin, and in Loretto I am called the Demon Dom Keely-Fay, but I prefer to think of myself as Her Majesty's private secretary, and her loyal servant."

I looked from one astonished face to the next, and then back to Roper. Behind me I heard the sound of our demilances unsheathing their swords, and the clicks of pistols being readied. "I regret to inform you all," said I, "that in the name of Her Sovereign Majesty Floria the First, I must command you to lay down your arms and surrender your persons to her clement justice."

I half expected Roper to lead a resistance, and if not Roper his son, who wore armor, commanded the Trained Bands, and looked hardy enough to fight an army. And if not these, then the coronel from Loretto who commanded in the Citadel.

But it was not any of these who resisted, but one of the aldermen—a gray-haired fellow who emitted a shriek from between toothless gums, drew a dagger, and leaped at Coronel Kosma, who was so surprised by the assault of this lean-shanked dotard that he was almost struck down. One of Kosma's demilances stepped forward and slashed with such force that his broadsword became lodged in the attacker's skull, and he had to make a gruesome effort to pull it free.

It was clear from this episode that Kosma's men cared not whether any of our captives lived or died, and so Roper and the rest surrendered peaceably, let their knives and swords fall, and then consented to stretch out on the flags until they could be bound and delivered to a place of confinement.

The cannoneers and others on the roof of the gatehouse followed the examples of their leaders, and quietly surrendered.

We watched as the column of soldiers continued to pour into town. Kosma's mercenaries ran along Royal Street, which ran the length of the entire city south to north, and poured through the open gates of the Citadel. We heard a few shots as some of the Loretto garrison were killed, after which the rest—outnumbered nearly ten to one—surrendered. The flag over the Citadel, with its Loretto shield inescutcheon on the flag of Duisland, was lowered, and replaced with an enormous Duisland banner four fathoms long, one sewn to fly in battle over *Sovereign*'s quarterdeck.

Campion's men were assigned to secure the gates, and as they entered split into several parties. The west gatehouse, which overlooked the Long Bridge across the Dun Esk, was taken without a single shot. Some guards in the north gatehouse tried to resist and were cut down, after which Campion's men ran down the mole to the

Causeway Fort, which with its great guns was swiftly occupied. The gate leading into the east harbor was taken easily, and the soldiers then went on to storm every ship in the harbor.

Afterward soldiers went on to occupy the Hall of Justice, the town hall, and every one of the city squares, for the Trained Bands and anyone else inclined to resist would use the squares as rallying points. Then Campion sent heralds through the city proclaiming the restoration of the Queen's government, and saying also that anyone having a complaint against the Lord Mayor or his administration should present that complaint tomorrow, at the Hall of Justice.

As the city seemed secure, we bound our prisoners and marched them to the Hall of Justice, where we also released those of the Fernyhaugh faction we found there. These were sent home, and the Ropers and their allies stripped of their jewels and chains of office and confined in the same noisome cells to which they had condemned their enemies.

My little fleet of eleven ships sailed into the eastern harbor, under the command of Tate, and horses were taken ashore, along with the field artillery and the supplies.

I occupied the Lord Mayor's office and spoke long into the night with the sad remains of the Fernyhaugh clans and with prominent citizens of the town. The heralds had told them to come tomorrow, but they saw no reason for delay, or thought themselves too important to wait their turn. As a result of these meetings, I wrote many names on many different lists.

I had never run a city before, and now I had one in my charge. I had never commanded an army, yet now four thousand soldiers attended my commands. I owned ships, but I had never commanded them, and now eleven ships were under my orders.

I did not know whether I was blessed or cursed, but I supposed I would find out soon enough.

CHAPTER NINETEEN

en days after the capture of the city, I wrote to Floria:

Such is my love for Your Majesty that I cannot refrain from bringing you one victory after another. As an early gift to mark the second anniversary of your coronation, please allow me to present you with your city of Ferrick, now restored intact to your realm. My little army, released from its bondage in Loretto, has taken the city without loss, and the renegados who delivered Ferrick have been dealt with, as I shall relate.

Your Majesty will no doubt be relieved to discover—(and here I gave a history of the feud between the Ropers and the Fernyhaughs)—*so the city was not lost in consequence of some enmity toward Your Majesty or a misplaced loyalty to Loretto, but the animus of small-minded fools who would rather rule a molehill than accept a lesser place in a just and prosperous commonwealth.*

Well, they are dead now. As the city is now laid under martial law, I asked Sir Cadwal Campion to form a drumhead court-martial—I am not familiar with the procedure, but I know there was an actual drum involved—and he passed sentence on the Ropers and their party. While the trial went on, the accused were treated to the sound of their scaffold being built, and upon sentencing they were bound, then brought into sunlight to be despatched.

Ferrick's executioner had been given much practice by the Ropers, and he had their heads off with deft efficiency, charging a fee of three crowns for each blow of the axe. It was quicker, apparently, to behead them in swift succession than to hang them one-by-one.

I am not overly troubled by the speed with which the sentences were imposed and carried out. Thousands of soldiers had been cut down when Roper had refused to open the gates to them, and their deaths were far more brutal than his. Roper's allies may or may not have had a part in the decision to close the gates against our army, but they had all supported him afterward, and profited by his confiscations. I found myself offended by this business of treason for profit, and I was pleased to make it less profitable. We are now confiscating their wealth, and will use it for the relief of their victims' families.

The heads were stuck on pikes and placed atop each of the city's gatehouses, a lesson for those who were of a mind to learn it, while the bodies were left in the square for their families to claim, which they did with wailings and shrieks and the rumble of carts. I did my best to harden my heart against the extravagant sounds of mourning that echoed from the square, and reminded myself that the mourners who wailed now had not wailed so when the Fernyhaughs were killed.

We have not announced to the countryside that the city

has changed hands, and so dispatch riders to and from Admiral Mola have been riding through our gates, and we have all their letters.

Mola demands more powder and shot for his siege guns, and complains about the quality of the food sent from home. He also demands medicine for his sick troops—I am not surprised that his men are falling ill, for they have been fighting and working for months in boggy country, sloshing in trenches half-flooded with water.

Mola reports that he has a little over fifteen thousand soldiers in his army, of which nearly eight hundred are wounded and three thousand are sick. His Boreal Fleet has forty-five galleons of two hundred tons or more, large enough to stand in a line of battle against Coneygrave. The sailors are far healthier than his soldiers, and he is keeping them continually at sea, both to avoid catching sickness from the land and to ward off our privateers, who plague his ships of burden.

The dispatches going to the admiral are for the most part promises that Mola's demands will be met at some point in the future, a point which, though indefinite, is pledged to be soon.

The riders carry also letters from individual soldiers to their friends and family, and these testify candidly to the miseries of the siege, to the sickness among the troops, and to the raids and continuous bombardment that keep anyone from rest. Their spirits are poor, and with luck I hope to make them poorer.

Some of the promised foodstuffs sailed into port two days ago, two galleons filled with salt beef, cheese, and biscuit, supplies intended to be disembarked and carried to Stanport along the old Aekoi road. One of the city's pilots brought them through the shoals and into the eastern harbor, and the ships were stormed by our troops as soon as they tied up at the quay.

The next day came a ship full of cannonballs and gunpowder. This anchored well offshore, to avoid blasting the town by accident until arrangements could be made for a safe offloading. We did not inform the crew of the recapture of the town, but acted as if the enemy were still in command. The dangerous cargo was transferred into lighters, then rowed to the quay and carried very carefully to the town's powder stores. The ship we did not keep, but sent on its way to bring us more provender.

I know not how Admiral Mola will react to the loss of the city, but a hostile Ferrick athwart his lines of communications will put him in a dangerous position, and he will need a port on the north coast if he is to survive the winter. I suppose it is too much to expect that he will embark his army and sail home, but he may try to retake Ferrick, or may continue the siege of Stanport in order to win himself a new harbor. If your officers, particularly the Lord High Admiral, contrive to keep Mola entertained on land and sea, I would be very grateful.

I am trying to organize the defense of the town, and I think we stand in good stead. Before his death the Knight Marshal made certain the walls were in good repair. The harvest is in and the granaries are full, so we will not be starved out. We disarmed Roper's Trained Bands, and now we now raise a militia of our own under reliable officers. The walls are furnished with plenty of artillery, but we have few cannoneers, and we are trying to recruit those who crewed the guns under the Knight Marshal and even earlier.

Do you recall the two siege guns that His Grace of

Roundsilver cast for the Queen's Army during Clayborne's War? They were marvels, as much works of art as artillery, each made of ninety hundredweight of bronze. Cast laurel wreaths encircle the breech, the handles are in the shape of leaping dolphins, and over the barrel crawl the images of gods and goddesses hurling lightning or puffing out their cheeks to blow the shot toward the enemy. Spells of deadly power are inscribed on the barrel, Roundsilver's shield is displayed, and the cypher of your royal sister is blazoned near the touchhole.

Forty horses or mules were required to move one of these masterpieces from one place to another, and it required forty pounds of gunpowder to fire a sixty-pound stone roundshot that had to be raised to the muzzle with a special hoist.

The guns were cast by Engineer Ransome, who sprinkled the molten metal with diamond dust and other ingredients of his alchemist's art, and the results were so impressive that Ransome was appointed to his present office of Queen's Gunfounder.

I found one of these guns on the roof of the Citadel's donjon tower. The other is not in the city, which is a pity, for the guns were made for sieges, and we may have a siege on our hands very soon.

I beg Your Majesty's pardon, and I must leave off writing for the moment—a large warship of Loretto has appeared off the port, and signals for a pilot. I shall capture that ship as a gift to Your Majesty, and I beg your indulgence until I have accomplished this task.

That last brave statement should be a lesson to me, and brings to mind the proverb about counting one's bullion before the ore has been refined. (Or is it chickens that are counted? While I own that I know a little about mining, my knowledge of fowl is lacking.)

All the ships in the harbor were readied for battle, and every cannoneer that could be found crewed the guns in the Citadel, the east harbor walls, and the Causeway Fort.

But the galleon—five hundred tons, I think, with a distinct raked poop, and the leopards of Loretto painted on the main topsail—took the pilot aboard, and then sailed away in the direction of Stanport. I think that Mola now knows that he has lost Ferrick, and he now has a pilot that can take his fleet through the mud flats right into the harbor.

The pilot was abducted yesterday. It has been more than a day since I last took up my quill, and for this I apologize. I had forgot that Sir Cadwal Campion's mistress was giving a dinner for me and for the officers. To this feast I wore the newly made chain of office that marks me out as Your Majesty's Lord Governor.

This lady of Campion's rejoices in the name Guilhelma, and is a native of Loretto. Like Sandicup she has hair of blazing red, though to better effect, and she is framed rather like a stately bluff-bowed galleon, tall and impressive, her motions as purposeful as those of a warship. She cannot read or write but speaks the languages of Loretto, Duisland, Thurnmark, and at least one of the dialects of the Three Kingdoms. Despite her Lorettan birth, she seems popular among our troops, and she is a loyal supporter of Campion.

It must be admitted that Guilhelma knows how to please soldiers. The dinner was plain but the food was served in enormous quantities, the drink—plundered from the Ropers' stores—overflowed like the Falls of Wendover, and Guilhelma's booming laugh echoed down the table as she *laughed at one jest after another. By the end of the evening she was leading us in song, and the songs were bawdy.*

And now, as I write, I hear that clarion voice again, for she and Campion are having an argument, and as their apartment is near mine in the Citadel, I know that their arguments are frequent. As soon as this letter is done, I shall escape the merrie couple and get about the business of preparing the eastern harbor against attack.

I confess that Selford seems very far away. It is the height of the hunting season now, so I suppose Your Majesty is out most days pursuing hart or boar, flying your falcons, or shooting pheasant and black grouse. I long to return home to the castle, or to my Haysfield Grange, but sadly I must do my duty to Your Majesty, prepare for Mola's arrival, and hope not to become prey myself to a foreign lord as merciless as Death itself.

I hope this letter finds you well and free. I labor incessantly for your freedom and sovereignty, so that you are not forced into choices that are obnoxious to you.

I tender you the love and obedience due from a subject, and I dare hope that ere long my eyes and heart will be gratified by the sight of your royal person.

—Demon Dom

There was much more that I wished to say, of how much I adored Floria and hated Gandorim, how I despised the nobility who were pressing her about marriage, how I longed to hold her in my arms and kiss her on the lips; but I dared not put such things in a letter, for the letter would be a gift to the enemy if it were intercepted. They would publish extracts that would make Floria seem a trull and I a seducer, and proclaim to a scandalized world Floria's lack of chastity.

I had yet to be convinced that Floria's chastity was in any way the world's business, but the world disagreed.

I could have put the letter in cipher, I suppose, but ciphers can be broken, and the result would have been just as dismal. Instead I had to send my message in a kind of code that Floria would understand but that I hoped would be opaque to anyone but the Queen.

I sealed the letter, then closed my eyes and saw Floria slowly appear before me, sitting on the settee in my room in the castle in her transparent gown of golden sarcenet, her eyes glittering in candlelight as she laughed at some jest. I fancied I could sense her bright galbanum scent.

My heart turned over with love. I wanted her desperately, and I felt that for a few moments with Floria I would sacrifice ten years of my life.

I wanted her free, free of the dances of the court, the intrigues of Gandorim, the demands of the lords.

I wanted her free to spend the rest of her life with me.

I watched as the phantom Floria faded as if being carried away on a tide, and then I opened my eyes, read the message again, and then sealed the letter. I gave it to a messenger to carry to the winter capital of Howel, and thence to Longfirth and Selford. I told him to place it only in the hands of Her Majesty, and I gave him money, an escort of two troopers, and an extra relay of horses. In hopes of avoiding Mola's patrols, he would ride south before turning west to Howel, and if the fates were moved to provide good weather and fair winds, Floria might have my letter in eighteen or twenty days, though it might take as long as a month. A reply would take as long, and so it might be December before I heard from her.

By that time, the fate of Ferrick would probably be decided, one way or another, and so I resolved not to expect relief, and to fight on with what fortune had given me, and not to surrender, not least to despair.

CHAPTER TWENTY

I watched from atop the west gatehouse as Mola's army heaved itself along the road, moving like a blind worm creeping over flagstones wet from the rain. When my own little army had marched into the city, we were gay beneath bright banners; but Mola's forces barely showed a flag, and their armor was dull even in the bright sun. They looked as if they'd been living in rain and muck for months, and I supposed they had.

I was considering ordering the guns atop the gatehouse to try a shot at the head of the column, but instead the column parted as a troop of demilances came riding up under a white flag. Their leader, a lean man of middle years, rode up to the Long Bridge and paused for a moment as he saw that I had taken up the planks, and there was no way to cross the river. Trumpets blew a sennet, and the ensign with the white flag waved it overhead.

I cupped my hands and shouted. "Shall I send a boat?"

The leader considered this for a moment, and then made an imperious gesture, as if summoning a lackey.

It took a few minutes to organize a boat's crew, during which the soldiers and their leader subjected our defenses to intense scrutiny.

A whaleboat was sent across the river, and took aboard the leader, his ensign, and an escort of four troopers to support the officers' dignity. These came to the landing, and I opened the gate and stood with Campion and Kosma to welcome the new arrivals.

"This way, my lord," said I, in the language of Loretto.

"I must speak with the city's commander." The man's speech was clipped and precise. He wore blackened armor inset with brass, and gold spurs on his boots. His beard, cut to near-stubble in the Loretto fashion, surrounded a mouth prim with disdain. His small company was not covered with the muck of travel, but seemed to have made some effort to put themselves in order before presenting themselves before the gatehouse.

"I am governor here," said I. "I am Dom Keely-Fay, Conte de Selford. My comrades are Coronel Kosma and Dom Cadwal Campion, who here commands the Army of Duisland that once fought for King Priscus."

I watched them carefully as I said this, and though the leader was at pains to present an impassive face, I saw something shift in his eyes when I mentioned my name. The young ensign was not so guarded, and looked at me in frank surprise; while the demilance troopers gaped at me, and one of them made a sign against evil.

I felt obscurely complimented, and suppressed a smile.

"I am the *Duque* de Murtro," said the leader. "My ensign is Dom Silvio Solas de l'Espan." He did not bother to introduce the private soldiers.

"Your Grace is welcome," said I. "If you would accompany me, I would be happy to offer you refreshment after your long ride."

"That will not be necessary," said Murtro. "My message is brief." He adopted the formal pose used in the Loretto court, one leg advanced, his chest thrust out as his body bent like a bow. "Admiral Mola has charged me to say," said he, and here his voice changed slightly, as if he were delivering his message in another's voice, "that he demands the surrender of His Majesty Aguila's city of Ferrick. If this demand is refused, the loss of life and destruction of property will be entirely on your own conscience."

"If Admiral Mola wishes Ferrick," said I, "he may come and try to take it"—I smiled—"but this time there will be no traitors inside the gates, but a force more than capable of defending every brick and stone of the city. There is no question of yielding Ferrick, not after Mola's abuse and assassination of Lord Gadsby and the men who surrendered at Stanport Levels."

"We have heard enough, then," said Murtro. He began to turn away, but I shouted after him.

"I have not finished, Your Grace!" said I. "For I charge you to carry my message to Admiral Mola."

He turned and drew in a long breath through his nose, as if he were inhaling a great stink.

"Be brief," he said.

"Tell Admiral Mola that I name him a coward and murderer," said I. "He is not a gentleman but a caitiff lout, not a knight but a churl, not a nobleman but a beast with the blood of innocents dripping from his chops. Let him but come and I will serve him justice at the point of a pike." As I spoke Murtro turned white with rage. I favored him with a skeletal grin. "Will you remember that, or should I put it in writing?"

"That is enough," Murtro said. Again he made as if to go, but I lowered my voice and spoke in a friendlier tone.

"Let me offer you a word or two of warning," I said. Murtro hesitated, then turned partly toward me. "Your countrymen have favored me with the title of Demon Dom Keely-Fay," said I, "and your own statesman have named me a wicked and powerful sorcerer. While I dispute the moral imputation of the charge, nevertheless I do confess myself a great magician, perhaps the greatest since Setebos the Golden."

Murtro pursed his little disapproving mouth. His posture told a tale of restraint and patience, of a struggle not to call this nonsense by its proper name. I persisted, for he was not the target in my sights.

"Through my arts," said I, "I lured Admiral de Cuerzy onto the rocks with all his ships—rocks that were on every chart, rocks that he'd seen daily for weeks, rocks to which my spells made him blind along with all his men. His ships were lost, de Cuerzy died, and thirty thousand men drowned."

I made a motion with my hand to indicate Ferrick, its walls, the gatehouse in which we stood. "As for this city, I but waved a hand and the gates were opened to us. No blood was spilled in recovering Ferrick—and indeed you may examine the town, inside and out, and find no evidence of fighting."

"Sir," said Murtro icily, "you make of yourself a mountebank."

This was an accusation I did not bother to dispute, for it was true. I modeled my performance on that of Doctor Smolt, a necromancer once in the service of the Queen Floria's mother, the divorced Queen Natalie.

"Admiral Mola will have three days to take Ferrick," said I, "for I retire now for a three-day working, after which my thaumaturgy will make this city impossible for you." I reached out as if to touch his arm, and then hesitated. "But I implore your lordship to beware the blue mist, which is deadly to all your countrymen. Remember—the blue mist is deadly—the azure mist will be your bane." In these last phrases I deepened my voice as I stared unblinking into Murtro's eyes, one hand raised in a dramatic gesture.

Murtro's reply was an impatient grunt. "Are you done with this foolishness now?"

I smiled, I hope ominously. "Call it foolishness if you like; I say it but for your benefit. Whether you heed the warning or not, I trust you will remember the choice words you carry from me to Admiral Mola."

His jaw worked, as if masticating upon a reply, but he chose not to deliver it. Murtro bowed to me, and then he and his party turned for the whaleboat. I watched them leave with some satisfaction, for even though Murtro affected to disdain my claims of sorcery, that had not been the case with others of his party. All four of the demilances had made a sign against evil at some point during the interview, and the ensign had clutched at a chain around his throat, a chain that I guessed dangled an amulet concealed beneath his cuirass. By the next morning, word of the Demon Dom and his blue mist would have run through the camp like a virulent plague.

"I do not know if it was wise to insult Mola in that way," said Campion as we watched the whaleboat stroke across the river. "He may come raging at us."

"I hope he does," said I. "If he attacks in a rage, he will fall afoul of our traps."

"In that case," said Campion, "we must hope we have sufficient traps."

"I just laid one," said I, "if you hadn't noticed."

It was three days before Mola's army settled into its camps on the east side of Ferrick. If I had actually used that time to work up a spell, I would have cast it in good time.

As the enemy could not cross via the Long Bridge, they had to march upstream to a ford, and as the river was high due to several days' rain, it was too dangerous for the foot soldiers to cross. They marched not on an Aekoi military road but on a country lane used for local traffic—for the real road was the river, and to travel upon it boats were required, and I had ordered all the boats carried to the east bank, where the Lorettans could not reach them.

As they toiled along up the river, they were subject to harassing fire from masked batteries on our side of the river. By the time the enemy got their artillery in position to reply, ours had been harnessed and withdrawn.

When Mola finally arrived he set up camps on the firm ground east of the city, then began fortifying their camps and digging a parallel just outside of the range of our guns. Lorettans swarmed like locusts over the hills behind their camps, cutting down every tree and bush, demolishing houses and barns, and destroying many a fine orchard.

"Do they need so much firewood?" asked I.

"They also make fascines out of brushwood," said Campion. "For their men to hide behind, or to throw in our ditch to fill it, so their soldiers can cross."

I had seen no siege guns, though I thought the enemy were building magazines, and then I realized that the heavy artillery would come by sea. This surmise proved correct, for a few days later the great mass of Mola's fleet hove over the horizon, and sailed past us to the Bay of Basford, where I had landed my own men just weeks before. Platforms were already being constructed for the guns, protected by gabions, which were large wicker rollers filled with rocks or earth, to absorb the force of our cannon shot. More gabions guarded saps that were advancing toward us with right good speed. Mola's army was practiced at siege work by now, and the ground was more suitable for the work than the bogs around Stanport. They worked mainly at night, when it was impossible to see to shoot at them. Kosma led a few sorties to kill their engineers, which succeeded twice before the enemy stationed soldiers near the sap heads to repel us. In the end the saps continued to advance, though perhaps more of the enemy lost sleep than would have otherwise.

. The enemy had carefully placed their batteries where the giant Roundsilver gun in the Citadel could not reach them, for they were hidden from it by rising ground or by buildings in the town itself, which would have to be demolished to provide a field of fire. I thought we were not in such desperate straits that this would be necessary.

Mola's fleet cruised offshore, gray wooden fortresses on the gray sea. The ships looked beaten down. They had been in service for months, and during that time no one had brightened their paint or buffed the gilt ornament. They had been in action against Coneygrave's flotilla, and I thought I saw evidence of damage, windows covered with planks, gunports beaten into one, sails patched, damaged yards fished. I could only hope that Mola's foot soldiers were in as battered a condition.

Sunlight glittered from telescopes on the enemy's quarterdecks. They were marking out all our dispositions, all our defenses.

I knew that they were looking at the eastern harbor, which was our weakest point. If they got into the harbor and began to land troops, the city was lost.

Ferrick had originally been built on a kind of broad peninsula, with the river on the west side and a deep natural harbor on the east. As the city grew and prospered, wharves and warehouses appeared on the far side of the east harbor, and—because Ferrick was always in danger of attack from our traditional enemy of Loretto—this port was enclosed to a stout wall. The round Citadel, for its garrison of royal troops, was built on the northern end of the city, with its round donjon tower offset slightly to the north, and the city made as impregnable as possible.

Defense of the city was made more complicated when siege guns began to appear in the world. The wall built along the Dun Esk River could be demolished by guns firing from the opposite bank, but to storm the city an enemy would have to get across the river, and in the present instance I had made this impossible by confiscating every boat I could find.

The walls to the east and south had been fortified against cannon fire with a glacis made of packed earth and backed by a stone buttress. The glacis made a gradual slope leading upward toward the top of the wall, and soldiers in a storming party would be exposed to the fire of the defenders all the way to the brink of the glacis, at which point they would be confronted by a deep ditch at the foot of the old city walls. Guns might fire at the narrow ribbon of wall exposed above the glacis, but their shot would most likely overshoot, be buried in the earthen glacis, or bounce high to land somewhere in the town. Only if a gunshot managed to strike the very top of the wall would it have any effect, and that would only happen by luck.

The walls were also safe from undermining, for the city sat in watery country, and if anyone tried to drive a tunnel beneath the wall, he would drown ere he came near the city.

To help defend the harbors from ships armed with cannon, a mole had been built northward from the Citadel with the Causeway Fort at its end. Yet the eastern harbor remained the most dangerous point, for if large warships could sail into the harbor, they could knock down the harbor walls with gunfire, then land troops to storm the town. The walls were old and not built to sustain gunfire, and the concentrated fire of an entire broadside could turn the masonry to dust.

I had four large warships, including my own *Sovereign*, capable of standing up to Mola's big ships, and these I moored in a line across the harbor entrance. I had also captured the two big ships laden with supplies. I did not have full crews for these, but I moored them along with the four others, brought their guns up from the hold, whence they had been shifted to allow room for cargo, then moved enough cannoneers aboard so they could be used as stationary batteries. I sank ships in the channel to force any attacker to approach under our heavy guns.

I sank ships also in the Dun Esk River to the west, which I blocked completely.

The smaller ships, those from Thurnmark and the ships I had hired, I sent back to the Hook of Zomer to board more troops. These, alas, had not arrived in time, and I worried that they had been captured by Mola's cruisers.

Those six large ships moored in a line would, I thought, tempt

Mola to use fireships to clear his way, and indeed our ships were perfect targets for blazing ships drifting down among them. I wished
to close the harbor with a chain, but that would have set every black-
smith in town to forging the links on their anvils, and I preferred
the smiths working on weapons and armor. So I made up a boom of
barges and boats, all lashed together with hawsers, which could be
drawn across the harbor entrance like a curtain. At present I deployed
it only at night, to keep out fireships, and before dawn I withdrew the
boom so Mola's telescopes would not find it, and I let the boom lie
against the mole connecting the Causeway Fort with the Citadel.

As a final act of mischief, I shifted the aids to navigation, the
buoys and the long wands that marked the two-fathom line, driven
into the muddy bottom and topped with flags. Any ship following
those guides would end stranded on the nearest mud bank, directly
beneath the fire of our guns.

I had to hope I was not stranded myself.

My heart leaped into my mouth as I saw the first enemy shot rise into
the night sky, the burning rounds trailing sparks as they rose high,
arced, then stooped like a diving falcon to plunge into the city.

This was my greatest fear. Mola was firing carcases, hollow shot
covered with tar and filled with sulphur, antimony, saltpeter and
other incendiary material. With such ammunition he had burned
most of Stanport, and left the population with little shelter.

My mind was frozen by the memory of my own city of Ethlebight
set afire by Aekoi reivers. My parents and my sisters had died when our
home was burned over their heads, and thousands of my neighbors
had been murdered or carried off into slavery. The horror of that night
filled me as I saw the first fires blaze up in Ferrick, and I felt my hands
clench into fists. Roundsilver's huge gun loomed over my shoulder
like a shackled beast, unable to inconvenience the enemy fire.

The gun had been cast by the alchemist Ransome, Edith

Mountmirail's younger brother, during the war against Clayborne, which had been expected to be a war of sieges. So magnificent had been his achievement that he had been appointed Queen's Gunfounder.

But the war had ended quickly, without the anticipated siege, which only spurred Ransome in his ambition to cast the greatest guns in the world. And so he did: His guns were masterpieces, vast and ponderous, ornamented with the royal cypher in scrolling script, monstrous animals, gods and demons, astrological symbols, and spells engraved on the muzzle that promised destruction to any enemy. To this Ransome added his own alchemical concoctions of orpiment and diamond dust to add strength and deadly purpose. The greatest of these, the basilisks, could hurl a hundred-twenty-pound stone shot over half a league.

But these great guns required a train of nearly a hundred horses to haul them from place to place, and then only on good roads. The basilisks took the better part of an hour to load, and the cannoneers were obliged to construct a crane to lift and then tip the roundshot into the muzzle.

Once the war with Loretto had begun, I had managed to persuade Floria of the uselessness of these cumbersome masterpieces, and so the orders went out from Council for field artillery, particularly light guns, that could be used both on land and sea. It was intended that every battalion would have one or two of Mountmirail's leather guns attached to it, to smash up enemy formations before the infantry crashed together and the pikes locked.

Ransome, ever eager to retain the goodwill of the monarch, made no objection to this change of plan. He was casting more guns now than Duisland had at any point in its history. And curiously enough, as the guns grew thinner, Ransome waxed greater. He must by now weigh three hundred pounds, which increased the contrast between himself and his gaunt elder sister.

In Ferrick we had anticipated the use of incendiaries in the siege, and had organized a fire watch in the town, a watch ultimately composed of all the citizens who weren't carrying arms—young and old, women and men, boys and girls. Lookouts stood on the roofs of the public buildings to see where a shot might land, and others equipped with scaling ladders and hooks and buckets of sand stood ready to rush to any threatened building and battle the flames wherever they broke out. I stood on the battlements of the donjon and mentally urged the fire-watch parties to rush to their work.

As the night went on, my apprehension began to ease. Few of the fires caught a lasting hold. The fire watch did its work, smothering the incendiaries with sand or water, or using hooks to tear burning thatch off the roofs of the buildings. When a carcase set fire to an outbuilding, or even to a house, the fire watch ran up with their hooks and iron crows and hammers and tore the building to pieces before the fire could spread to its neighbors. They had orders also that when a house was fully alight and could not be saved, the neighboring houses were to be torn down to keep the fire from spreading, but this proved not necessary.

As daylight rose on the city, only a few columns of smoke rose into the pale sky. Relief rose in me like a flood tide.

The bombardment did not cease. Now that they could see what they were shooting at, the siege guns shifted to roundshot and began at once to pummel the glacis. Our own guns answered from the walls, but little damage seemed to be done either way. The enemy's shot for the most part buried itself in the city's glacis, and the return fire failed to penetrate the gabions and fascines that protected the siege guns.

I looked seaward, to the dark shades cruising like sharks on the darker water. When Mola's real attack came, it would come by sea.

CHAPTER TWENTY-ONE

I felt a strong hand shaking my shoulder, and I opened my eyes to see Boatswain Lepalik. "The fireships, my lord, they come," he said.

I was awake at once, and reached for my jerkin and my boat cloak. "How many?" I asked.

"I do not know."

It was the second night of the bombardment. Again carcases had dropped into the city, but the fire watch was more practiced now, and none of the incendiaries set a building alight. The enemy batteries fell silent after midnight, so perhaps they were discouraged, or had run out of incendiary ammunition. I had gone to bed.

I dressed, stamped my way into my boots, and took my broadsword and a pair of pistols. We hastened our way out of the Citadel's water gate, and there Lepalik had my whaleboat and its crew ready. The Citadel's alarm bell was a persistent clamor, and I heard the tramp of the cannoneers as they ran to their guns. The tide chimed against the old stone pier.

The night was dark, with low skimming clouds that sealed away the stars. A cold autumn wind blew from the northwest and rippled the black water. The waning crescent moon hung low on the eastern horizon and was partly obscured by cloud. Yet something glowed a dull red against the bottom of the cloud, and when I saw it I felt a surge of dread crawl up my spine.

The water was dark and cold, and the tide was running in, so the oarsmen had to stroke hard as we raced out along the mole. The six warships defending the harbor entrance were black silhouettes against a horizon that was growing ever brighter. We shot between two of the ships and heard the challenge of a nervous lookout after we had already passed. I answered the challenge in a distracted manner, for before me I saw a ship ablaze coming down at us, its topsails aglow with reflected fire.

We now had to get past the boom, which was stretched between the Causeway Fort and the King's Bastion on the north end of the eastern harbor wall. Any ship coming into the harbor would run afoul of the boom, and that might save our ships and the harbor from a conflagration, but I thought it possible that a fireship could burn through the hawsers holding the boom together, then drift into our warships, and this I was determined to prevent.

The whaleboat scraped against the stone of the Causeway Fort as we passed between the fort and the nearest barge. We had to bend down level with the gunwale in order to slip under the cables that ran to the fort, and then just as I straightened, one of the fort's culverins went off just a few yards away, a vast plume of orange fire blossoming in the night. I felt its hot breath strike my face like a blow, pain lanced my ears, and the air filled with the overwhelming stench of gunpowder. I tried to blink bright blooms from my eyes, and my ears sang a high soprano shriek that faded only gradually.

Once we were past the boom, and out of the shelter of the mole and the Causeway Fort, the cold wind bit harder, and the whaleboat rocked on a steep chop. Spray spattered my face. Ahead a burning pinnace blazed in the dark night, the flames teasing the masts and sails with bright fingers, then retreating. Behind that ship I could see fire kindling in another ship, orange light glowing through the gunports.

"Trumpeter!" I called. "Blow my sennet!" The three descending notes, *Quil-li-fer, Quil-li-fer,* sounded in the darkness. I meant the call to alert the three guard boats which, after drawing the boom into place at nightfall, now patrolled outside the boom as a guard against fireships. I meant them to know that I was on the scene, and was ready to mark and reward their bravery.

As I had expected fireships, I had queried Gaunt and the other sea-captains about them, and also studied a copy of *A Trew Historie of the Armed League of the North,* by Belmason, in which was described the naval war between the League and King Stilwell, Floria's oft-married father. Fireships had been employed by both sides, and from this I concluded that whether fireships succeeded or not depended entirely on the courage and audacity of the men involved.

Fireships were ships of modest size, or larger ships worn out and at the end of their lives, stuffed with combustible cargoes like pine-wood, oil, tar, old rope, turpentine, rosin, and sometimes kegs of gunpowder. They carried small crews, just enough to kindle the fires and steer them toward their targets. After the fire took hold, the crew would lash the helm onto its course, jump into boats towed astern of the ship, and make a dash for safety and the open sea. Any guns aboard were loaded and run out, would detonate as the fires reached them, and discourage anyone trying to interfere with their mission.

The fireships' crews needed a good sense of timing, to know when to set their vessel afire—if they lit the fires too early, the ship might burn out before it reached the enemy, or the fire might advance so quickly the crew would be forced to abandon ship before their time and allow the ship to drift off course. And of course the crews needed courage to remain on a burning ship as long as possible, for the temptation to abandon early was always present.

Bravery and audacity were required also in those opposing a fire-ship attack, for this could only be accomplished by coming alongside a blazing ship, grappling it, and towing it off its track, or by putting one's own crew aboard to steer it into safe water.

And so I had come onto the water myself, to make certain the guard boats did their duty—or if necessary, to do that duty myself, though I hoped there would be no opportunity for me to display any heroism.

Another culverin fired from the Causeway Fort, and there was a horrid howl as a twenty-pound solid shot cleaved the air over my head. I almost threw myself onto the bottom boards, and for a moment I was paralyzed with shock. Ahead of me, I saw a burst of flame on the blazing fireship as the shot struck home.

"Play that sennet again, trumpeter!" said I. I wanted the cannoneers in the fort to know that I was a friend, and that I did not wish to be decapitated by a speeding iron ball.

We saw a guard boat ahead and pulled alongside, and I told it to take the flaming ship in tow and drag it onto the nearest mud shoal. I could see the eye-whites of the mate and his crew, very wide in the darkness, and I knew the fireship had already spread its terror among them.

"I shall follow you!" I said, my words intended both as a threat and a reassurance.

The mate gave his orders, and the oars of the guard boat dipped in unison as it turned for the burning ship. We were at least two hundred yards away from the fireship, but already I could feel its heat on my face.

I opened a hatch in the stern sheets and drew out a grapnel and line to make fast the enemy pinnace. I looked up as an explosion blossomed on the quarterdeck of the fireship, exactly the place where the timoneers would be standing at the helm, and I realized that the ship could not possibly be under command. The crew had set its fires too early, and had been forced to abandon the vessel before it neared its target. I shouted this information to the mate on the guard boat, and I saw him give a wave of acknowledgment.

I was looking over the water for sight of other vessels, and saw two more pinnaces with fires beginning to glow from their gunports. They were farther up the channel, moving slowly under reefed topsails. Behind them, I saw their firelight reflecting off the sails of at least one additional ship.

We were nearer the blazing pinnace now, and my nerves gave a leap as a gun fired from its forecastle. The heat from the burning ship scorched my face, and I held up a gloved hand that my face not be blistered. The guard boat swept in under the fireship's bowsprit, and two grapnels were flung through the air to catch on the spritsail rigging, after which the crew leaned on their oars to drag the head of the pinnace around to starboard. Slowly the pinnace edged its bow around as my own whaleboat stood by to assist if it proved necessary. As the fireship swung its head around, I realized that its larboard broadside was now trained on us, and I ordered our oarsmen to bend to their oars and speed us under the fireship's stern before any more guns went off. We accomplished this just as another gun discharged, and the wind blew pieces of flaming wad aboard our whaleboat. These were easily enough extinguished.

The guard boat had successfully pulled the fireship around so that it was now heading out of the channel, and I thought the boat would not need our help, so I directed Lepalik to take us farther out into the channel, toward the next fireships. I had the trumpeter blow my sennet again, as a signal to the two guard boats I had not yet seen, and which I hoped were engaging the enemy.

Behind me there was an enormous flare as the fore and main topsails of the pinnace burst into brilliant towers of flame. The other vessels were illuminated, and I saw that four, not three, were still bearing down at us. Then there was a bang and a flash twenty yards off the starboard side of the nearest vessel, and I realized that at least one of the gunboats was in action. Return fire crackled out as the crew of the fireship fired down into the boat.

The guard boats were each armed with a swivel gun, but my whaleboat had only small arms and swords aboard, and I did not care to be in a situation where an enemy could fire down into us with impunity.

"Take us along their larboard side," I told Lepalik, and then I turned to the trumpeter in the bow. "Hook on to the mizzen chains."

The crew of the fireship were distracted by their battle with the guard boat, and they didn't see us as we came sweeping along the flank of their vessel, the crew drawing their oars inboard as we closed. The boat hook snagged the mizzen chains, and the trumpeter was almost pulled clean out of the whaleboat as he found himself the yielding elastic link between a sixty-ton vessel sailing south and a light rowing whaleboat sweeping north. The whaleboat swung very suddenly about as the fireship dragged it over, a gout of water leaped into the air between the two craft and soaked us all, and then we banged against the fireship's bilge with a tooth-rattling jolt.

"Good man!" I said, and stood. "Keep holding on!"

I jumped for the mizzen chains and landed with both feet on the wooden platform that served to anchor the mizzenmast's shrouds. Others followed, and I stood on the tips of my toes and peered over the fireship's bulwark.

The timoneer stood by the whipstaff in the glow of the fire rising from the main hatch. Five other men crouched by the starboard bulwark, madly trying to reload their assortment of pistols and calivers.

The guard boat on the other side of the ship let fly with its swivel gun, pieces of the starboard bulwark leaped into the air, and one of the enemy sailors fell cursing to the deck while he clutched his bleeding forehead. The others pointed weapons over the bulwark and fired.

I looked left and right and counted five men standing with me on the platform, including Boatswain Lepalik. "Let us take them!"

I said, and we swarmed up the shrouds, then swung to the deck. The crew were somewhat forward of us, blinded by the rising flames, and did not see us at first, which gave me time to draw my broadsword and untie my boat cloak, which I wrapped about my left arm as a shield against cuts.

We came storming across the quarterdeck toward the unsuspecting enemy. The boat's crew cut down the timoneer before he was aware of our presence, but the larger party had a little more time—a man loading a pistol saw us and cried a warning, then threw the pistol at me and drew a whinyard. I batted the pistol aside with my cloaked left arm, then cocked the broadsword over my shoulder.

My opponent lunged with the whinyard, I turned the thrust aside with my heavy cloak, and then I hacked down at him, and to my immense surprise cut off his hand at the wrist. We both stared at the bleeding stump for a frozen moment, and then fighting erupted all around us, and I lashed out left and right, concerned in the main with protecting myself—and then the fight was over, my boat's crew was throwing dead bodies into the sea, and the man I wounded was still staring at the place where his hand had been.

"Surrender, if you please," said I, in the tongue of Loretto, and then I turned to Boatswain Lepalik. "Bind his wound, if you would be so good."

I turned and tried not to step into the blood and brains of the timoneer as I took my place at the whipstaff. I was a little surprised at the bloodthirsty character of my whaleboat's crew, and their being so efficient at the art of murder, and I resolved not to forget this somewhat unsettling fact.

I took the whipstaff and looked over my shoulder for the fireship I knew was somewhere behind me, and I saw it a hundred yards off my starboard quarter. Its berth deck was well alight by now, the flames glowing through the hatches onto the sails, and I could see that the vessel was a ketch-rigged crumster, a smaller vessel than the one we had just seized. I began to wonder what mischief I could manage against the other ship, and I leaned on the whipstaff a little to bring the fireship's heading to larboard, sailing away from the crumster at an angle to allow it to catch up.

Lepalik was now in a shouted conversation with the guard boat, and I could see by his gestures that he was sending it on to one of the other fireships.

Now that I had swung the fireship wide in the fairway, I pushed the whipstaff over the other direction, and we began a lazy turn to starboard. The crumster grew closer, moving as we turned from the starboard quarter, then right abeam, then creeping forward.

I was thankful the fireship didn't have a spritsail set, for that sail is also called a "blind," for it blocks the helmsman from seeing directly ahead. I wished to see the ship I planned to run down.

There was a burst of light forward as a hatch on the forecastle blew off to allow a gush of flame to shoot skyward with a loud, sustained hiss. The explosion set off several of the broadside guns, and they fired both left and right. I heard shouts of alarm, possibly from the crumster, possibly from the guard boat, and possibly from my own boat's crew.

The blasting guns apparently caused the crumster's crew to notice my fireship for the first time, as I began to hear someone aboard hailing us.

"Turn aside! Put your helm up! You'll run us down!"

I held the fireship on its current heading, and I shouted in the Loretto tongue. "You're sailing out of the channel, you fool! Put up your own damned helm!" And I followed this with every term of abuse I could think of, and these were a great many, for the language of Loretto is rich in curses.

The crumster put up its helm and began its turn, but too late.

"Brace for collision!" I called out to my own crew, and then the fireship shuddered as we struck the crumster amidships, a collision that felt and sounded as if the entire ship had been hoisted a couple fathoms into the air, then dropped back onto the hard, flat surface of the water. The sails slatted, the timbers screamed, and belowdecks objects collapsed, causing gouts of fire to shoot out the hatches. Burning-hot tar rained down on the deck. The crumster was rolled onto its flank, and I could see the bilge as it wallowed up, weed and barnacles streaming with seawater. The crumster somehow came back upright, but we were now locked together, for fireships are covered with grapnels to seize and hold enemy warships, and the grapnels on our ship's bowsprit had got a hold on the crumster's rigging. The two vessels spun in a slow circle as the crew of the crumster lined the bulwark and hurled at us a torrent of inventive abuse.

"Gentlemen!" I cried. "To the boat!"

We ran to the mizzen chains and found the whaleboat still clinging to the fireship. The trumpeter, still hanging on to the boat hook, looked up at us with a hopeful expression, his face scarlet in the light of the flames.

"My lord!" Lepalik shouted into my ear. "What do we do with our prisoner?"

I looked at the young sailor whose hand still rolled on the fire-strewn deck. He was pale, and was barely able to remain upright.

"Take him with us," I said. "He may furnish information."

I hardly thought the information would be worth anything at all, yet I could not leave a wounded man to burn to death on a doomed ship, even the man who had tried to run me through the heart.

I jumped down into the whaleboat and took my place in the stern sheets. Lepalik lowered our prisoner into the boat, and he sprawled next to the trumpeter in the bow, his head lolling on the gunwale.

Lepalik joined me in the stern sheets and tucked the tiller beneath his arm. "Shove off!" he called. "Give way together!"

We sped away from the two spinning ships. The pinnace we had just abandoned was truly blazing now, torrents of fire shooting up the masts, fingers of flame beginning to dance up the topsails. The crew of the crumster, having concluded their situation was hopeless, now leaped into their own boat to make their escape. I looked about in an attempt to get my bearings.

Behind me blazed the first pinnace we had encountered, its reflected fire turning the waters around it to gold. It had been towed onto a mud bank by the guard boat, and was now burning merrily. The tide might yet float her off, but for the moment she was harmless, and might burn to the waterline well before she became a danger to any other vessel. The second pinnace and the crumster, locked in their slow spinning dance, were being blown by the wind across the channel, and would go aground ere long.

That left two fireships remaining, so I had the trumpeter blow my sennet and told Lepalik to take us to the nearest target. This proved to be a herring buss, a sturdy two-masted vessel of forty tons, designed to stay at sea for weeks as it followed shoals of herring on their long migrations. I had often seen whole fleets of busses passing my home city of Ethlebight, trailing their long gill nets. They would fish all day, at night haul in their catch, and immediately the gibbing and salting would begin. The busses' round, bluff-bowed hulls could hold ten kipper lasts, each of ten long hundreds or twelve thousand fish, a total worth a thousand royals when the fishers finally returned to port. Since herring spawn in every month of the year, the busses were constantly at work in all seasons, greatly to the profit of the master and crew. Herring had been the foundation of many a fortune in Ethlebight, and in every port in Alford.

This buss-turned-fireship was probably a prize of war, captured at sea by Mola's fleet and now prepared for sacrifice. The glow of the fire was just beginning, and I could see the crew moving over the decks as they carried their torches and slow-matches, setting their flammable cargo alight.

There was a bang, and I recognized the sound of the swivel gun on one of the guard boats. I didn't see the boat or the flash, but I saw the crew of the herring bus become more animated as they abandoned their torches and ran for weapons. Then another swivel went off, and this time I saw the flash, and heard the cheers of Duisland sailors as they closed with the enemy.

By the time my whaleboat arrived, the fight was over. The buss had been boarded from both sides, and its crew either killed or fled into their own boat, now fighting the tide as it thrashed its way to safety. The mate in command of one of the guard boats had taken control of the tiller, and was turning the buss out of the channel and onto the nearest reef.

The mate of the other guard boat got his men back into the craft, then pushed off and joined me in rowing for the fifth fireship. I could not quite make it out in the darkness, for it had not yet set itself alight, and all I could see was the other ships' fires glinting off the sails. I thought it had but a single mast, like a hoy. As I peered into the darkness, straining my eyes against the night, I saw the oncoming craft transform into an expanding sphere of light, and a few seconds later the great sound of the explosion came speeding toward us, a vast noise that pummeled my ears and was followed by a hot wind that struck me in the face like a slap from a silken glove. A wave rolled toward us like a silver serpent writhing over the water, and the bow bucked high as spray spattered my face. I tasted salt and burning on my tongue.

The blast stunned us all, and the oarsmen missed their stroke and the boat slewed to larboard. Falling bits of the enemy vessel began to dot the water ahead of us.

"By the Pilgrim's eyes!" said Lepalik. "That was no fireship but a hellburner!"

Which meant that instead of incendiary material, the craft had been packed with gunpowder. It had been intended to lie alongside its target, after which the crew would light the fuses and make a dash in their boat for the open sea.

But gunpowder, night, and confusion had instead led to a catastrophe, and the hellburner had blown itself to bits well before it got near any of our vessels. All that was needed for such an outcome would have been an unlucky spark struck by a hobnailed boot.

The whaleboat pitched as it was knocked about by wind and the tide, and Lepalik sorted out the oars and turned us for the harbor. I looked at the four flaming wrecks lying canted on the mud reefs, and at the sight I felt relief, satisfaction, and exhaustion in equal measure. As we sped into harbor, we pulled next to one of the guard boats, and I told them to make sure that if the tide lifted any of the fireships, they were to be brought aground again immediately. Then I congratulated the crews, and my thoughts turned to my warm bed.

I felt I should congratulate myself as well as the sailors, for I had repelled an attack without the necessity of engaging in any heroic actions. (I do not consider attacking an unsuspecting crew from behind the act of a fearless paladin.)

But Mola and his thousands were still outside the gates, and the Boreal Fleet still prowled the sea. At first light the siege guns would begin again to batter our defenses, and when the tide and wind suited those offshore cruisers would make an attempt on the port.

This was only the first attack. There would be more.

CHAPTER TWENTY-TWO

Siege guns boomed as Campion looked at me over the dinner-table "I am sad to say those insults you offered Mola have not driven him into a mad frenzy," said Campion. "They have but increased his determination."

"Not every stratagem succeeds," said I. "Yet here we dine in safety while we wait for the first blast of winter to blow our enemies home."

The siege guns began firing at first light and continued all the morning. I had been asleep in my apartment with a warm quilt snugged up to my ears, and no one had considered the renewed bombardment important enough to wake me. Our casualties were few, and the damage slight.

"It has become obvious where Mola intends to breach our defenses," Campion said. He forked a piece of lamb somewhere into his black beard, where it vanished. "His batteries aim at only two points," said he. "I think we should make ready in case he carries one or another of these breaches."

"And what would you do?" asked I.

"I would fortify the areas behind the intended breaches. The build-ings are warehouses, or sailors' hostels, bear pits, bawdy houses, or other places where amusements for sailors may be found. The buildings can be loopholed, trenches can be dug, stout wooden walls built to confine the enemy. We can emplace guns on their flanks, and prepare infernal engines to blow them to pieces. In some places canals can serve as moats."

I waved a hand. "Let it be done."

"Very good, your lordship." He drank from his cup of ale, then took a second draft. "This is a fine brew, sir," he said.

"The Citadel has its own brewhouse, to serve the soldiers," said I. "I will convey your compliments to the brewster in charge, a Mistress Tucket."

He raised his glass. "Here's to Mistress Tucket, then," he said. "Long may she ease the burdens of this siege."

"I hope the siege may not be as long as that," said I.

Campion left to arrange his traps for Mola's soldiers. I put on my cheviot overcoat and climbed with Rufino Knott to the top of the Citadel's tower, where I patted the breech of Roundsilver's great gun, put my eye to a telescope, and surveyed the Flota Boreal prowling the seas. At low tide the mud flats stretched for half a league into the sea, like the land's brown fingers grasping for Mola's ships but falling short. Piles of blackened timber rested on the reefs, the melancholy remains of the previous night's fireships. Beyond, the warships were gray specters haunting the deep ocean. The tide had only just turned, and would soon advance over the mud reefs—and if the enemy were to come today, they would come in with that tide.

The wind now favored such an attack. The breeze had backed that morning to blow out of the east, and its force had moderated. Mola needed a favorable wind to enter the port, but if his attack went amiss he needed also to be able to leave. The east wind would allow him to come in on a reach, and to sail out the same way.

The tide advanced and foam-streaked water boiled over the reefs.

The clouds were high and scattered, and a bright sun glittered on the waves. I saw a puff of smoke, heard the sound of the signal gun seconds later, and then I saw flags rise on the enemy masts. With slow deliberation, a squadron of enemy ships turned their bows toward the land and came on a reach toward the entrance of the channel.

"Ring the alarm," I ordered, and the bell clattered while the cannoneers ran to their guns. I turned to the captain of the enormous bronze gun that shone brilliant in the afternoon sun.

"Load, master gunner," said I, "and let us discover what this fire-breathing monster can do."

The gun's crew were delighted to begin their work—they had never fired the gun, but practiced by loading and firing in dumb show, and they were eager to see their weapon in action. They began the business of ladling forty pounds of powder down the barrel. While this went on I studied the enemy through my telescope. Ten of the largest high-charged galleons were coming into the channel, led by a ship flying a vice-admiral's flag. The fore- and aftercastles glinted with sun reflecting off steel, and I supposed they were crammed with soldiers. The ships felt their way up the channels at a very deliberate pace, topsails reefed so that they wouldn't charge onto a reef at full speed.

I imagined the kidnapped pilot in the lead ship, picking his way up the channel by taking bearings on the land, on the donjon or the Causeway Fort or some other landmark. A glance in the channel would have shown him that I'd shifted the buoys and other markers.

"My lord!" Campion had returned. "Do they come now, at last?"

"Ay," said I. "Shift some of your men to oppose any landing in the port."

He narrowed his eyes and stroked his black beard with a gloved hand. "How many soldiers are aboard, d'you think?"

"Three or four hundred on each ship," said I. "Three or four thousand, in total."

His eyebrows rose up his forehead. "That is the size of our entire army, not counting the militia."

"Then I had better not let them into the port," said I. "And if I fail, you must make certain that our militia counts in any battle."

"I will do what I can, my lord." The ashlar hastened away, moving with the same swift purpose as when he marched over the camp to run his sword through Aspasio's breast.

The gun's loaders had finished ladling powder into the barrel, and now rammed down a wad made of rope. Others of the crew set up the winch to hoist the stone ball to the lip of the barrel. The ball having gone down the barrel and being rammed home, another wad was driven in to keep the ball from rolling out, a danger as Mola's ships were below us and the barrel would be very slightly inclined downward. Dropping a sixty-pound ball onto the flagstones below would not serve as a mark of military genius.

The gun captain busied himself with his quadrant and level, and had his crew roll the gun back and forth from the embrasure until he had precisely the bearing he wanted. I posted myself at another embrasure upwind of the gun, so that the wind might blow the smoke away from me, and I could judge the fall of shot.

"Prepare to give fire!" called the gun captain. The crew stepped away so as not to be caught in the recoil—all but for one crewman who had mounted the carriage by the breech, and who poured powder into the touch hole. The captain, standing far behind the cannon, peered along the barrel, then jumped away and signaled for the gun to be fired. A crewman dropped the linstock onto the touch hole, and bright fire shot skyward as the slow-match lit the powder.

I had the good sense to clap both hands over my ears, but this mattered little, for the sound was overwhelming. Pain lanced through my ears, and I heard saw crewmen stagger as their hats went flying and they clapped their hands to their heads. Rufino Knot stared at me in shock.

The enormous gun recoiled with startling speed and crashed into the rampart to its rear. The single crewmen who had ridden the carriage in its recoil put a leather-gloved thumb over the touch hole, to keep flame from spurting out and wearing away the bushing.

The vast explosion was followed by a strange sawing noise that dropped in pitch as the ball receded from the tower. I peered out through the embrasure, and through the haze of powder smoke I saw the ball strike the water a hundred yards in front of the first enemy ship, bound over the waves, touch again, then leap up only to vanish from sight. A few seconds later I heard the crash of the ball striking the Loretto galleon somewhere on its starboard bow.

Brimstone stung my mouth and nose. "A hit!" I cried, and then I coughed while the crew cheered.

Flames still licked from the muzzle of the great cannon. "Swab her out!" called the gun captain, and the crew began the long business of reloading the gun. Though the enemy ship had been struck, it continued to sail up the channel unimpeded. With the telescope I could see leadsmen on the ship's beak, testing the depth of the water to make certain they remained in the channel.

We would have to keep shooting.

A shot cracked out from the Causeway Fort, and I watched as the ball struck short, skipped over the waves a few times, and then sank in white foam. I hoped that this example might encourage the other guns to hold their fire, but they banged out regardless, and all missed. If I were the vice-admiral on that lead ship, I would have laughed in scorn.

I told the gun captain to carry on, and with Knott I ran down the spiral stair to the Citadel, where the gun captains lay watching the enemy through the ports, and by comparison with the Causeway Fort were displaying an admirable restraint by not firing on an enemy not yet in range. The guard on the sally port recognized me and let me out, and on the mole I saw the three guard boats that had acted to frustrate the enemy's fireships.

"Gentlemen, it is time to place the boom," said I. "Once that's done, shift to the other side of the causeway and stand by for orders."

They saluted and leaped into their craft. I returned to the Citadel and began trudging up the winding stair to the roof of the donjon.

"Master Knott," said I, "I hope you are taking notes for the ballad you shall write on this battle."

"I am, my lord," said he. "But that gun makes louder music than ever I will."

"Let us trust we play the enemy a merry tune on that instrument," said I.

I was out of breath as I gained the roof, and dots of sweat had broken out on my forehead. The gun crew was deploying the hoist used to lift the shot to the barrel. Standing nearby I found Lieutenant Tate, his hat pulled down over his forehead against the wind. He saluted with his one hand.

"Coronel Campion has sent me to you, my lord," said he. "I am to be the bearer of messages from your lordship to the coronel."

"You are welcome," said I. "How stands Sir Cadwal?"

"He is shifting companies to the harbor walls," said Tate. "But that will take time."

"I will try to give him that time, then."

I glanced out an embrasure and saw the guard boats pulling the barge boom into place, white foam streaming from their oars as they battled the incoming tide. The boom had been withdrawn just before dawn, as usual, and had been lying against the mole since then.

This, I reckoned, would be the first time the enemy had seen the boom, since none of the fireships had got close. Getting over or through the boom had not been a part of their plan till now, and they would have to improvise a solution. As the enemy had plenty of soldiers aboard, I assumed they would be able to put enough of them onto the barges to cut the boom's cables, but this would expose both the ships and the soldiers to our fire for a time, with little chance of the enemy being able to properly reply.

The great gun was now being run up to an embrasure, and I took my place in the same embrasure I had occupied before, and gestured for Tate and Knott to stand by me.

"Prepare to give fire!"

I clapped hands over my ears, and the others did as well. Again the great gun spoke, again the roundshot moaned as it dove toward the enemy flagship. It did not skip across the water this time, but vanished into the dark silhouette of the Loretto galleon—and then came the crash as it went home, and the mizzenmast gave a lurch, then toppled over to starboard, carrying the lateen sail with it. Apparently the roundshot had cut the mizzen away belowdecks, because there was no break above the deck.

On the tower roof we all cheered, bounding on the flagstones like lunatic children. I ran to the muzzle of the gun and looked up at the spells blazoned in bronze relief on the barrel, and I reached out to touch them and found them blazing hot. I remembered the day the gun was cast, the twenty-four monks that had chanted over the metal for twenty days. . . . I had thought it nonsense at the time, but now I wondered if perhaps that chant had succeeded in instilling some deadly virtue into the weapon.

The crew bustled about the gun as they began the procedure for reloading, and I hastened out of their way and returned to my embrasure. The fall of the mizzen had unbalanced the ship's equilibrium with regard to the wind—without the lateen to keep the stern pushed down, the wind caught the foresails and pressed the bow down instead. The flagship made a curve to larboard, aided perhaps by the lateen or some of its tackle fallen into the water and helping to drag the ship around. The bonaventure was too small to do the lateen's job, and the timoneers were helpless to keep the ship on course.

The flagship went gently aground, and the crew ran to launch boats, perhaps to carry a kedge anchor astern to pull the ship off. The oncoming tide would float them off eventually, I thought, but unless they got their lateen up, they wouldn't get far. At this moment the water-battery of the Citadel, on the ramparts below the tower, went off in one great salvo, and I saw forty-two-pound roundshot skip over the water to slam home aboard the enemy ship.

Tate, that melancholy man, grinned. "Adding insult to injury," he said.

"Injury to injury," I corrected. "Let us injure them some more."

The Causeway Fort fired again, as did the guns on the King's Bastion across the harbor, and feathers of white appeared in the waters around the stricken flagship.

When Roundsilver's great gun had reloaded I directed it to fire at the next ship, for by that time it had passed the flagship and was well into the channel. The shot struck the forecastle, and I saw weapons and armor fly through the air as the ball cleaved a path through the close-packed soldiers. The batteries of the forts shifted their fire as well, and billows of white powder smoke drifted across the water as the fire continued.

The leader absorbed another sixty-pound ball from Roundsilver's gun, and dozens of hits from the batteries, before it came up against the barge boom. It drove into the gap between two of the barges, intending I supposed to ride over the hawsers and come to grips with our warships, but the boom only flexed inward, then gently pushed the galleon back.

At that moment the four warships in the center of our line opened fire, powder smoke filling the space between the boom and the line of warships. I could hear the sound of shot hitting home, and in my imagination I saw the raking fire driving through the ship's bows and along the gun deck, cutting through the crewmen, upending guns, and wreaking charnel havoc.

For the first time the enemy returned fire, one broadside directed at the Causeway Fort, and then a few minutes later at the King's Bastion across the harbor. They had not crew enough, I thought, to fire in both directions at once, and so had run the crew across the deck, starboard to larboard, to fire guns already loaded. But now they would have enough crew only to reload and fire on one side.

A few minutes later another galleon came up to the boom, not trying to break the boom but coming up broadside, so it could fire over the barges at our ships. The galleon's broadside was wreathed in smoke and flame as it fired, and I heard the crash of shot lodging aboard our ships. Soldiers from the two Loretto ships spilled over the bulwarks onto the boom, hacking at the cables with swords and axes. These were caught in the fire directed at the ships, and greatly suffered—not merely from the cannon but from the soldiers that garrisoned the forts alongside the cannoneers, who directed fire from their hackbuts and calivers at the frantic men on the barges.

A third ship joined the others at the boom, and then a fourth. There was no room along it for the others, so they anchored in the channel, which did little but make targets of them.

The crash of cannon and the rattle of the handguns was now a continuous din as the ships pummeled each other across the boom, and the scene was buried in white drifts of powder smoke.

Roundsilver's gun had reloaded, and now was jockeyed by its crew to a different embrasure, so that it could bear directly on the line of enemy, so close that it could not miss. I was so riveted by the spectacle below that I forgot to cover my ears, and as the gun went off I felt as if my crown had just been struck by a threshing flail. The gun was aimed at the ship that had been first to the boom, and when the ball struck, there was a rending cry of tortured timber, and the foremast pitched over, with the fore topmast yard hanging in its slings.

Shrouds and stays prevented the mast from toppling completely, but I knew that if the battle favored Duisland, that ship would not easily escape to the open sea.

For another few minutes the guns continued to hammer at the enemy caught on the boom, and then finally the boom parted. The Loretto ships did not sail in perfect formation up the harbor to engage with our ships but spilled into the harbor like fruit tumbling from a shattered bowl. The easternmost ship crashed into the quay below the King's Bastion, and the cannoneers fired directly into it as it scraped its way along the stone. Unable to get under command, it swung completely around and ended up drifting toward our ships stern-first, with our shot crashing through the stern windows and tearing a bloody path through the length of the ship.

The boom failed so swiftly that dozens of enemy soldiers were stranded on the barges, unable to regain their ships. The enemy came crashing into our line in a jumble, the easternmost coming stern-first on the tide, another spearing my *Sovereign* amidships, its bowsprit locked with the foremast stays. The others came down more or less broadside onto our ships, but they overlapped awkwardly with ours, their midship guns alongside a Duislander's forecastle, or their forward battery overlapping Duisland stern. Many of the guns on either side would not bear on the nearest foe.

One battery of the Citadel was able to fire down the length of the entire Loretto squadron, and so was Roundsilver's gun, though it could not depress low enough to fire on the ship closest to us. The roar of battle increased, and the crackle of small arms swelled as the soldiers on the fore- and aftercastles engaged at close range. At the sound I felt a disquiet, for I thought the enemy held more soldiers than our ships, and that they might carry ours by boarding.

Then I noticed the quay opposite me was packed with soldiers, with Duisland flags flying among them. They were climbing into the boats moored along the quay, and setting out toward our fleet.

Someone—Campion, I supposed—was sending soldiers to reinforce those on our ships. My apprehension eased.

One of those brief and inexplicable lulls fell on the battle, and even with my ringing ears I could hear the *clack-clack-clack* of capstan pawls—and in the brief moment before gunfire once more broke out, I realized the five unengaged enemy ships, moored in the channel, were raising their anchors to come down into the fight. White feathers leaped around them, for some of the batteries on the King's Bastion and the Causeway Fort did not bear on the main battle, and the stationary ships in the channel were a perfect target.

I thought there was not room for all of them in the battle line, not with the irregular way the first wave of enemy ships had come into battle, but perhaps one or two would be able to wedge their way into the fight.

Roundsilver's gun was loaded again, and the crew sawed it back and forth as they aimed it for a new embrasure. I went to the gun captain—pale trails of sweat tracked across the dark stains of gunpowder on his face, and there was a black mask around his eyes. I suspected that I looked no better.

"Can you aim at the waterline?" asked I. "Can we sink one of them?"

"I see the waterline of only one ship," said he, and pointed at the ship that had run its bowsprit into *Sovereign's* foremast rigging. "The rest are bow- or stern-on to us, though plunging fire may serve to drive a hole through their bottoms."

"Do what you can," said I.

"Very good, my lord."

There was more jockeying as the gun was aimed at the new target, and the quoin was driven in under the gun's breech, to depress the muzzle.

This time I remembered in good time to stop my ears, though my skull still rang like a bell when the gun went off. The range was perhaps a hundred yards, point-blank for any cannon, let alone a gun so enormous. A fountain of water leaped high from the waterline of the target ship, and my heart leaped skyward with it. The single hole would probably not sink the ship—they could stuff a sail into it, I suppose—but I hoped it might encourage the enemy to flee the scene before they were holed again.

The five unengaged Loretto ships came on slowly—uncertain, I suppose, where it was possible to join the action. The ship that had come stern-first onto our line only to be raked from stern to stem, managed to get under way and limp toward the open sea, and that gave one enemy a chance to come in broadside-to-broadside with one of our ships. Two other Loretto ships shouldered their way into the fight, though they could fire full broadsides only with the danger of hitting their own ships, and were only partially engaged. The remaining two ships anchored under our guns and tried to fight against the forts, but accomplished little and were battered in return.

The next shot from the Roundsilver gun struck an enemy that was bows-on to us, and landed on the forecastle, cutting a searing path through the soldiers massed there. It then plunged belowdecks, though it was impossible to determine whether it put a hole in the hull.

Trumpet calls arose from one of the enemy ships, and I looked in surprise to see the vice-admiral's flag rising on the mainmast. The enemy commander had managed to get himself rowed from his flagship, still aground, to one of the engaged ships.

"Let us shoot at that one," I said to the gun captain, and he grinned, white teeth flashing in his powder-blackened face.

"Ay, sir," said he.

The battle roiled on, the ships' masts rising above the drifting gunsmoke like staves thrust into a snowbank. Roundsilver's gun went off every fifteen or twenty minutes, all its fire directed at the new flagship, which began to list to larboard. The sun hovered in the west, and the long shadow of the Citadel and its tower darkened the scene of battle. The volume of fire decreased as the gun crews battled exhaustion as desperately as they battled the enemy.

I longed for the high tide to turn and help the enemy leave the scene, but I knew the tide would not begin to run out for at least another hour, and the pounding would continue for all that time.

The turning point came when one of the Loretto ships rolled over and sank. It went over very slowly onto its beam-ends, crew and soldiers scrambling onto the side that remained above the water, and then the ship vanished very quickly in a boil of rising bubbles, taking almost all the crew with it. Once it got under the surface, it must have gone upright again, for the upper masts remained above the water despite the harbor's depth of ninety feet. A few lonely, sodden sailors clung to the masts, sad survivors of the five hundred aboard.

We were too exhausted to cheer.

One of the reserve ships drew up its anchor and made an attempt to take the sunken ship's place in line, but the masts thrusting up from the water kept it from getting close, and the ship passed along the line, fired at whatever targets it could find, and then turned out into the channel.

At last the Lorettan vice-admiral realized that his venture had failed. Trumpets called out the retreat, flags went up his battered masts, and he set his canvas and managed to sail himself out of the line, which meant he presented his stern to the ship he had been fighting and was raked repeatedly. His ship had been smashed repeatedly by the Roundsilver gun and sailed low in the water, with the lower gunports closed to prevent the sea flooding in, and rivers of blood poured from the scuppers.

The other Loretto ships managed to get under way, with the exception of that engaged with my *Sovereign*, which still had its bowsprit tangled in *Sovereign*'s rigging. It had been reduced to a shambles, for only part of one broadside bore on the enemy, while every gun on *Sovereign*'s broadside was able to fire. As I learned later, many attempts to board had been repelled at enormous loss of life. Abandoned by his admiral and his comrades, the brave captain was compelled to surrender.

The original enemy flagship had been floated off the mud by the incoming tide, but with its damaged rigging proved unmanageable, and so warped itself out of the fight by putting an anchor in a boat and sending it as far away as the cables would permit, after which the capstan was manned and the ship dragged atop its anchor. This was repeated again and again until the ship vanished into the growing night.

The new enemy flagship, on the verge of sinking, grounded itself under the guns of the King's Bastion. Another ship anchored nearby and—under fire the entire time—rescued the officers and crew, after which the abandoned ship was set afire. Its brilliant flames illuminated the scene for an hour before the fire reached the magazine, after which we were treated to the sight of cannon weighing four tons apiece trailing sparks as they tumbled from the sky to rain down on the sea.

And so the enemy straggled away. It was not a great victory like that of the Races, or a battle that decided the outcome of a war like Exton Scales, but more like a combat between exhausted prize-fighters staggering and leaning on one another for support—but still it was a victory for all that, and considering the odds, I was obliged to find myself satisfied with it. Our six warships had been attacked by ten and taken one as a prize, sunk another, stranded and blown up a flagship, and badly battered the rest.

While the enemy ships were still trailing out of the fight and into the gathering darkness, I gathered men to take prisoner the soldiers who had been stranded on the barge boom. I then found crew to rebuild the boom, for I feared another fireship attack. Having done this, I went in search of a boat to row me to *Sovereign*.

It was not difficult to find one, for the boats that had rowed reinforcements to the ships were now carrying off the dead and wounded, and I, along with Knott and Tate, was able to take one of these vessels from the quay to my ship.

Captain Gaunt met me at the entry port. He and I had sailed to Tabarzam together, and been shipwrecked together on the return, and we had discovered one another's worth on that voyage, and become friends. He was a large man with a graying beard and fists as big as kegs, and though unschooled he had taught himself the philosophy of the Compassionate Pilgrim, and sincerely argued in its favor though he prayed to Pastas Netweaver at sea. I was very happy to see him hale on his own quarterdeck, and when I came through the port I embraced him, his armored cuirass digging into my breastbone.

"We have beaten them!" said I. "They fly from us on the tide!"

"There are thirty more ships where those ten came from," said Gaunt. "I don't know that we could fight such a battle ever again."

"Mola sent us his best," said I. "We can thrash the remainder with half the effort."

Gaunt did not seem convinced. "I pray you are right," he said.

I grinned at him. "Now tell me what you need, and I will make certain you have it."

"The dead and wounded are being carried away," Gaunt said. "But now I have taken a prize, this *Aguila*, and this ship is full of prisoners, and they must be taken to shore and mewed up."

"Master Tate." I turned to the one-armed lieutenant. "Can you ask Sir Cadwal for an escort for a few hundred prisoners?"

"Of course."

"We will also need powder and shot," Gaunt said. "Carpenters to make repairs, and sailors who can haul a rope."

"I will see that you have them."

"By the Pilgrim's toes," Gaunt said, "this fight was a close one. It could have gone either way, but that big gun on the donjon knocked them all to pieces."

I toured *Sovereign* so that I could view its condition for myself and know how best to send aid, and then I visited the other ships of my little flotilla. I was shocked at their condition, for they were in far worse case than *Sovereign*, with the dead lying in heaps and the decks slippery with blood. The gun decks reeked of burning, for the enemy ships had come right alongside, bilges touching, and the enemy cannon were so close that they scorched the ships' sides when they fired. Holes had been blasted in the sides of the ships, cannons were upended, and severed limbs lay unregarded on the deck. Two of the captains had been killed along with many of the lieutenants, and I received reports from whatever officers had survived. I now felt that the confidence I had expressed to Gaunt was misplaced, and I felt doubt that my ships could withstand another such attack.

I decided that second attack must not happen.

CHAPTER TWENTY-THREE

The next day I wrote to Floria and told her of the battle.

Now that the fight is over, you may consider it odd that your Lord Governor should concern himself with paint. But I looked down at our little fleet this morning and saw all the ships alive with people making repairs, some dangling over the side on lines, others lowered on stages over the side, others aloft reeving new rigging. The constant sound of hammering echoed from the city walls.

And the first word that came to my mind was paint. For the raw wood planking over the scars of battle were obvious to any enemy with a telescope, and I wished the ships to look like a brave wall standing against Loretto, not battered flotsam that might fall to pieces in the first strong wind. And so I sent Master Knott to the ships to inquire if they had sufficient stores of paint, and if they did not, to find paint for them.

I hope Your Majesty considers it auspicious that the enemy galleon captured yesterday was Aguila, named after

Loretto's infant king. Long may that king's endeavors meet the same fate as his namesake ship. I would rename the vessel Floria, but at present the ship is a wreck, and I would not put your name on a ruin. It has been towed into the harbor and will be repaired as soon as I can spare the men.

The siege guns began to boom at dawn this morning, so it may be that Mola will try to take the city through an attack from land. I have every confidence that our defenses can keep him out, though if Your Majesty could send us reinforcements, or Coneygrave's fleet, our victory would be certain.

After sending Knott for paint I went to visit the hospitals, and did what I could to cheer the wounded, and to thank them for doing such great service against our enemy. Wounds in naval actions are so ghastly that my task was nigh impossible, yet Duislanders will always put up a brave front, and the courage they displayed in their misery buoyed me more than I cheered them.

This is why we must never allow Loretto to conquer us, for it would make a mockery of those who have sacrificed so much to keep us from being enslaved by the likes of Viceroy Fosco and Admiral Mola. Your own freedom depends much on these men, and I hope you will do what you can for them, and not let them beg on the streets for their bread.

In the hospital I paid also a visit to my own prisoner, the man who I rescued from being burned to death on the fireship. He suffered a fever, but he recognized me, and thanked me for his life. So in saving this man I have done at least one good thing in my life. I hope he will survive the fever.

Afterward the indomitable Guilhelma gave another dinner for the officers. This was much like the one I have described in my previous letter, save that it was attended also by one prisoner, Dom Doroteo de Gres, Conte de Routerra, captain of Aguila. Routerra is a small man with a beard that curves up like a hook, and he seems a half-comical foreigner out of one of Blackwell's plays; but according to Captain Gaunt he was fearless, and led several boarding parties onto Sovereign's foredeck, all of which were shot down or otherwise repelled. He has several small wounds, but his armor preserved his life.

Routerra did his best to emulate the good spirits that were seen at the table, but he could not conceal the melancholy brought about by his situation. I shall regret extremely the necessity of asking a large ransom for his release.

It must be said that these fighters of Loretto are very brave, and skilled in war. Of course, they have had more practice than we.

I hope this finds Your Majesty merry and free, and secure from every form of oppression. Every victory in your realm releases you from constraint upon your will, and so I strive ever on your behalf.

Your Demon Dom

CHAPTER TWENTY-FOUR

I sent my letter with a rider and escort, then went to the top of the donjon for another view of the enemy. The siege guns growled off to the east, their positions marked by plumes of white, and though the tide was now running, Mola's fleet showed no inclination to come in but continued to cruise offshore. Perhaps the paint I had slapped on the hastily repaired ships was keeping them away.

More encouraging were the pains I felt in my crooked little finger, confirmed by the dark clouds I saw sweeping up from the west, promising a storm that would make military operations impossible.

The storm broke early the next morning, a dismal cold rain pelting down while thunder growled louder than the siege guns. The siege guns ceased fire shortly thereafter, for it proved impossible to keep their powder dry.

Anticipating a day of rest, I sent for wine and built up the fire in my office. At mid-afternoon I received a visit from Lieutenant Tate. He stood in my doorway in dripping oilskins, having with exemplary courtesy decided not to sluice rainwater on the floor of my office.

"The enemy have come up against our walls," he said. "They are filling the ditch with fascines."

"I suppose we are shooting at them," said I.

"Ay, but the storm hampers us."

I sent to my boat's crew, put on my old cheviot overcoat and my oilskins, then went out to the quay. Here Tate and I joined Lepalik and the others in my whaleboat, and I was rowed across the eastern harbor. Once ashore, Tate led me to one of the towers on the eastern city wall, and I climbed to the top, where I met Campion and Kosma. They stood miserable in the rain, bear-shaped, oilskins over their armor.

The tower was the same height as the rest of the wall, for anything taller than the glacis would have been knocked to pieces by Mola's siege guns—and indeed there had been a wooden roof to keep sentries dry in bad weather, but the enemy fire had destroyed it. But the tower needed no wooden roof to accomplish its military purpose, for it projected out into the ditch and could direct an enfilading fire on any attacker approaching the wall.

Kosma's spreading beard was so wet that it looked as if moss had sprouted across his chest. He threw out an arm. The rain was beating so hard on my sou'wester that I barely heard his words.

"Here! You may see for yourself!"

The siege guns had been concentrating on two sections of wall, one north of our tower, and one to the southwest where the wall began its curve to the south gate. Now the siege guns had ceased fire, and instead two columns of men, bent double under the weight of the fascines, toiled up the glacis as the rain flooded down on them. When they reached the brink of the ditch, each hurled his fascine into the gulf below, then dashed down the glacis to safety, where I suppose each then picked up another fascine and again began the march up the glacis. It looked as if we were being attacked by a legion of woodcutters.

The glacis was already black with corpses. Though slowed by the downpour, the guns on the walls and in the towers were spattering the attackers with hailshot and grape, and handgunners pointed their hackbuts through the merlons to pick off the enemy. The range was so short, they could scarcely miss.

Campion shouted into my ear. "In normal circumstances," said he, "we would pour some oil down onto those fascines and throw down some torches, and that would be the end of them. But the rain is giving them a mighty great soaking, and they will not catch fire."

I peered into the ditch and saw fascines tumbled atop one another at the bottom. When enough of the fascines had been thrown down to reach the top of the ditch, the enemy could walk across the improvised bridge onto our battlements.

"How long before the ditch is full?" asked I.

"I would expect an attack at dawn tomorrow," said Kosma. "Possibly earlier."

"Have we carcases in our armories?"

Kosma scratched his pug nose as he considered the question, and then Campion answered.

"Ay, I have seen some. But I know not how old they are, or whether they will work."

"We could fire some into those heaps of fascines, and see if burning munitions might set them alight."

Campion stroked his black beard. "Ay, I will send for them."

It took some time for the carcases to be brought, and then they proved to be of a gauge that could only by fired by a culverin, and there was only one culverin in the tower, which faced directly out of the tower and not to the flank where it could shoot at the fascines, so it had to be hauled to the right embrasure while a smaller gun was shifted out of the way. We fired two carcases into the southernmost of the fascine piles, and there was a glow and a deal of smoke, but nothing blazed up, and the rain continued to pour down.

"If they come," I asked, "can we hold the wall?"

"If a battalion comes up in a great column," said Kosma, "one line of men on the battlements will not stop them."

I turned to Campion. "You said you would prepare another line of defense behind the city walls," I said. "That work must be sped if it is not already done."

"Much has been accomplished," said he. "And I will do more. Will you come with me to see the new lines?"

Indeed, his efforts had greatly improved our defenses. Strong buildings were loopholed, weaker buildings guarded by chevaux-de-frise, walls of wood or uprooted flagstones were built across lanes, and ditches were dug, then filled with stakes to channel an attacker into a place where they could be raked by fire. Small cannon were ready to slash into the enemy's flanks as they descended the wall.

"I hoped to implant infernal devices to blow the enemy to bits," he said, "but there is no laying a powder train in this weather."

"Are the special munitions in readiness?"

"Ay," said Campion, "but again this arrant weather is against them."

I adjusted the visor of my sou'wester as I peered up at a large warehouse. "That stands too close to the wall," I said.

"It is loopholed and barricaded, and I have stationed a half-company of good soldiers there."

I pointed. "The enemy could leap from the battlements to the roof, and then dig down through the thatch, or jump to neighboring buildings. It is like a bridge to carry Loretto into the harbor district. You must tear it down, Sir Cadwal."

Campion sighed. Rainwater dripped from his nose. "Ay, those soldiers will not enjoy giving up their dry, warm quarters."

"That may be true," said I, "but none of us shall enjoy Mola's forces capturing the city."

The ashlar reluctantly went to make the arrangements, and Kosma and I returned to the tower. I looked at the growing heap of fascines in the ditch.

"Is it possible to undermine them from below?" I asked.

Kosma peered at the fascines, and then at me. "I do not understand this *maldrait*," he said.

We conversed in the language of Loretto, and I realized I had used the wrong word. Mistreating the fascines was desirable but gave an unclear impression of what I intended.

"Is it *sapé*?" asked I. "To dig it out?"

"*Aï*," he said. "The sappers *sapé* at the saphead."

"We could put fellows in the ditch," I said, "with hooks. They could tear at the fascines from below, pull them away."

Kosma made an equivocal gesture with his stubby fingers. "It might work for a time, until our men are seen. Then the enemy have but to throw rocks at them, or shoot them down from the glacis."

I considered this. "Let us try it at night, then. Our folk may not be seen in this wretched weather."

In truth, I was growing vexed with Admiral Mola. He had found a method to use the downpour to his advantage, and I hoped most sincerely that he and his whole crew might soon be struck by lightning.

"I will leave it to you to arrange for our sappers to *sapé*," said I. "You and Campion have my authority to shift soldiers to where they will be needed. I shall return to my quarters for now, but look for me at midnight."

"Very good, my lord."

The rain turned to hail as I returned to the Citadel, and so we rowed across the harbor on water dancing to the impact of falling pea-ice. The stuff formed drifts against the quay. I told Lepalik to make sure the boat's crew got a good hot meal, and then be ready before midnight.

I followed my own advice and had my supper of pottage, roast chicken, and an almond tart, all washed down with mulled wine, and then I went to my room, told Knott to wake me at eleven, and rolled myself in my blanket.

When Knott shook me awake, he helped me into my buff coat and armor, and handed me my pistols, sword, and oilskins. Last of all I equipped myself with a pollaxe, then stepped out into the rain. The hail had ended, and the rain was lighter than it had been. I looked in vain for stars, but the low clouds still stretched across the firmament.

The trumpeter who had joined me in the skirmish with the fire-ships had arrived with four of his fellows, and they huddled in the boat as we were rowed across the harbor. Every so often I could hear a cannon boom from the walls. The whaleboat was snugged to the quay, and my boat's crew and the trumpeters followed me as I sought Campion, who I found in a tavern with his boots off and his feet in their particolored stockings propped before the fire. Tate, huddled beneath an overcoat, lay asleep against the wall. Rain beat against the windowpanes, and wind sighed against the thatch.

"Stay, Sir Cadwal," I said as he began to rise. "I will join you. But first, allow me to introduce Boatswain Lepalik, the crew of my whale-boat, and a small but clamorous orchestra. Master Knott you know."

"You are welcome all," said Campion. "Bestow yourselves about the room; we shall be here a while."

I took off my helmet and my oilskins, and propped myself against the wall near the hearth. "How go the enemy and their fardels?" asked I.

"Apace. We are undermining them, but they are building their bridges faster than we can tear them down."

"I am astonished at the courage of those men," I said. "They trudge up the glacis bearing their burdens, and we shoot them down in heaps. Yet on they come."

"In a siege, soldiers are little more than beasts of burden," said Campion. "And if we have killed a thousand brave men today, there are thirteen thousand still to come over our walls."

I offered a weary laugh. "You cheer me so, Sir Cadwal."

"We shall kill them all, if we must," Campion said. "Fear not for the city, we shall hold it."

By and by Knott helped me out of my armor, and I slept on the floor in my thick suede buff coat until a blast of gunfire rattled the windows. A pale dawn leaked in through the diamond panes, water-droplets on the glass reflecting little rainbows. I saw streaks of blue sky through the windows, and it seemed that the storm was over.

Within seconds the room clattered with activity, and I was locking myself into my cuirass while Knott stood by ready to fit the gorget to my neck. The trumpeters had snatched up their instruments, my boat's crew loosened their whinyards in their sheaths, and Campion dragged on his boots.

We splashed through cold standing water on our way to the fight, and I found my heart thrashing in my chest. Sweat prickled my forehead. Grim, cold soldiers opened doors for us as we passed into the strip of desolation behind the walls, where we hoped to trap the oncoming storming parties. The air was filled with great ripping sounds as the enemy's iron overshot the parapet to land somewhere behind us. Our own guns fired back, and the chill air was scented with brimstone.

We climbed the tower, and there found Kosma surveying the enemy with a telescope. "They fire at us while their storming parties are forming," he said. "You may see them in those brown fields, just this side of the tents."

I was panting for breath. I borrowed Kosma's telescope and viewed the enemy columns forming, pikes a pale forest in the dawn, banners a wink of color against the somber background. Behind them, the sun was a scarlet blot behind a screen of mist.

I turned to Campion. "The special munitions are ready?"

He nodded. "Of course."

"Where shall I station myself?"

Campion turned to Tate. "Show his lordship to his perch." His eyes turned to me. "I will join you by and by."

My station turned out to be a sailors' hostel of two storeys. It had been erected by hands accustomed to building boats and ships, for inside and out the walls had a subtle curve, outside the walls were clinker-built, with the planks overlapped like strakes, and the roof was a boat inverted, ribs arching overhead.

The special character of the place had been thoroughly ravaged by Kosma's Radvilans, who had turned the hostel into a fort, with loop-holes bored through the planks, the doors and windows barricaded, and holes hacked into the roof, so that soldiers in the attic could fire into the crowds below.

I climbed to the attic and peered out the improvised embrasure into the bright sun that had just risen above the mist. My hackles rose as enemy shot moaned over my head, disturbingly close. With the city wall directly in front I could see very little, and so I decided to avoid being beheaded by an iron shot and dropped down the ladder to the ground floor to await events.

I had not long to wait. The siege guns fell silent, and I heard trumpets call and drums beat, and I imagined the enemy columns now headed for the walls, feet swishing through the sodden, trampled grass.

There was a knock on the door, and it was unbarred to allow Campion and his staff to enter. He nodded at me, and we went up the ladder again, and peered out the embrasures cut into the roof. His ensign unfurled his banner over our heads. Off to my left, where one of the storming parties was expected to cross the ditch, I saw the knight-and-roses of Kosma's banner rise over a fortified warehouse. Handgunners stood in silence near us, blowing on the matches of their hackbuts.

Our guns had not fallen silent and were now slashing the advancing enemy with solid shot and grape. My heart was in my mouth, for

I could imagine those advancing columns all too well, the lead ranks in their cuirasses, bearded faces glaring out beneath helmet brims. They marched over their own dead, and I supposed that this would harden them and turn their thoughts to vengeance.

Hackbuts began to crackle, and I knew Mola's soldiers were within a hundred yards.

Looking out from the embrasure on the roof, I saw their flags first, for the pikes had already been leveled to the charge. The flags faltered as they came to the ditch, for it was not a metaled road they had built but an untidy pile of irregular stick-bundles, and the footing was uncertain enough that the charge faltered somewhat. Yet soon enough I saw heads appear over the battlements, and a clatter rose as the mortal business of hand-to-hand combat began. There was a moment in which the enemy were held on their bridge of sticks, but then they began tumbling over the battlements, and our defenders ran for their lives, or hung off the catwalk to drop to the ground below.

Soon the enemy began to follow them. Flags swept over the battlements, and troops poured down the stone stairs that led to the ground. Our own handgunners fired from loopholed buildings and from behind new-built walls. The soldiers sharing my embrasure stepped forward, leveled their hackbuts, and fired, then stepped back to reload.

At this point I heard someone calling my name, and I looked down the ladder to see a soldier staring up at me.

"My lord," he said, "I'm from the Citadel. I'm to tell you that enemy ships are heading into the harbor."

"How many?" I asked, while an image of a tide table rose in my mind. The tide had been coming in for the last four or five hours, and should now be near its height. The enemy were not coming in with the tide but on top of the flood.

"Three big ships, sir," said the soldier. "And a host of small craft."

Three large galleons would not serve to break into the eastern harbor. The smaller ships I wondered at, for they could not stand in line of battle. Perhaps, I thought, they would try fireships again, this time in daylight—but that would be difficult without a tide to carry them in.

"Thank you," said I. "Tell your captain to prepare for fireships."

He saluted. "Ay, sir."

"And keep me informed."

The attic filled with gunsmoke as our handgunners fired down into the enemy. The enemy poured into the soggy no-man's-land that Campion had prepared to trap and kill them, and I could see their officers conferring about where to lead their soldiers. Handgunners continued to fire through their loopholes, and masked guns blasted them with hailshot, knocking over half a dozen at a time.

Mola's soldiers came surged up against our defenses, fell back, came again. More continued to tumble over the battlements. I could hear them cheering, *"We're in! We're in!"* I could see some using pikes to dig through the wall of a fortified warehouse—not a difficult task, for the walls were half-timbered, and the infill was mere wattle-and-daub and easily broken through.

Explosions burst among the enemy. The blacksmiths of the town had prepared iron tubes filled with scrap iron and gunpowder and capped at both ends, with a fuse ready to be lit by a slow-match. These now were hurled down, trailing a spiral of sparks, to explode among the enemy soldiers. I could hear the thunder as the enemy hammered at the walls of the hostel below.

I looked at Campion. "Now, Coronel?" asked I.

Calculation flickered through Campion's eyes. He nodded. "Before they break through somewhere," he said. "Ay."

I turned to the soldiers. *"Special munitions!"* I cried, and then pointed to the trumpeters. "Play the sennet!"

All five trumpeters raised their instruments to their lips, and their cheeks puffed out as they blew as hard as they could. The sennet was repeated three times: *Quil-li-fer, Quil-li-fer, Quil-li-fer.*

"Keep playing!" I told them, for in the great noise of battle I did not know if they had been heard.

But the first of the special weapons was already on its way, rolled down the gently curving surface of the roof to tumble down amid the soldiers trying to break into the hostel. There was the crack of an explosion, the weird sob of scrap iron tumbling through the air, and then . . . *the blue mist.*

"*La neblina azur!*" I shouted in the tongue of Loretto. "*La neblina azur!*" With a fist I beat a rhythm, and the others around me took up the chant. Other bombs tumbled down from the roofs and burst in clouds of blue smoke. I heard shrieks of terror from the soldiers below.

The colored smoke was not hard to produce. The bomb was exactly the same as those we had been throwing, an iron tube filled with powder, save that shavings of copper had been mixed with the gunpowder, along with a piece of lye wrapped in linen.

I had thought that since copper turns green when it is exposed to the elements, it would produce a green color when burnt, but in fact it burns blue, as I discovered when I consulted a maker of fireworks shortly after my arrival in Ferrick.

The lye did not change the color, but it was intended to produce a throat-searing smoke that might convince the enemy that they had been poisoned.

Panic was instantaneous. Mola's soldiers were courageous professionals who had been employing every possible trick to smash through our defenses, but the instant my fell sorcery was deployed against them, their bravery was overthrown, and they turned, abandoned their weapons, dropped their standards, and fled. Those officers not overcome by horror tried to turn them, shoving them back toward the fight or lashing them with their swords, but it proved impossible to return the desperate soldiers to their duty, and in the end the officers fled too.

"La neblina azur! La neblina azur!" The whole army was chanting it now.

It proved more difficult for the enemy to escape than it had been to break in. There were only a few stone stairs that led up to the battlements, and these were not near the bridge of fascines. The stairs were soon packed with struggling figures clawing their way to the parapet. Our handgunners shot them in the back as they ran, and once on the battlements they knocked each other off in their desperation to escape.

Once they reached the bridge of sticks, they ran into the column of soldiers who were still trying to come in, and there was a mad struggle atop the fardels before the entire enemy force broke and ran as if my sorcery would pursue them to their homes.

Some of the foe had not even tried to reach the fascines, but had gone over the wall and dropped into the ditch, where they could not climb out. We captured several hundreds in the ditch after the fight, many with broken limbs.

"La neblina azur! La neblina azur!"

I found myself laughing as the last of the blue smoke writhed away in the wind. The scene below was appalling, a blood-soaked landscape of torn flags and shattered armor, where bodies lay in heaps and the wounded sobbed out their final breaths—but I had wrung a victory out of it, and I had survived along with the army, and I felt a blaze of life rise within me as the army ceased its chanting and its cheers rose clamoring into the sky.

"Sir! Sir! Lord Governor!" The shout came nearly in my ear. Startled, I turned to find the messenger who had come from the Citadel with a warning about enemy ships.

"What is it?" I said, still grinning merrily.

"The enemy ships!" he said. "They've broken into the harbor!"

My laughter died. "They got past our *warships?*"

"Nay, sir! They're not in the east harbor; they're in the Dun Esk! In the *river*!"

I believe my mouth dropped open. I had blocked the Dun Esk with a barrage of sunken ships, but that had been days ago, and I had paid them scant attention in the time since. But in that time a strong tide had come in twice a day, then poured out again; and a day-long storm had caused the river to rise.

It is a fact of nature that wood desires to float. Sinking a wooden vessel is more than a matter of knocking some holes in the bottom, for it may capsize but will not sink until the wood grows waterlogged. So I had anchored the ships in place and filled them with stone ballast to keep them on the bottom—but still they were made of wood even after they were holed, and wood remains buoyant even if some great weight is holding it down. Perhaps some of the sunken ships had been dragged out of place by the tide, or torn apart so the ballast spilled—or perhaps the river had risen so high that the enemy were able to sail right over the barrage. That, I thought, was why they had brought so many small vessels that drew little water, and why they came on the flood tide.

They were attacking the city at its weakest point. The river walls were old and weak and unprotected by a glacis, for to build a glacis would have meant extending it out into the river. Also, the wall was held by our weakest troops, some of the Trained Bands that had only served together for two brief weeks.

I turned to Campion. "Did you hear that, Coronel?" I said.

He nodded. Again calculation flickered through his eyes.

"You must bring troops to the river wall as soon as you can," said I. "I will leave all that business to you, for I must return to the Citadel. Put Kosma in charge here."

"Ay, my lord."

"Bring also some of the special blue-mist bombs." I feigned a laugh. "Who can say? They may work their magic yet again."

"Ay." His lips drew a grim line amid his black beard. "I will come. You may depend on it."

"May I have Lieutenant Tate?"

"Ay, of course."

I turned to the messenger. "Come with me."

In the ground floor I found Tate, Knott, and my boat's crew, and together with my trumpet orchestra we hastened to my whaleboat.

Getting soldiers from the warehouse district on the east side of the city was not simply a matter of marching them straight to a new position. The east harbor was in the way, and the soldiers would have to march in a long curve to the south, or somehow be carried across in boats. Once they had got around the east harbor, they would still have to cross the bulk of the city to get to the wall—for the area between the Dun Esk and the east harbor was the original city of Ferrick before it expanded to the south and east, and home to most of the city's eighteen thousand inhabitants.

I could not count on Campion coming with any great speed. He would have to re-order his troops, form his columns, turn them about, and only then commence his roundabout march. I hoped he would not arrive to find the city already held against him.

When I arrived at the quay, I saw gunsmoke towering over the city, and heard a constant thunder of artillery. Amid the roaring I heard the great searing crash of the Roundsilver gun atop the donjon, and so I knew that the city's defenders were fighting back.

Once in my whaleboat, I did not travel straight to the Citadel but instead went to the line of six ships stretched across the entrance of the east harbor. "Send all soldiers to the Citadel!" I told them. "They will be needed there!"

When I arrived the ships were cleared for action and ready for a fight, with the soldiers already mustered on the castles fore and aft. There were many boats moored alongside the ships, so I thought it would not be long before another four or five hundred soldiers joined those defending the Citadel.

The whaleboat tied up at the Citadel's quay, and I picked up my pollaxe and ran for the entry. The sentries above the gate recognized me and opened the stout iron-bound doors of the sally port. I did not climb up the tower but instead dashed across the gun platform that overlooked the Dun Esk and ran into a bartizan, a little one-man turret projecting from the rampart, and intended as shelter for a sentry.

The bartizan had a good view, and through clouds of gunsmoke I could make out the three large galleons, each of six hundred tons or more, lying near the quay and smashing at the river wall with their cannon. The galleon in the center carried a vice-admiral's flag, the same commander who had attacked two days before. Not counting swivel guns and murderers, each ship had over fifty guns, which meant at least twenty-five on the broadside, with cannon firing forty-two-pound roundshot on the lower deck and culverins on the upper deck firing eighteen-pound balls.

If you remember that a battery of siege guns is made up of eight cannon, you can easily reckon that each of these ships had the equivalent of three or more batteries on a single broadside—so that firing all together, they made up the equivalent of at least nine siege-gun batteries, all firing point-blank at a single piece of curtain wall.

I could see cables rove from the stern windows of the ships, which meant the galleons had anchored on a spring, and could use the capstan to rotate the ship so that its guns would bear on the target.

Behind the three galleons were a swarm of smaller craft, crumsters, hoys, pinnaces, and flyboats, all of them crammed with soldiers who would launch themselves through the breach once it was made.

I wondered why Mola had sent only three large ships, for the quay was long enough to hold three more, but then perhaps after his losses two days before, he did not wish to risk more galleons than necessary—and indeed three ships were enough to batter a breach in the wall.

The harbor wall had been built centuries before the advent of gunpowder and was about twenty feet high and six or eight feet thick. It consisted of an outer and inner casing of dressed stone filled with a mixture of rubble and mortar. The dressed stone might resist the iron shot for a short while, but once the guns started smashing into the rubble, the wall could fall to pieces very quickly.

And indeed there was already a pile of rubble on the quay, stone and mortar blasted from the wall, and when the enemy shot struck, debris tumbled to the quay, and a gray eddy of dust was whipped into ribbons by the strong western wind.

The fight was not entirely one-sided, for there were bronze guns on the west gatehouse and other guns on the wall itself. A battery of eight culverins bore on the quay from the Citadel, and were raking the stern of the nearest enemy galleon. In addition there was the Roundsilver gun firing from its perch in the tower, plunging fire capable of smashing clean through enemy hulls. The galleons had all been more or less battered, for they'd had to pass the Causeway Fort and the Citadel to get into the river.

There were handgunners on the wall as well, and I could see the white smoke spurting from their hackbuts as they took aim at the soldiers on the ships.

But none of this would be enough. Soon there would be a breach in the river wall, and there were not enough defenders to keep the enemy out of the city. Campion had not cleared a no-man's-land behind the wall, nor had he filled it with traps, and as soon as the enemy came through the wall, they would find themselves in the city itself.

I left the bartizan and found the Warden of the Citadel, one of Kosma's officers named Kowal. "Sir," said I, "I need your soldiers. Kindly summon them from their stations and make sure they have weapons suitable to fight in the city."

"Well, sir, well," he said. "We are the garrison, you know; we must hold the Citadel."

"More soldiers will come from the ships to help you hold the walls, and Coronel Campion is on his way with reinforcements. Please have your men ready in the courtyard as soon as possible." I recalled another item, and held up a hand. "I will also need a flag and an ensign to carry it."

The Roundsilver gun punctuated my words, followed by the sawing roar of the shot, which ended after a second with a great crash as it struck one of the enemy ships. The crash seemed to tip Kowal's mind toward obedience.

"Very well, my lord." He began calling his handgunners from the crenellations, and ordered a trumpeter to sound the officers' call.

I was about to return to the bartizan when I saw Captain Gaunt marching through the postern with a score of soldiers drawn from the *Sovereign*. I ran from the rampart down into the courtyard to join him.

"Captain," I said, "I will take your men, and leave you here to put in order those who follow. The enemy are making a breach, and will storm the town unless we can prevent them."

My words seemed to strike him a little like a slap, and I saw him wince. His big fists clenched. "What do you intend, my lord?"

"I will put a stopper in the bottle, if I can," said I. "When sufficient soldiers come off the ships to form a respectable company, I need you to send it after me. Then the next company, and the next."

"Ay, my lord."

Warden Kowal, having finished his conference with his officers, dismissed them to bring up their troops. Gunsmoke drifted over the scene, and the pounding of guns was constant. Kowal's Radvilans formed in the Citadel courtyard, and I sent the soldiers from the ships to join them. I placed myself at the head of the column with Tate, my boat's crew, and the trumpeters, and last of all a young ensign came trotting up with a Duisland standard.

"You are welcome," said I. "Your name, young sir?"

He gave me an uncomprehending look. I repeated the question in the language of Loretto, but he spoke it not, so I took him by the shoulders and placed him gently near me in the front of the column, and waved to open the gates.

We passed through the north gatehouse at a brisk walk onto Royal Street, the wide thoroughfare that spans the length of the city. The street was for the most part deserted, the shops were shuttered, and the few people on the street had a furtive aspect about them, as if they hoped not to be observed.

The first welcome sight came when we marched to the first square and found there a company of the Trained Bands, listening to the thunder of the guns and wondering if they would ever receive orders. Their lieutenant was a youth who wore thick spectacles and boots too large for him, and I supposed he owed his appointment to being a member or client of one of the great merchant families. I told him to form his soldiers and follow us. This he did, and I found it a pleasant surprise that half his company didn't desert at the first opportunity.

We had reached a place about two-thirds of the way to the west gatehouse and the Long Bridge, and I thought I was now parallel to the section of wall pounded by the enemy guns. But the roads off Royal Street were narrow and twisted, and I did not want to lead my column down one of these lanes for fear that I would get lost, or have to turn everyone around and march them back out again. So I took Lieutenant Tate with me, and we sped down a side street as fast as Tate's limp would permit.

The private dwellings were typical for an old city, tall narrow buildings of three storeys, the ground floor built of stone, and the upper floors built of timber jettied out over the street, so close together that the sky was visible as only a narrow stripe of blue directly overhead. Tate and I hastened down the street, and then to my surprise a wooden fence replaced the buildings on our left, and we discovered a pen filled with cattle.

Over the scent of manure I could detect traces of sweet wood-smoke, and I knew at once why the cattle were here—for they were penned in the yard of a butcher, a residence very like the house in which I had been raised.

When Mola's army approached, the country people had fled into the town, and they had brought with them their livestock. There was little fodder in the town, so the animals had to be slaughtered as speedily as possible, before they starved. The butchers could kill them quickly enough, but any meat that could not be sold fresh had to be smoked or salted, and that took a deal of time—to salt with brine took at least a week, preferably longer, and a dry salt took a month, and in all that time the meat would sit in barrels, and the barrels took up space and would have to be stacked somewhere. I'm sure the butchers and theirs apprentices were working eighteen hours per day, and keeping coopers just as busy making barrels; but in the meantime the butchers' yards were overflowing with live animals.

Yet I hardly had time to purchase cattle or salt the flesh, so Tate and I continued till we saw the curtain wall directly ahead of us. There was already a great bite taken out of the rampart, fifteen yards wide at least, and the earth shook with every impact of the guns. I turned to Tate.

"Bring up the handgunners first," I said. "We'll put them in all the houses roundabout, and turn them into forts if we can. Then send up the pikemen."

"Ay, my lord," Tate said. "May the Pilgrim have mercy upon us."

"Indeed." I was thinking of that butcher's yard and the cattle, and then I gave an involuntary leap as part of the harbor wall crumbled and crashed in a great cloud of billowing dust. I coughed and wiped the dust from my lips.

"Hurry," I said, and then backed away from the wall while I considered what to do.

More pieces of wall fell in ruin as the soldiers were bought up. The handgunners Tate assigned to the houses nearest the breach, and told them to barricade themselves in the buildings and to make loopholes to fire through. Pikemen I placed left and right of the breach, to keep the storming party confined to a narrow channel, and I placed myself with my boat's crew, backed by Gaunt's soldiers with boarding pikes, farther down the narrow lane, with the ensign and his flag directly behind me.

I looked down at the end of the lane and contemplated the horrors I had so recently seen—the carpet of soldiers on the glacis, the dead lying in their blood in Campion's no-man's-land, the charnel decks of embattled ships. All war was brutality, but sieges were the most terrible of all, with attackers and defenders battling at close quarters, luring one another into traps, firing into one another's faces, standing shoulder-to-shoulder hacking at each other with sharp steel while their boots slid in gore.

Yet here I was in the front rank of my column—I, who was not a soldier, and who had no wish to be my country's paladin—because my little experience in war had led but to one conclusion.

It was madness to join in war, to hazard life and safety, to know that soldiers died of sickness, by pike and gunshot and halberd and misadventure, that they risked mutilation and might spend the rest of their lives begging for coppers on the street. Madness. And yet for my Queen whom I loved these sacrifices were necessary, and the only way to make certain the soldiers did their duty was to lead them, lead them onto the enemy spears, into the enemy guns, into the enemy's ditch.

While the guns pounded, the river wall tumbled down piece by piece, and I considered my own situation, standing with my pollaxe against the thousands who would soon storm through the breach. I had a memory of the Festival of the Burning Bull in Howel, where a bull was set on fire and allowed to trample through a crowd as a sacrifice to a god whose name had long been forgotten. I thought again of those cattle packed in the butcher's yard, and then I ordered my column to back down the lane just far enough to open the gate to the pen, and to let the cattle into the lane. I sent some of Gaunt's men up ahead to keep them packed in the road, and not free to wander at will. "When you hear the trumpets," I told them, "get out of the way, for the kine will charge like a wave down a tidal bore."

A few minutes later, there was an enormous, resounding blast of thunder, and though I couldn't see what had happened, the billowing cloud of dust rolling toward me told me that the river wall was down.

Urgent, staccato trumpet blasts echoed on the air. The enemy were calling their soldiers to the breach. I could hear their cheering and the blast of the Roundsilver gun in answer.

As the cloud of dust cleared, I could glimpse bright daylight ahead of me where once there had been a wall.

It was some time before the enemy ventured into the breach, for their soldiers still had to land from the ships and form on the quay under the lash of the enfilading guns of the west gatehouse and the Citadel. But then I heard them cry out—"*Aguila! Aguila! À Loretto et Aguila!*"—and there followed a long, continuous cheer as they came pouring into the breach. In the narrow slice of daylight ahead of me I could see banners mounting the ruin of the wall, and I heard the crackle of hackbuts and calivers.

I allowed the enemy to advance into the lane—the blue-and-gold flag of Loretto waved at the head of the column—and then I called to my own trumpeters. "Play the sennet!"

The brass call of *Quil-li-fer Quil-li-fer* echoed down the walls enclosing the narrow lane, and I swatted the nearest cow with the butt end of my pollaxe.

"*Hai!*" I called. "*Hai, hai!*"

At the head of the column of cattle, Gaunt's men leaped into door-ways as the herd began to move, then run, then charge. I gasped for breath as I followed at a run. The cattle moaned and roared, bucked, and in a frenzy tried to leap over the animals before them and reach the front.

I heard sharp cries of warning from the enemy ahead, and then the flood of cattle struck them and trampled them into the road like broken dolls. The blue-and-gold flag fell. I saw men tossed high on horns, then fall into the lane to be crushed between hooves and cob-bles. The enemy broke and tried to run but could not get away fast enough, and were blocked by those still pouring through the breach.

In their frenzy the cattle charged for the daylight at the end of the lane, mounted the heap of rubble that had been the wall, and then bolted out onto the quay.

The trampling did not cease once the cattle had passed, for my col-umn of sailors and pikemen trampled the enemy again as we charged on, then swept left and right to strike in the back the soldiers battling with the pikemen I'd placed in the lanes to either side of the breach.

Breathless, I stood at the rubble that had been the wall. I had steeled myself to fight hand-to-hand in the lane, but instead all I'd done was to swat some cattle on the rump. Relief sang like wine in my blood.

The daylight at the end of the lane called to me, and I climbed over dust and shattered stone to gaze for a moment at the quay, all in disorder as the cattle dashed with frothing lips among the masses of soldiers—and then I saw one of the enemy ships, the one in the middle of the line that carried the vice-admiral's flag, suddenly fall away from the quay, the great masts rolling over as if a giant hand had swept them to the surface of the water. The ship rolled, revealing gashes in its planking torn open by the Roundsilver gun, until the galleon was on its beam-ends. . . . It hesitated for a moment and then plunged in a froth of water to the bottom of the river. The shrieks of trapped and drowning sailors sounded on the air like a chorus of the damned.

Something snapped and cracked over my head. I peered up past the peak of my burgonet to see the flag of Duisland, which the ensign was waving over me. It occurred to me that this might attract unwanted attention, and indeed I saw some of the enemy looking at me and pointing; and so I gave them a civil wave and climbed down to the lane, taking the flag-bearer with me. My soldiers stood in the lane, still breathless from their chase.

"They will come again," said I. "Back, my bawcocks! And let us find some way to block the lane."

As we drew back we took the enemy flags from the lifeless hands of the standard-bearers. Carts were found and turned over, and the pikemen massed behind these improvised fortifications under the cover of handgunners in the buildings above. I saw Tate on an upper storey of one of the houses close by, and he gestured at me to join him.

I thought I should find a better view than I would get sheltering behind a wagon, and I entered the house—the inhabitants had long fled—and I went up the stairs to join the Tate and the handgunners leveling their pieces out the windows of the topmost floor.

"My lord," Tate said. "Is there anything you need? A message to Coronel Campion, or—?"

"If you could find another herd of cattle, I would be grateful."

He considered this request. "This might be possible. We are on the edge of the Flesh Shambles here; there are butchers aplenty."

"Let us send some fellows to look."

"Ah. Sir." A memory had returned to Tate. "I have sent a lance-pesade back to Royal Street, to direct reinforcements to you. You should establish a headquarters here so that messengers and men may find you."

"I thought to join the fighting."

"That is not your place," Tate said.

I confess I felt relief as he said this, and thought that for all my resolution to lead the soldiers in person into the mellay, his suggestion was probably the proper one. Yet something in me remembered my earlier resolution to lead from the front, resisted Tate's suggestion, and wondered if my relief was prompted by cowardice.

I was still inwardly debating this when trumpets called out a sennet, and my heart leaped at the sound.

"It is Coronel Campion," said Tate.

We went down to greet the coronel, and I discovered he had come ahead of the foot soldiers with two squadrons of cavalry. I blush to say I had nearly forgot the cavalry, for they were hardly suited to the brutal necessities of siege warfare, but now I viewed them with rising delight.

When we had put the horses into the ships to transport them from Thurnmark, they had been thin, sad animals, their ribs visible, their sharp hips jutting from their hide. But now, after a month of grain and good fodder every day, they looked like formidable chargers, bright-eyed and glossy, high-spirited and ready to meet the enemy.

"I am right pleased to see you, Coronel," said I. "And I am pleased also to observe that a troop of horse is nigh as good as a herd of cattle."

Campion was puzzled at this, but brightened as I explained. The pikemen were withdrawn into side streets, the carts were righted, and the first troop of demilances were put into a column of fours and aimed toward the breach.

This came just in time, for the enemy trumpets were again sounding the attack, and again we heard the cry of *"Aguila! Aguila! À Loretto et Aguila!"*

I had no wish to be trampled in a cavalry charge, and so I went to Tate's nest on the top floor of the house, and I was followed by Coronel Campion and members of his staff. My ensign held the flag out one of the windows, to mark the headquarters, and Campion and I leaned out just in time to see the gunpowder smoke jetting from the hackbuts and calivers in the upper storeys of the buildings near the breach, and then we saw soldiers spilling from the breach into the lane.

Campion let Mola's men come on, the fire of the handgunners turning their mass ragged, and then Campion leaned out the window and urged the troop on with a shout and a wave of his hat. The first rank of the demilances clapped spurs to their chargers' flanks, and were almost immediately at the gallop, hurling themselves at the enemy. The next ranks followed at a more sedate pace, for they didn't want to crash into the first rank if its advance was retarded.

That was hardly necessary, for that first rank of four troopers rode like demons into the enemy, sword arms rising and falling. One horse dropped, but at the gallop it had such driving power that it sprawled into the attackers and bowled them over like ninepins.

The demilances drove the attackers all the way to the breach, then turned and trotted proudly back to their starting-point while the observers broke into wild cheers. They had not lost a single man, for even the trooper who had lost his horse had rolled to safety, and walked back at the tail of the column, limping slightly with his broadsword still in his hands.

The enemy had been driven back to the quay, where they were again subject to flanking fire from the west gatehouse and the Citadel. It was an untenable position, and in their situation they must either advance or retreat. They determined to make another attempt on the breach, and again they cheered and came on, at a more deliberate pace this time with their long pikes lowered to the charge and presenting a hedge impenetrable by cavalry. Again the handgunners picked at their formation as they came on, and again Campion sent the demilances at them. The cavalry were less successful this time, for the horses flat refused to advance against the pike-hedge, so the cavalry performed what is called the caracole, in which each rank fires their pistols into the enemy at close range, then turns their chargers to retire to the rear of the column to reload. There was scarcely room in the lane for the ranks of horsemen to pass one another, but the enemy were coming on slowly so as not to disorder their pike formation, and failed to take advantage of any disorder amid the demilances.

In the meantime the handgunners continued to fire into the attackers, lead and steel shot pelting down from above and either side.

Our opportunity came as the attackers advanced across a side lane, for our pikemen waited there and attacked the head of the enemy column from both sides. The pike hedge was disordered, and the first rank of horsemen must have seen their opportunity, for they discharged their pistols, threw the empty pistols at the enemy, then drew their swords and charged.

Soon there was a wild melee, the swords slashing right and left, the horses rearing and trampling as they pushed deep into the enemy formation.

Again the cavalry drove the mass of soldiers back, but this time the enemy made a desperate effort to resist them, and horses and troopers fell in the crush and were killed. Yet the enemy gave way, at first grudgingly, then swiftly, and then in complete terror as they fled through the breach and onto that deadly quay swept by our fire.

After that the enemy made no more attempts to storm the city but only tried to get their soldiers back on their boats and make an escape on the ebbing tide. One of their battered galleons, holed several times by the Roundsilver gun, ran aground on one of my blockships, and was forced to surrender after it was abandoned by the rest of their force. The rest suffered greatly as they retired under the fire of the Citadel and the Causeway Fort, and several of the smaller craft were sunk with the loss of nigh everyone on board.

Let us meet them in the field, I remembered Floria saying, *and there give them such an abundance of war, such a storm of Fornland iron,*

Bonille steel, and Duisland courage, that they will turn in horror from the fray. . . .

Ay, we had cut them down in heaps and sown horror among them, a horror so profound that they had fled at the first whiff of harmless blue smoke.

I left Campion at the breach and returned to the Citadel before the last shots were fired, followed by my boat's crew carrying a forest of captured flags over their shoulders. These we displayed on the parapet where they could mock the enemy.

I marveled that so much had happened, and that it was not yet noon.

CHAPTER TWENTY-FIVE

The next morning, fog wrapped the city close in a chill embrace, and through the fog we heard the deep boom of gunfire. The fog magnified the sound so that it seemed as if the cannon were going off but a hundred yards away, but no enemy attack was reported on the city, and standing atop the donjon with my hands cupping my ears, it seemed to me the sound was coming from far off the land. Coneygrave and Mola were doing battle miles out to sea.

I paced the battlements of the donjon while cold wet drops of condensed fog dripped off my hat and worked their way under my collar. The great bulk of the Roundsilver gun loomed over my shoulder, and its crew huddled in their overcoats and worried whether their powder was keeping dry.

From the city came the sounds of both destruction and fabrication. The bridges of fascines had been torn down, and the enemy would not cross the ditch again without cutting down another forest's worth of timber to carry them over. Behind the river wall Campion was now constructing a second line of defense, with stake-filled ditches designed to channel the enemy into narrow lanes strewn with deadly traps. Repairs continued on our ships, and we were running out of places to confine our prisoners.

The gunfire sounded off the sea for hours, even as the fog slowly burned off the land. When we could finally see the northern horizon, we saw another dense bank of cloud, though in this case it was not made of mist but gunsmoke.

The battle went on till early afternoon, after which the sound of cannon dwindled away and the line of smoke gradually dispersed. Two sets of ships clustered in different quarters of the ocean, and they drew apart. One set of ships disappeared over the northern horizon, and the other came toward the land. Anxiety gnawed at me as I wondered if Mola had been driven off his station, or if he was going to resume his blockade of the city.

Relief came when the telescope at last revealed details of the oncoming fleet, and I recognized *Imperial* with its tall castles and vermilion hull. I laughed and stepped back from the telescope.

"Lord Admiral Coneygrave has driven off the enemy!" I said. "We should prepare to fire a salute!"

A few hours later the salute was duly fired, and Coneygrave and some of his officers stepped out of their barge to greet us. That night they were my guests at supper. Coneygrave's underslung jaw, baring his lower teeth, made his wide grin seemed particularly feral.

"We sent them running, Lord Selford!" said he. "And we have taken three prizes!"

"We did our best to soften them for you," said I. "For we took two galleons and sank three more, and battered several others."

"I see you have much to relate, then. But before you do . . ." He reached into his doublet and produced a letter. "I carry a letter for you, from Her Majesty, that she gave me when she ordered the fleet to Ferrick in your support."

It was all I could do not to snatch the message from his hands. But I was compelled that night to sit at the table and converse with my guests, offering and receiving toasts while we told stories of our campaigns, and for all those hours I could scent Floria's galbanum fragrance wafting from the letter now lodged in my own doublet.

More frustration came later, for when I opened the letter I found that she had written it in cipher, and I had to get out my book and work out the message letter by letter.

> *Your message has arrived by the fisherman* (meaning Barbosa) *and I have ordered Coneygrave to sea as soon as he can resupply his ships.*
>
> *Rest assured that you have not been forgotten in Selford. The rescue of Coronel Campion and our army has been celebrated with bells, gun salutes, and illuminations, and we anticipate your next dispatch, and the news of the salvation of one of our cities.*

It did not surprise me that she hadn't yet received either of the messages I had sent from Ferrick, and I was gratified that she had sent the fleet out as soon as Barbosa's lugger had touched at Innismore.

> *I have every confidence that your project will bring results. There is a reason beyond politics that you were given this commission, and that reason is simple, for I knew you would succeed.*
>
> *I will treasure your message, and keep it ever close to remind me of you.*

> F.R.

Post Scriptum: The Constable has arrived in Howel to take command of the reinforcements waiting there. He is a hasty man, and I think you will see him ere long.

F.R.

Constable Scutterfield-or-Drumforce would arrive after he was no longer needed, but at least his arrival would serve as an excuse for me to leave Ferrick and sail to Selford. I could turn the city over to the Constable with a clear conscience, and he could set his soldiers to repairing the damage Mola had inflicted on the city.

I hoped he would not be so foolish as to march out of the city and attack Mola's forces, and if he did, I hoped to be well away before the battle took place. I had no great confidence the Constable would take the victory.

While I was thinking these thoughts, one of Kosma's men came to tell me that a messenger had arrived claiming to have been sent from the Constable. I invited the courier into my office, and saw that he was wet through and through.

"I hoped to get over the Long Bridge," said he, "but the planks were taken up, so I had to cut inland and swim my horse over the Dun Esk."

"At night?" asked I. "And with the river in flood? Surely that is a feat that should be celebrated in song."

"It was my duty, my lord."

"Your dispatch must be urgent indeed. Give it to me, and I will send you to a fire to warm you, and send as well a warm brandy punch."

"No dispatch, sir," said the courier. "Just a message verbal. The Constable expects that he and his army will arrive tomorrow at noon."

The message was welcome but was hardly worth risking the life of the messenger. I rose from my chair.

"I thank you for the news," said I. "And now let us find you that fire."

I left the messenger wrapped in blankets before a fire, with his clothing steaming on a line, and a leather jack of spiced punch warming by the hearth. I returned to my quarters and went to bed, and I put Floria's letter beneath my pillow, so that her galbanum scent would waft through my dreams.

I woke to the sound of cheering. I was swimming into my shirt when Rufino Knott knocked on my door and entered.

"What's ado?" asked I.

"Mola drew his siege guns out of position during the night," he said. "Everyone thinks he's retreating."

I first thought he might instead be repositioning his guns, but on reflection I decided that Knott was probably right. "I think I am too weary to cheer," I said, "but I will do my best."

Before breakfast I arranged for the planks on the Long Bridge to be restored to their places, a task which required a barge with a crane on it, and during breakfast I sent for red-haired Guilhelma, and asked if she would arrange for a feast that day, with the Lord Admiral and Constable Scutterfield as the guests of honor. She was pleased to be asked, and immediately set about the work.

After breakfast I sent for Captain Gaunt. "I intend to leave for Selford tomorrow," I said. "And if *Sovereign* can swim, I intend that you will carry me."

"I will be right pleased to see Selford again," said Gaunt.

"Take on such supplies as you need," said I, "and the tide will take us out mid-morning."

When the banners of the Constable's armies came over the western horizon, the Long Bridge still lacked two spans, so I sent my whaleboat across the Dun Esk to bring Scutterfield-or-Drumforce to the gatehouse. We had decorated the gatehouse and the river wall with flags, the colors of Duisland flying over captured enemy banners.

As the whaleboat crossed the water, I recognized some of the men aboard—the Constable, with his fair hair and drooping mustaches, my friends Bill Lipton and Lord Barkin, respectively the Lieutenants-Generals of Artillery and Cavalry, tall Lord Morestanton in a peacock-green doublet covered with embroidered red poppies, and—dismayingly—the Marquess of Stayne, who had once hired a gang of rudesbys and prizefighters to kill me and had been exiled from court, but who had redeemed himself in the eyes of the nation by his ferocious defense of Stanport.

My eyes, however, were not those of the nation, and there was no redemption there to be found.

Boatswain Lepalik brought the whaleboat smartly against the quay, and his passengers stepped out. I donned my smiling heartylad face and stepped out from the gatehouse. "Welcome to Ferrick, gentlemen!" said I. "You are most welcome. I bring you good news— Mola has been defeated on land and sea, and this morning began his retreat to his own country."

Constable Scutterfield's chin jerked upward at this news, and I saw fierce determination enter his eyes.

"We must pursue, then!" he said. "Pursue immediately!"

As long as I had known him, Scutterfield-or-Drumforce had simmered with anger, and disdained inaction. I do not know if he was so disposed before his father had been murdered by Edevane, but he had certainly adopted a ferocious, uncompromising mien in the time since.

"It will be some time before the bridge is ready for your army," I said. "In the meantime you may enjoy our hospitality in the Citadel."

I introduced Campion, Kosma, and Coneygrave, and together we walked up Royal Street to the Citadel. Campion insisted on making detours to view the breaches that we had defended the previous morning, reeking narrow places that still smelled of gunpowder and were stacked with corpses, and with great pride he described each action in some detail. He then asked me to explain the ruse of the blue smoke, which I did with a degree of reluctance, as I saw Stayne's eyes on me.

Stayne was a lean man with long gray hair and a well-trimmed gray beard that framed a pursed, disapproving mouth. He listened to my tale with what he probably imagined was feigned patience. I did my best to content myself with the knowledge that I had enjoyed his wife Amalie—and furthermore that Amalie had enjoyed me.

"So you won by a trick," he said with disdain.

"Tricks are better than hard knocks," said I. "We were outnumbered four to one, and we needed every trick in the world to keep them out."

"There was no chance for tricks at Stanport," he said. "There was only hard fighting, face-to-face in the ditches."

"I am told you defended every ditch valiantly," I said. I thought of his wife in my bed, her head resting on my shoulder, strands of pearls tangled in her tawny hair.

"Let us go on to the Citadel," said Coneygrave, his eyes turning from me to Stayne and back. Perhaps he remembered that Stayne had been sent to his seat at Allingham for trying to murder me.

He took Stayne's arm and steered him toward Royal Street. I walked beside the master of artillery Bill Lipton, who had forsaken the grand uniform of his office and wore merely a brown suede jerkin and on his bald head a shapeless cap that fell around his pink ears. His beard was grizzled, and he leered at me.

"That Stayne is a peevish fellow, sure," he said.

"He tried to have me killed," I said.

Lipton laughed. "Is there anyone in the peerage who has not?"

I considered my recent history. "Some," said I, "but if they are tardy, we must give them time." I looked up at the Citadel's tower rearing at the end of Royal Street. "Do you remember the great siege guns that Roundsilver cast in the last war?"

"Of course I do," he said, "For I watched them being cast, with all that chanting monkish mumbo-jumbo, and then I had to certify them as acceptable for the Royal Armory."

"One of those guns is on yonder tower," I said, "and placed so high it was able to direct plunging fire onto the enemy ships and drive straight through their bottoms. It sank three and badly damaged others."

"I am glad some of Ransome's big guns were at last of use," said Lipton. "We had two of his cannon-basilisks at Castras, but the enemy never came within range of them."

Campion directed the party onto the battlements of the Citadel, where the Constable viewed Mola's retreating army with a telescope. Mola had sent his siege guns and supply train ahead, and hovered in the distance with his fighting men, well out of range of any of our guns. I could see Scutterfield's lips moving as he counted regimental standards and estimated their strength.

"I think our numbers are equal," he said, "if we bring Coronel Campion's men forward with us, and Captain Kosma's."

"I do not think you are seeing his entire force," said I. "He will be hiding some of them."

"By the time we get the army across the bridge and through the town," said Barkin, "it will be too late to fight a battle, and night will fall before we reach a decision. Best to start a pursuit at first light tomorrow."

"There is a feast awaiting you in the hall," said I, "if you gentlemen would care to join us."

"I will send my quartermasters to find places for your soldiers to sleep," said Campion.

The Constable withdrew reluctantly from the battlements and came to the hall, where he and Coneygrave were set in the place of honor at the head table, flanked by Campion and Kosma. I found myself farther down the table, with Morestanton on my left and Stayne on the right. I resigned myself to furnishing my own company for the evening.

Mistress Tucket's fine ale was brought out and served to the company, and I rose with my glass in my hand, and offered a toast to the gentlemen of the Queen's Army and Navy, who had come to the relief of Ferrick and rendered us safe from Mola's malevolence. There were cheers and applause.

The Constable rose and offered the loyal toast to the Queen. Coneygrave then stood, and thanked me and the garrison of Ferrick for our hospitality, again to applause and cheers.

Then, to my great surprise, Morestanton rose with his cup. "I pledge this cup to Lord Selford, who by taking and holding Ferrick forced Mola's retreat, and saved Her Majesty's city of Stanport from Mola's murdering crew."

Stayne, on my other elbow, reddened with rage. "You know nothing about it!" he snarled to Morestanton as applause and cheers rang out. I acknowledged the ovation with a wave of my cup while I looked at Morestanton in surprise. I had not expected such praise from Pontkyles's son.

Morestanton drained his cup, wiped his lips with a napkin, and returned to his seat. He looked at Stayne across me.

"I know enough, I think," he said. "I know that if Selford hadn't taken Ferrick, you would still be squatting in a ditch at Stanport, dining on a fine meal of spit-roasted rat while Mola's guns knocked the town to bits over your head."

Morestanton, I thought, had always been well-spoken, though I had never thought that eloquence would be used in my defense.

And Stayne, I concluded, must have been making friends among the Constable's officers in his usual charming way.

"You are a fool, Morestanton," said Stayne. "You have never been in war, and you know nothing."

"I will soon amend my ignorance," said Morestanton, "if we are to engage with Mola tomorrow. And—"

He was interrupted by the arrival of Guilhelma, who swept into the hall with the first remove of pottage on a wheeled table, and who was greeted with applause. She wore a gown of bright yellow velvet, trimmed with dark gray fox fur, and a blue ribbon over her shoulder embroidered with the word *Victory* in gold thread.

"Gentlemen!" she cried in her booming voice. "We are right glad to see you here, and I want you to know I love you all!"

Then she marched up to the head table, took the Constable's head in both her hands, and kissed him fiercely on the lips while the room broke into astonished cheers. Then she reached for a bowl, poured pottage into it with her own hands, and set it down before the astonished commander.

Everyone at the high table was treated likewise, first with a kiss on the lips, and then a bowl filled and served by Guilhelma.

"Is this your whore, Quillifer?" Stayne asked. "Her gross vulgarity suits well with your own."

"Ah, Stayne, you have just put your lordship's life in my hands," said I. "For she is Sir Cadwal Campion's mistress, and if I report that you slandered her so, he would pistol out your brains before you could cry 'misunderstanding!' "

Stayne gazed speculatively at Campion and sneered, but nevertheless suffered Guilhelma to kiss him, and to offer him a bowl of pottage. I myself kissed her right gladly, and so I think did Morestanton.

"I thank you for your defense of me," I told Morestanton.

"I did not know what to make of you, I confess," he said. "You are not like anyone I have ever met. But after I saw you ferret out the poisoner, I realized that whatever you might be, you are Her Majesty's true and faithful servant."

"I almost poisoned you," I pointed out.

Morestanton made an equivocal motion with one hand. "I own that

I resented it at the time," he said. "I understand now that an experiment needed to be made. And now that you have rescued Duisland's army and taken Ferrick, you have a claim to every honor Her Majesty gave you."

Stayne laughed. "Enjoy your honors while you may, Quillifer," said he. "You have in store for you the fate of all your climbing sort—you will fall, and then the merest breeze will blow you away."

I looked at him. "Your family name is de Ferrers, is it not?" asked I.

"It is. We are among the oldest noble families in the realm."

"But de Ferrers is surely a corruption of 'farrier,'" I said. "One of your noble ancestors made his living shoeing horses."

He made a contemptuous snort. "Don't be absurd."

"Stayne," said I, "there are horseshoes on your achievement of arms."

"That is because several of my ancestors held the office of Count of the Stable," said Stayne. "We commemorate that honor on our shield."

"Ah," said I. "And here I thought you were proud that one of your ancestors made a useful living with his hands."

His disdainful little mouth pursed, no bigger than a blackberry. "That is a slanderous accusation," he said.

"What? That your ancestor was useful?"

"You understood my meaning, Quillifer."

Afterward Stayne fell silent and brooded to himself for the rest of the meal. No doubt he felt himself greatly imposed upon.

I took a spoonful of pottage and tasted it. It was made of chicken and leeks, with a spicy admixture of ginger, and I thought it fine.

In my mind I conjured an image of Floria, and this time she seemed to be drifting closer, almost within reach of my arms. Silently I raised my cup and pledged to her. I would be on the sea tomorrow.

CHAPTER TWENTY-SIX

Nature provided seven days of mild autumn weather, sunshine and fresh breezes. My crooked little finger never ached, and we came into Selford on the afternoon tide on the twenty-ninth of October, and once the *Sovereign* moored to its buoy off Innismore, I was away with my boat's crew within ten minutes. We arrived at the Marygold Stairs by Selford's great bridge at mid-afternoon, and I looked up to see the bridge jammed with wagons and coaches, and I knew well what this implied. The Queen and the entire court had gone to the royal hunting lodge at Kingsmere for several days' hunting, and now, bloodlust sated, they trekked wearily back into town.

"Come with the baggage when you can," I told Knott. "It is a pleasant day, and I will walk to the castle."

I went up the stair to the road and walked along the road, passing carts loaded with baggage, tents, carpets, barking hounds, mattresses, firearms, hooded hawks on their perches, grooms, footmen, cooks, pages, postillions, lawyers, pages, whippers-in, henchmen, ostlers, singers, kitchen drudges, the terrier-man in his little cart, musicians, choristers, bakers, stewards of this-and-that, and hopeful office-seekers (a term which embraced everybody).

It was good they had practice, for in a few weeks they would have to pack up and move again as the court journeyed to the winter capital of Howel and the meeting of the Estates.

I saw no actors, as they all lived in Mossthorpe and needed not to cross the bridge to go home.

I strolled along, and as I was dressed as a sailor, few recognized me. I turned into Chancellery Road and walked up the street toward the castle, on the way buying a pearmain from a greengrocer. The crisp green-skinned apple with its tart white flesh had been my mother's favorite, and the taste brought back memories of autumns in Ethlebight, when I was a schoolboy free of care and full of mischief.

I passed by the square pale building covered with the shields of the cities and corporations of Duisland, and stopped when I heard a frantic tapping on a window. The window opened, and Sir Robert Hillier, the King of Arms, leaned out to greet me.

"I was on the verge of sending a package to your office," said he. "Come in, and I will give it thee, and a glass of brandy besides, an you can spare the time."

"I will come right willingly," I said.

I joined Hillier in his crowded office, beneath that window painted with the most elaborate heraldic achievement in history. He had already put out two glass goblets and was pouring brandy. He handed me a glass and raised his own.

"I drink to you, Lord Selford," said he, "for I have news that will please you."

"And I will be happy to hear it."

We drank. Brandy fumes lodged in my nose, and I barely avoided a sneeze.

"Sit you, sir," said Hillier, "and take a look at this. I have just finished it."

He handed me a leather tube capped at both ends. I uncapped it and drew out a rolled vellum of the highest quality, soft as wool, with the veins of the calf which had donated its hide still inscribed faintly on it. I unrolled the vellum and looked in bewilderment at an interlocking net of lines, names, places, and illustrations of heraldic achievements.

"What is this?"

"You remember that you sent out old Redbine to Ethlebight to investigate your ancestors? I am pleased to tell you that Redbine has succeeded in his mission. Unfortunately he fell and broke a leg, and at his age this is a serious matter, so he sent the documents on to me, and I have here illuminated your family tree, as you see, with your own device at the top."

"Succeeded?" asked I. "He found I have noble ancestors?"

Hillier laughed. "Better than that, my lord!" he cried. "You are of royal blood!"

I had always assumed that I was, because I had assumed that *everyone* was. Kings have many children, and those children have children, and so on down the ages. I once worked out the figures on an abacus, and found it is mathematically unlikely that, after the space of a thousand years, any person is *not* descended from at least one king, probably more.

The problem, I surmised, was proving it.

"Which king?"

Hillier tapped some lines on the bottom of the scroll.

"Herefrid the Seales," he said.

I looked up at him. "And who is Herefrid the Seales? I never heard of him."

"He was King of Acclock about nine hundred years ago."

"One of the Sea-Kings, then? Where was Acclock?"

"A kingdom on the lower Ostra."

"He ruled in Ethlebight, then?"

"Indeed, his seat was at Ethlebight, which was why the city is named 'Royal Bight.' As you see, Herefrid was married to Earcongota of Sutgill, and they had seven children. Now their daughter Bealdthryth married Berhtric, who is described in the annals as a *Comes rei Militaris,* like our own Count of the Stable or Constable . . ."

He went on to explain that Berhtric was a famous champion who served not only Herefrid but his two successors, and whose grandson Eadwine, another celebrated warrior, married again into the royal family and was the father of Inguburh, who the Council of Counts or Witenagemot elected King after every other eligible male died in battle.

"Hold, Sir Robert," said I. "Where is this recorded? Because I have heard of none of this, there is no legend of Bealdthryth or Berhtric in my family, and I'm sure no records of that period have survived in Ethlebight. That was, what?—seven hundred years ago?"

"We know about Inguburh from the people who killed him," said Hillier. "He died defending Ethlebight from one of the Osby Lords, a fellow named Aslak, who led an army of reivers known as the Scramlings. Inguburh was burnt to death in his own tower, but his son Osred survived, and was adopted by Aslak and given the name Otkel.

"Now, if you have ever read any of the annals of the Osby Lords, they all begin with the genealogy of the central characters, and they include as well the genealogy of everyone they fought, to prove their enemies were mighty paladins who could only be killed by the greatest of heroes. So the tale of Aslak and Otkel is recorded in *The Annals of Hosvir.*"

"Hosvir," I said. I took a swallow of brandy. "And who is he?"

"Hosvir was Aslak's great-grandson, King of what had been Acclock but was renamed Langana by the Osby Lords. Otkel and his descendants feature in the story, as friends and supporters of Aslak's family."

"Langana at least I have heard of," I said. "It is an old name for the country around Ethlebight."

"During the time of Hosvir," Hillier continued, "he was friends with Trigg, who was Otkel's twice-great grandson. In a particularly bloody battle, Hosvir was badly wounded, and Trigg carried him away from the field on his back, running so swiftly that he eluded all pursuit. For this service Trigg was nicknamed Konungsfotr, or King's Foot."

He pointed at the scroll. "The name Konungsfotr continued in the family, long after the rule of the Osby Lords ended. But over time the name was corrupted—" Hillier looked at me with bright eyes. "Can you guess into what?"

"Cannon Fodder," said I. "And in the last few months I have demonstrated the aptness of that name."

He laughed. "Guess again."

I looked at the scroll. "It is Quillifer, is it not?"

"Redbine has been able to trace your family for all these centuries. Your people remained in the lower Ostra for all that time, though you ceased to be great warriors and became instead respectable burgesses."

I looked at the great scroll and took another drink of brandy. I had sent Redbine to Ethlebight in hopes of finding some noble ancestor that might make me more acceptable as a husband to Floria, and now I had succeeded beyond my dreams. I was descended from two kings, Herefrid and Inguburh. My royal line was senior even to that of the Queen. For a moment I was dazzled, and then I returned to my senses.

"I don't know who would believe this story, even if it is true. *The Annals of Hosvir* can't be reliable history, can it?"

"There is only one person in the realm qualified to accept this genealogy and its supporting documentation," said Hillier, "and that person is the King of Arms." He touched his glass to mine. "With this toast I thus accept your royal ancestors." He laughed. "Congratulations, my prince!" He sipped from his glass, then put the glass on his desk. "Now I think we should discuss amending your achievement of arms to reflect your distinguished royal ancestor. Perhaps you could quarter your galleon argent with a willow tree, for that is the meaning of 'Seales.'" He frowned. "Herefrid of the Willow is an odd name for a king, don't you think?"

"Perhaps he was born under a tree."

Hillier considered the matter. "And perhaps some chronicler was unfamiliar with the complexities of the genitive case in our ancient tongue."

"Quillifer is an odd name for anyone," said I. "In my name it seems I follow long-established family tradition." I swallowed the last of the brandy. "You must forgive me, but my ship just landed, and I must report to Her Majesty about the situation in Ferrick."

"Congratulations on that succor of that city, by the way," Hillier said. "It was a feat worthy of your great ancestor Berhtric."

I rolled up the scroll and placed it in its leather sheath. "I thank you, Sir Robert," I said, "and I look forward to discussing my arms with you as soon as my duties permit."

I stepped out into the sun and walked up the road. Elation rose in me, and I felt myself rise almost bodily into the clouds. I was royal, and all objections to espousal with the Queen could be safely dismissed, at least in my own fantasy.

I glided past all the carts, wagons, and royal servants I had passed earlier. They were at a standstill, and looking ahead I could understand why, for the Outer Ward of the castle must have been filled with carriages and carts unloading and turning around, and some would have to leave before room could be found for any more vehicles.

I looked over the line of carriages, carts, and drays waiting to turn

into the castle and recognized one of the carriages for the splendor of
its scarlet body and gold wheels, and for the carved demigods perched
on the corners of its roof. I stepped off the curb and peered in, and
the Duchess of Roundsilver looked at me with surprise in her brilliant blue eyes.

"Quillifer!" she said.

"I hope I am not being rude in peering into your coach," said I.
"I assure you that I'm not a freebooter, or trying to sell pasties or
cakes."

"Please join me."

"Your Grace is kind." I opened the door and seated myself across
from the duchess. Roses in porcelain vases filled the carriage with
their sweet scent. Over her usual finery the duchess wore a travel
cloak of brown fustian, to preserve her clothing against the dust of
the road.

"I hope the hunting was fine," I said. "I surmise the weather was
good, for we had fine days at sea."

"The hunting was good, but I was not well." She spoke with unusual care, while her eyes gave me a long speculative look. I found
this searching gaze a little unsettling.

"I'm sorry you are ill," I said. "Where is His Grace? Is he not taking care of you?"

"He had to ride on ahead—some business awaited him. And there
was nothing he could do about my illness in any case. I expect I'll be
ill every day for the next few months."

"Ah. I comprehend. Let me offer my congratulations."

She put a hand over her abdomen. "The babe weighs less than a
dream," she said, "and already it torments my digestion."

When she had been carrying her son the Marquess of Ethlebight,
she had been miserable, at least for the first five or six months.

"I hope this child will be easier than the first," said I.

"I will petition the Pilgrim daily."

"My mother had a recipe for a posset that settles the digestion. I shall have it sent to you."

The duchess leaned forward, and excitement danced in her eyes. "I wish you had seen the celebrations for the recapture of Ferrick! The Queen ordered a day of celebration. Every cannon was fired, every trumpet gave voice, and every firework in the city was fired from the battlement of the castle! Your name was on the lips of everyone in the city."

"I am pleased to be remembered. It feels as if I've been away for a long time."

She reached out and touched my hand. That speculative look still hovered in her eyes, a look I could not read.

"You must have news," she said.

"Mola abandoned the siege of Stanport to retake Ferrick. We fought for six days, and the enemy were defeated on land and the sea. Mola is retreating to his own country. The Constable is in pursuit, along with the Lord Admiral. I no longer had any business in Bonille, so I came home."

Her smile rose brilliant as a sunrise. "I hope Her Majesty has been buying more fireworks," she said. "There will be more guns, displays, and celebrations."

"One of your guns—one of the two sixty-pound cannon you cast for the war on Clayborne—was mounted in Ferrick's Citadel. It was in no small way responsible for the victory."

"My husband will be happy when I tell him." Her speculative look deepened. I began to be alarmed.

"Have you had any news from Selford at all?"

"None," said I. "But just now I had good news I had not at all expected."

"Yes?"

"Hillier, the King of Arms, has looked into my genealogy." I lifted the leather tube. "I now have a vellum scroll with the last seven or eight hundred years of my family history inscribed in a minute hand, and it demonstrates that I am descended from a king."

She blinked. "Which one?"

"Herefrid the Seales."

The duchess blinked again. "Who?"

"That's exactly what I asked. He was one of the Sea-Kings, ages ago. It now seems my royal house is the oldest in the realm." I smiled. "Don't worry; I won't insist on your calling me 'highness.'"

My jest did not seem to amuse her. The blue-eyed searching look was back, and in it I detected a soft glint of compassion.

I felt a cold shiver go up my spine. "What is wrong?" I asked.

She shook her head, and her hand tightened on mine. "My friend, I would give anything not to be the one to tell thee," she said. "But before you go into the castle, you should know."

"Prince Oriol," I said.

"Ay. The treaty is signed. Floria will marry Oriol after his ship arrives from Varcellos."

I felt my heart tear itself to pieces and fall tumbling into my boots. "That is why I went to Ferrick," I murmured. "To relieve Floria of any obligation in the matter of Oriol or anyone else."

"She is the nation," said the duchess, "and the nation needs an heir."

"But not this week. This month." I shook my head. "I wish she had more faith in me."

Tears shimmered in her eyes. "A woman—even a Queen—has little choice in our world."

"I strove for her freedom," said I. "But she chose not to take it."

"Duisland is at war," said the duchess. "The enemy were on our soil, and Varcellos offers armies."

"At too high a price," said I. Suddenly the carriage was too small, the rose-scented air too cloying, and my own company too crabbed and ill-tempered.

"I am sorry, Your Grace," said I. "But I must walk in the sun for now." I took her hand and kissed it. "Thank you for your goodness and compassion, but I must be alone."

I left the carriage, and as I walked along the cobbles I considered turning around and going back to *Sovereign*, and with Captain Gaunt sailing to the farthest corner of the world.

Instead I walked through the gate of the castle, and made my way to the Inner Ward. The guards recognized me, and their startled expressions showed that I had not been expected. As I walked across the courtyard I saw Ambassador Gandorim walking with Sandicup and Baron Scarnside. I approached and bowed. Gandorim's mild brown eyes surveyed me with interest.

"My lord ambassador," said I. "I thought I would ask whether the Marquesa dels Altimirs is still available."

Amusement lightly touched the ambassador's mouth. He spread his hands. "Alas, my lord of Selford, there is a time for everything. That time is passed."

"Such a pity, for a fine wind now blows from the south. From your nation." I gave Gandorim a smile. "Your Highness is to be congratulated, for you have managed a thing that everyone thought impossible—you have persuaded the highest nobility of the realm to sell their Queen to a foreigner in exchange for a jackboot full of silver."

Scarnside, who had not only taken that boot but had probably kissed it, looked outraged. Sandicup offered an insolent smile, and I knew what he was thinking: *Riot at my theater, and I take your Queen away. What think you of that?*

Gandorim merely nodded. "I acted for the good of my nation," he said. "And for yours as well. Soon your Queen's succession will be secure, and we will be your firm allies against Loretto."

"I hope we prove as firm an ally to you," said I. "But now you have shown to the world how easily our great men turn whore, so we must see who buys them next." I looked at Scarnside and Sandicup. "Ere long they could work for Loretto. Or Littov. Or the Man in the Moon. But they must sell themselves quickly, before their good name is devalued and worth nothing at all."

Scarnside had turned white with rage, and his eyes seemed as deadly as those of a basilisk, ready to flash me to stone. I looked at him, and I hoped he would choose to resent my words. In the last months I had killed tens of thousands, and one over-proud nobleman more or less would scarcely shift the balance, and would leave the world cleaner.

But Sandicup put a hand on Scarnside's shoulder and said, "Let us go. This man is no longer worthy of our attention."

He drew Scarnside away. Gandorim regarded me again with his solemn brown eyes, then bowed and walked after his minions.

As I slowly came back to myself, I saw that we had not been alone in this colloquy, but that a number of people had overheard. Some were shocked, others seemed to approve of my sentiments. I bowed to them and went to my apartment.

I changed to clothing more appropriate to the court and donned some of the rings I'd left in my strongbox. I poured myself a cup of brandy and drained it, and then walked to the Great Reception Room. Many courtiers were present, but I saw not Floria, and I sent a page to Her Majesty to let her know I wished to see her. Short after that, the page returned, and took me to Floria's cabinet. I glanced through the hagioscope as I entered and saw Lady Mellender with her embroidery, and the devout lady named Holdsworth, who mouthed chants while her fingers counted her prayer beads.

I took off my cap and held it over my heart while I bowed.

"Majesty," I said, "I see I must congratulate you on your impending nuptials."

For the first time I looked at Floria, who sat in her brilliant gown of satin and velvet, jewels glittering in the sun, her face and hands softly glowing with that sublime light thrown back by the ground pearls in her cosmetic, an embodiment of semi-divine majesty enthroned on a carven chair. In the hazel eyes I detected a flash of pain, and a mean little part of me rejoiced.

"We thank your lordship," Floria said. "And we are happy to see you again. Sit, an you have a report, please tell it me."

I sat and told her of the fighting at Ferrick, the bombardment, the fireships, the naval assault, the attack over the glacis and in the harbor, and lastly—only a little late—the arrival of the Constable and his army.

"The victory was perilous but complete," said I. "When I left, the Constable and his forces were marching out of the city in pursuit of Mola's army."

"Has your lordship any knowledge of how that pursuit fared?"

"Your Majesty, I hope Mola escaped entirely. He is a slippery antagonist, resourceful and full of tricks, and I feared he would ambush the Constable if he was pursued too closely."

"We shall hope for the best," Floria said. "We will send out heralds this afternoon to let the city know that your lordship has driven Mola from Ferrick, and we shall appoint a day for celebration in Selford."

"I am given to understand that you have already complimented me with some days of celebration. I thank Your Majesty."

Her eyes turned to mine. "Those celebrations in your name were entirely deserved," she said. "Your service to the realm is inestimable."

On the contrary, I felt that my service had been very finely estimated, and that it had been reckoned not worth a penny.

"Your Majesty is kind," I said.

The heralds went out into the city with their trumpets, but first the announcement was made in the Great Reception Room and in the courtyard of the Inner Ward, and so when I went into the court I received many congratulations. I was asked again and again for an account of the campaign, something that I would once have considered an opportunity to burnish my reputation and put any rivals in the shade, but this day I lacked the heart to boast to anyone, and soon retired to my apartment. Rufino Knott had arrived after bringing my dunnage through the great tangle on Chancellery Street, and was shifting my gear from my trunks to the wardrobe. I considered ordering a bath to be brought up, but the castle was in such a bustle after the return from Kingsmere that I feared it would be midnight before the hot water arrived.

While I debated this with myself, a page appeared and told me that the Queen intended that I should take her in to dinner next noontide, so that I might make a report of my adventures to the court, and to the common people in the gallery.

So now I was to be trotted out before the meiny as an example of the triumphs brought about by Floria's policy. I had no wish to be a puppet on display, and I had never felt so miserable in my life.

I told the page I would right willingly join Her Majesty for the following day's dinner, and decided to postpone the bath till tomorrow morning.

CHAPTER TWENTY-SEVEN

I wondered if you would come," said I. "I had decided you would not."

Floria stepped through the secret door into my apartment, her candle in her hand. She blew out the candle, closed the door, and put the candle on the mantelpiece carved with gloxinia and camellia. Her disordered hair framed her face, which had been washed clean of the cosmetic that had given her such an unearthly, regal appearance . . . now, looking at her face alone, she looked like an ordinary young woman who could be anybody, possibly even the bride of a butcher's son.

Though her clothing offered a contrary impression, for she wore a gold satin dressing gown with a high collar that shimmered like precious metal in the light of my lantern.

I had been working on papers I'd brought from the Secretariat, weeks of correspondence that had waited for my return. I gathered the papers from the cushions of the settee, put them in their folders, and placed them on a side table.

"Would Your Majesty care to sit?" asked I.

"My majesty would." She picked up the leather tube containing Hilliard's scroll. "What is this?"

I took the case from her hand and took out the scroll. "Take a look; it might amuse you." I picked up the lantern I had been reading by and held it nearer Floria so that it illuminated the scroll. "The King of Arms presented me with this," I said, "in which he proves that I am the descendant of a king—two kings, in fact. I had thought my doubly royal blood might aid in convincing the world I could make a suitable consort for a sovereign, but as the present sovereign is promised to another, I will have to find another majesty somewhere."

Floria glanced at the scroll for a moment, then rolled it again and tossed it on the bed. "Royalty is not found in genealogies," she said, "but in what you can convince the world to believe." In a rustle of satin she placed herself on the settee. "I usurped the throne from my nephew," she said, "but millions willingly own themselves my subjects, and foreign nations treat with me as if I were born with the crown imperial empaled on my brow."

"True, much is illusion," said I. "I had thought to surround myself with an illusion of my own, but I had not the chance." I looked into her eyes. "Could you not have waited?"

"I delayed as long as I could," said Floria. "I hoped for a miracle, but—"

"The Battle of the Races does not count as a miracle?" I asked. "I caused an enemy fleet to disappear."

"The miracle needs to be in how people regard you," said she. "You could have turned that genealogy into a scroll fifty yards long and hung it from the highest tower of the Castle, and it would not have convinced anyone that you were royal. Those who mislike you consider you a freak of nature, an unnatural monster, and even those who love you—like the Roundsilvers—love you as a being of singular wit and talent but could never envision you on a throne."

"So you will make this Oriol our King." I could not hide the bitterness in my words. "This prince selected by Gandorim to master you, to dictate policy, to curb your womanly weakness, and to make you a servant of King Anibal's policy."

Her lip curled in disdain. "Oriol will never be King!" she said. "I accepted Oriol for the sake of his father's soldiers, not because I desire a master. I will not imitate my sister's mistakes, nor will I part with an ounce of my sovereignty."

I was surprised. "Surely Oriol and Gandorim expect otherwise."

"Then they will be disappointed," she said. "I'll make Oriol a duke—he's already a prince, after all—and I will assign him some estates from which he may draw a competence, but he will never have a finger in state policy." She gave me an appraising look. "But now we must decide what to do with my lover."

There had been too many surprises in the last minutes for me to absorb them all, but I knew Floria well enough to respond.

"You would not have raised the subject if you had not an idea."

"I do, but only with your permission. For you see, Oriol comes with a dowry of soldiers, and also with a city."

"What city?"

"It sits on Terra Nostra in the empire of the Aekoi. Varcellos conquered it from the pirates three generations ago. They have not really prospered there, and willingly gave the city away."

"Axcolo," said I.

"Yes. I thought to make you viceroy there, and setting you free to wreak what mischief you can on Loretto, or on the reivers who killed your family—or simply to sit in the shade of the cypress trees and play your guitar, if that would suit you." She offered a shrug. "It will be awkward to have you here when Oriol arrives, but after two or three years, it will not matter. You can be recalled and take your place in the House of Peers and on the Council."

I looked at her. "And if I should wish to play my guitar somewhere closer to home?"

"You may, but you may not play it at court. Play it at Ethlebight, and build your canal." She frowned down at her hands for a moment, then looked up at me. "In Axcolo I would make anyone else a mere governor, but the title of viceroy I mean as a compliment to you, and as a promise that you will be honored now, and on your return. I think Axcolo would offer your abilities greater scope than you can find here, but you know best what you desire."

"And what do *you* desire, my Queen? I asked you once, and you could not reply."

She looked at me, and lantern-light shimmered in her eyes. "I would live in the shade of that cypress tree, with you and your guitar. But that is not possible, and so I must make other arrangements for us."

I felt my heart break, and I wondered at it, for it had broken so many times already.

She took my hand and kissed it. "I said that even with Hillier's scroll, you could not convince anyone that you were in any way royal. But that need not be the case with our child."

For a moment the very spheres of the heavens seemed to pause in their course, and my consciousness flew from my body to hover in some weightless void. I believe my heart simply stopped. But then, in a great rush, the world came flowing again into existence, shining as if all were perfectly new, and I looked at Floria in a kind of rapturous surmise.

"You're with child?" I said. "But surely people would have noticed—I've been gone for three months."

"I do not carry a child," said Floria. "But we have some weeks before you must leave and Oriol arrives. I propose that you put away your sheaths, and I will forego my cream of silphium, and so we let Fate decide if some new being is created and then lodged in my womb."

I found myself unable to speak. Floria seemed an entirely new person, a near stranger, so uncanny and astonishing that I might take her for a changeling.

"Dear heart," I said, "I find I do not know you."

She drew close. "Would you not like to know me better?"

In truth I did not know if I wished to touch this new Floria or not, for the last hours had shattered my being and my hopes, and I wished not to render myself vulnerable to even greater agonies. But Floria kissed my lips, and I felt her ardor—and so I complied, as ever, with the wishes of my Queen.

Yet a part of me hovered above the scene, observing and marveling at this scene of love and desolation, and I wondered what would come of it, if the heavens would open, the earth crack, and kingdoms slide down in ruin, or whether the ruin was not of kingdoms but of myself.

CHAPTER TWENTY-EIGHT

Quillifer sailed serene through the rocks and the spume
Led the foe to the Races, and de Cuerzy to his doom.
The sailor Coneygrave is now a viscount brave,
But what did Quillifer get?
What did Quillifer get?

Your Grace," said I to Pontkyles. "At Ferrick I saw your son Morestanton, and he was well and sends his regards."

No regards had been sent, but I felt that Morestanton would have sent them if he'd remembered, and so I repaired his negligence.

Pontkyles regarded me with his swinish calculating eyes. "Stands he well with the officers and men of rank?" he asked.

"The Constable chose him as one of a party of a very few men to accompany him to the city. Stayne was jealous, and called him an ignorant fool, but Morestanton silenced him with a fine eloquence."

"Stayne was ever a jealous dog." Pontkyles growled the words, as if he, not Stayne, were the hound.

It would do no harm, I thought, should my enemies Stayne and Pontkyles decide to hate each other.

We stood in the lobby outside the banqueting hall, waiting for the Queen and her ladies to come to their dinner. I held a cardboard folder in one hand, tied in the red ribbon that signed the matter had reached a happy conclusion. The lobby was crowded, for the word had gone out that I would make my report of the defense of Ferrick, and many would want to know how the city had been saved.

The doors to the royal apartments boomed open, the guards froze at the salute, and Floria entered with her ladies as the room bowed. Three strands of my rubies burned like coals across the front of her satin gown. She walked straight to me through the silence and held out her arm.

"Lord Selford, if you please."

I rose from my bow, shifted my folder to the other hand, and took Floria's arm. The doors to the banqueting hall opened, and I took the Queen to her place at the head of the table, then took my own place at her right side. The other guests spent the usual amount of time working out their precedence with regard to one another, and then entered in the correct order. I found the Roundsilvers on my right, with Chelmy and his duchess beyond. I saw Pontkyles, Gandorim, Scarnside, Sandicup, Thistlegorm, and the Philosopher Transterrene, Fulvius. The gouty Lord Campion, Sir Cadwal's father, was half-carried in by a pair of attendants. Eventually we all stood at our places, and I helped the Queen into a chair, which allowed the rest of us to sit. As the ewers came round the table, and we each washed our hands, the doors to the gallery above were opened, and the common people entered. The gallery filled quickly, and by the time the first bowls of pottage came up from the kitchens, the gallery was a mass of curious faces peering down at us.

I felt my conversation constrained. After the events of the previous day I could not be at ease with Floria, who had dismissed me, loved me, and strove to carry my child all at the same time; while on the other side of me was the duchess, who had last seen me when I stormed out of her carriage on Chancellery Road.

I would deliver my report at the end of the meal, but there were ten removes to get through before I could speak, and so I endured the pottage, the salmon, the cod, the pigeon, the goose, the lamb, the pork pies, the tenderloin of beef, the custard, and the pudding doused with brandy and set alight. I found myself without appetite, and ate only a bite or two out of each dish.

At length the golden platters were all carried away and the ewers reappeared. We washed our hands, and Floria gave a signal for a trumpeter to blow a sennet, which ended all conversation.

"My lords, ladies, and gentlemen," she said into the silence, "we are here to listen to Lord Selford's report on the recent battles in Ferrick, and the defeat of Admiral Mola. It is my desire that Lord Selford offer us that report now."

I rose and untied the red ribbon from my cardboard folder. The folder held my report, but I did not read from it, but used it as an outline for a more expansive verbal narrative, beginning with my meeting with the Hogen-Mogen to discuss Priscus's army stranded on the island, then my first meeting with Sir Cadwal Campion, and the results of the revolt on the island of Briese. I described the state of the army that I found there, and likewise the condition of Kosma's mercenaries on Gravelinye. I told of the trip to Genk to view the silver, and of the Hogen-Mogen's kindness in arranging for us to be supplied on the march to Houbek.

I spoke of the treachery of the Ropers in delivering Ferrick to the enemy. I told of my meeting with Mayor Roper at the gate, and of our storming the city under false colors. I related the fate of the traitors, and the preparations for the defense of the city.

I then told of Mola's approach, the siege, and the assaults he made upon the city. I gave full credit to Campion and Kosma for their stout defense against the assaults by land, just as I praised the ships of the Navy for their courage in holding the port. I turned to the duke as I mentioned the Roundsilver gun and the great execution it had done against the Loretto ships, and recommended that other giant guns be placed on elevations overlooking ports, to direct their plunging fire onto attacking ships.

I kept to myself the trick of the blue smoke, for I thought I might want to use it again.

I described Coneygrave's victory in the sea battle, followed by the arrival of the Constable, and his march to drive Mola out of the country.

"And with the arrival of the Constable, Ferrick's freedom was assured, and so my duty was done," said I. "Therefore I took ship for Selford, that I might let the people of the realm know that Duisland is now completely free of the enemy, that traitors and rogues have been dealt with as they deserved, and that our soldiers and sailors are victorious and stand like a wall between a free people and those who would enslave them."

The applause was enormous, particularly from the gallery, who waved their hats and handkerchiefs and deafened us with their cheers. Floria stood to applaud, which obliged everyone else to stand as well. Even Pontkyles applauded my conclusion with a will, though Sandicup and Scarnside barely touched their hands together. Scarnside leaned to Sandicup and spoke into his ear, and I imagined him saying, "But *anyone* could have done that!"

A mob burnt your house, Floria had said, *and two nobles tried to murder you. That is how your popularity stands now.*

I thought that my popularity now stood on a somewhat *greater* foundation.

Because I had taken Floria in to dinner, I was obliged to escort Floria from the banquet room. Afterward I stood in the lobby while others came to praise me, but I had never wanted to be alone so much in my life.

The army of Duisland was prison'd on an island bleak
Till Quillifer their trail like a hound did seek
He took them on the sea, and now the army's free.
But what did Quillifer get?
What did Quillifer get?

It is no small thing to be a Viceroy, I discovered. I needed to assemble a household—I needed secretaries, scribes, a major domo, a butler, a cofferer, a steward, a comptroller, a notary, maids, ushers, bailiffs, grooms, footmen. I had Harry Noach as my cook, Oscar as my groom, and Rufino Knott both as a musician and my varlet, and I could recruit from the staff at Haysfield Grange, but not all wished to travel, and though I did my best to tempt the steward, Master Stiver, Stiver decided to remain in the service of Lord Rackheath, from whom I had leased him, along with Rackheath House in Howel.

It was not hard to find ordinary servants, but the skills of a Master Stiver, or a comptroller or a notary, were not so easy to come by. Under normal conditions I would have been happy to consider candidates recommended by prominent men in Her Majesty's service, but the recommendations did not come so easily, for no one wanted to promote a friend or relative into the service of a royal favorite who had been dismissed to some foreign land. I settled for young, ambitious men with little experience, and who otherwise would not be promoted into such an office for years. When possible, I chose from among the hopeful Ethlebight natives who were always knocking on my door in search of employment.

It occurred to me that the Gentleman Pensioners were blessed with experience in government service, so I chose some from among those who were not totally decrepit.

I also needed folk who could speak the language of Varcellos, which was the common language of Axcolo, and I needed a tutor who would teach me the language. With the help of the Mercers Guild, which had contacts throughout the world, I found such a man, a Master Rosas who had run into trouble in his own country and couldn't go home.

Fortunately I had no need to recruit an army. Axcolo was defended by two regiments of mercenaries who would shift their allegiance to the Queen as soon as I arrived, and who the Queen would then be obliged to pay.

At the Mercers Guild I met also with Kevin Spellman and his father Gregory, who represented Ethlebight in the Burgesses. Two years ago I'd had the idea of creating a new joint stock company controlled by those merchants who traded in the East, in Tabarzam, the Candara Coast, or along the fringes of the Empire. These men were now at the mercy of local despots, princes, or pirates, who might throw them into prison for no reason, or hold their cargoes for ransom, or demand large gifts. There was little a single shipowner could do to prevent this, but I thought that if the eastern traders formed a single association—and in effect became a well-armed, well-commanded fleet—they could go much farther in demanding fair treatment from these petty tyrants.

This would require the Estates General giving the Association of Eastern Traders a monopoly in trading with certain parts of the world, and also allowing the Association to issue stock in its own name, and that in turn required another bill passing the Estates. I had introduced such a bill in the House of Peers during the last session, but the idea was too novel, and the war had occupied everyone's attention, so the bill had been tabled.

A bill dealing with trade were better introduced in the Burgesses rather than the Peers, and Gregory Spellman agreed to do this along with some of his merchant colleagues. The ground had been better prepared over the last year, and we could evoke the demands of war by pointing out that ships traveling in convoy, and providing a common defense, would be far safer from enemy privateers than ships traveling singly. Master Spellman thought the bill stood a good chance of passing, and I pointed out that Axcolo would make a fine rendezvous for our merchant fleets, for watering and resupply. Perhaps the Mercers could establish their own outpost there.

I was not worried in the event that the bill failed to pass. Private merchant adventurers needed no permission to convoy or to deal with foreign princes from a position of strength. They would not have their monopoly, and they would not be able to issue stock, but there were only a few merchants who traveled so far to the east, and if most or all were of a mind to collaborate with one another, there was little anyone could do to discourage them.

After all, it was entirely in their own interest.

A few days after returning to Selford I traveled to Philpott Square to pension off Lottie Forde. I gave her three months' allowance, and also three months' free lodging. She surprised me by offering to buy the house from me, and in the end I was happy to sell it to her.

Clearly she had more resources than I had surmised.

Before I could even decide whether or not to raise the subject, Lottie declined to accompany me to Axcolo. She had lived her whole life in Duisland and had no wish to go abroad.

She offered to introduce me to a younger member of her sorority who might be inclined to travel, but I declined.

The afternoon being pleasant, we took a drive in her open carriage, so that we could carry out our deception one last time. Afterward we supped together, then had a musical evening in her house, I playing on my guitar, and she on her virginals. I kissed her cheek for the last time, left her rose-scented bower, and took my carriage to the castle.

"I suppose I should not be surprised," said I, "for one of Orlanda's bodements was that I should lose you."

"Bodements?" asked Floria.

"It is a new word. I made it up."

Her brows knit as she regarded me. "Do you still see her?"

"Orlanda? Nay. Not since that day in the spring, when she made her prediction and vanished, saying that my fall was inevitable and that she need not lift a finger to assure my ruin."

Floria propped herself up on an elbow and gave me a fierce look. "You are hardly ruined, Quillifer," she said. "And though you may have fallen somewhat in the estimation of the court, you will rise again. I promise it."

"In the meantime I must put up with the sneers of Scarnside and Sandicup."

"When have you ever cared about their sneers?"

We lay in my great carven bed after another of our nightly attempts to engender a child. Candlelight painted Floria's body in bands of gold, and her galbanum scent floated in the room.

I found that our meetings lacked their old intimacy, and their old savor. Part of me watched and listened and wondered while the rest of me acted more or less as I had always done. I spoke, I jested, I relayed the gossip of the court, but now I was aware that it was a performance, though sometimes the performance was convincing enough that even I believed it.

I frowned. "I have intelligence that may interest you. I now have the exact tally of the bribes that Gandorim scattered among Your Majesty's friends and councillors."

"I would be interested to see it."

"You might use this knowledge to assure the compliance of your nobility, by threatening to expose them, or even indict them as foreign agents."

"Difficult to manage," Floria judged, "as Varcellos is now an ally."

I closed my eyes and pillowed my head on my hands. "On the other hand," I offered, "you might interview each of these gentlemen, and suggest that a donation to the treasury equal to the sum paid by Gandorim will assure that word of their duplicity will not be revealed."

Behind my closed lids I sensed Floria's smile. "That might be amusing. Scarnside is so proud—it would be gratifying to see him knocked down a little. What is that word you invented? *Disapprobate.* I would *disapprobate* him."

"I approbate this line of conduct."

"Oh, Quillifer." She laid her head on my shoulder, her disordered hair warm on my arm. "I shall so miss these, our nights together."

For myself, I was already missing them. Near everything that had been joyous about our meetings—our secrets, our intimacy, our shared joys and amusements, our conspiracies against the world and the court—was now gone, replaced by a shadow-play.

"What do you intend for the future?" I asked. "When I return from Axcolo, will I again be granted this apartment? Will I receive you now and again in secret?"

"I cannot say," said Floria, "but I may hope. Oriol may be the man Gandorim says he is, or he may prove a beast, or an imbecile. You and I may have a child, or we may not. I have hazarded our hearts on a cast of the dice, and we must see how the dice land."

I thought that the dice had already landed, and that my poor wagered heart was lost.

It was decided that Judge Travers, who had occupied my office while I was gone, would follow me onto the Council as Principal Private Secretary. He and I met in my office to sort through the intelligence that had arrived when I was away, and while we sipped our fragrant ginger and honey tisanes, I briefed him on the spies I had inserted into the households of the powerful men of the realm, as well as the guilds, the moots, and the army and navy.

"Most comprehensive," he murmured. "I am surprised so many are women."

"Men do not notice women," I said. "That is particularly the case with powerful men. A female servant is nearly invisible, and so is a poor relation living in the home on sufferance. Yet they hear things, and know who is going in and out, and they share information with one another, because it helps them survive in a household in which they have very little power. If a woman can read and write well enough to send letters, she can make an excellent spy."

Travers seemed troubled by the thought that women in his household might be judging him much as he judged them. He tugged his white beard.

"You have the reputation of always noticing women," he said.

"It is pleasant to notice them."

He turned his blue eyes to me.

"Have you a spy in my household?" he asked.

"Nay," said I. "But now that you are to have a seat on the Council, I am sure every foreign ambassador will come sniffing around your household, looking for someone to corrupt."

Travers was troubled by this news as well.

"If you sit on the Council," I told him, "your life will be lived in public. You may have secrets, but these will be the secrets of others, discovered by you. You will have no secrets of your own but that they are trumpeted over the town."

"Well. So." He sighed, fidgeted with a ring on his finger, and then a thought seemed to come to him. "I have a success to report," he said. "You may remember that we caught a man from Durba with pamphlets writ against you and the Queen, and that I put him in a cell, with one of my own men in the cell adjacent. There was a chink through which they could communicate, and my man claimed to be in the service of Loretto, and as his friends would soon secure his release, he offered to bear messages to the prisoner's friends. The prisoner was completely gulled, and now we have the entire webwork in our hands."

"Excellent well," said I.

"I have used the trick more than once now," said Travers, "and always with good effect."

"I congratulate you," said I. "It is a fine, subtle device, and I wish I had thought of it long ago. I never liked employing those machines in the undercroft."

"I will use them as little as I may," said Travers. "For we may trust nothing revealed under compulsion, and it is always better to have a confession in a man's own words."

"Very true, sir," I said.

I did not have a spy in Travers's household, but now I would have my agents in his office. Duplicates of many of his reports would be sent to me, and I would receive regular packets from Jeronimy Bledso. In Axcolo I would not be in a position to much affect the business of the realm, but I could send some advice to Floria or Travers or anyone else that might need it, and it would also be useful to keep track of my enemies.

After all, I would some day return, and I wished to know what sort of welcome might await me.

Two days before my departure I held a dinner for my friends in a rented dining room at the Loyall and Worshipfull Societie of Kissers, Cordwainers, and Workers in Leather. As befit a room in the leather-workers' guild, the room itself was clad not in panelling but in top-grain leather, beautifully worked and ornamented with sorcerous and astrological devices made of leather of different grades and colors. The table was covered in dark brown leather stretched out with brass tacks, and the chairs were cushioned with wool stuffed into fine soft leather.

I invited their graces of Roundsilver, Kevin and Gregory Spellman, Blackwell, Edith Ransome and her Gunfounder brother, and Sir Robert Hillier the King of Arms. Harry Noach supervised the cooking, and though there were no marchpane dragons or centerpieces draped in gold leaf or coqz heaumez, the food was good, and the wine better.

"My friends," said I, when we were all seated. "I am soon embarked on a new adventure, and it may be that I will not see you for some years. I invited you here today to tell you how much I treasure your friendship, and to let you know that I will miss you terribly when I am gone from Duisland. Should any of you venture as far afield as Axcolo, you will receive a hearty welcome. But now"—and here I raised my goblet—"I would drink to our friendship and to our continued association. Long may we thrive!"

They echoed my toast and drank. I saw tears in the fierce eyes of Edith Ransome, and the duke dabbed at his cheek with a handkerchief. His duchess raised her own glass and responded.

"We shall much miss your mischief here in the capital, Lord Selford. I hope that from Axcolo you may raise some mischief against Loretto, but whether or not that is the case, I have every confidence that in Axcolo you will thrive." She brandished her goblet. "This glass to you, Quillifer."

And with that she drained her cup. I looked at her in some surprise, for I had never known her as a great carouser. Yet she was not alone, for the others drank off her pledge, and as the dishes came up from the kitchen, we all grew merry. At the end of the feast I presented each of my friends with a ring inset with a gem from Tabarzam, and I embraced them and kissed their cheeks. As people began to leave, I returned my genealogy to the King of Arms.

"Keep this for me, Sir Robert," said I. "It came too late to be of use to me, and to make it public now would constitute nothing but pretension. Yet I shall look forward to someday meeting with you and discussing whether or not to augment my arms with the willows of Herefrid."

"I shall be delighted to have such a discussion," said he. "And we might also discuss whether your shield might carry reminders of your exploits among the Aekoi."

"I may do nothing there worth remembering. Axcolo is distant and may only be, as the poet Bello might say, 'the sad cockpit of ruined ambition.'"

"Yet people can make money at a cockpit," said Hillier, "if they put their money on the right gamecock."

"I shall try to be a gamecock worthy of the wager, then."

We embraced and he departed. I wondered if I was a gamecock worth the wager, or just a mere coqz heaumez, a stuffed dead bird in cardboard armor.

Only time would tell, but I knew that I would not care to lay a wager on myself.

> *Ferrick groaned in distressing strait*
> *Till Quillifer slipped past the enemy gate*
> *Ferrick he stormed and a government formed*
> *But what did Quillifer get?*
> *What did Quillifer get?*

When I first heard Knott sing that song in the castle's Middle Ward, I almost struck him. But then I reflected that he was a free man of Duisland, and was entitled to his opinion. If anyone objected, let the matter be referred to me.

I approached him after it was over. "That was wretched doggerel, Master Knott," I said.

"I will refine it by and by," said he. "Besides, it is all in how I sing it."

"Be careful where you let your voice take flight," I said. "The precincts of the castle may not be the wisest place."

"On the contrary," he said, and gestured at the box he'd placed on the cobbles. Copper and a little silver gleamed in its interior.

"You have many friends here," said he. "They seem most grateful to have their own feelings so well expressed." He put a finger beside his turned-up nose. "And I have sold the ballad to a printer, who will make it available at every bookstall in the realm."

"The Master of the Revels will not sanction it."

"We will not trouble the Master of the Revels for an opinion."

I considered this. "It is lucky we soon leave Selford," said I, "for otherwise you might be hanged."

I left the Middle Ward for the Outer, on my way to the Secretariat, and then saw a familiar one-armed figure approaching, limping along in the wake of a two-wheeled cart carrying turnips to the Castle kitchens.

"Lieutenant Tate!" said I. "I am mighty pleased to see you. Do you bring messages?"

"I left them at your office, with a Master Bledso. I hope that was all right."

"That was perfectly correct." I took Tate by his empty sleeve and drew him out of the way of an oncoming carriage. "Must you now return to Ferrick?"

"Nay," he said. "I have left the army. I cannot fight, and I can barely sit a horse. I have learned to write with my left hand, but not well enough to turn scribe." He gave me a melancholy smile. "I have come to Selford to seek my fortune."

"This is the place to do it," said I.

"I wonder if you might be able to employ me in some way." He offered a diffident shrug. "I could turn a spit, or scatter feed for chickens, or keep children quiet by telling them tales of my life."

"I can employ you in the character of a military advisor," said I, "but you will have to come to Axcolo with me."

He seemed taken aback. "I know not where Axcolo is."

I laughed. "No one does, but you will be welcome there."

I took him to the Secretariat, where I wrote a note to Captain Gaunt to let him aboard *Sovereign* and find him a place to sleep. He thanked me and turned to go.

"Wait, Lieutenant," I said. I held out my left hand. "We have known each other awhile, and fought the realm's enemies together. May I know your forename?"

He smiled. "Rumbald," he said, and shook my hand.

"Rumbald Tate," said I, "it is a pleasure to meet you."

The fireships came and bore down on our fleet
Quillifer boarded and drenched their red heat
Our ships were saved and the foe was amazed
But what did Quillifer get?
What did Quillifer get?

"I will make Cadwal Campion a baron," said Floria. "His father is already Baron Campion, and his older brother will inherit that title, so Sir Cadwal will be Baron Campion of . . . of Ferrick?" She raised her eyebrows and looked at me.

"Why not?" I said.

"Coronel Kosma is a foreigner and there would be complaints if I ennobled him, so I shall make him a Knight of the Hippogriff."

"I am sure he will be grateful. And if you are handing out honors, don't forget Judge Travers. If he is to sit on the Council, he must have some kind of award or the nobles will ignore him."

"He's from Bonille? Another Hippogriff, then."

It was our last night together in my carven bed. The next night I would spend on *Sovereign* in order to sail on the morning ebb. Floria sat up in bed, propped on pillows, and sipped at her sloe cordial. My mind was half at sea, and I could not stop myself from itemizing in my head, making certain that the ships would be loaded with every-thing needful.

Tendrils of melancholy drifted through the both of us, though by way of distracting ourselves from our sadness, we kept up our conver-sation, for the most part about trifles.

The tide indeed was changing, and neither of us knew whither it would carry us.

"There will be another appointment that you will not like," she said. "Stayne will be Knight Marshal."

"He will be the most grandiose, overripe occupant of that office," I said. "And I suppose he will try to kill me again."

"He commands an army in the field. He is too busy to murder you now."

I looked at her. "Have you his assurance on that point?"

"He will not run mad again. He has a son to live for, and now his new position."

"You assume an arrant fool has a choice in whether or not to be an arrant fool," said I. "He will not be an ornament to your court."

"He held Stanport for five months. He fought in the trenches alongside the common soldiers, and earned their devotion. No one else could have done it."

"I could have done it," I said, with a memory of my blue smoke. "And it wouldn't have taken five months, either."

A pensive silence descended on us. Her hand sought mine be-neath the blanket. "When Oriol comes, I will have to pretend to be a virgin," she said.

"Just lie still and do nothing," I said. "Afterward tell him how won-derful it was. He will believe you."

She gave a soft little laugh. "You are more cynical about your sex even than I." She looked up at the bed canopy, with its softly glowing woven stars. "In former times they hung up the bedsheets to satisfy the curiosity of the public," she said. "I thank the Pilgrim that such customs are no longer followed."

"Your Majesty," said I, "I beg you to speak no more of your wedding night. The subject toucheth me too closely, and I prefer not to think of it."

She turned to me. "I hope you do not hate me."

I turned my gaze away from her. "I am angry, and resentful, and jealous. But I cannot hate you." I shook my head. "I love you but you are sending me away, and I go not like a lover, but as a dutiful and pitiful subject."

She raised my hand, and touched it to her cheek. "You have a right to your anger," she said. "What I suffer is not anger, but fear."

I looked at her. "You are afraid? But why? You have braved a thousand dangers. You fled Fosco's tyranny to rally the nation, and on the way you pistoled a pair of bandits to the ground. The enemy armies have been driven from the realm, and though the war will continue, the freedom of your realm is no longer in doubt. Why be afraid now, when you were not before?"

Her hazel eyes gazed into mine. "Because I now take up the principal task of a Queen, which is to provide the nation with princes. I am a small woman, my hips are narrow, and I fear that I may not survive childbirth. My sister was so much taller and robust than I, and birthing Aguila so weakened her that the first fever carried her off."

I turned toward her and kissed her cheek. "You are young and in good health," said I. "The Duchess of Roundsilver is smaller than you, and she gave birth without any trouble."

She offered a slight smile. "I half-expect you to offer me a posset of your mother's, to assure a successful delivery."

"I wish I knew of such a posset," said I. "But I should say that you should pay attention to the midwives, and as little to the physicians as you can. My father always said that you should not go to physicians unless you're dying, then at least they can't make it worse."

"My sister blamed the physicians and their bleedings and purges for her miscarriages."

"She was probably right. You should ignore them and do whatever seems right to you."

"I will follow your advice, then. Though I wish I had your mother's posset." She shook her head.

We gazed at each other at a range of a few inches for a few long seconds, and then I leaned forward and kissed Floria's sloe-seasoned lips. A pang of longing and loneliness drove through me like a flaming spear, and I kissed again. A tremor shivered through her frame, and I put my arms around her and kissed her a third time.

Passion seared us both. I clung to her out of desperation, out of a yearning never to be away from her for an instant, out of a need born of untamed love and shattered dreams.

Afterward, as I lay broken and gasping in her arms, I felt as if I had never been so lonely in my life

> Mola sent in his forces by land and by sea
> Quillifer picked up his pikestaff and charged to the quay
> Stayne is judged great, has the Knight Marshalate
> But what did Quillifer get?
> What did Quillifer get?

Once before, banned from the life of the court, I had taken ship to seek my fortune, and I found it abroad, then came home with a hull full of spices and silks and a coffer of gems from the Street of the Shining Stones in far Sarafsham.

I thought I would not find much of a fortune in Axcolo, but I hoped I would find something besides despair.

On my last morning in the castle I ordered up a bath, knowing that it would be some time before I had another. I lay in hot, scented water while Rufino Knott packed my belongings and readied them for the long journey, and then after my bath we went down to the river, where Boatswain Lepalik waited with *Sovereign*'s whaleboat. Captain Gaunt gave me a hearty welcome as I went aboard the ship, and then the day became very busy, for there was a deal of loading to do. My carriage had been broken down and stowed in the hold, and my horses also had to be swayed up on slings and lowered into place. Phrenzy thrashed and bellowed as he swung up into the air, but my groom Oscar calmed him, and he was put into his stall on the maindeck. I had no intention of being kicked or bitten and so kept my distance.

Five other ships would accompany *Sovereign* to Axcolo—two from the Queen's Navy, to support the dignity of the new Viceroy and help carry my suite over the sea, and three merchant ships bound for the Candara Coast, which would convoy with us for the sake of protection. The Association of Eastern Traders was turning into a reality whether or not the Estates approved.

I stood under the great brass stern lamps that overhung the poop, listening to the pumps as fresh water was taken aboard from the lighter, when the chief mate approached.

"My lord," he said. "There is a man at the entry port, and he asks for you."

"Did he give his name?"

"Nay, sir. He is a lank rogue, and he came on the water-lighter."

"Very well." I went down to the spar deck and looked out the entry port, and found myself looking into the indigo eyes of the poet Blackwell.

Blackwell looked ill, and his blond hair was disordered, along with his clothes. Perhaps he had been up all night drinking.

"Selford," he croaked. "I need to speak with you."

"You are welcome aboard, Master Blackwell."

He hesitated to put a foot on the battens that made up the stair leading to the entry port, but he visibly steeled himself, took hold of the lines, and came up to the port in a rush. Once through the port he swayed, and I tried not to flinch, for he smelled of brandy and sweat.

"What is it you need?" I asked.

"Speech," said he. "Private speech."

I took him into the owner's cabin, with the graceful row of stern windows and the gilded stern gallery, and I led him to a chair.

"What is the matter?" asked I.

"In brief . . ." he said, and then his voice failed him. His color was ashen. He essayed again. "In brief, I've stabbed Wakelyn to death." He gave me an imploring look. "Can I voyage with you, overseas? Until the hurly-burly is over?"

I regarded him as if I were still Secretary, as if I were at an interrogation. "Tell me what happened."

"I was drinking at the Hog Sty with some friends," said he, "and Wakelyn came in with some of his actors. He was already drunk."

Since Florla had commanded Wakelyn to return Blackwell's foul papers, Sandicup's Players had not fared well. It was two months before they could mount a play, and then it failed, as did their next. Since then they had done nothing new but revived old plays that had been popular in our fathers' time, and had achieved a modest success.

"Wakelyn took a table near me, and he and his friends offered a series of leering insults intended to be overheard. I responded with remarks that Wakelyn chose to resent, and he came to my table to harangue at me. I stood and pushed him away, and he drew a knife, and so did I." He passed a hand over his face. "I have sent him to his grave, my lord."

"You're sure he's dead?"

"Ay. I put the knife through his throat. There was blood everywhere."

"Do you still have the knife?"

Mutely he reached into his jerkin and produced a dagger. He had made some effort to clean away the gore, but still there was dried blood marring the good steel.

I took the dagger between thumb and forefinger, walked to the door that led to the stern galley, opened it, then flung the knife into the Saelle. I turned back to Blackwell.

"I will have Captain Gaunt find you a hammock," I said. "Try to stay out of everyone's way, and if liquor comes near you, I expect you will turn it down. Come with me."

I made the arrangements, then went out onto my stern gallery for a last, longing look at the city. We were lying alongside the crowded wharf in Innismore, and the pumps were still thumping as they emptied the water-lighter into the water casks in the hold. The mainyard creaked as it swung cargo aboard. I looked to larboard and saw the white towers of the castle in the distance, shimmering like an apparition in a fairy tale, unreachable.

I turned and there you were, your brilliant red hair framing your perfect face, your figure outlined by a green gown with scarlet collar and sleeved, the whole sewn with pearls and yellow diamonds. Bright stones glittered on your fingers, each a nobleman's ransom.

"Well," said I. "You have come to rejoice at my fall. Forgive me if I think it a little mean of you."

Amusement flashed in your emerald eyes. I remembered your words: *You may not live in a world of whispers and enmity without suffering some loss. And in your position, to suffer any loss is to lose all.*

"I came not to rejoice, but to reassure," you said. "I wish to affirm that I have kept my promise. I have not interfered in any way with the course of your defeat, though of course I feel free to rejoice in it."

"You are not alone in your rejoicing. Half the Council now sing and skip about like Queens of the May."

"Those fools know not why they dance," you said. "For they never regarded you as anything but an ill-bred nuisance or a freak, and best swatted away like a fly." A smile touched the corner of your lips. "Whereas I know you better, Quillifer—I know you as a man of wit and resource, a man clever and ambitious, a man many steps above fools like Scarnside and Sandicup. They may jest at your dismissal, but only I know the delicate, intoxicating scent of tragedy that follows your downfall—the tumbling-down of a man great in his way, perhaps even noble, but who must be cast down for reasons of state."

"Blackwell is aboard," said I. "He may yet cast me as the hero of a tragic play, or an epic poem."

You pursed your lips, and touched your fan to your chin. "There is another element of the tragedy," she said, "of which—charmingly— you remain unaware. Which is how Floria managed not only your rise but your fall."

You smiled, a green triumphant glitter in your eyes. "She is the heir to a great house, and great houses do not succeed through an unwillingness to use the tools available to them. She used you in her bid for the throne, she used you to help set the realm in order, she sent you to command her armies, and your victories became *hers,* part of the glory that surrounds Her Majesty."

Your fan traced a picture in the air. "But if you failed—if Pontkyles trampled you, or if you were drowned at the Races or killed on the ramparts of Ferrick—what had she lost? A butcher's son, nothing more." The fan swept through the air and pointed southeast, toward Axcolo.

"Now Axcolo," you said. "You may have some hope of a recall, or of accomplishing something brilliant that will bring you back to Floria's arms, but I say to you"—and here the fan swept through the air and pointed at me—"that this is also a part of Floria's calculation. Hers is the glory, yours is the sacrifice." Your lips offered a scornful twist. "She is a calculating bitch, this Floria. I admire her exceedingly, for she brought you to your knees and broke your heart, and still you love her."

I looked at you coldly. "I think Floria is everything you say," I said, "but ever so much more."

You laughed. "Oh yes, Quillifer. And you will find that out by and by."

I stared at you in dumb anger, and you stared back as your green gaze seemed to draw a line through the air between us. You stood proud in your victory and spoke no more, for you had said all that was needful.

I stared at you until you were glutted with your triumph, and then you faded from my sight, fading like a lost hope.

The tide began its ebb at five in the morning, but a thick mist had wrapped the Saelle and we worried that we might collide with other ships if we moved, and so we waited until the rising sun burned the fog away. Then we fired two guns and raised a flag as a signal to the other ships, and we sheeted home the topsails and let the wind and tide carry us away.

As we sailed on wavetops aglitter with the rising sun, we heard a hail from behind and saw a galley speeding after us, its oars flashing foam, its bow glowing with gold leaf. Above the stern flew the royal ensign.

My heart stirred uneasily in my breast. Had Floria come to wish me farewell on my own quarterdeck?

But nay, it was only a young, beardless ensign of the Yeoman Archers, with a message. He came aboard through the entry port, bowed politely, and presented me with a letter. I recognized Floria's personal seal, and I put the letter into my doublet.

This is also a part of Floria's calculation, I thought.

"Will there be an answer, my lord?" asked the ensign.

"Nay," said I. "If a reply is necessary, I will send it with a ship coming into port."

The ensign bowed and returned to his galley. I ignored the firm presence of the letter inside my doublet and instead walked about the poop, viewing the green country as it floated by, my native land that I might see again in years, if ever.

As we floated down the estuary, we heard the sound of gunfire, and saw smoke wreathing the forts guarding the river's mouth as they fired their salutes. A ship stood proud in the fairway waiting for the tide to turn. Its gilding was ashine, and the hull was not painted but bright with varnish. Over the ship flew the flags of Duisland and Varcellos. Prince Oriol had come to the scene of his victory.

I resisted any inclination to pick up a telescope and try to pick him out from amid his glittering suite on the poop. Instead I turned my back on him, and went to my cabin for my dinner.

I took Floria's letter out of my doublet and placed it near my plate. I would read it, I thought, at my leisure.

Sent out the back door to a desolate shore
Out the back door to a desolate shore
That's what Quillifer got.

Sent out the back door to a desolate shore
Out the back door to a desolate shore
That's what Quillifer got.

"For God's sake, Knott," I said. "I have heard that song enough. Play another."

ACKNOWLEDGMENTS

With thanks to Ada Palmer
For letting me know the difference
Between "finxi" and "feci"